THE ECHO FROM TIRNMOOR

RIPLEY LARROW

For my family.
Without your encouragement,
this book would have never happened.
Thank you from the entirety of my heart!

I would also like to thank all who purchased, read, and loved this book. Every one of you helped make a dream come true!
Thank you!

Trigger Warning

Abduction
Alcohol Consumption
Betrayal
Death
Gaslighting
Identity struggles
Imprisonment
Loss of family
Manipulation
Oppression
Religious Persecution
Self-doubt
Supernatural horror and dark magic
Tobacco Use
Torture
Violence
War

THE ECHO FROM TIRNMOOR

Darkness may swallow the weak,
but those who endure learn to wield it.

Part I: Nemeah

Chapter One

The rhythmic tapping on the thatched roof pulled Nemeah from a restless sleep. If she could even call it sleep. Another nightmare left her feeling drained as she pulled the heavy down comforter over her head. Curling into a ball, she tucked her knees to her chest, seeking any warmth her thin body could muster. Outside, a gale whipped against the pine-framed window, its cracked glass and rusted hinges rattling in protest. The shutters clattered against the stony walls as the wind howled, and a cold stream of autumn air seeped into the room. The hissing rain against the hot coals in the chimney felt like a defeat. The fire had long since gone out, and she knew she had to relight it. But with her eyes still tightly shut, she willed herself into a deeper sleep, wishing to ignore the cold, the fire, and the hellish dreams that haunted her.

She longed for the simpler dreams of her childhood, a time filled with warmth and free from troubles. The clatter of dishes echoed from the first floor, a sharp reminder that her parents were up and starting their chores. Nemeah could almost picture her mother bustling about in the kitchen, the smell of breakfast wafting up the stairs, while her father headed out to tend to the animals. Outside, a rumble of thunder grumbled ominously in the distance, signaling the beginning of a gloomy day. Frustration bubbled within her, a fierce rage that ignited in her heart and coursed through her limbs like wildfire. She clenched her fists, every muscle in her body tightening as she fought against the overwhelming tide of emotions. It felt as though her entire being was a coiled spring, ready to snap. The torment of the strain built until it

was almost unbearable, and she shook violently, her muscles screaming for release.

Yet, she held on, hoping to drown out the noise of the world below
and the chaos swirling in her mind. Nemeah focused on her breathing. She listened to each breath; the rise and fall of her chest seemed
to bring with it a sense of relief as the tension slowly subsided. She lay
still, exhausted, with sweat slicking her skin. She decided that pout-
ing would not bring her the comfort she craved, and procrastination
would only irritate her parents and delay the day's work. Frustration
felt like a waste of the already dwindling energy she had. The rage that
had consumed her moments ago had now shifted to a heavy sadness.

With a resigned sigh, she peeled back the thick wool and heavy
feather blanket from her face, allowing the frigid morning air to rush
in. The faint smell of smoke tickled her nostrils, a reminder of the fire
that once burned warmly. The cold sensation filled her chest as she
inhaled deeply, sending goosebumps racing across her skin. The sweat
on her forehead instantly cooled, and she stifled a groan, knowing she
would have to leave the warmth of her bed. She slowly sat up and
became struck by the chill in the room, a stark contrast to the cozy
comforter she was reluctantly leaving behind. Nemeah let her eyes adjust to the faint light filtering through the window. Thick gray clouds
loomed in the endless sky while raindrops waged war on the already
saturated earth below. A shiver coursed through her as she shifted her
gaze from the window to the hearth, where the once roaring embers
now weakly flickered, their red glow pulsing as the wind from the
chimney breathed new life into them.

She slipped out of bed, and her stockinged feet met the icy floor.
The cold seeped into her skin, enveloping her bones like an unwelcome embrace. Stealing one last envious glance at her pillow, she
reluctantly folded the comforter over it and smoothed out the wrin-
kles with a wistful touch. She moved carefully across the small room,
avoiding the creaky floorboards that threatened to betray her. In the
corner by the hearth lay a stack of dried logs and a basket brimming

with kindling, waiting for her to coax the warmth back to life. Nemeah sprinkled a handful of thin shavings and small twigs over the glowing coals and blew gently to encourage a spark. Smoke twirled upward in delicate wisps until a flicker of flame danced to life on the wood. She carefully added the most miniature log she could find. She watched as it crackled and popped, quickly engulfing in a bright blaze.

Satisfied, she placed two more logs atop the first and leaned back, holding her hands out toward the fire to soak in the warmth. Nemeah closed her eyes as she longed to crawl back into bed, burrow under the covers, and let sleep claim her for the rest of the day. The allure of that warm cocoon tugged at her, but the fire crackling beside her reminded her of the responsibilities waiting just beyond the warmth. Another fierce wind howled through the window like a banshee wailing for its next victim. Nemeah glanced at her sister's bed, where a small pale figure lay undisturbed by the storm's fury. Watching her sister's chest rise and fall with each breath. Her nightmare filled her head.

Nemeah always remembered the dreams. For years, they had played out the same way, every detail etched into her mind like a scar. She was eight years old again, standing in the dark, dripping barn. The smell of damp hay mingled with the sharp tang of rain as the storm outside raged. The wind howled through the gaps in the rotting boards, giving the barn a voice, a groaning, creaking *thing* that seemed alive. In the distance, the explosions began. She had not understood them then, those thunderous booms that shook the ground and rattled her tiny bones. All she knew was chaos, hurricane-force wind and rain slamming to the ground, the world trembling around her, yet her gaze fixed on *it*. A field of flowers. It stretched impossibly across the barn's far side, a sea of purple and white blooms swaying gently in an unseen breeze.

Bees hummed lazily through the air, flitting from one blossom to the next, and the scent of honeyed sweetness hung thick. This glowing world of light and color did not belong here amidst the gloom. Nemeah stepped closer. Always closer. The line was clear where the rotten hay gave way to fresh, green grass.

Her shoes brushed the edge as she stared into that strange other world, only half a step away. Then came the scream. It split the air like a knife, dragging her back to the barn. Nemeah felt a clawed hand on her shoulder, cold, too strong. She turned, her wide eyes meeting the figure looming behind her: a tower of shadow, black smoke, and ash swirling where its face should have been.

Her scream mingled with the subsequent explosion. She fell backward, her vision spinning as the vibrant flowers melted into darkness. She felt herself falling, fainting, but she could still hear everything: the horse's frantic grunts, her mother's anguished cries, stomping of feet, and clanging metal.

"*Go away!*" her mother's voice screamed, cracked with pain.

"Ma?" Nemeah tried to call, but no sound came.

More explosions. More screams. And then, silence. She woke on the cold barn floor, disoriented. The air smelled of blood, metallic and sharp. Her head spun as she sat up, her trembling hands finding the dark, sticky patch on the ground. She wiped her head, and her hand came away with bright red blood. Her head throbbed as she frantically looked around her.

"Nemeah." Her mother's voice broke through the haze, soft, calm, but strained. "Nemeah, can you stand?"

She nodded, her legs wobbling as she pushed herself up. Around her, the barn was broken. The roof sagged inward, the horse was gone, and blood streaked the floor like some terrible painting.

"Ma." Her voice cracked.

Her mother sat slumped against the stall, her face pale and her round belly taut with pain.

"Nemeah," she whispered, her voice soothing despite her anguish, "I need you to fetch towels and water. Can you do that?"

Nemeah blinked, her vision clearing just enough to see it. A baby. Her mother was having a baby. She spun on her heel and bolted through the barn doors into the storm. The rain was relentless, sheets of it beating her small frame as the wind threatened to throw her off her feet. She stumbled to the house, the door banging open behind her. The kitchen was dark, with no warm fire, no stew simmering on the stove, and no father whistling in his rocking chair. Everything felt wrong. She grabbed the linens from the cupboard, careful not to soil them with the blood on her dress, but she hesitated at the water. The pigs' slop bucket would not do. The thought made her head throb even more. In desperation, she crept into her parents' room, somewhere she was never allowed to go. Her father's muzzleloader was gone from its place on the wall. A reminder that her father was busy with the war. The washbasin sat heavy on the dresser, its water jug next to it. She grunted under its weight, nearly dropping it to the stone floor before dragging it out the door. She could not run; the ceramic jug was too heavy, and her arms burned with the effort as she tried to carry all the supplies at once. Halfway back to the barn, she heard her mother's cry, a wail that froze her in place. Rain streaked down her face as she listened, unmoving. Only the patter of rain and distant rumbles of the dangerous storm.

Her fear brought a ringing to her ears, and then the smell came again. The sweet scent of flowers and hot earth on the wind. Slowly, she turned her head, and there it was: the valley of blooms. Her heart leaped into her throat. The vision shimmered before her like a dream.

How easy it would be to step away. To walk into the light and beauty. To escape this gray, broken world. Her feet edged toward it. Her flesh was riddled with goosebumps from the overwhelming heat that poured from this portal before her. Excitement danced in her belly as her lips formed an involuntary smile. The hairs on the back of her neck rose as a blast of frigid air kissed her skin. She turned, and there it stood. The shadow figure, its claws outstretched, tendrils of ash curling toward her. She screamed, stumbling backward. The water jug slipped from her grasp, crashing to the ground with an ear-splitting crack. The linens fell to the mud as she shielded her small body with her hands. A blinding flash of lightning struck the ground. Her body felt a buzz with the energy as the thunder deafened her ears. Desperate for safety, she ran, sobbing and whimpering, back to the barn. The creature and portal were gone; only the raging storm remained. When she reached the stall, her mother's face was waiting, furious, disbelieving.

"The linens, Nemeah? Where is the water?" Her voice trembled.

She could not answer her mother; her body shook, and her head thrummed with pain. A soft cry pierced the silence, a wail, small and fragile. Nemeah turned and saw the infant cradled in her mother's arms. Tears poured down her face as she stumbled back into the barn's shadows, frantic. She needed clothes. *Something.* A flash of color caught her eye. A single purple flower lay in the dirt, vibrant against the gloom. Nemeah's breath caught. Beyond it, the figure waited, its black form swirling, its claws stretching toward her. Her final scream always woke her up.

A snore from her sister pulled Nemeah back from those memories. Thanks to the crackling fire, the room felt warmer now, but a noticeable chill still lingered in the air. She moved to Orla's bed, gently pulling the blanket up to her sister's chin and tucking the sides snugly under her petite body. With a reluctant sigh, Nemeah retrieved the blanket from her own bed, wincing at the thought of her careful arrangement going to waste. Nemeah draped her blanket across Orla's bed before heading to the wardrobe. She dressed quickly; the enticing smell of morning porridge wafted into the room. Her stomach growled softly, muffled beneath the layers of clothing as she braided her hair and tied a handkerchief around her head. Anticipation built within her, urging her to hurry downstairs.

The main room welcomed her with a burst of warmth; the fire here was much larger than in the girls' room. The heat thawed her chilled bones, and she relished the tingling sensation in her toes as she slipped her feet into her leather clogs. Her mother furiously stirred the creamy oatmeal in the pot hanging above the fire while her father piled fresh wood next to the stove, a comforting routine that felt like home. The sweet aroma of oats and fresh-cut pine filled the house, and when it mingled with the crackling of the fire and the bubbling breakfast, it wrapped Nemeah in a warm embrace of comfort and familiarity. Outside, the thunder rumbled, but within the thick stone walls and with a fire to keep them warm and dry, it felt more like a distant memory than a threat.

She walked to the cabinets and pulled out three bowls, setting the table as she had done every morning for as long as she could remember. Leftover bread from last night's supper sat in the center, and she sliced several pieces to complement their meal. Once the porridge was ready, the three gathered at the table, murmuring grace before her mother spooned the steaming oatmeal into each bowl. Nemeah drizzled honey over the warm lumps, and the sweet aroma brought with it a rare sensation of calmness.

Just as they were about to dig in, a loud rapping on the door echoed through their cozy cottage. With a mouthful of oats, Nemeah's father pushed his chair back, the wooden legs scraped against the stone-patched floor. He limped to the heavy pine door and pulled it open, revealing a soaked, shaken figure draped in a baggy coat.

"Oh, Mr. Noctis, I am so sorry to intrude on you and your family at such an hour."

Nemeah's heart sank as she recognized the old Ashford woman. With her frizzy brown hair and large nose, she reminded Nemeah of a potato, her mole-speckled skin adding to the resemblance. The short woman shook out her coat at the door, water dripping onto the floor, disrupting the cozy atmosphere of their home. Nemeah felt the simmering anger in her chest return as she watched this intrusive figure mar their peaceful morning.

"Our heifer is in the middle of having her calf, but it seems to have gotten itself stuck in the canal." Mrs. Ashford hurried over to the small pine table that comfortably seated four, greedily snatching a slice of bread as if it were a lifeline. "Would you come to help us get the damned thing unstuck? We cannot afford to lose another cow."

Nemeah sprang up from her chair, the force sending it crashing against the wall with a thudding knock.

"But it is market day, Mrs. Ashford. Pa and I must..."

Her mother cleared her throat loudly, cutting her off.

"I will pack you a lunch, Eoghan."

"Oh, thank you, Maeve, dear." He replied.

Maeve shot Nemeah a stern look before heading to the cupboard for extra bread and some smoked meat. Nemeah clenched her fists and stared at her bowl. The once-steaming porridge had become a cold heap of food destined for the pig. Her mother quickly tied a rag around the parcel and handed it to her father, helping him with his jacket and hat before closing the door behind him as he escorted Mrs. Ashford to their wagon. Frustration boiled over, and Nemeah slammed her fist on the table, making the dishes rattle.

"Why should we help those people?" Nemeah fumed, feeling her nails dig into her palms. "They always need help with something, and Pa helps them for free. Yet if we needed help, they would surely send us a bill!"

"Mind your tone, young lady, or you will wake your sister." Her mother returned the pot of porridge to the fire, stirring its contents with a steady hand. "That is just the way they are and the way we are. You cannot choose whether or not to help someone if it buys favors later."

Rage boiled inside Nemeah. She wanted nothing more than to hurl her bowl across the room, to watch it shatter into a thousand pieces, and to listen to the debris rain down on the stone floor. But she knew that if she did, they would forever be short one bowl. Instead, she gritted her teeth and cleared the dishes from the table, scraping the cold breakfast into the slop bucket for the pigs.

"You will have to go to the market alone. You can take the small hand cart since your father took the wagon." Her mother scooped a fresh helping from the pot and offered it to her daughter. Nemeah shook her head, carrying the dishes to the sink. She plunged the bowls into the filled basin and watched bubbles rise from the depths of the frigid water.

"Why can I not wait for Pa to return before going to market?" She scrubbed the dishes with a rag, trying to loosen the sticky remnants of porridge. "Or why can you and Orla not come with me? Orla has been begging to see the town, and it is such a long way to go alone on foot. What if I get lost or..."

Her mother scoffed at the suggestion, filling a fourth bowl with the reheated remains of breakfast.

"Skip a whole day of tending to the farm so that you would have company. Pish posh." Maeve placed the bowl on a tray with a spoon and a cup of milk. "Come now, you are too old to be whining like an infant. Go to market today and be done with it."

Nemeah watched her mother carry the tray of food upstairs to her sister, a pang of jealousy twisted in her gut. She listened to her mother's soothing song, designed to rouse the sleeping child, the baby of the family whom everyone doted over and treated like a spoiled brat. Orla was frail, but Nemeah believed that was mainly because her mother never allowed her to do anything outside the house. She never made Orla help with the dishes or take part in cooking, coddling her as if she were made of glass. The spoiled girl never even had to make her bed. Nemeah rolled her eyes at the thought as she finished washing the dishes. Glancing at her reflection in the window, she saw her features illuminated by the firelight. Her heart-shaped face with high cheekbones framed a slender, pointed nose. Her perfectly arched eyebrows complemented her thin mouth, which was often set in a way that flatly concealed her emotions. As she stared into her dark blue eyes, the thud of her sister's feet on the floor above jolted her mind back to the present.

Nemeah went to the cupboard to prepare her own lunch for the journey: some bread and meat, a small wedge of cheese, and an apple. She wrapped her meal in three layers of rags and stuffed it deep into her own well-worn coat pocket. Fastening her hat to her head and tying the coat strap around her waist, she confirmed she had dressed for the weather. However, as she opened the door and looked out at the windy gray sky, she wished for clearer skies. The chill caught in her lungs as she swung the heavy pine door shut behind her and headed toward the barn.

The chickens clucked nervously and scurried away as Nemeah pulled open the barn door. The smell of fresh hay filled her senses, confirming that her father had tended to the animals long before she left her room that morning. She pulled the small cart out from one of the empty stalls and filled it with loose hay. With the muddy, gravel-strewn road ahead, the last thing she wanted was for everything in the cart to jiggle and clank about. Nemeah gathered baskets of eggs and crates of beans in clay jars. The dusty sacks of potatoes released clouds of collected dirt from the years of harvest into the air, making her cough. She managed to stack everything neatly before covering it with a large, waxed linen cloth. She silently hoped it would be enough to keep her goods dry until she reached the market.

Nemeah stood at the edge of the road, her anger simmering just beneath the surface, urging her to *do something*. Lash out, curse the world, anything to give her a second of earned release. Instead, she tilted her face to the gray heavens, mumbling a short, bitter prayer to the gods she never believed in. Whispering the quick words to steady herself. With a deep breath, she gripped the cart's handles and pulled it down the worn path. The road to the market was familiar. She knew it like the back of her hand, every rut, every muddy dip that could catch a wheel. She had been traversing it with her father for seven years, ever since the war ended, a couple of years after Orla had been born. No one truly understood why the Axis had come to Tirnmoor, marching across its peaceful farmlands as if it were their birthright. Potato fields trampled beneath boots, apple trees stripped bare, and the herds of dairy cows driven off. At first, the adults whispered theories behind closed doors: treasure hunters, they said. Others believed the Axis sought a specific person, a runaway disciple who had fled to the island for sanctuary. Eventually, all the stories merged into one tangled mess of rumor. But one truth remained. The disciples were ruthless. Nemeah had been only a small girl when the soldiers arrived at the shores of their small island. She remembered the merchant's stories: cannons rattling on carts drawn by heavy warhorses, perfectly polished muskets, and soldiers clad in armor that glimmered like dragon scales. For days, smoke lingered over the horizon, blotting out the sun. Though she had never seen the Axis army herself, she knew to be terrified of them. She had heard one of the neighbor boys muttering once, *saying they were only here to control the population.* When she had asked why, he had shrugged, eyes wide. *That is what my parents said.* The war had ended, but it left behind little more than whispers.

She had been ten years old when the disciples finally boarded their ships. Sails unfurled like pale wings against the slate-gray sky. They left for the lands far south, where the sun burned hot, and the soil ran dry, places Nemeah could only imagine. What must it be like, she wondered, to stand beneath a sky that was not choked with clouds? To feel the sun's rays, warm your skin until it tingles. To walk barefoot through sand instead of mud, the heat sinking into her arches and bones? She tried to picture it now as she trudged along the muddy road, her boots sticking with every step. Somewhere far beyond Tirnmoor's sodden fields and icy shores were golden deserts, warm winds, and skies so blue they looked painted. Unfortunately, that was not for her. The cart's wheel snagged on a rock, jerking it from Nemeah's grasp. The daydream of sandy lands and warm climates evaporated as her thoughts returned to her home's cold, wet grasslands. She trudged to the back of the cart to push the wheel free from the rock and continued her journey, each step making a suction that nearly tore her boot free from her foot. With great effort, the cart was free. She shielded her eyes from the rain and looked ahead to where she needed to travel. It usually took about half a day to journey with the horse and wagon, which meant a long day of walking for her. Nemeah glanced down at her pocket where she had tucked her food away, wondering if she had brought enough rations for the trip.

Chapter Two

Several hours had passed, and Nemeah felt the weight of the cart in her tired muscles. She knew she was close to the market, perhaps another half hour of walking if the cart did not snag on more rocks. She glanced down at her skirt, splattered with mud, evidence of the two times she had fallen. Her mother would be furious when she saw the state of Nemeah's dress. Her gaze shifted to her boots, caked in muck, and a sense of dread filled her. She knew it would take days to scrub the mud off them, taking care not to leave behind any dirt in the laces or the seams. A cold wind blew, sending a chill through her as she pulled the cart to the side of the road. She walked to the back and lifted the wax-covered linen to inspect her cargo. Everything was still dry, and she could feel the warmth radiating from the hay beneath the cloth.

She longed to crawl under the cover and sleep in the cart until morning, but that would mean returning a whole day late and undoubtedly worrying her parents. Sighing, she sat on the edge of the cart. The rain had stopped a while ago, but her clothes remained soaked, clinging uncomfortably to her skin. Nemeah pulled out the last of her food: soggy bread and a small, yellowish-green apple. Her stomach rumbled, echoing the stormy skies from that morning. In frustration, she tossed the bread onto the road and sank her teeth into the crisp skin of the fruit. The sweet, fragrant juice burst into her mouth, and she savored the ripe flesh as she tore a chunk away. She ate until only the core remained, continuing to nibble at the soft flesh around the stiff center. Once finished, she discarded the core beside the bread, her gaze drawn to a single seed that had dislodged. The wind picked up again, and the sun's rays managed to break through the clouds, bringing a splash of color back to the otherwise gray world. A small patch of green caught her focus, small clovers stretching towards the rare sunshine.

The smell of dead grass was not as pleasant as the fragrance of spring flowers, when they managed to bloom. Nemeah glanced back at the seed on the ground, longing for the fleeting warmth of springtime sun. She imagined the trees budding with blossoms, the air dry and inviting. She remembered being a girl as carefree as the larks. With her raven-black hair wisping behind her as she ran, dashing through the valley, her pale skin glowing in the sun. Arms outstretched, she would run through wildflowers and tall grass, watching as rabbits darted away, bounding off through the grass surrounding her. She remembered lying on the hill, breathless, watching the white clouds race across the blue sky.

How wonderful it felt to be younger then, before the Axis had come and disturbed their peace. Before the slaughtering of countless men, before her father became injured fighting alongside family and friends. Lying in the grass had made her feel spirited and wild, as if her life would always be this perfect and happy. Her mother's frustration and the cries of her baby sister could never touch her here in her field of swaying grasses and flowers. She would hum softly while plucking long, stemmed blossoms, weaving them into her lengthy, black hair. But then a shadow fell over her, a figure towering above, blocking the sun. Nemeah looked up, struggling to understand what her eyes were seeing. A metal claw reached down, grabbing her wrist and dragging her to her feet. She caught a glimpse of her reflection in the armor, her face pale with terror as she screamed and tried to wrench her arm free.

A deep, mocking laugh echoed from within the metal plate, sending shivers down her spine. At that moment, she knew she had ventured too far from home, ignoring her parents' warnings. Now, a monster twice her size had hold of her.

"This one is the right age." The metal man yelled to the other shimmering humans.

All wore the same reflective armor with the golden sun on the front in a proud display. Their long crimson capes trailing down their backs, flapping in the wind that would no doubt bring a storm any minute. The fear she felt was like none she had experienced before. A scream tore from her mouth, a shriek that echoed as the sound of twisting metal churned around her. She remembered cowering low to the ground. Pushing her hands to her ears and squeezing her eyes shut. The faint yells and guttural spurts disrupted the otherwise soundless field. When the world grew silent again, she slowly uncovered her ears. Sitting up hesitantly, she allowed herself time to take in what she saw now. A dense, dark fog was carried off with the wind, and bodies littered the field. Parts torn to pieces. Bloodied flesh blended with scraps of metal as the world around her now looked like a butcher's processing shed.

She stood on shaking legs. Her eyes were wide as she took in the carnage. The once peaceful field of no troubles was now a wasteland of human remains. Blood tainted the once-green blades of grass, and now, everywhere was touched by death. A coppery smell filled the air and stuck in Nemeah's nose. She gagged as the realization came to her—bodies, everywhere. Men who had once been alive seconds ago now lay dead. The frightening expression froze on their face, showing that they feared what had come for them.

A crack of thunder rumbled through the sky, bringing her back to the present and away from her remembered nightmare. She shuddered at the memory, just another horror to plague her sleep. Something thudded on the ground in front of her cart. It sounded heavy, startling her as her body gave an involuntary jerk. Nemeah searched the gray skies as she slowly rose to her feet. Turning and leaning around the cart, she glimpsed a mass splattered in mud just a few feet away. She inched closer, her heart pounding as she focused on the strange object before her.

"Is...it metal?" she questioned, her voice trembling with fear.

She quickly scanned her surroundings; no other human was within miles of her. So where did it come from? She found a stick on the side of the muddied trail to poke at the metal mass. It felt childish to poke and prod, as if she were a small girl again messing with an ant hill. How silly she must have looked, but how could she explain where it had come from? She was sure it had not been there just moments before. There was no way she would have missed this with her cart. With a shaky hand, she lifted the stick and tapped the metal; its hollow clang resonated with an eerie, almost musical tone. Pushing at another piece, she discovered the pile was firmly stuck together, twisted into an unrecognizable shape. Her curiosity grew as she inched closer and bent down to examine it, her blue eyes caught a glimpse of their reflection in the corroded metal. She froze when her eyes landed on a familiar insignia. A sun, carved into the breastplate of the monsters in her dreams.

"This is not real," she whispered, a chill running down her spine. "I must be dreaming."

Nemeah felt her heart fall as she forced herself backward, falling onto her backside. She felt a panic take hold of her as a churning sound filled her ears. First low, then steadily growing as the mass twisted and turned before her eyes. It stacked itself and spilled out onto the road like a fluid. It scraped along the rocks in the mud and creaked as the weight of the armor grew taller and taller. Still, Nemeah could not move. She watched in horror as the metal heap took on the shape of a mutilated soldier. Long, smoky tendrils clung and wept down the armored figure. The creature stumbled back and forth, struggling to find its footing. Then it stopped. It stood motionless just feet away from Nemeah, silently waiting. She dared not breathe, sitting perfectly still, anxiously awaiting its next move. Her eyes trailed up the distorted metal. The bent and warped panels with rust and

mud decorating its reflective surface. Two legs held up a torso. A helmet sat at the top, where the head should be, smashed and twisted.
Two arms that ended in claws rested by its side. Minutes dragged on,
and both Nemeah and the creature remained frozen like statues, silence enveloping them. Her mind raced with thoughts of escape.

She could scream, but who would hear her? Who would come to
her rescue? She could run, but with the cart behind her, she knew she
would not be fast enough. What if the monster caught her? Would it
hurt her? Or would it remain still, like a nightmare frozen in time?
A drop of rain fell on her cheek, icy and shocking, making her wince.
Then another fell, and another, the rain bouncing off the creature's
metal armor, creating a strange, melodic hum, a haunting lullaby amid
her terror.

As the rain grew heavier, pooling around her and soaking into her
clothes, Nemeah knew she could not remain where she was. With her
heart racing, she braced herself and slowly shifted her weight, gripping the cart's handle for support. Standing upright felt like a defiance against the fear that clutched her throat. She held her breath,
daring not to move again, her body a statue caught between flight
and fate. The monster remained motionless, the rain beading on its
armor like teardrops, cascading down and pooling at its feet. Nemeah
let out a shaky breath, a noise that was barely audible above the now
pouring rain. With a sudden jolt, the creature's helmet swiveled to the
left, then to the right, mimicking someone straining to hear a whisper
in the storm. It took a stiff-legged step forward, and Nemeah's heart
thundered in her chest. She carefully slid her foot around the cart's
handle, plotting her escape toward the town. But just as she shifted,
the squelch of mud beneath her boot treacherously revealed her position.

The monster lunged, its armored arms crashing down onto the
cart with a resounding thud, splintering the wood and sending the
hay flying into the air. Nemeah rolled away instinctively, adrenaline
surging through her veins. She scrambled to her feet, her eyes wide

with terror. The cart lay shattered behind her, the metal figure looming, still and menacing. Panic propelled her forward as she sprinted toward the safety of the town, her breath ragged and desperate, the sounds of the storm merging with the pounding of her heart. The jars of beans shattered with a sharp crack, sending shards of glass and the glossy contents spilling across the road. Crates burst open, their wooden sides splintering as sacks of potatoes tumbled out, rolling into the muck. The delicate baskets of eggs smashed against the ground, yellow yolks bursting forth and staining the brown mud like a splattered canvas.

Nemeah's heart sank as she glanced back at the chaos. The monster continued its destructive rampage, the once sturdy cart now a jumbled heap of broken wood and glass, remnants of her hard work strewn about in a grotesque display. The rain mixed with the spilled food, creating a slick, sludgy mess. She forced herself not to dwell on the destroyed continents, she needed to get to safety. With every ounce of her strength, Nemeah pushed herself to run faster, her feet pounding against the wet earth. Each step felt like a battle against her fear; the image of the twisted figure looming behind her burned into her mind. She could not afford to look back any longer; safety within the walls of the town was her only thought. The familiar sounds of life ahead urged her on: voices, the clatter of market stalls, the distant laughter of children. It felt like a lifeline, a promise of shelter in a world turned upside down.

Nemeah's heart raced as she stumbled forward, her knee landing hard on a rock. Radiant pain shot through her leg, but she could not stop. The monster's hollow clanks echoed behind her, a relentless reminder of the chaos she had just seen. She pushed herself harder, the familiar path to Fayridge becoming a blur of colors and shapes. The rain pelted the path, soaking her clothes and weighing her down, but she welcomed it. It masked her footsteps, making it harder for the creature to track her, she hoped. She could hear its heavy body behind her, like a storm gathering strength. The town was close, just beyond the next rise, but the thought of safe ground felt so far away. Nemeah navigated the slick ground, her boots slipping beneath her as she ducked low to avoid branches that hung like skeletal hands from the trees. Every instinct told her to look back, to see how close the monster was, but she could not afford to waste a moment. She had to get to the town.

"Help!" she shouted, her voice hoarse as the roar of the rain abruptly stopped. "Someone, please!"

The winding path finally opened, revealing the bustle of Fayridge. People moved about, blissfully unaware of the terror that chased her. She dashed toward the nearest stall, her lungs burning, praying someone would notice her frantic state.

"Please!" she gasped, waving her arms wildly as she reached the edge of the market. "Help me!"

One of the merchants rushed to Nemeah's side, his face marked with worry. He was tall and slender, carrying the scent of fresh herbs and earth. His arm felt warm around her shoulders, and his embrace offered a fleeting sense of safety.

"What is the matter, lass? What has happened?" An older woman came around an even older herbal cart, her apron patched in places that matched the knees of the man's trousers. Nemeah assumed they were husband and wife.

Shaking with exhaustion, Nemeah glanced behind her, desperate to spot the creature that had hunted her, but nothing appeared. The night had chased her along with the monster, yet now, bathed in the light of the market, she saw only an empty road. Her once peaceful Tirnmoor island grew darker by the minute as the small amount of light dipped below the horizon, leaving clouds heavy with rain to block the moon's glow. The temperature dropped quickly, and a dense fog settled over everything. Only the faint light from the market's torches cast an orange glow on the faces of those shopping there.

"Just there!" Nemeah pointed back to the path she had fled from. "It was chasing me."

"Chasing you?" The old man echoed, squinting into the dense mist. His wife joined him, straining to see.

A crowd of merchants and customers began gathering at the edge of the market, drawn by the commotion.

"What is happening?" a woman's voice cracked.

"Chasing? What is chasing who?" came another.

But as anxious eyes scanned the night, nothing stirred. There was no sound except for the restless shuffling of feet behind her. The metal-clad monster had vanished. The eerie creaks of scraping armor were now silent, leaving only the thick fog in its wake. The merchant tightened his arm around Nemeah and exchanged a glance with his wife.

"Poor lass just got a fright in the dark. Go about your business," he called to the crowd, waving them away.

"No!" Nemeah shook off his arm, stepping forward. "It was real! It broke my cart!"

Her voice cracked with desperation as she scanned the crowd but saw only doubt. The market returned to its usual noise, a cacophony of traders hawking wares, women exclaiming over new fabrics from overseas, men haggling over the price of pigs, and children running about with toys and skewered meat in hand. The smell of freshly baked goods and smoked meats filled the air, making Nemeah's stomach growl despite the anxiety gripping her.

"Come, sit." The old merchant guided Nemeah behind his cart and offered her a rickety stool. His wife rummaged through the herbs in their cart, tossing leaves into a kettle hanging over a small fire. The air was filled with the fragrant scent of spices. Nemeah noticed her knee throbbing, a sharp reminder of her fall during the frantic escape. She stared into the fire, the memory of the metal creature's pursuit sending shivers down her spine.

"My cart..." Nemeah murmured, trying to rise, but the pain in her leg stopped her.

The merchant raised a hand to calm her. His face, lined with age and wisdom, softened with a reassuring smile. Equally thin and weathered, his wife fetched the kettle, pouring its contents into a wooden cup and handing it to Nemeah with care.

"Chamomile and heather. It will calm your nerves. Be careful; it is hot," the old woman said. She filled two more cups, handing one to her husband, and they sat across from Nemeah, sipping slowly.

Nemeah followed their lead, blowing on the steaming tea. The sweet, mossy flavor, tinged with honey, eased its way down her throat, settling warmly in her stomach. A strange metallic taste lingered, but she could feel her muscles easing and the tension subsiding. Her terror began to melt away with each sip, replaced by a growing sense of calm.

"Thank you," Nemeah said, handing the cup back. "I have never tasted anything like that before."

The old woman smiled, her eyes crinkling with pride. "Old knowledge of the land." Her voice carried the weight of years, and Nemeah realized just how aged the couple were. The woman's thick gray and white hair hung down her back, tied in rags, and her skin was thin, marked with veins of blue and green.

"We gather herbs ourselves, dry them, make them into medicines," the old man said, his tone light. He glanced fondly at his wife as she busied herself with approaching customers.

"From one wayward soul to another." The woman rang out as the customers grinned and waved their goodbyes.

"Do you travel a lot?" Nemeah watched the woman fill a few more bags.

"We mainly stick to Tirnmoor and the mother continent, Nocthrea. But we have gone as far as Sylvara."

"Sylvara?" Nemeah's interest was instantly piqued. "What is it like?"

The couple smiled; their warmth was undeniable. "Taller trees and fairer weather. Everything else is the same."

Nemeah tried to imagine the forests of such a strange land. Trees towering, and the weather allowing for sunny days.

The old man finished his tea as he looked into the night, the path now swallowed by darkness and fog. He stood, draping his apron over a chair and pulling on a coat. After lighting a lantern, he turned to Nemeah with a reassuring smile.

"Let us go get your cart, shall we?"

Together, they ventured down the muddy path. Every step brought back the terrifying memory of the creature. The clanking, the scraping of metal—how could it vanish so completely? Nemeah glanced at the merchant, wondering if his thin legs could keep pace if they had to flee. His shuffling steps did not inspire confidence. As they walked, Nemeah's gaze fell on her footprints in the mud. There had to have been a mistake; had they taken a different route back? She ducked close to the ground, the old man bringing the lantern closer to her. No other tracks accompanied hers. No heavy, armored feet. No evidence of her horrid pursuer. Her heart sank. Was it possible she had imagined it all? A dream, no, a nightmare she had dreamt while awake?

"Is that your cart?" the merchant asked, pointing.

Through the mist, Nemeah saw it, her handcart, sitting upright as if nothing had happened. The wheels were intact, the goods safely tucked under their waxed linen. No broken glass. No scattered eggs. The realization hit her hard. There had been no monster at all. The day's journey and lack of food must have taken it out of her more than she realized. The merchant gave her a pat on the back and handed her the lantern. Together, they hauled the cart back to the market. Upon returning, Nemeah noticed that the noise had dimmed. The torches burned lower, casting long, flickering shadows on the cobbled street. The market was closing, and she had not sold her goods. She gave a reluctant sigh as she looked back to the road, the dense fog casting a white haze that obscured everything.

"Thank you for everything," Nemeah said, handing the old woman the lantern as her husband pulled the cart alongside their own. "I really should head back tonight."

The couple exchanged a glance, the old woman taking stock of everything in Nemeah's cart: eggs, potatoes, and jars of beans. The old man rummaged through his trouser pockets, producing a few shillings.

Nemeah's eyes widened. "What is this for?" She questioned as the man dropped the coins into her hand.

The woman laughed softly, already lifting the baskets. "For your produce and eggs. You did not come to the market just to return home with all this, then, now did you?"

Nemeah watched, stunned, as they emptied her cart into their own. She was undoubtedly relieved to have the goods sold; that had always been her father's task when they came to market, and she had no clue as to who she would need to talk to. Now, with the exchange complete, a sense of relief washed over her; her long journey had borne fruit. She held a demure composure as her insides sang with praise. She imagined her parents' pride when she showed them their earnings.

"I do not know how to repay you for your kindness," Nemeah said, feeling small in the face of their generosity. She glanced down at herself, at her soiled and damp clothes, wondering what more she could offer.

"No need to repay us, lass. We enjoy being able to help when we can," the old man said, his toothy grin kind, if a bit worn. He was missing several teeth along his bottom row, a detail Nemeah had not noticed before.

"Jacob," the woman said, pointing to the corner of the market. "Take her cart next to our wagon. She can stay with us tonight. It would be foolish to try heading home in this fog."

Nemeah hesitated. The offer was kind, but the thought of spending the night among strangers unsettled her. Then again, with the fog thickening and the memory of that monstrous metal creature still fresh, the idea of venturing back alone chilled her to the core. The old merchant did not wait for a reply. He pulled her cart next to their wagon, an old, covered thing with a small gray donkey snoring softly at the front. His wife retrieved a black iron pot from their supplies and handed Nemeah a small knife.

"I take it you know how to peel these potatoes of yours?" she asked with a chuckle.

Nemeah nodded and took the knife, settling down to work. They peeled the potatoes in silence; the rhythmic scraping of the blade against the skins was comforting in a way. The old woman diced the potatoes and tossed them into the pot with beans, and a mix of herbs Nemeah did not recognize. As the pot simmered over the fire, the market gradually quieted. The last torches were snuffed out, and the remaining shopkeepers brought in their wares and closed their doors. Nemeah watched and listened as the old woman hummed as she stirred the bubbling pot. The smell filled Nemeah's nostrils and made her mouth water.

The old woman ladled the thick, hearty stew into bowls, and the three of them ate in companionable silence. The rich flavors, far better than anything Nemeah had ever tasted, filled her belly and eased the lingering aches of her body. She felt warmth spread through her, settling her nerves.

"I am afraid we do not have room for you inside the wagon," the woman said as they finished the meal, scraping the bowls of every last morsel, "but we can make you a soft bed of hay underneath. You will be warm and dry until morning."

"That will be more than enough," Nemeah said gratefully.

The women cleaned the dishes as Jacob snored softly in his chair beside the fire. Nemeah packed hay beneath the wagon as the old woman rummaged around inside her wagon above. Thuds and chimes flittered through the air before the woman gave out a triumphant, "Ah-ha!" When she emerged, she held in her hands a thick woolen blanket. The smell of cinnamon clung to its fibers.

"This should keep you warm." The woman smiled as she turned to retrieve her sleeping husband.

As they clambered into their wagon, Nemeah crawled underneath, grateful to have a warm place to sleep. She looked out at the fog that bordered their encampment. Its dense walls sent a shiver down Nemeah's spine despite her now dry clothes and cozy sleeping arrangements. Above her, the old woman murmured prayers softly, her voice a soothing hum in the stillness. Nemeah closed her eyes, trying to recall any of the gods she might send her own prayers to, but sleep overtook her before she could begin.

Chapter Three

Cannon fodder rumbled beneath her feet, shaking her small frame. The sound was deafening as gunpowder exploded, sending metal projectiles tearing through the air, leaving chaos in their wake. Bodies fell, people screamed, and the night was filled with the cries of children calling for parents and animals shrieking in fear. The sound of war was a symphony of terror, relentless and unforgiving. Metal monsters, clanking, grotesque machines, crawled over the rocky hills, inching ever closer to what had once been a peaceful town.

"Run, Nemeah! Run! Do not let them find you!"

A voice called out to her, faint but desperate, barely cutting through the panic thrumming in her veins. She bolted, legs burning as she sprinted through the field, heading toward the barn. The air was thick with smoke, blood, and sweat. She threw herself into the pile of freshly gathered hay, burying her trembling body deep into its warmth, trying to still her rapid breathing. Her heart thundered in her chest, pounding loud enough that she feared it would give away her position. The barn door creaked open, the sound echoing through the suffocating stillness. Then came the laugh, dark and ominous, followed by the steady, clanking steps growing louder and closer. The golden armor with its large gauntlet hands and crimson cape came into her vision as Nemeah desperately tried to blink away the horrible monster that had followed her.

BOOM!

Nemeah awoke with a start, a gasp of smoke filled air sucked deep into her lungs. Sweat ran down the back of her neck, cold and sticky, as she stared at the underside of the wooden wagon. Her throat was dry, her body tense, and for a moment, she struggled to remember where she was. Then it all came back: the market, the merchants, the fire. Her senses sharpened, and she lay perfectly still, listening. A strange noise caught in her ear, as she tried to calm her breathing and strained to listen. She heard it again—another boom, faint but distinct. The noise seemed to drift in and out of earshot, carried on the shifting air. She let out her breath and whipped the hair from her face. The market was silent, and the fire reduced to weak, glowing embers. From inside the wagon, she could make out the slow, even breaths of the old merchant couple sleeping peacefully.

The sound came again, soft but unnerving, a metallic groan, almost like a whisper carried by the wind. Was it her imagination? A remnant of the nightmare still clinging to her mind? The fog lay thick around the wagon, dense and swirling like a living thing. It curled across the ground, its damp tendrils snaking through the camp. The fire's faint glow barely pierced the heavy mist, casting long, flickering shadows that danced like specters in the night. She strained her eyes, scanning the darkness, but the fog was impenetrable, swallowing everything beyond a few feet. The world felt far too quiet; no animals stirred, and no night birds called. Something was out there.

A strange pull urged her to move, to investigate. She tried to ignore it, but it filled her brain with thoughts of what could be out there. Slowly and carefully, Nemeah crawled out from under the wagon, ensuring not to disturb the sleeping couple. The cold night air hit her, heavy with the scent of wet earth, smoke, and the faint tang of saltwater. She glanced around. The donkey blinked at her, its dark eyes watching her every move as its ears twitched.

"What is out there, huh?" Nemeah whispered as she rubbed the donkey's side.

Its warmth was a comfort in the cold, still night. But her mind was restless. That strange noise was not in her head, right? She thought back to the metal creature. She shook her head; she would be foolish to wander in such a fog just because she thought she heard a noise. She patted the donkey and turned back to her makeshift bed when a voice whispered her name. "Nemeah." She jumped and turned, the voice sounding as if it was whispered in her ear. It sent chills racing down her spine as her feet rooted firmly to the ground. The sound of her name hung in the air like a warning. The fog shifted, twisting, and a dark figure emerged from the mist for a split second. Nemeah's breath caught in her throat. Her heart pounded wildly in her chest as she squinted, trying to focus on the shape. The figure disappeared, retreating into the shifting fog, leaving behind a strange doorway, an eerie tunnel of mist.

"I am still asleep." She murmured as she rubbed her face with her hands.

The air hummed with tension. She felt the pull again, stronger this time, urging her forward. Her legs moved independently, carrying her toward the tunnel despite the fear tightening her chest. This was not part of her usual nightmares. The clang of metal echoed faintly again, distant but undeniable. She took another step. Then another. Before she knew it, the fog lightened, and the scent of the ocean filled her senses. The salty breeze greeted her, mingling with the freezing night air. The sound of waves lapping at the shore reached her ears, soft and rhythmic as if the sea was calling to her. Then, as if by magic, the fog dispersed, revealing a cloudless sky. Thousands of stars dazzled the black sky, filling Nemeah with amazement. The full moon hung high, casting a silvery glow across the beach. The sand shimmered, wet and glistening, while scattered shells caught the moonlight, reflecting like a thousand tiny stars.

Ahead, a light flickered a bright, orange-white beam that cut through the night like a beacon. It was warm, inviting, like the glow of a torch. Yet, this light felt different. Unnatural. As Nemeah moved closer, the sound of clanging metal grew louder, echoing off the rocks and the water. The wind whipped against her, stinging her skin as she drew her arms tighter to her chest. Her hair flew wildly around her, the sea's mist freezing to individual strands. She cursed herself for leaving her coat behind, the cold biting deep into her bones, but she could not turn back now. Not yet. The light beckoned, and her feet obeyed. Her only goal was to reach the light and the source of the noise. As she grew closer, she could see something bobbing on the waves that washed ashore.

"A box?" Nemeah whispered, her voice barely audible over the crashing water.

She blinked, trying to make sense of what she was seeing. A small, weathered box, no larger than a jewelry case, sat nestled in the sand, partially buried beneath layers of seaweed. Another wave washed over it, sending it rocking against a nearby stone. The sound it made was impossibly loud for something so small. Nemeah crouched down, her fingers tracing the edges of the metal box. It was warm to the touch, unusual and unexpected from the ocean's icy tide. The surface was corroded, worn down by time and the relentless beating of the waves. Beneath the patches of rust and barnacles, she could make out intricate scrollwork, delicate designs that hinted at craftsmanship long lost to the ages. Her emotions pulled at the sight of it. It was more than just a box. There was something about it, something that called to her, pulling her deeper into its mystery. She wiped the sand away with the edge of her sleeve, uncovering more of the design. It must have been beautiful once, a work of art in a world that had forgotten it. The waves lapped at the shore, the steady rhythm calming her momentarily as she turned the box over in her hands.

The hinges were stiff, and the clasp resisted her touch as she tried to pry it open. Frustration mingled with curiosity. Was it stuck because of the rust, or was something keeping it shut, something more powerful than time and decay? She shook the box lightly, hoping to hear a rattle, something to give her a clue about what was inside, but the sound that emerged was silence: no shifting contents, no hidden treasures clinking inside. Whatever was sealed within was locked tight, as if it had been waiting for her to find it.

As she fiddled with the box, a strange feeling washed over her, a deep sensation to open it, to free whatever was within. The panic inside her grew stronger, more insistent. A thirst that needed to be quenched. There was power here: ancient, forgotten, and sleeping. She could feel it humming through her fingers, a faint vibration just beneath the surface of the metal. She tried and tried, the metal clasp digging deep into her fingertips. Suddenly, the sky above darkened. The moon, so full and radiant moments before, was now obscured by a thick layer of cloud. The fog returned with alarming speed, swirling in from the ocean like a living thing, faster and denser than before. It had enveloped her in seconds, and the beach disappeared from view. Nemeah stood, clutching the box tightly to her chest, her breath shallow. The sound of the waves faded into a distant murmur, replaced by an oppressive silence. She glanced back toward the shore, hoping to glimpse the path that had led her here, but there was nothing, just a wall of swirling ghostly mist. The camp, the merchants, the warmth of the fire, they felt like distant memories now, too far away to reach. She was utterly alone. Her fingers tightened around the box as if it were her only anchor to reality. Then, out of the stillness, came a voice.

"Nemeah."

It was further, now more urgent, whispering her name like a soft wind brushing past her ear. She turned sharply, searching the fog, but saw nothing—only the endless, rolling mist.

"Who is there?" Her voice wavered, small and unsure. She took a step forward, her feet sinking slightly into the damp sand.

The box felt heavier in her arms.

"Nemeah..."

The voice came again; this time, it was unmistakable, a woman's voice, low and commanding. It sent a shiver down her spine, but not from fear. It was familiar, as if the voice had always been a part of her, buried deep within her memories. A figure emerged from the fog. At first, it was nothing more than a shadow, a dark outline against the white backdrop of fog. As Nemeah strained her eyes, the figure took shape, tall, graceful, and cloaked in black.

The woman's face was obscured, hidden beneath the folds of a hood, but there was an unmistakable aura about her, something ancient and powerful. Nemeah's heart skipped a beat. The woman raised a hand, her fingers long and pale, and pointed toward the box in Nemeah's arms.

"Free me," the woman said, her voice both soft and sharp as if it cut through the fog.

Nemeah took a step back, clutching the box tighter to her chest. Her instincts screamed at her to run, to flee back to the safety of the camp, but her legs would not obey. She was rooted to the spot, drawn toward the figure, unable to look away.

"Free me." The woman's command echoed in her mind.

"How?" Nemeah's voice was pleading. "Who are you? How can I free you?"

The long, slender hand reached out again from the shadows and pointed to the box in Nemeah's grasp. She eyed it, heart quickening, but the mysterious figure had vanished when she looked up. The beach and the rhythmic pulse of the waves all faded. She blinked, and the world had shifted back to the camp. The gray donkey lay on its side, braying softly in its sleep, exactly where she had left it. The soft crackle of the fire and the scent of humid air replaced the salt-brined sand of the beach.

Nemeah turned toward the fog, half expecting to see the woman again, but the fog hung thick and unmoving. A hollow feeling settled in her chest. Who was she? And why had Nemeah felt so seen in her presence? Shivering, she crawled back under the wagon, clutching the corroded metal box to her chest.

The warmth from the box seeped into her skin, the metallic tang of saltwater inhaled in her nostrils. She nestled into the soft hay bedding, wrapping herself in a woolen blanket. The warmth from the box comforted her and lulled her into a deep, dreamless slumber.

Morning broke with the smell of sizzling eggs and potatoes filling the crisp air. Nemeah stirred, her body sore, but the aroma coaxed her from the hay. The old merchant woman was tending to breakfast, her hands swift over the iron pan as the fire crackled beneath. Nemeah propped herself up on her elbow, rubbing the sleep from her eyes. Her head ached, and her throat was dry as she tried to remember her dream. A panic swept through her as she flung back the blanket to reveal golden hay beneath.

"Just a dream." She murmured to herself.

She slowly crawled out from under the wagon before she joined Jacob, helping him to load up the wagon. The gray donkey was harnessed, and the merchant's herb cart was secured at the back, ready for travel. They sat down to eat, the food warm and filling.

The old woman had cooked more than seemed possible, yet not a crumb was left by the time they finished. As Nemeah tidied up the dishes, Jacob eyed her curiously.

"Heard you talking in your sleep last night," he said, picking his teeth and rubbing his full belly.

Nemeah hesitated, unsure of how to answer. In all her years of being plagued by nightmares, never once had Orla or her mother mentioned her talking in her sleep. What had she said? Her cheeks reddened at the thought.

"I have nightmares, most nights actually," she said, offering a weak smile. "I am sorry if I woke you."

Jacob shook his head and continued to rub his full stomach. The old woman, however, nodded knowingly and disappeared into her wagon. After a few minutes of clattering, she emerged with a small jar and handed it to Nemeah.

"Here, take this," The old woman forced the jar into Meah's hand.

"What is it?" she eyed the speckled outside of the brown, gray jar.

Its cork was pushed deep into the opening.

"It goes by many names, but we old travelers call it silvervane root. I also threw in some chamomile and heather, the same mix you drank last night," she said softly. "Brew a small amount of it into tea before bed. It will calm your mind. Help you sleep." She patted Nemeah on the shoulder.

Nemeah accepted it gratefully, guilt gnawing at her for not offering payment. She gripped the few coins in her pocket, knowing she could not return them. Her mother would fuss if she came back with less than she already had.

"A gift." The woman said quickly. "From one traveler to another." As if she knew what burdened Nemeah's mind.

She hugged the woman tightly, grateful for her warmth, then watched as the wagon and donkey trundled away down the muddy road, both its occupants waving goodbye. A pang of loss hit her like she was saying farewell to family.

The day was cold, the sun dim behind the ceiling of thick gray clouds. The wind tugged relentlessly at her skirts, urging her in the wrong direction. Still, her spirits lifted. She had earned money for her family, made new friends, and was eager to return home to her chores and normal farm life. The world did not feel so heavy today despite the storm rumbling in the distance, and the grass seemed more vibrant, with mid-autumn's touch of various browns and oranges, even yellow tints here and there. As the afternoon wore on, she pushed the cart homeward, her pace quickening with the thought of her family. She imagined her parents' faces, the warmth of their hugs, and the relief in their eyes when they saw her safe return. The coin she had earned from the kindness of strangers. She had done well, in spite of everything. She looked down at the cart.

No broken wheels, no splintered handles. Yet, despite her cheery mood, her legs ached, and hunger gnawed at her belly. She pulled the cart along at a slower pace, her brain thinking of the dream from the night before. The woman cloaked in black. The brilliance of the moon and stars. The warmth of the box in her hands. The tarnished metal was beautiful, though some of it was corroded and rough against her skin. "Free me." A strange shiver passed through her as the wind picked up and the looming storm grew closer. With renewed determination, she pushed against the biting wind as she made her way home. The cart creaked as Nemeah pushed it forward, her muscles protesting the strain. The wind whipped against her relentlessly, but she pressed on. Her dry clothes balanced the chill in the air, giving her enough comfort to proceed.

Finally, she crested the hill, and her family's tiny cottage came into view, nestled between the rolling hills like a hidden treasure. The sight filled her with warmth. Smoke curled from the chimney, and the front door was propped open, letting the fresh air flow through. Her mother would be bustling about inside, likely preparing for her return, and her father would be working in the garden, always tending to the land or the animals. Nemeah quickened her pace, a smile spreading across her face. The weight of the journey fell away, replaced by the simple joy of coming home. As she neared the cottage, the familiar sound of clucking hens and the faint scent of freshly baked bread filled the air. Her legs wobbled with exhaustion, but the promise of rest and food urged her forward. She sloshed along the muddy trail through the farm's gate. The horse and cow chewed the grass lazily as they both watched her pull the cart alongside the field. She looked back to her home, where a figure now filled the doorway of the cottage.

"Nemeah!" Her mother's voice rang out, full of warmth and relief.

Nemeah let out a giggle of delight as she quickened her pace and bounded down the trail that led to their house. Her mother hurried down the path, her apron flapping in the wind. Her arms were open wide, and Nemeah gladly fell into them, feeling the comfort of home wash over her.

"What in all of Ardoria took you?" her mother said, pulling back to inspect her daughter. "You gave me a dreadful fright!"

Nemeah grimaced as she recalled the metal creature and the relentless downpour that had delayed her journey to the market and, ultimately, her journey home. The memory of trudging through the muck still clung to her, but her mother's sharp gaze quickly pulled her back to the present. Maeve eyed her dress and boots. Her stained coat and wrinkled hat. Then her eyes fell to the cart suspiciously, noticing a few bulging lumps beneath the linen cloths.

"Sold everything?" Her voice was laden with accusation as she tugged back the cloth, revealing the old, speckled jar of herbs and a corroded metal box.

Nemeah felt shock surge through her as her eyes landed on its rusted surface. Where had it come from? Did she actually go to the beach last night? Her head whirled with questions that needed to be answered. The sun's dim rays gleamed off the exposed silver, its intricate designs catching the light in a way that made Nemeah's stomach twist with anxiety.

"And spent it all?" Maeve's tone grew sharper, her face shifting from her brief greeting smile to the all-too-familiar look of discontent whenever it came to Nemeah's ventures.

Her brow furrowed, her lips thinning into a tight line. The pale skin of her cheeks flushed crimson. A splotchy rage spread down her neck like an unchecked fire, her temper simmering beneath the surface, ready to burst.

"No," Nemeah stammered, fumbling as she pulled a few coins from her pocket. "I sold everything to a couple of herbal merchants. They sheltered me for the night and gave me this jar of herbs in return."

She handed the shillings over, her heart fluttering in a desperate hope for approval. Maeve snatched the coins from Nemeah's hand, her fingers clenching tightly around the shillings as she counted them with a scowl.

"So, you gave everything to a couple of bedlamite vagabonds," Maeve spat, the disdain dripping from her words, "and in return, you bought a scrap of rusted metal and a jar of weeds?"

Maeve seized the jar and yanked the cork free, the sharp pop filling the tense air. She shook a few of the dried roots into her palm and brought them to her nose. Her expression soured further, and her lips curled in disgust as she tilted the jar, letting its contents spill carelessly onto the ground.

"Just as I thought," Maeve muttered bitterly. "Useless grass roots. Foolish girl!"

Nemeah stared in disbelief, her heart sinking into her stomach. She had smelled the contents herself and knew them to be something more by their pungent, sweet scent. The contents the old merchant woman had given her were far more bitter and foreign than any grass roots she had ever smelled. How could her mother not know the difference? Her thoughts were interrupted as Maeve's hand shot out toward the metal box, snatching it up with a rough grip. Nemeah's heart pounded in her chest as Maeve rattled the box, shaking it with unnecessary force, but the contents, if any, remained silent, just as they had when Nemeah tried the same.

"An empty box," Maeve sneered, inspecting the silver scrollwork and the corroded dents.

"I found it." Nemeah quickly interjected. "I thought it was nice."

Maeve turned it over, examining it with a critical eye.

"We will see if your father can clean it up. It looks to be silver... or close to it. Might be able to sell it and make back what little profit you failed to acquire."

Before Nemeah could respond, a faint cry echoed from the doorway of their cottage. Maeve and Nemeah both turned to see Orla standing barefoot, clutching one of her ragged dolls in her little hands. Her too-large dress hung from her thin frame as she stared at her sister with a wide grin.

"Did Nemeah bring me back anything from the market?" Orla's voice was sweet and innocent, and she was completely unaware of the tension between her mother and sister.

Maeve quickly dropped the box and rushed to the door, yelling about Orla's bare feet on the cold cobblestone floor. Nemeah watched her mother escort her sister back inside and shut the door. At that moment, Nemeah felt a familiar sting of inadequacy. She had sold all their goods at the market, yet her mother made her feel like her efforts were not meeting expectations. She felt worthless in her mother's eyes. Despair washed over her as she fought the tears that burned in her eyes. Her attention fell to the ground where the box had fallen; she was surprised to find the latch unclasped and the lid ajar. Nemeah slowly crouched down, bunching her skirt and apron in her lap to avoid the muddy ground. The icy chill wrapped around her legs and sent goosebumps erupting from head to toe. She cautiously peeked over the hand cart to check if her mother was watching, relieved to see the door still firmly shut. Nemeah slowly lowered her hands to the box, its warmth seeping into her thin fingers as her heart gathered speed. She carefully pried the clasp free of its hook, and the lid of the old metal box creaked open. A gasp escaped her lips.

Inside was a beautiful mirror. Its glass was perfectly intact, reflecting the sky above in a gleaming, almost magical finish. Carefully, she wrapped her fingers around the mirror's handle and lifted it from the box. The back and handle displayed intricate scrollwork that matched the designs on the box itself. To her surprise, the mirror was spotless, with no corrosion or rust, no tarnish blemishing its silvery metal. She gazed into her reflection, captivated by her deep blue eyes flecked with lighter hues reminiscent of a night sky with a dancing aurora.

Her raven-black hair shone like polished silk in the radiant sunlight, while her delicate features were dotted with freckles that lent her an air of youthful innocence. As she admired herself, a strange surge of energy flowed through her, igniting a feeling of triumph and a familiar pull deep within her chest. It was the same ache she had felt the night before on the sandy beach illuminated by the moon. The creak of the front door startled her, and she instinctively glanced back to see her mother standing in the doorway, arms crossed in disapproval.

"Get that cart to the barn and fetch your father. It is time to eat." Her mother's voice was sharp, cutting through the wind like a knife in a cake before she slammed the door shut again.

Nemeah sighed, her heart heavy with disappointment. She turned her attention back to the mirror, and shock coursed through her when she noticed another face staring back at her. This face mirrored the hooded figure she had encountered on the beach the previous night. The woman had luminous eyes that shone like the full moon from under the shadow of her hood. Hair as dark as the void of night spilled out around her shoulders and down her arms. Mysterious felt like an inadequate word to describe the figure who gazed back at her. With a serene smile that was just barely visible, the woman spoke, her voice echoing in Nemeah's mind. "Free me." The words startled Nemeah out of her daze, causing her to tumble backward onto her bottom, nearly dropping the pristine mirror. Her movements came in shaky jolts as she hurriedly placed the mirror back inside its box and closed the lid. Heart racing, she peeked over the hand cart again, checking to see if the coast was clear. The door remained firmly shut, a small comfort amid the whirlwind of emotions.

She quickly rose to her feet, tucking the box back under the waxed linen and pushing the hand cart toward the barn. Inside, her father was now brushing down the old golden mare, whistling a low tune as he worked. The steady control of each note always impressed Nemeah, evoking a hint of jealousy within her. She had tried her hand at whistling but could only manage a single high note on rare occasions, much to her frustration. The mare's dark eyes followed Nemeah as she rattled the cart through the wide barn, which smelled of hay and old wood, a scent that had always felt like home. Eoghan glanced up and nodded to his daughter, a warm smile gracing his face as she passed him. She returned the cart to its empty stall, taking a moment to hang the linen over the stable wall, her thoughts still preoccupied with the mirror. She found herself staring, mesmerized by the shining box nestled among the hay in the cart. Who was the woman she had seen? Where did the box come from? What did the woman mean by needing to be freed? A thrill of excitement mixed with fear danced in her chest, and she wondered what kind of magic was at play. Nemeah's mind swirled with questions. The mirror felt significant, almost as if it had a life of its own, a connection that beckoned her to explore further. She could still picture the woman's luminous eyes and the gentle yet urgent plea that had echoed in her mind. Was this woman trapped somewhere?

"Everything all right, Nemeah?" Eoghan's voice broke through her reverie, his brow slightly furrowed with concern.

Nemeah quickly shook her head, brushing away the thoughts as best she could. "Just... tired from the market. It was a long trip on foot."

Her father nodded, returning to his work, but the warmth of his concern lingered. Nemeah watched him for a moment as he methodically groomed the mare and felt a wave of affection. In this cozy barn, surrounded by familiar scents and sounds, she wanted nothing more than to share her discoveries and seek advice, yet a sense of unease held her back. She let her eyes wander around the barn. The patch in the roof that had been mended when she was smaller. She remembered helping fetch tools her father needed and climbing the tall, wobbly ladder to hand him nails. The new shingles that had cost a fortune stopped the Tirnmoor rains from seeping in. Her father's fresh wounds were on the mend as he stifled groans while hauling the heavy beams and lumber around.

"Heard a commotion." Her father's gravelly voice pulled Nemeah from her thoughts as she put away the cart.

"Umm, yes. Ma was not happy with the amount I got from the market." She bunched up some hay and sprinkled it in the stall where the golden mare usually stayed at night, her fingers working mechanically as she spoke.

"We never get that much from the market. Your mother knows that." Eoghan replied, still focused on brushing the mare on the other side of the stall.

Nemeah felt a small spark of relief at his words, but it was not enough to wash away the weight of her mother's reaction. The disappointment lingered like a shadow over her.

"I heard something about roots, and maybe a box to sell?" Eoghan's brow furrowed as he stared at Nemeah over the horse's back, his brush strokes steady and methodical.

"A couple of nice merchants gave me some herbs to try. They also let me sleep under their wagon last night since it was so late by the time I got to the market. I guess I walked a bit too slow." She thought of the metal monster her imagination had conjured, the fear and wonder mingling, and decided it best not to mention it to her father. "The herbs are supposed to help with nightmares, but Ma said they were just old grass roots. I guess I got swindled, though they were given freely." She shrugged her shoulders.

Her father raised an eyebrow, pausing his work as he set the brush aside and wrapped a blanket around the mare's back. "Thought you stopped having nightmares."

"Well, I did, for a little while," she stammered, feeling the flush of embarrassment creep up her cheeks.

Eoghan limped over to her, his strong arms enveloping her in a comforting embrace. "It will pass. Just like it always does."

A tear threatened to spill from her lower eyelid, but she blinked it away, quickly pushing out from his embrace.

"Anyways, I found a silver box on the beach last night. It is rusted shut, so Ma suggested you look at it and see if you could clean it up and make back some of what I lost at the market." She rushed to the stall where the cart had been stored, her heart racing as she stared down at the box.

She carefully lifted it and brought it to her father, who took it with a careful hand and examined the battered exterior of the small chest. Eoghan ran his calloused fingers over the intricate scrollwork and the corroded surface.

"This is quite beautiful," he mused, tilting it to catch the light of his lantern. "Could be silver, but we will need to clean it up properly to see."

He scrutinized every corner and detail until, at last, he tried the clasp. Nemeah's eyes widened as she watched her father open the lid. She leaned in, desperate to peer inside with him, but froze as she looked into the box. The mirror was gone. Panic surged through her. Had she imagined it just as she had with the metal monster? Dreaming when awake? She recalled the weight of the mirror in her hand and the surge of power that had coursed through her. A wave of disappointment washed over her, leaving her breathless.

"Seems to be just fine to me, no problem opening," her father said, examining the latch and hinges with a curious glint in his eye. "I would say it is silver. Precious Metal does go for a pretty amount to the right buyer. I can see what I can do as far as cleanup." He looked at Nemeah with a slight grin. "How about I split the money with you since you were the one to find it?"

Nemeah's heart soared at the thought. She had never earned money before. Excitement bubbled up, bringing visions of new shoes, a beautiful dress, perhaps a parasol, or a necklace adorned with shining earrings. She could dress like the princesses in her storybooks. To look beautiful and elegant as her dress swayed back and forth as she walked, but then she quickly shook the thought away, a frown replacing her earlier enthusiasm.

"No, I did not fetch enough at the market. It should go back to the farm," she murmured, her eyes falling to the ground.

Her father gently patted her shoulder, his smile unwavering despite her protest. "We will split it. You for finding it, and me for cleaning it up."

Nemeah met her father's gaze and felt warmth spread through her chest. She smiled back, grateful for his understanding and kindness, even if she felt a twinge of guilt. Just then, Maeve's voice rang out, calling from the house, "Dinner is getting cold!" Together, Nemeah and her father walked to the house, where the enticing smell of food brought some life back to Nemeah's weary body. Her nostrils flared as she inhaled deeply, savoring the aroma of freshly cooked chicken and warm, crusty bread. The scent of sprouted greens pan-fried with bright orange carrots and boiled potatoes wafted through the air, promising a feast befitting a nobleman. Her stomach rumbled fiercely in response as she pulled her chair out from the table.

"Now that is a sound I recognize and can relate to," Eoghan chuckled, tugging on her long braid playfully as he sat beside her.

"Go clean up first," Maeve commanded, her eyes fixed on Nemeah from across the table. "The both of you."

Nemeah glanced at her father, who nodded in agreement and hurried away to his room. She groaned under her breath as she slid her feet onto the cold cobblestone floor, dragging herself step by step until she reached the base of the stairs. Her tired legs protested with each stomp up the fourteen steps to her and Orla's room, and her frustration grew. The sight that greeted her was chaos. Orla's toys were scattered everywhere, mingling with Nemeah's books and ribbons.

"Orla!" Nemeah shouted down the stairs, irritation bubbling over.

"No yelling, young lady," Maeve called back, her tone firm.

"But she messed with my stuff! I have asked her so many times not to touch it, Ma!" Nemeah countered, exasperation creeping into her voice.

"Did she mess anything up? Can the books still be read and the ribbons used?" Maeve's voice was stern, and Nemeah could sense the rising temper.

Nemeah felt the heat of rage surge through her as she looked around the room, and her frustration morphed into defeat when she did not notice any damage to her belongings.

"No," she groaned through clenched teeth.

"Then wash up, young lady. I will not tell you again."

Nemeah sighed, gathering her things and placing them back on her shelf and in the drawer of her bedside table. She removed her shawl and handkerchief, untied her apron, and threw it onto her bed. As she did, she noticed that its weight felt unusual.

"I must have left something in a pocket," she muttered, curiosity flooding over her. She lifted her apron, now taking note of just how much mud covered it. She quickly scanned her blanket, grateful she had not soiled her bedding. She reached a hand into the first pocket and came up empty-handed. She reached her hand into the second and froze as her fingers encountered something smooth and cold. Her heart raced as she recognized what it was. Her hand trembled as her fingers curled around the handle and pulled out the mirror.

"But how?" she whispered, confusion swirling in her mind.

The mirror's reflection returned her own visage, the familiar deep blue of her eyes staring back, and its weight was comforting in her hand. Nemeah stepped back, her foot meeting one of Orla's many toys, which sent her stumbling slightly. She quickly glanced around the room, anxiety prickling at her skin. Where could she hide the silver mirror without her little sister finding it? She knew that if Orla laid eyes on it, she would want it for herself, and with her mother's favoritism, Nemeah feared she would lose it. Acting swiftly, she lifted her mattress, struggling under its dense weight, and slipped the mirror carefully underneath. She replaced the mattress and smoothed her bedding, ensuring it was hidden from sight. Satisfied, she moved to her wash basin, washing away the remnants of the day's labor and her frustrations. Once finished, Nemeah headed back downstairs, ready to feast like never before.

After supper, Nemeah was tasked with the cleanup. Even though her stomach ached with how much she had greedily stuffed down her gullet, she was happy to be busy and not under her mother's watchful eye. She stepped outside to bring the hogs their buckets of vegetable trimmings and the scraps that Orla had refused to eat. The wind whipped around her, cold and biting, but she could not help but feel a spark of exhilaration at the secret she held close. With each bucket she carried, thoughts of the mirror danced in her mind. How had it ended up in her pocket, and what did the mysterious woman mean by "free me"? The hogs grunted eagerly as she set down the buckets, their snouts diving into the scraps. Nemeah watched them for a moment, her thoughts swirling. Maybe, just maybe, the mirror was more than just a beautiful object. Or perhaps she was losing her mind after all? Perhaps there was no woman, no mirror. Maybe she had fallen and hit her head without remembering? She ran her fingers along her scalp, searching for any evidence of a wound, and found none. She looked up to the thick clouds, the moon's light peeking through as the ever-familiar sound of thunder rumbled in the distance. She looked back down at the pigs, who had already devoured the contents within the bucket.

"A storm is coming." She murmured as she retrieved the buckets and headed back inside.

Chapter Four

T he deep, ominous laugh of the armored soldier rumbled in his metal shell as it sifted through the hay in search of a young girl, one who had just been frolicking in a field and had witnessed a massacre. His massive, heavy hands edged closer and closer until she heard a familiar voice.

"Nemeah? Where are you?" Her father called, panic threading his tone.

Fear found her buried beneath the hays shelter as she squeezed her eyes shut and wished the man would leave her alone. A hissing sound filled the barn, the man's hands flexing as his body tensed and quaked inside the armor. Smoke spilled out from the metal skeleton as a deep growl replaced his voice. The metal creature now stood, shadow spilling from its plated casing. It shifted its attention to a new target and swiftly left the barn. Nemeah poked her head out from the hay, her heart pounding. The deafening ringing of gunfire echoed around her, and even as she covered her ears, she could hear the desperate cries of her neighbors and family fighting against the enemy that had trespassed onto their land.

Slowly, she walked to the opening of the barn door. The young mare was kicking and thrashing in its stall, begging to be freed from its confined space. Its neck and chest were scratched by its efforts, red welts surfacing under its hair. Feeling the same dire need to escape the madness, Nemeah tugged on the bolt and released the mare.

She watched as it galloped out of the barn into the sunlight, the smoke of gunpowder billowing around its shiny coat as it raced to-

ward her father. The mare reared back and knocked the large man to
the ground before her father.

He wore the shining armor and crimson cape. His sword flew free from his hand. A swirl of smoke moved quickly around the soldiers.

Each one falling to the ground, their lifeless bodies halting any movement. She watched in horror as the creature moved like an animal, yet was dressed as one of their own. Shots rang off, yet no bullet wounded it. The screams started then, with her own being drowned in the chaos. That is when her vision focused, and she saw it: the blood running down her father's leg and forehead, the anguish on his face as he carefully aimed his muzzleloader.

"Father!" Her little scream was no match for the explosion within his gun. The metal ball whizzed through the air and struck the ashen monster in the chest.

It froze, a man speared on its claws, blood dripping down the golden armor. The creature turned, its eyeless face focusing on the man who had shot it. It gave a beastly roar as it charged her father, its razor claws swinging low to the ground. Time seemed to slow as Nemeah watched her father's body fly through the air, landing with a thud on the ground. His body going still.

"No!"

Nemeah woke in a trembling state of panic. Her body shook as she quickly sat up in her bed, covering her face with her hands. Her tear-soaked cheeks felt feverish under her fingertips, and she realized she was soaked with sweat. She glanced at the hearth, still crackling with fire, indicating that she had not been asleep for long. Her eyes drifted to her sister's bed, where a small lump stirred momentarily before soft snores filled the silence of the night. Nemeah wished she had the herbs with her to ward off the painful nightmares that replayed every night without fail. Her imagination morphed into terrors of the days the Axis stalked their land. Of the stories she had heard from others, and the anger she felt every time she remembered her father was hurt fighting far away. She held her head in her hands while her thoughts slowly calmed.

"Maybe I can find the pile in the yard?" Her voice was scratchy as if she had actually been screaming with all her might in her dream.

She tried to clear her throat to no avail. Easing her shivering body out from beneath the covers, she stepped into her leather clogs and draped her shawl over her shoulders. Before she crept downstairs, Nemeah felt the space under her mattress and was relieved to touch the mirror's cool metal. Knowing she did not imagine the box or mirror the day before was a comfort. She carefully opened the heavy pine door and inched one foot along the knotted stairs until she found the edge with her toe, making sure not to trip in the darkness. She eased herself down slowly, feeling as if it took hours to descend from her bedroom. Stopping anytime she heard a noise that was not her own. Once her heel hit the cobbles of the lower floor, she quietly walked to the front door, retrieved her coat, and pulled it on before sliding out of the cottage's massive door. As she stepped into the yard, she noted that the moon was full, just as it had been in her dream the night before. She remembered the smell and taste of the ocean's mist on her skin and lips. She stared at the sky, momentarily forgetting her mission.

The moon's white light brightly illuminated the dark exterior of the world. Stars twinkled in the black sky as she tried to sear every detail into her brain. Clear nights like this were very rare, and she did not know when she would see the stars again. Nemeah crouched low to the ground, skimming her hands just over the grass and mud. She knew the searching would yield nothing in return, considering Tirnmoor's heavy winds. She also knew she would be a mess when she went back inside, but she figured she could wash up in the morning and avoid trouble with her mother. She searched and searched until her back grew tired and her knees ached. The night's temperature felt like it had dropped several degrees while she looked for the discarded herbs. Just as she was about to give up, she heard a faint voice behind her. Slowly, she stood and turned to see the hooded woman standing between her and her home. Nemeah's heart raced as her wide eyes remained unblinking.

The woman stood motionless as seconds ticked by, and with them, the sky began to change. The stars flared brighter as though the universe itself had taken a sharp breath. The world around Nemeah twisted, whirling away into nothing, leaving only an endless void. Space. She was floating, suspended in the silence of a place she could not begin to comprehend. Nemeah screamed, her voice raw and desperate, but no sound came. Panic clawed at her chest as her gaze darted frantically, searching for solid ground... for *anything* to hold on to. Her black hair floated wildly, strands twisting in slow, weightless arcs. The thin fabric of her chemise tugged against her skin as if eager to escape into the vast nothingness around her. Cold seeped into her very bones, an unforgiving, unnatural cold, and her breath caught in her chest as she felt the liquid in her eyes begin to freeze. She blinked furiously, forcing herself to focus, to stay awake. The silence was unbearable. It was not just the absence of sound; this *place* seemed to swallow noise entirely. Even her thoughts felt stifled, reduced to a dull hum beneath the crushing weight of the void.

What is this place?

A surge of fear and helplessness rippled through her, and she finally fixed her attention back on the hooded woman. She had not moved, serene and still, her presence almost ethereal. It was as though the chaos of this strange place could not touch her.

"There is no need to be frightened," the woman said, her voice breaking through the silence like warmth into winter.

The sound startled Nemeah. It was gentle and calming, like sunlight on a cold morning, and for the first time, the panic in her chest began to ease. The woman smiled kindly and softly, and Nemeah felt something strange bloom within her: trust. She did not understand why, but suddenly, she was at ease with not being alone. Nemeah's breaths slowed, her chest rising and falling in deliberate, icy inhales as she forced herself to look around. The stars were close now, burning and blazing with a wild brilliance she had never known. In the night sky, they had always seemed distant, indifferent. But here, they were alive. Fiery reds and glacial blues pulsed around her, light shimmering in slow, sweeping waves. Comets streaked past with great, blazing trails that rippled like water disturbed in their wake. Their tails lingered for moments before dissolving into a million silver sparks, which drifted lazily into the darkness. It was beautiful. It was terrifying.

Nemeah felt tiny, a speck lost in a glittering ocean, suspended between wonder and dread. This place was otherworldly, untouched by mortal hands, and the stars themselves seemed to hum, vibrating faintly in her chest as though whispering secrets she could not yet hear. She pulled her chemise tightly to her skin, taking another slow breath to steady herself. Her eyes flicked back to the woman, who remained still as though she belonged here and was part of this endless expanse. *Who are you?* Nemeah wanted to ask, but her lips would not move, and her voice disobeyed. The stars burned on, and the woman smiled. She stood closer now, so close Nemeah could see the details that made her unreal. With deliberate grace, the tall figure removed her hood, and Nemeah's breath caught. The woman's eyes were a marvel, twin voids like black holes, yet within their depths, Nemeah glimpsed the far reaches of time, fractured visions of stars being born, dying, and reborn again. They were vast and unknowable, a paradox of light and darkness. She had a fierce and unwavering gaze, and though her voice was soft, it carried the weight of ages, commanding attention with every unspoken word.

Her hair, impossibly intricate, fell in smooth pleats woven with shimmering chains and etched runes. They caught the light, glittering like constellations strung through the night sky. Nemeah's eyes followed their patterns before tracing the woman's robe, layers upon layers of silken fabric that fell like raven wings. Black feathers rippled and shimmered, delicate yet sharp, as though stitched from shadows and moonlight. Her skin seemed to glow faintly, a soft shimmer like stardust scattered across her form, and in the face of such beauty and mystery, Nemeah felt her heart falter. Fear curled low in her stomach, but so did an unshakable longing, a desire to understand, to *know*.

"Who are you?" Nemeah whispered, her voice fragile as frost.

The woman smiled softly and comfortingly, though her presence remained as overwhelming as the stars around them.

"My name is Kallemena Vaelora," she said, her voice melodic, as if shaped from song and wind. I come from a land far away and long ago."

Long ago? What did that even mean? And how was it she was here, with this strange woman floating through what she could best guess was space itself. This was impossible. This was a dream.

Nemeah held the questions on her tongue. Before she could ask, the mysterious woman waved her hand through the air. Their surroundings started to shift once again and change. The stars fell slowly as if snow caught in a current of air. The blackness of space lightened to reveal a snowy landscape, barren except for a few cypress trees. Nemeah looked down. Snow was up to her waist, and she could feel the ice melting against her thin gown, soaking the cotton through. She began to shiver as a harsh wind sent her hair whipping about her face. The strands of her loose hair stung her skin, and ice clung to her lashes. She was sure she would freeze here, in a land of blinding white. She looked around for the woman who had brought her to this freezing landscape when her eyes caught sight of tall peaks that kissed the sky. Snowcapped and gray and blue. They, too, looked as if they were carved from ice.

"Mountains?" Her teeth chattered against her will.

They rose like titans in the distance, their peaks piercing the sky. They were stark and silent. The sight stole her breath, and she could do nothing but stare. A hand settled on her shoulder, warm and steady. Nemeah flinched at first, but as soon as Kallemena's touch met her skin, a pulse of warmth coursed through her body. It spread quickly, chasing the cold from her limbs, thawing her frozen toes, and quieting her shivers. Her frantic breaths slowed, and a strange, soothing calm washed over her. Her gaze shifted upward to meet Kallemena's face, serene, unreadable, yet somehow reassuring. For now, the freezing wind felt distant. The snow beneath her feet no longer seemed intent on swallowing her whole. And the mountains, those great, looming sentinels, stood watch.

"Where is this?" Nemeah's voice was almost carried away by the wind, but the woman heard her and answered in that same melodic, haunting voice.

"This is my home. This is Glacia."

Nemeah looked up and studied the face of her strange traveling companion. A tear slowly fell from her eye and froze on her soft, delicate cheek. Kallemena extended a long arm, her thin, elegant fingers parting like the blades of a fan. The world shifted again. The icy mountains crumbled into nothing, their snow lifting like mist and scattering upwards to form stars once more. Space reclaimed them, swallowing the landscape in its black and glittering expanse. Nemeah stumbled as the sudden change stole her footing. Kallemena released her shoulder and paced a few steps away. The tall woman rubbed her temples wearily, her graceful composure fraying for just a moment.

"Glacia?" Nemeah whispered. "The frozen continent? Were we really there?" Nemeah's heart pounded, her excitement growing. "How did you do that? Do it again! I want to see the deserts of Aetheria and the canyons in Solara!"

The woman waved her hand, and a chilled warning swept through Nemeah. It felt as if her lungs had frozen, every breath a struggle to warm her insides. She looked back at the woman. Fear kept her silent, but if this was a dream, she needed answers before she woke up. Nemeah managed a sliver of courage.

"What do you want?" She scrubbed at her now-thawed cheeks, erasing the last trace of frozen skin.

Kallemena turned to face her again, her expression calm but her voice weighted. "I need your help." The rich and unfamiliar accent coated her words like a song half-remembered. "I need you to free me."

Nemeah remembered the words she had heard when she first found the box. "Free you?"

She looked around her. From what she had just seen, this woman could do anything and be anywhere with the wave of her hand. Free her? Free her from what? Again, as if reading her mind, Kallemena answered her question.

"This realm is my prison. I am stuck here against my will by a power from long ago. I have lost everything, and I need you to help me get out of here."

Nemeah turned slowly in place, absorbing the vastness of this so-called prison. It seemed infinite, beautiful, even. Compared to her cramped, one-windowed room back home, where the floor creaked, and Orla's snores echoed through the night, it hardly seemed a prison.

"This does not look like one. There are no bars or chains."

Kallemena's gaze sharpened, and the air around her fell still. "Imagine," she began, her voice deliberate and careful, "that all your loved ones were taken from you. You do not know where they went, if they were safe, if they were allowed to grow old, surrounded by warmth and family, or if they perished alone. You are stuck, frozen in time, with no one to speak to. No touch. No sound. No life. For over *five hundred years*. Taken from your home, forced into a life you never wanted!"

Kallemena's words pierced the silence as she circled Nemeah. Her presence was magnetic, and though her steps were measured, Nemeah felt as though she were being pulled into the woman's orbit.

"Now," Kallemena continued, "would you still say this is not a prison?"

Nemeah swallowed thickly, the weight of those words pressing into her chest. Slowly, she nodded.

"But you can see me. Talk to me," she murmured as if testing the truth of her own statement.

"Yes." Kallemena's eyes softened. "But only because I have been found."

"Were you lost?"

"Yes, and you found me."

"Why me?" Nemeah turned in her spot as Kallemena continued to circle her.

"Because you have a power growing inside you that links us together. The mirror, my prison, felt you in the world and has been slowly making its way to you after so many years of lying dormant at the bottom of the sea." Kallemena looked at Nemeah with sympathetic eyes. "This road will be dangerous, and your journey will test your strengths and fears."

"Wait, road? What road?" Nemeah's voice trembled as she stared at Kallemena. "I am not going anywhere. I am just a farm girl! I have to help my family."

Kallemena said nothing. She lifted a hand, and the void shifted once again. Nemeah was suddenly bombarded with visions, war and peace, destruction and rebuilding, fields blooming under sunlight, and cities burned to ash. She felt joy so pure that it brought tears to her eyes and then anguish so sharp that she gasped for breath. Scenes flickered faster and faster: laughter, screams, children playing, soldiers dying, faces she had never seen yet somehow *knew*. Emotions crashed over her like waves, relentless and unending, happiness and pain, love and heartbreak, terror and hope. Tears spilled down Nemeah's cheeks, though she could not say which feeling brought them on. She clutched her head as if to hold herself together.

"Stop," she choked out. "Please, stop!"

The visions faded as quickly as they had come, leaving her panting and unsteady. Kallemena's low and unwavering voice cut through the silence.

"This is what our people felt," she said. "Day in, day out. When chaos broke out. When war after war brought people like *us* to our knees, to be slaughtered and forgotten. You are one of the few who remain, Nemeah. One of the few who can walk this road."

She raised her hand in another sweep, her voice a symphony of sorrow and resolve. "Free me. Free the souls of those who once flourished in these lands, souls who sought peace, who built kingdoms and harmony. *You* are the key."

Nemeah let out a strangled sob, her body curling in on itself. "No! No, I am dreaming! I fell asleep in the yard. Yes, that is it! Any second now, my parents will come to wake me up, and Ma will scold me for ruining my nightgown, but that is all right; I will wash it in the morning."

She crouched low, pressing her hands against her face to shield herself from the impossible. Her words sounded childish, even to her own ears, but she clung to them like a lifeline. This could not be real. Kallemena appeared beside her, the sharp edges of her features softening in the void's dim light. There was a glow to her, a presence that both comforted and overwhelmed.

"I know this is much to ask," Kallemena murmured, her voice wrapping around Nemeah like velvet. "And I know you are afraid. I can feel it saturating you, your body shaking from it." Slowly, Kallemena reached out, her fingers drifting through Nemeah's tangled hair. The touch was feather-light, almost soothing. "I will be with you," she promised softly. "And your *creation* will guide you. Protect you."

Nemeah's head shot up, her tear-streaked face etched with confusion. "Creation?"

Kallemena smiled faintly, then snapped her fingers. A mound appeared before them in the void, its jagged edges catching the faint light of distant stars. Nemeah's breath faltered. She *knew* that shape, the twisted, rusted hulk of metal lying in a broken heap on the invisible ground. Her pulse quickened—the *monster*. Nemeah scrambled back as fast as her body would allow, raw terror in every movement.

"No," she gasped. "No, no, no. It is a monster! It attacked me, it chased me! Send it away!" Her voice broke into a shriek that echoed through the silence.

But Kallemena did not flinch. She knelt beside the mound, her long nails tracing its rusted edges with a reverence that made Nemeah shudder. The metal groaned faintly at her touch, the sound like some ancient, wounded beast. Kallemena shook her head, her voice calm but unyielding.

"No, Nemeah," she said gently. "It is not a monster."

Nemeah continued to stumble backward as Kallemena snapped her fingers again. The sound echoed through the void, and the *creature* groaned to life. The noise struck her like a hammer blow, the grating screech of twisted metal, the scrape of claws against unseen ground. The monster rose with a horrible creak, its hulking body unfurling until it loomed at its full, grotesque height. Another snap. It took a waddling step forward, each movement grinding and rattling through the air. Nemeah tried to run, but her feet refused to move as though rooted to the nothingness beneath her. Panic surged through her chest, and her cries rose to desperate wails. The monster came closer, step by agonizing step, its shadow swallowing her whole. It reached out with one jagged, clawed hand. Nemeah's eyes slammed shut, and for a moment, she was certain this was the end. Her pulse hammered in her ears, her bladder threatening to betray her. Then, a gentle touch. A few strands of her hair were brushed back and tucked softly behind her ear. Nemeah gasped, her breath coming in a sharp, ragged burst. Her eyes blinked open, tears spilling down her cheeks, her terror giving way to shock. The creature stood perfectly still before her, its massive form like a statue of steel and shadow. It was silent. Unmoving.

"He is your protector," Kallemena said. "He has been with you since you were very young. Protecting you when the Axis came to your home."

Nemeah jumped, spinning to face her. She raised her hand instinctively to strike, but Kallemena caught her wrist with an icy grip. Ne-

meah froze, staring into eyes that had gone solid black, bottomless
voids that swallowed the starlight.

"Calm yourself," Kallemena said softly, lowering Nemeah's arm.

"The Axis never came to my home. They stayed along the outskirts
of the island. They were looking for a runaway. Nothing more." She
wiped away her tears.

Kallemena just stared, an eyebrow arched. "You know they came to
your home."

"No." Nemeah shook her head. "They did not."

"The nightmares you have, they are memories." Kallemena waved
her hand.

Nemeah was thrust into a storm. The rain soaked her through and
clung to her hair. The wind blew with a force that was deafening. She
was just outside her family's barn, the dark gray skies rumbling above.
Her mother's wails of pain. A small girl stared at a field of violet flowers and green grass, edging closer and closer as a thunderous boom
rang out. A creature of smoke and ash pulled the small girl out of the
way as the ceiling of the barn collapsed. Her mother was yelling again
as golden armored soldiers marched across their farm, taking note of
a small girl lying motionless on the ground.

"Go away!" Her mother screamed as she slid down the stall walls,
clutching her stomach in her hands.

"No. This is a dream. A nightmare." Nemeah's voice faltered.

Kallemena waved her hand again, and they were back in the void
of space. "It is a memory of when you were very young."

Nemeah staggered back, staring wide-eyed as Kallemena circled
the monster, her knuckles rapping against its helmet with a hollow
clang.

"He protected you," Kallemena continued. "Your powers were evident even back then. Now is the time to embrace it."

Nemeah continued to stare at the monster, still unmoving in its
blemished armor.

"He is harmless." Kallemena knocked on his breastplate.

"*Harmless?*" Nemeah spat, her voice raw with disbelief. "It chased me! Scared me half to death! The whole market thinks I am mad because of *that!*"

"And yet it never harmed you. Or anyone else at the market." Kallemena waved a hand.

Nemeah's cart appeared beside her precisely as she had left it, waxed linen and all. She blinked at it, then back at the motionless figure of metal. Her mind swirled, struggling to make sense of the impossible.

"This is not a dream," she whispered, her voice hoarse. "And that *thing*, it will not hurt me?"

Kallemena shook her head. Nemeah sank onto the edge of her cart, tucking her trembling hands beneath her legs.

"Then explain."

Kallemena's expression softened, though her face remained pale and strained.

"You have the same power I carry in me. Born during the same cosmic occurrence that leads to us becoming what we are. Our powers manifest at a young age, and before, in my time, we would learn to harness that power with masters to teach us, but I am afraid that is not the way anymore." She rubbed her head. "I am sorry, I am running out of time. This," She gestured around her, "takes a significant toll on me." She looked at Nemeah, her face blank. "I will have to give you more of the history later; right now, you need the facts."

She waved her hand, and the stars disappeared. No light could be seen anywhere, and no noise could be heard, and Nemeah wondered if this was what death felt like.

"I need you to go on a faraway journey and find eight other mirrors, like the one that imprisons me. You must find them and bring them together before you can free me. The next Eclipse Veil will happen in one year's time. Which is not ideal, but it is all we have. If you cannot free me before then, I fear something even more terrible is going to happen. The stars and planets are aligning. I can feel them. This will be a celestial event like no other, and someone seeks to gain more power than he understands at that time."

Nemeah opened her mouth to protest, but screamed instead. Something seized her wrist. A searing pain shot through her arm like fire, and she thrashed wildly, striking at whatever held her. Her blows hit nothing, just empty air. The pain vanished as suddenly as it had come, leaving her gasping and trembling. Her fingers flew to her wrist, probing the tender skin. She winced as her hand brushed against something, a raised bump of raw flesh as if a brand had been seared into her.

"What did you do?" Nemeah's voice was barely a whisper, shaking with fear.

"I am sorry, but that needed to be done." Kallemena's voice was faint now, brittle as if the words were splintering in her throat. "Think of it as a gift... to help hone your powers."

A dim orb flickered to life above Nemeah, its golden glow bathing her in soft light. She was still perched on the cart's edge, her fingers clutching its wooden edge.

"Your powers are projections of what your body needs," Kallemena continued, her voice drifting like smoke through the void. "Think of them as a defense."

Nemeah squinted into the shadows where Kallemena's voice echoed, straining to see her, but the woman was hidden, her form swallowed by the darkness.

"Your metal monster," Kallemena said, "is a guardian. It manifested because your powers knew you needed protection, even when *you* did not." Her words trembled with weakness now, each syllable heavier than the last. "You must learn to project it. To use the gift I have given you. Practice."

Nemeah shook her head violently, a shiver running down her spine. "I, I do not want to make that *thing* again. Not now."

A soft, amused chuckle drifted through the silence, unexpected and strangely comforting.

"Very well," Kallemena murmured. "Let us start with something smaller. Easier. A bird, perhaps?"

Nemeah hesitated, her wrist still burning uncomfortably. *A bird.* Her mind latched onto the image: A black bird with a white belly, red trimming its wings. A black bill with a red dot between its eyes. A common valley bird. She held the thought in her mind, careful and deliberate, as though shaping clay with her imagination. Her eyes widened when the image shimmered to life. A bird sat before her, its feathers a perfect shade of shadow and night. It twisted its head to look at Nemeah sideways before twisting to look at her with the other eye. It hopped along the ground, pecking at the dark flooring before expanding its wings and taking flight. Nemeah ducked as the bird swooped down towards her, the wind from its wings rustling her hair. She watched it fly around before instinctively holding her arm out for the bird to land. It perched on her hand, its talons digging into her skin, but doing no real damage. His glossy wings were delicately tucked behind its back.

"Very good," Kallemena wheezed.

A sharp *snap* cracked through the void like lightning. In an instant, the world around Nemeah shifted, and her family's farmyard sprang into existence, the familiar shapes of the barn and farmhouse standing solid under the morning sky. The pinks and oranges of sunrise streaked the horizon, glowing faintly against the lingering shadows. Kallemena stood at the center of it all, hunched over as if the weight of the world had bent her spine. Her face was pale as snow, her eyes sunken and ringed with darkness.

"Are you all right?" Nemeah's heart lurched. She rushed to Kallemena's side and slipped an arm around her. The woman's body was light, far too light, as though she might dissolve into mist.

"Just... a side effect," Kallemena whispered, her breath uneven. "From the prison, I was sealed in. It drains me." She looked at Nemeah then, her gaze soft but searching. "I must rest now, but before I do, I need your answer."

Nemeah hesitated, her pulse thudding in her ears.

"Will you help me?"

The question hung between them, fragile as a spider's thread. Nemeah's eyes wandered across the farmyard. The sunrise bathed the fields in gold, and for a moment, everything felt untouched, unchanged. But in her heart, something had already shifted. She thought of distant lands, vast oceans, and strange cities. She imagined sights she had never seen and people she had never met. An adventure beyond anything she could dream of. Her gaze fell to her wrist, where a pink scar had formed. It was tender and fresh, the shape delicate, like petals etched into her skin.

"It looks like a flower," she whispered.

Kallemena's lips curved into a faint smile. "A snowdrop. My mother used to call me that."

A moment passed between them, fragile, quiet, and unspoken. Nemeah felt her heart ache for this woman she barely knew. She felt the thrill of something new unfurling inside her, a whisper of purpose mixed with longing. Before she could think, before doubt could stop her, the words spilled from her lips.

"I will help you."

Kallemena's smile blossomed, and for the first time, it was reflected in her eyes. Her face seemed almost aglow with warmth as if the promise had breathed life back into her.

"Keep the mirror close," she said softly. "It will show you the way. For now, practice your gift."

With a final wave of her hand, Kallemena was gone. Nemeah looked around. The house sat silent as the rooster in the coop began to crow. Still reeling from the encounter, she crept carefully back upstairs to her room before her mother could wake and find her outside in her chemise. She was relieved to see hardly any mud on the white cotton dress and sighed in relief as she pulled her leather clogs from her feet. Pulling back the thick, feathered blanket, she was surprised to see the speckled jar the merchant woman had given her. She pulled the cork from the jar with a satisfying pop, and the sharp, sour smell of the herbs seeped out. Holding the jar close, she muttered a quiet thank you, then set it on her bedside table before crawling under the covers. She went to sleep with her thumb rubbing over the minor burn on her wrist.

Within the hour, Maeve was up, collecting eggs from the chickens and gathering a few fresh vegetables from the garden. A couple of purple and yellow peppers with a stalk of green onions sizzled in the pan, making Eoghan's mouth water as he entered with a bucket of fresh milk. He gave his wife a quick kiss on the cheek before ladling the milk into glass bottles and setting them aside.

"You were too hard on Nemeah yesterday," Eoghan murmured, his voice barely louder than the sound of the sizzling vegetables.

Maeve's temper stirred as she cracked three eggs hard against the side of the pan, tossing the shells into the pig bucket.

"Well, she should not have given away our hard-earned goods at the market," she replied, slipping an oven mitt on to pull out a loaf of bread. She tapped the top, pleased with the thick golden crust, though a few smears of flour still clung to the surface.

Eoghan finished his task and walked to the table, dragging a wooden chair across the cobbled floor before sitting down with his lame leg stretched out.

"Maeve, we both know she got slightly more than we usually do. You need to stop being so hard on her."

Maeve spun around, her face flushed from the heat of the stove.

"She could have gotten *more* for those potatoes and eggs! Our hens lay the best eggs. And if she would have gone to our usual buyers..."

"She would have gotten *less*," Eoghan interrupted, his voice louder now. "Everyone sells eggs, Maeve. Anyone's hens can lay just as good as ours. You scold her for everything she does! If I had gone with her, maybe we would have gotten a shilling more because people know *me*. They do not know her, and maybe if you had let her wait for me to return from the Ashfords, I could have gone with her."

A sudden thud from the ceiling silenced them both. They looked up at the floorboards that supported their daughter's room.

"Let her be, Maeve. It was not her fault." Eoghan stood abruptly, his face red with anger and embarrassment. Hobbling to the door, he paused before leaving.

"She is starting to remember again, Maeve." He forced the door open with a heavy shove and slammed it behind him, leaving Maeve with only the smell of burnt eggs and overcooked vegetables.

Upstairs, Nemeah awoke groggy. The few minutes of sleep she had managed seemed to do more harm than good. She rolled over and saw her little sister playing with her wooden toys on the floor. Orla's brown hair hung in her face, unbraided and messy. Nemeah propped herself up on one elbow, rubbing her sore eyes. She froze. Did that really happen? Was last night real? Slowly, she opened the drawer on her bedside table, and nestled among her ribbons was the jar of roots. A smile crept across her face as she closed the drawer quietly.

"Those smell awful," Orla said, wrinkling her nose as she pretended to feed her wooden horse with grass from the yard.

Nemeah groaned. "Why were you in my things again?"

"I let you play with my toys, so it is only fair for me to play with yours." Orla grinned mischievously at her older sister.

"I do not have toys, Orla," Nemeah muttered, dragging her hands down her face. "I just have *things*. My things, and I do not play with your toys. At least not in the last five years."

After dressing herself, Nemeah braided Orla's hair and helped her slip into a thick dress and even thicker wool stockings. Together, they went downstairs, where the smell of burnt eggs greeted them. Their mother sat at the table with her head in her hands, the wood damp where her tears had fallen.

"Mama, what is wrong?" Orla asked, wrapping her thin arms around Maeve's shoulders.

Startled, Maeve quickly wiped her eyes and composed herself, clearing her throat. "I just burned the eggs, Orla, dear. Silly old woman mistake." She patted Orla's hand, gesturing for her to sit.

Her eyes drifted to Nemeah, who was fetching cups from the cupboard and pouring the milk Eoghan had brought in earlier. Maeve felt the urge to apologize, to say anything that might mend the long fraying bonds between her and her eldest daughter. She watched as Nemeah moved carefully around the kitchen, cutting a few slices of bread and dividing the charred eggs into four portions.

"Nemeah..." Maeve's voice was weak and flat. Nemeah looked up, waiting for her mother to speak.

"Your father will not be joining us. You can have his portion if Orla does not want it."

Orla took a bite of the blackened eggs and vegetables, then immediately stuck out her tongue in disgust.

Chapter Five

Nemeah watched intently as her father polished the silver box after prying off the old barnacle shells. Using a mixture of old ashes and water, he scrubbed the surface until every inch was coated. The gritty paste stained his hands and clothes as he scrubbed the tarnished surface. To their surprise, all the darkened spots lifted, revealing intricate scrollwork that shimmered in the light. Eoghan gave her a wink, then carried the box to the water barrel and rinsed it off. After drying it carefully, he examined the gleaming metal one last time before handing it to her.

"You know, you could keep it," he said, leaning against the barn door's frame as he wiped his hands with a rag. "Since you found it."

The clouds hung low in the sky, and a gentle breeze rustled the leaves. Nemeah looked at her father, his calloused hands and weathered skin resulting from years of working out in the Tirnmoor elements. His once-dark hair had faded to a light brown, with long strands of white lining his temples. His squinted eyes scanned the fields where their cow and horse grazed on sweet clover while the hogs lay lazily in the mud. The chickens pecked furiously at the freshly scratched dirt, with their heads bobbing as they did so.

Nemeah's thoughts drifted to her strange encounter with Kallemena; the realm in which she was imprisoned was so different from the farm. She looked out over the fields, her mind flickering to the powers she possessed. The abilities that were supposed to be hers. She focused on the image of a rabbit, imagining a twitching nose and long ears just as she had done with the bird the night before. But nothing appeared in the field. No rabbit. No magic. Only the grass swayed in the breeze. A storm building on the horizon. She sighed and turned back to her father.

"We should sell it," she said, offering him a faint smile as she returned the warm box. "Besides, I have nothing worthwhile to put in it anyway."

Eoghan considered her words for a moment and nodded. "Then maybe you can buy something nice at the market when we sell it." He gave her a nudge before disappearing into the barn to tidy up his tools.

She watched him favor his right shoulder as he picked up the rags and scrubbed the work surface. She remembered the healing process after the war. The doctor was no more than their neighbor, Mr. Callan, and he mainly worked on animals, not humans. The scars left behind on her father's skin showed proof that Mr. Callan did not worry about pretty lines and clean sewing. He ensured Eoghan was back in one piece before leaving their farm.

Nemeah wandered toward the fence, watching the mare and cow graze peacefully. She folded her arms on the railing and smiled as she felt the hot sun warming her dark hair. The clouds parted ever so slightly above her. It was a welcome change from the rainy, gray days they had been having. Even the songbirds seemed to be enjoying the weather by swooping through the sky and chirping their melodies above, the world around her calm and ordinary. But inside, a storm brewed. She remembered the power she had felt the night before, the strange sensation of being something more than just a farm girl. And now... nothing. She studied her wrist where the flesh now lay flat and pink, her little gift from Kallemena. She balled he fists and focused again, this time with more determination. She pictured the rabbit, willing to bring it into existence with all her might. A small gray lump flickered in the grass, but before she could react, it was gone.

Frustration welled up inside her. Her mother's words echoed in her mind: "You are too old to act like a child. You have spent all our hard-earned money." A surge of emotion burst from her, and the mare suddenly shrieked, a high-pitched, bone-chilling sound that sliced through the air. The horse's nostrils flared wide as it bolted in fear. Nemeah looked up to see the cow, startled, let out a deep bellow, low and rumbling, filled with panic. Nemeah's heart raced, her pulse pounding in her ears. She scanned the field and saw it then, the metal monster, the same one that chased her to the market, the one Kallemena said would not hurt her, but would it hurt others? She watched in horror as it stalked toward the cow.

"No!" Nemeah screamed, climbing, half-falling over the fence, and running toward the growing disaster. "Get away from her!" She yelled as she waved her hands frantically.

Her feet flew over the ground, but terror clung to her like a weight. She clapped her hands and let out barks of noise, trying to scare the cow into moving, but the poor creature was frozen, its wide eyes locked on the approaching smoky beast. Then, with one final cry, the cow collapsed onto its side, still and silent. Nemeah skidded to a stop, watching in horror as the monster turned its attention to the mare, who ran terrified along the fence line, neighing wildly. Desperation filled Nemeah. She shut her eyes and focused.

"It is not real," she whispered. "It is not real. It cannot hurt them. It is not real!"

She opened her eyes and willed the metal creation away. It dissolved into the air as if carried off by a stray wind.

"Nemeah?" Her father's voice called out, sharp with concern. He hurried toward the fence, his face filled with alarm. "What happened? What is going on?"

Nemeah froze, unsure of how to answer her father's questions. "I... I thought I saw a wolf," she lied, the words tumbling out before she could stop them. "It scared the animals, that is all."

Eoghan studied her, his brow furrowed, before turning to the cow lying motionless in the grass. They walked in silence, approaching the hulking animal, Nemeah wishing with all her might that it would stand and trample off. It did no such thing. Her father knelt beside the animal, his hand running over its still body. The cow's eyes were wide and empty, its chest no longer rising and falling. A thin trickle of blood ran from its nose. Nemeah's heart sank as guilt washed over her. She had killed it. Her monster had terrified the cow to death. Tears spilled down her cheeks, and she fell to her knees, grief gripping her chest. Her father knelt beside her and pulled her close. He let out a soft whistle, and the mare cautiously approached, sniffing at the body of her fallen companion.

"Go tell your ma I need my butcher's knives," Eoghan said gently, rising to his feet. He slipped the bell off the cow's neck. "And tell her I will need salt."

That afternoon, Nemeah's father carved up the cow. He set aside thick slabs of meat to be salted while hanging thin strips in the shed to smoke. Inside, her mother, Maeve, fried large steaks for supper. As they ate, the only sounds were the crackle of the fire and the scraping of cutlery against their plates. A sad meal on what should have been a happy day. Later, Nemeah took on her nightly chore of slopping the pigs. She scattered the scraps and watched their greedy snouts dive into the mix. Standing outside, she glanced up at the lightning that raced across the sky. The sound of raindrops hitting the earth was starting to fill the quiet night. Anger and guilt twisted in her stomach. No matter how hard she wished and prayed, she could not bring their cow back or erase the terror she had felt earlier. Her father would now have to go to the neighbors for milk or spend money they could not spare on another cow, one mature enough to calve and produce.

Her gaze shifted to the pigs again as they snorted and jostled each other for food. When she turned toward the house, she saw her father crossing the yard, carrying a bedroll and his muzzleloader. He planned to sleep in the barn tonight, watching over the mare in case the imagined wolf returned. Nemeah ducked inside, the guilt gnawing at her. Inside, she could feel her mother's eyes on her back as she tidied up. Maeve's stare followed her daughters' every movement, sweeping dirt from the floor and placing a few logs on the fire. Perhaps she had been too harsh, too demanding. But seeing Nemeah so quiet and defeated made Maeve ache in ways she did not know she could. Nemeah was about to head upstairs when her mother's voice stopped her.

"Nemeah, wait."

Maeve, her brown hair streaked with silver, quickly rose from her chair and came to the stairs. She hesitated, struggling to find the right words. She thought back to when Nemeah was a baby, cradled in her arms, or five years old, proudly presenting a jar of crickets for the chickens to eat. And she thought of that terrible day when Nemeah was just eight years old, her daughter's face smeared with blood, shaking, and crying profusely. Her newborn was in her arms with no one to help as the Axis left their farm behind in ruins. Maeve had been so strict ever since, but now, looking at her daughter, she felt a pang of regret. Maeve pulled Nemeah into a tight embrace, tears slipping down her cheeks.

"I am sorry," she whispered. "I am so sorry I was so hard on you for all these years."

Nemeah stood in shock as her mother drew back, wiping her eyes.

"I will go out tomorrow and find more herbs for you," Maeve added, her voice soft. "For... your nightmares, if it helps. I hope it helps. Anything to keep..."

Maeve shook her head and finished brushing away the few tears that managed to escape her eyes. She composed herself and hurried back to her chores.

"I... I actually found some already," Nemeah stammered, hesitant to explain how exactly. "Out in the yard."

Maeve stiffened. "Then I will put the kettle on. You can make some tea and head off to bed." She filled the kettle and hung it carefully from the hook over the fire.

She stoked the flames with the iron poker and continued to busy herself around the kitchen. Nemeah wanted to ask her what brought on the bout of kindness. She wanted to be pulled into another hug. The affection she rarely saw from her mother was begging to be relived. Instead, she held her tongue and climbed the stairs. Maeve watched her daughter go. She sighed to herself as she felt the pang of fear in her chest. How do you raise a daughter correctly when you are so afraid of her? Fearful of what she is? Of what she could become? She sat at the table and remembered that day in the barn. The day the Axis came for her. The things she saw that carried no explanation. She had heard stories of people who could do the things she saw, but she refused to believe her daughter was one of them. One of the people born on a starless night. The whistle from the kettle brought her out of her memories as she slipped a rag around her hand and fetched the boiling water. Nemeah came down with the speckled jar that Maeve had emptied the day before. She looked away as her daughter pulled the cork off and stared inside.

"How much do I use?" She looked at her mother.

Maeve's heart heaved when she saw the face of her grown daughter. Where did the years go? Why had she been so angry? Why did she not try to understand her daughter and her gifts? A scream ran through her head. The flash of the terrible day when her waters broke, and she was alone with a daughter who made unnatural things happen. She blinked the memory away and took the jar from Nemeah. She shook out a small amount and dropped them into a mortar bowl.

"We will try a little and adjust as needed." She crushed the pieces under the weight of the pestle and sprinkled the powder into the hot water, stirring slowly. As the earthy aroma filled the room, Nemeah took the mug. "Thank you, Ma," she said quietly.

"Get ready for bed now," Maeve replied, smiling softly. "That tea should be ready to drink by the time you are done washing up."

Nemeah paused at the bottom of the stairs. She looked back at her mother, a question looming, but unsure of what or how to ask.

"Ma, when I was younger, did the Axis ever come to the farm?"

Maeve froze as her cheeks reddened. She wiped the sweat from her brow and relaxed her face the best she could. "No, they stayed on the outskirts of the island. Why do you ask?"

Nemeah shook her head, "No reason. I think I am just getting the nightmares confused with memories." At that, she carefully made her way upstairs with the hot mug. After washing her face and arms in the basin by the wardrobe, Nemeah slipped on her chemise and climbed into bed. The tea was pungent, its mossy sweet taste lingering on Nemeah's tongue long after she had drained the mug. She laid her head on her pillow, pulled the blankets snugly under her chin, and stared at the roof above. The thick layers of grass insulated the cozy room from the freezing wind outside. The relaxing effects of the tea took over, and soon, she drifted into a deep sleep. In her dream, Nemeah floated effortlessly through the cosmos, surrounded by millions of burning stars. Their light washed over her, filling her with a sense of power. She danced across the moon's dusty surface, her bare feet kicking up the regolith, as she skimmed her hand through the icy tail of a comet.

"It is a defense."

Kallemena's voice cut through the dream, snapping Nemeah back to a dream based more on reality. She found herself standing once again in the field with the cow, just like before. The monster looming.

"No!" Nemeah shouted, racing toward the animal. But before she could reach it, Kallemena's voice returned, commanding.

"Do not fear your creation!"

The power of Kallemena's words made Nemeah falter. She covered her face with her hands, trembling, as she heard the cow's labored bellows and the heavy thud of its body collapsing to the ground.

"Control it, Nemeah!"

Her heart pounded in her chest, but something stirred within her. She waved her hand, her voice breaking through her fear. "Stop!" she cried, feeling the strength behind her words. The intensity of the power that rocked from her core and out to her extremities. Instantly, the monstrous projection froze, the world around them fading away until it was just her and the beast.

"Do not fear what you make," Kallemena's voice echoed, ghostly and distant as it faded.

Nemeah stood, her rapid breath filling the silence. Her thumb ran over the scar on her wrist, the snowdrop-shaped burn. The monster remained still. She waited, expecting it to turn its helmeted head toward her, to raise its deadly claws and lunge at her, but it did not move. She took a tentative step forward, then another, cautiously circling the armored creature. Still, it remained frozen, unmoving. Despite this, fear lingered in her trembling legs.

"Do not be afraid," she whispered, taking another step. "It is here to protect me."

Her declaration felt more like a question, uncertainty still clinging to her words. Determined, Nemeah waved her hand, imitating Kallemena. The metal beast suddenly clanged and scraped as it danced in place. A small smile broke across Nemeah's face. With another flick of her hand, the monster vanished. Her mind turned to the field and the simple joy of summoning something harmless. With a wave, the gray rabbit appeared, bounding across the stars, leaping from one bright burning dot to the other. A burst of excitement lit up her heart as she started to grasp the full extent of her powers. She imagined the silver box and the money her father would share with her. The things she could buy. A beautiful gown, shimmering jewelry, and all the books in the store. With another gesture, her plain white chemise transformed into a deep red dress adorned with black silk and delicate ruffles. She twirled, laughing, as her dreams of grandeur took shape. Another wave and glittering jewels appeared, hanging from her ears and decorating her wrists. The possibilities felt endless with the power she now wielded. The rest of the night passed in a blur of conjuring forgotten toys, lost books, and ribbons from childhood.

When she awoke, the sun was high in the sky, hidden by thick fluffy clouds, a storm peaking over the horizon. She could hear her mother fussing over Orla's hair downstairs and the familiar sound of the horse neighing outside. Rushing to the window, she saw her father hitching the wagon, loading it with crates and the silver box. She clutched her head, a headache booming through her brain, making her feel off-balance. She heard her mother's warning to Orla again and continued her hasty start. Throwing on her clothes, Nemeah quickly tied her unbrushed hair into a low bun and half-ran, half-slid down the stairs. She was about to dart out the door when her mother stopped her.

"That tea must have worked well," Maeve commented, eyeing her daughter's tangled hair. "Maybe too well?"

"Where is Father going? Is he off to the market? Can I go with him?" Nemeah asked, trying to duck around her mother's arm.

Maeve gently pulled her back, forcing her into a chair Orla had just been in. She grabbed a brush and began undoing the tangled mats of Nemeah's hair.

"You cannot go looking like you have been living in the woods," Maeve said as she detangled a mat with her fingers.

"But he might leave without me." Nemeah protested.

Maeve impatiently tugged the brush through the knots. "He will not leave without you. Now, hold still."

Nemeah squirmed under the brush's pull, frustrated by her mother's lack of hurry. She felt like time was slipping away.

"Oh, stop wriggling," Maeve scolded lightly. "I have already packed you a lunch."

Nemeah froze in surprise, relaxing as she realized she would not be left behind. She endured the rest of the brushing, listening as Orla hummed quietly by the hearth, content with her doll. The old familiar rag was well-loved with an old stocking sewn into a tight, discolored dress. The button eyes had fallen off and been lost the year before, while the bald spot on its head grew more prominent each day. With a small smile, Nemeah knew what she would do with some of the money she earned from selling the silver box.

The journey to Fayridge was undeniably quicker with the horse and wagon, though the day carried a foreboding weight. Thick, gray clouds loomed overhead, casting a dim pallor over the gold mare as she pulled the wagon steadily across the creaking wooden bridge that led to the town's gateway. Anticipation coiled in Nemeah's stomach as they approached the square, the air rich with the tantalizing scents of fresh food wafting from nearby stalls. The busy streets were alive with movement, giving Nemeah a sense of excitement. She grinned as the wagon made its way slowly through the hordes of people.

Eoghan brought the wagon to a halt in front of a shop marked by a weathered sign swinging gently in the breeze. **"Relics Vault"** was painted in peeling black letters above a flaking door, its once vibrant red now dulled to uneven rust color. A large glass window, hazy with dust and spiderweb cracks at its corners, offered a glimpse inside. Behind the grime, pocket watches, well-worn hats, and other heirlooms seemed to beg for freedom as if silently lamenting decades spent gathering dust. With a grunt, Eoghan carefully lowered himself from the wagon, wincing as his weight pressed on his bad leg. He straightened with effort and turned back to Nemeah.

"Hand over the box."

From the wagon's bed, Nemeah retrieved the silver box, wrapped tightly in an old gathering sack that reeked faintly of damp earth and mildew. Eoghan tucked it securely under his arm, glancing toward the shop with visible hesitation. His sharp eyes flicked back to her.

"Stay here. Mind old Milly." His tone was stern, a command rather than a request, and the pointed look he gave Nemeah left no room for argument.

Before she could voice her protest, Eoghan had already limped to the shop's entrance. The tarnished bell above the door gave a weak chime as he stepped inside, and the weathered door shut behind him with a soft but resolute thud.

Inside, the shop was a maze of forgotten treasures, its walls and shelves crammed with relics from another time. Ornately carved wooden pipes rested in equally intricate stands, while fountain pens and half-filled inkwells occupied a narrow shelf below. A thin layer of ancient dust covered nearly every surface, muting the colors of the cluttered wares. The floor groaned beneath Eoghan's steps, the warped boards creaking as if voicing their discontent under his weight. The smell of the place was a peculiar blend of aged fabric, neglected wood, and the faint tang of freshly lit tobacco.

A counter was barely visible under stacks of weathered trunks and boxes, and the sound of a raspy cough came from the depths of the shop. Heavy footsteps followed, accompanied by the dull thud of items being shifted. The proprietor was clearly busy, rummaging through the organized clutter. Eoghan paused, his grip tightening on the silver box as his eyes scanned the room, his senses alert despite the tranquil appearance of the shop.

"Come in, come in!" wheezed the overweight man, his troll-like features twisted into an expression of strained politeness. Without ceremony, he raised the hem of his stained tunic and blew his nose on its underside, leaving a fresh smear. "What can I help you find today? Heirloom sold during hard times? A watch that was nicked while your attention was elsewhere?" The man eyed Eoghan. "A ring for a lady friend, perhaps?"

"No. Thank you.' Eoghan stuttered, unease pooling in his gut as he approached the hulking man. He carefully placed the wrapped silver box on the counter, his shoulders stiffening as he glanced around the dim room. The light filtering through holes in the ceiling was weak and gray, adding to the store's oppressive gloom. A single gas lamp on the counter cast a dim orange glow, barely illuminating the merchant's coarse features. The rest of the shop seemed to resist the light, as though even the relics wished to remain hidden in the shadows.

"My daughter found this about a week ago," Eoghan said, tapping the top of the box.

The weight of the canvas bag that had concealed the silver was oddly comforting in his hands, a shield against the suspicion creeping into his mind. He braced himself, half-expecting the man to snatch the box, rob him blind, and throw him into the street.

"A box?" the merchant mocked, his voice thick with sarcasm. "Well, why did you not start with that. I have been meaning to find a box of my very own, and you just happened to bring one straight to me." He fluttered his eyelashes as he took a slow, deliberate drag of his stubby cigar, the burning tip flaring bright. A moment later, he exhaled a cloud of acrid smoke that stung Eoghan's eyes.

"You know how many times I have heard *that* before? No, no. Take your wooden box and get out of my shop."

"It is not wooden," Eoghan blurted out, his voice sharp and defensive. "It is silver. I think."

He slowly unwrapped the box, revealing its polished surface beneath the bag's folds. The merchant's eyes widened, the mocking sneer on his face replaced with a flicker of intrigue. He leaned closer, adjusting the gas lamp to feed more wick to the flame, the brightening glow revealing more details of the box's flawless craftsmanship.

"Well, paint my hide pink and stuff an apple in my mouth..." the merchant muttered, his tone softer now. He patted his pockets, his expression turning frantic as he searched for something. "Where did she find it, you say?" he asked, still rummaging.

Eoghan nodded silently, watching the man's bulky hands dig through boxes, papers, and drawers, scattering dust into the stale air.

"Ah-ha!" the merchant exclaimed triumphantly, pulling out a small, rounded lens. He hunched over the box, bringing the magnifying glass to his eye and inspecting every curve of the intricate scrollwork. "The scrollwork..." he muttered, his voice a low rumble of disbelief. "No... I do not believe my old eyes."

He glanced up at Eoghan, his expression unreadable, then ran his fingers reverently over the box's surface. Its delicate clasp and meticulously crafted hinges shone under the lamp's flickering light. When he lifted the lid, the box radiated a faint warmth. The mirrored finish gleamed so brightly inside that the light reflected across the ceiling, briefly highlighting splintered rafters and thick cobwebs that sagged under the weight of decades of dust.

The merchant whistled softly and turned back to the cluttered shelves behind him, yanking out scrolls and books coated in grime. He slapped a scroll down on the counter, unrolling it with a flourish to reveal a map of the continent of Kalyra, its discolored paper marked with faded ink. His stubby finger tapped a spot in the map's center as an eager grin spread across his face.

"This is from skilled magic from long ago," he declared. "This type of craftsmanship has not been seen since before the Axis was re-formed. And your daughter found this? Where?" He grabbed another map and laid it on top, this one detailing all of Tirnmoor. "Point it out for me." His finger traced the island's edge with greedy intent.

Eoghan hesitated, rubbing the back of his neck as questions churned in his mind. "Magic? Maybe we should find you some fresh air?"

The merchant gave a dramatic sigh, clearly insulted. He jabbed at Eoghan's sternum, each poke resulting in a dull stabbing pain, his tone clipped with exasperation. "This world used to be crawling with people who could do incredible things. Grow trees with a sneeze and calm the tides of a cyclone with the air that rumbled their backsides! Do you know nothing of history?"

Eoghan's blank expression prompted another round of frustrated rummaging. The merchant dragged out more maps and dust-laden books, releasing a cloud of particles that made Eoghan cough. "Honestly," the merchant muttered, "people today have no culture."

Flipping through one of the books, he stopped on a page and pointed triumphantly. "Here! The Drakenfell Mountains used to be known for harboring one of their dragons in its jagged peaks. And the king of Highspire was said to have hidden his sons' gifts from his entire kingdom."

"The dragon in the mountains?" Eoghan coughed, skepticism lacing his voice. "The bedtime story?"

The merchant's face twisted in disbelief. "Not a bedtime story! People used to travel from all over the world to lay eyes on that mountain and the hideous beast that dwelt inside. Most would never return, but the ones that did swore..."

Eoghan held up a hand, cutting off the merchant's tirade. "Is the silver box worth anything?"

The merchant let out an incredulous laugh. "Worth anything? *Silver?*" His expression shifted, his giddy grin returning as he picked up a rusty pocketknife. Eoghan tensed as the man scraped the blade against the box, the screeching sound making his ears ache.

"What are you doing?" Eoghan snapped, but the merchant waved him off.

"Look!" he said, his excitement uncontainable.

Eoghan leaned closer, and to his astonishment, there was not a single scratch on the box's surface. Heat rippled across the box as the merchant lifted it above the gas lamp, revealing intricate, starlike patterns beneath the polished finish. Crimson hues shimmered and pulsed across the surface, giving the impression that the box was alive.

"This is not silver," the merchant said, his voice now heavy with authority. "This is *Celestium*. It was forged by the hand of the ancient enemy, an Echo demon they claim! A cursed one from the damned that is said to bring the worst of luck to any who possess it. Your daughter did not find just some *trinket*. She uncovered a relic of unimaginable value."

Eoghan's chest tightened. The merchant's expression darkened. "If the Axis finds out this was just lying around on Tirnmoor, they will send their disciples back here in force. Mark my words, this is not just a relic. It is a piece of history they will kill to reclaim."

Chapter Six

Eoghan emerged from the shop, limping heavily, with a large burlap bag slung over his shoulder. His furrowed brow and puzzled expression sent a ripple of unease through Nemeah as she instinctively reached for the bag. Its weight caught her off guard, and she felt as though she was lifting a sack of iron nails, solid and unyielding. She staggered briefly, throwing a foot out to steady herself.

"Goodness, Pa," she puffed, setting down the bag with a heavy metallic *clunk* against the wagon floor. "What did you buy? Rocks?"

Eoghan did not answer immediately. Instead, he heaved himself onto the wagon with a groan and snapped the reins sharply. The gold mare jerked forward, her hooves clattering against the cobblestones, as the wagon lurched into motion before Nemeah could properly settle into her seat.

"Pa?" she pressed, her eyes darting between the mysterious bag and her father's tense expression. "Did you sell the box? What did you buy? Nails? Supplies?"

Her questions hung unanswered in the cool, thick air. Eoghan's eyes remained fixed on the road ahead, his posture rigid as he scanned their surroundings. The hustle of the town square faded behind them, but her father's unease lingered like a shadow. Nemeah turned her attention to the bustling streets as they passed. Her gaze caught on to the familiar toy store with its inviting, colorful display. She smiled wistfully, remembering all the times she had pressed her nose against the window but was never allowed inside.

"Pa, maybe we could stop?" she ventured, her tone light. "Orla could use a new dolly. Her old one is falling apart, and I know she would love it..."

"No."

The single word, firm and unyielding, cut through her suggestion. Nemeah's grin faltered as she turned to her father. His eyebrows knitted together, his eyes dark with worry, and something else. Fear? The wagon wheels rattled over the wooden bridge, the rhythmic clop of the mare's hooves punctuated by the soft roar of the swollen river below. Nemeah tilted her head toward the sky, where thick, bruised clouds churned ominously. The scent of rain was heavy in the air, humid and frigid.

"Pa?" Her voice softened. "Is everything all right?"

Eoghan shifted uncomfortably, his hand briefly brushing the old injury at his hip as though it pained him anew. He leaned forward, his voice low and urgent. "Keep your voice down."

Without warning, he snapped the reins again, urging Milly into a brisk trot. The mare's gait quickened, her hooves slapping against the dirt road as the town disappeared behind them. Nemeah's stomach knotted with unease, mirroring her father's growing tension. Thunder rumbled faintly in the distance as they turned down the narrow, muddy track that led to their farm. The first icy drops of rain began to fall, landing on Nemeah's nose and sending a shiver down her spine. She jumped from the wagon and hurried to open the gate, the cold drizzle soaking through her cloak as she fumbled with the latch. By the time she rejoined her father, he had already unhitched Milly from the wagon. The mare, her nostrils flaring and sides heaving, snorted warm breath into the crisp air. Eoghan led her toward the barn for a cooldown walk, his expression grim and unreadable.

Nemeah fetched a bucket of oats, a few handfuls of hay, and two buckets of fresh water, setting them near the trough. After such a grueling pace, Milly would drink greedily, and Nemeah could not blame her; the old mare had not run that hard in years. The wagon creaked as Nemeah pushed it to the center of the barn, where it would sit until the next market day. Her eyes drifted to the mysterious bag, still sitting where she had placed it. She hesitated, her fingers twitching toward the leather ties of the sack, but stopped when she heard her father's boots squelching through the mud outside. The barn door creaked open, and Eoghan entered, drenched to the bone. Water dripped from the brim of his hat as he led Milly to her stall. Nemeah stepped back, her questions biting at the tip of her tongue. Whatever was in that bag had rattled her father, and she was not sure she wanted to know why.

"I will go see if Ma needs any help," Nemeah said, heading for the barn door.

"Not just yet."

Her father's voice stopped her cold. It was not loud, but it carried a weight that made her pause mid-step. She turned back, her pulse quickening as her father's commanding stare rooted her in place. Nemeah's mind churned. Was she in trouble? Was he finally realizing what had happened with the cow the day before? Did he know there had not been any wolf? Or was this about something else entirely, the antique shop, maybe? Why had he come back so quiet and nervous? Reluctantly, she slumped onto a nearby stool. Eoghan pulled another one across from her and sat down heavily, his knees bumping against hers. His expression was unreadable, but his steady gaze made her fidget.

"Where did you get that box?"

Nemeah blinked. "The box? I told you, I found it the night I went to the market."

"That is what you said," Eoghan said evenly, his eyes narrowing. "But where did you really get it?"

"I *did* find it... on the beach," she confessed, her voice going up in pitch.

Her father's hand came down hard on his knee with a sharp *smack*, making Nemeah jump. His face flushed a deep red, and his breath came quicker as he struggled to rein in his temper.

"Do not lie to me," he growled, his voice icy and low.

"I am not lying! I did not lie!" Nemeah stammered, her voice quivering. "I found it on the beach. I promise!"

"The beach is half a day's journey in the other direction from Fayridge!" Eoghan's face was red and his voice was trembling. "Now, where did you get the box, Nemeah?"

She straightened on her stool and folded her hands in her lap as she looked at her father. "I found it on the beach. That is why it was covered in barnacles. I am not sure how long it took me to walk there, but that is where I found it. I promise."

"Were there any others?" Eoghan pressed, his voice soft but cutting. "Anything else on the beach that night? Something you kept for yourself? Something you...made perhaps?"

Nemeah now held a puzzled expression. "Made?" She repeated.

"Was there anything else?" Her father's question made her freeze.

Her stomach twisted into a knot as her thoughts darted to the mirror hidden beneath her bed. *The mirror... he cannot know about the mirror.* She swallowed hard and shook her head.

"No. There was nothing else. Just the box."

Technically, she had not lied. She had just found the box on the beach, and the mirror was hidden inside. She held her breath as she watched her father's face grow from suspicion to concern. Eoghan studied her for a long, heavy moment. His jaw tightened, but he said nothing as he rose to his feet. Limping slightly, he made his way to the wagon parked in its usual stall. He untied the bag, reaching his hand inside. Nemeah heard metal clinking as her father pulled his hand out and shoved something quickly into his pocket. He did this two more times before closing up the bag, throwing it over his shoulder, and bringing it back to where she sat. He dropped it into her lap with a loud *thud.* The weight hit her thighs like a hammer, making her yelp and clutch at the bag before it toppled to the floor.

"Ouch!" she squeaked, looking up at her father in surprise.

"That is your half," he said, his tone matter-of-fact.

Nemeah's eyes widened. "My... half?"

Her fingers worked quickly to untie the leather cord securing the bag. As the mouth of the sack opened, her breath caught in her throat. Gold. More gold coins than she had ever seen in her life, their brilliant shine reflecting the dim light of the barn. She stared, slack-jawed, then darted a bewildered glance up at her father.

"But... this, how? How much is this?" she stammered, her voice barely a whisper.

Eoghan slumped his shoulders and dipped his head. Water that had pooled on the brim of the old straw hat was now rushing off and dripping onto the dirt floor.

"Promise me there was not more," he said, his voice steady but laden with a gravity she could not ignore.

Nemeah's heart raced. The mirror. She could not give it up, not when Kallemena was imprisoned inside. She bit her lip, willing her face to remain calm as she met her father's eyes.

"Pa, I promise," she said with as much conviction as she could muster. "There was only the box."

Eoghan held her gaze for a moment longer, then nodded. His shoulders slumped slightly as if he were satisfied or perhaps just too tired to press her further.

"That is about four hundred gold coins," he said as he turned toward the barn door. "Your half."

The words hit her like a thunderclap. Nemeah gasped, her head snapping down to the bag again as her fingers skimmed the edge of its fortune. *Four hundred gold coins?* Her mind spun with the possibilities, with questions she dared not ask aloud.

"Nemeah, hide it. Never let your Ma, Orla, or any of the town's folks know you have it, either. Do not tell them how you got it if they find out. Do not let anyone know about that box. From this day forward, we never speak of it again." Eoghan's voice was low and urgent, and his eyes locked with hers, a shadow of fear passing through them.

He shook his head, a mix of frustration and something darker clouding his expression. "We must start going to Thornwatch for our goods now." His voice carried a sadness now.

He left, heading to the house with the heavy burden of their secret. Nemeah was still dumbfounded as she sat alone in the barn, the soft neighs and sighs of Milly, the golden mare, in the background. What was she to do with so much money? Where was she supposed to hide it all? Had silver really been that expensive? And why was her father so angry with the small fortune they had just acquired? What was it about the box that set him on edge? What had that merchant told him? Her mind raced as she tied the bag back tight and stood. She looked at the barn's wooden beams, her thoughts a whirlwind. The bag of gold was heavy with answers she could not yet understand. She had to be careful, she realized. The last thing she wanted was for the townsfolk to ask questions.

That night, Nemeah lay staring up at her ceiling. She had carefully hidden her bag of gold in the floorboards under her bed, along with the mirror, now wrapped in cloth, its heat a quiet beacon she feared would call attention. She had moved both to that secret spot, hoping Orla's innocent curiosity would never lead her there. She thought of everything that had happened in the span of just a few days: finding the box, meeting Kallemena, and discovering the power within herself, a power she had never known she had. She raised her arm and looked at the crusted-over burn on her wrist. The flower that Kallemena had branded her with. She had a responsibility now. Kallemena's expectations loomed over her, and Nemeah had yet to grasp just how heavy a responsibility she had now stacked upon her shoulders. Where was she supposed to go from here? The island of Tirnmoor was small. Undoubtedly, the missing mirrors were not hidden in the familiar corners of her homeland. Would she need to cross the ocean to Tirnmoor's mother continent of Nocthrea or venture further to places she had never heard of?

She recalled the feeling of her father's suspicious gaze the moment his anger flared. She thought she understood his concern now. If one silver box could bring them eight hundred gold coins, where did a farmer's daughter get such a thing? Nemeah's logical conclusion would have been thievery as well. She could see the doubt in her father's eyes, the unease, as if the coins themselves were cursed.

"Do not let them know you have it." Those words rang in her ears, advice she would keep close to her heart. There was no going back now.

Over the next few weeks, things at home seemed to improve. Her father used some of the coins to buy two new cows and a donkey to help pull the cart across the farm. Maeve bought new fabrics to make both girls new dresses, and Nemeah was even able to buy Orla a new doll, just like she had wanted. The doll had brown hair and pale skin, just like Orla, and wore a green dress; Maeve promised to recreate it for Orla so she could match her new toy.

Nemeah kept her gold hidden in the floorboards, and aside from the doll for Orla, she had not spent a single coin. After finishing her daily chores of cleaning and tending to the animals, she would run off to the apple orchards. Under the branches of the once-fruiting trees, she would practice her ability. When she first started, she would manifest the rabbit and the bird. Long ears and the silent grace of wings were a nice, easy first projections. She eventually worked up to larger woodland creatures like foxes and wolves. She managed a few larger birds she had read of, but could never get them to sing their sweet melodies. Then, on a cloudy day, she braved her fear. She projected the metal monster. It stood still like a statue as she circled it. She prepared to run if it turned on her, but it never did. The first few times she projected it, she made it stand perfectly still. Taking in its appearance and growing used to its smoky wisps that spilled from its armored shell.

Then, the next time, she had it follow her around the woods that lay at her family's property line.

When she became comfortable with the metal soldier following her, she started work on its appearance. She made the rusted metal flawless. She smoothed the dents and polished the scratches. Every time, it stood a little taller and a little straighter until, at last, it stood at attention with a flawless sheen and perfect posture. It would walk a few paces behind her as she foraged for wild mushrooms and herbs. Its presence made her feel like she was a princess in some faraway land she had only read about in one of her storybooks. The first flakes of snow began to fall as the air turned colder. Winter was on the horizon, and Nemeah's heart ached with longing for the familiar festival dishes, songs by the warm fire, and the comfort of her family. She looked at her metal creation, now standing silently beside her. With a wave of her hand, she made it vanish, the projection dissolving into the air like mist.

"See you tomorrow," she whispered, a promise to the magic that had become a part of her.

She rubbed her wrist where the scar was and stared toward the house, where she knew her mother would be busy cooking supper and Orla would be complaining about whatever vegetable she had to endure that night. As she walked, she looked up into the heavens. The moon's pale surface was just beginning to rise in the evening sky. The moon would be full in a few more nights, but she did not know when Kallemena could offer more advice on what to do next and where to go. A shudder of anxiety coursed through Nemeah at the thought of leaving her childhood home behind for a world-bound journey. An adventure that would take her to unfamiliar places and new people. Her thoughts drifted to the gold she had hidden away.

She had enough money to keep her from starving or sleeping on the streets. But how would she tell her family? How would she tell her father that she would not be there to help him with the farm or at the market? How would she tell her mother she would not be there setting the table for a while? And how would she tell Orla that she could have the whole upstairs to herself? Not that her little sister would mind that at all. Nemeah shuffled into the kitchen, the frigid wind picking up outside. Inside, the warmth of the hearth embraced her, and the smell of fresh food greeted her senses. A mountainous pile of food sat on their small family table. Her mouth watered as her eyes scanned the assortment.

"Go wash up and tell Orla to come down and set the table," Maeve instructed, finishing the crust on her famous apple pie.

Nemeah's heart swelled with joy at the thought of feasting like royalty, thanks to their newfound fortune. She quickly skipped up the stairs, humming to herself along the way.

"Orla, time to wash up for dinner!" Nemeah sang as she rounded the corner, only to stop dead in her tracks.

Orla stood in the middle of the room, holding the mirror, fluffing her mousy hair, and smiling at her reflection.

"Orla!" Nemeah shouted, her voice sharp.

The little girl jumped, nearly dropping the mirror.

"I was just looking at it," Orla shrieked, holding the mirror up defensively.

Nemeah's eyes went wide as she noticed gold coins scattered around the room, the leather bag draped across her bed.

"Orla," Nemeah whispered, her voice tight with panic. "I am not mad. I just want my mirror back."

"You promise?" Orla whined.

Nemeah's stomach twisted. She tried to keep her voice calm, but it was hard to disguise the panic and rage building inside. "Yes, I promise. Just give it back."

But Orla quickly darted behind Nemeah's bed and clasped the mirror tightly to her chest.

"Ma!" Orla shouted, her voice shrill.

"Quiet! Just give it back!" Nemeah urged, stepping forward.

The stomping of their feet and the raised voices caught Maeve's attention. She had just placed the pie in the oven.

"Wash up and come eat," Maeve called, but her voice faltered at the sound of Orla's cries.

Orla jumped onto Nemeah's bed and then off the other side, sprinting for the door.

"Ma! Nemeah has..." Orla never finished her sentence.

She stumbled and fell on the landing at the top of the stairs, the mirror flying from her hands and tumbling down the entire flight of fourteen steps. Nemeah winced as she heard the harsh thud of the mirror at the bottom of the stairs, where her mother now stood.

Maeve rushed up the stairs, scooping Orla into her arms. "Oh, my goodness! Are you all right? Let me check."

Nemeah tried to squeeze past her mother to race downstairs, but froze when her eyes met her father's. He was standing at the foot of the stairs, staring down at the mirror that now lay on the floor. Nemeah could not see if the glass had broken, and her heart sank. She knew the mirror was likely shattered.

"Where did you get this?" Eoghan's voice was sharp and quick. "Where?"

"It was under Nemeah's bed, along with a bunch of gold coins," Orla blurted out, her voice trembling.

Maeve's gaze flicked from Orla to the open door of the girls' room. Inside, she could see gold coins scattered across the floor, shimmering in the light from the fireplace.

"What? Nemeah?" Maeve's voice shook as she looked back at her daughter. "Where did you get all of this?"

Nemeah could not tell if her mother's voice quivered with worry or rage. She was leaning toward the latter.

"Where did you get the mirror, Nemeah?" Her father's voice rang through the house, loud and angry.

The three girls stood frozen atop the stairs, staring at Eoghan in disbelief. He had never raised his voice like that, not even during the days of the Axis.

"It came from the box," Nemeah whispered, her voice barely audible.

"The box?" Eoghan bent down and picked up the mirror, turning it over in his hands as if inspecting it for damage. "Do you know what you could have done? You promised me there was nothing else."

He stormed out of the house, and Nemeah's thoughts raced. She followed him quickly, not knowing what else to do. Her father, who usually moved slowly with his limp, was now moving twice his usual speed. Each step was hard and purposeful. His shoulders were tense, and his knuckles turned white as he gripped the mirror tightly.

She followed him into the barn, where the hammer and anvil stood. "Pa, no!" Nemeah yelled, panic rising in her chest.

Maeve and Orla rushed up behind her, their faces pale with fear as they watched Eoghan strike the mirror with a force they thought had been lost to him after his injuries. Sparks flew from the glass with each strike, and the old mare in her stall neighed and fussed in distress. Eoghan's hammer fell again and again, each blow more desperate than the last. With a final, furious swing, the wooden handle cracked. The thud of the hammer hitting the floor echoed through the barn as the air grew thick with tension. Eoghan stood there, panting, wide-eyed as he stared at the mirror, miraculously still intact despite his effort. He let out another guttural yell and threw the mirror at the wall with whatever strength he had left. Before it could strike the wooden paneling, a suit of metal armor whirled into view, catching the mirror in midair. Maeve gasped, and Orla screamed. Eoghan staggered backward, steadying himself on the anvil, eyes wide in disbelief at what he had just witnessed. Nemeah's heartbeat quickened as she glanced from her father to the armored figure.

"Run!" Eoghan shouted.

He grabbed his family and herded them toward the house with a speed that defied reason. Nemeah tried to pull away, but her father's grip on her wrist was ironclad, dragging her behind him as though she were a sack of grain. He pushed them inside and slammed the door shut, placing the heavy bar across it.

"Grab my muzzleloader!" he barked at Maeve.

Orla huddled under the table, sobbing uncontrollably, as Nemeah watched the panic on her parents' faces as it grew by the second. Smoke was wafting from the oven.

"My pie!" Maeve screeched as she dropped Eoghan's gun on the floor.

The room was alive with frantic cries and angry yells.

"Pa, it will not hurt us," Nemeah pleaded, her voice trembling.

Eoghan shot her a furious look over his shoulder as he slid the lock closed. "It is your fault he is here!" he spat as he worked to fill the gun with powder.

Nemeah froze, stunned by his words. Had her father known about her gift? The confusion and fear she felt churned inside her. A shadow fell across the kitchen window, and she did not know if she should feel relief or more anxiety.

"You have nothing to worry about, I can..."

Her father cut her off with a sharp motion. He aimed his gun at the shadow and fired. The explosion of the shot deafened them all. Nemeah's ears rang as she heard her father shouting more instructions: get upstairs, stay together. Her guard remained motionless by the window, the bullet now lodged in its breastplate without any visible effect. Nemeah's mother tugged at her, pulling her toward the stairs. They hurried into the girl's room, her father reloading the rifle in the kitchen. Another bang roared, and the sound of the table crashing to the floor and dishes breaking echoed up the stairs.

"I can make him go away, Pa," Nemeah insisted, her voice strained. "We do not have to be frightened."

Maeve wailed a sickly cry, and her voice was strained and panicked. She was holding Orla close. The young girl was trembling, a blanket now wrapped tightly around her shoulders.

"Every time they come, it is your fault," Maeve whispered, her voice teetering as tears slid down her cheek.

Nemeah's breath hitched. "Ma, it is all right. Everything is going to be..."

Maeve stood, her posture rigid. "It was you who led them here when your father was hurt!"

Nemeah opened her mouth but could not find a response.

"We told you to stay out of the field. We told you to stay close to home, and yet you disobeyed us and led the Axis to our farm!" Maeve almost screamed as her trembling grew. "They had already come searching once, but you had to lead them here again. Just had to be your carefree self! Why could you never listen?"

A memory from when Nemeah was eight flashed in her mind, sharp and painful.

"And they are here now because you made that box!" Maeve's words were like a slap. "The mirror, too!"

Nemeah's eyebrows shot up. "Made the box? I did not make the box. I told you I found it."

Eoghan raced up the steps and slammed the pine door shut. He pulled Orla's bed in front to barricade them inside.

"Making things appear is one of the curses! The Axis hunts people like you! It is your fault they are here!" Maeve was starting to sound mad, the terror consuming her. "Look, look! They hunt for you again! Now they are here to arrest us, or worse! Kill us!"

At Maeve's words, Orla's tears flowed heavily. Nemeah's gaze darted between her mother and father, her mind reeling.

"You knew? Both of you? You both knew I could...make things appear?" Nemeah shouted, frustration and anger bubbling over.

Her heart pounded as a crash echoed from downstairs. She tried to calm her racing thoughts, drawing in a shaky breath.

"Yes, we knew," her father answered grimly. He loaded the muzzle-loader again, his eyes scanning the door.

Nemeah could feel her world falling apart. Hurt and betrayal rooted deep in her heart.

"My nightmares? They are memories?" She looked from her father to her mother. "The day the Axis came? The day Pa was hurt? A monster of smoke and ash attacked him...that was real?"

The silence from her parents was painful. She felt her insides twist and bile spring up her throat. Her guardian, her monster, had been the one to hurt her father. Had killed those Axis soldiers in the valley. Had pulled her away from a portal when she was small. Everything that had happened was because of her. Of who or what she was. She looked down at her hands, appalled by the flesh that housed her veins and blood. She felt tarnished, broken, and disgusted by being different from her family.

Heavy footsteps thudded up the stairs, each step deliberate and ominous. Nemeah felt dizzy from the overwhelming truth and the weight of the moment.

"Why lie to me all this time? Why not tell me what I am?" She yelled the words as she tried to speak over the deafening thrum of her heart beating in her ears.

Then, the guard's fist pounded against the door with a force that shook the house. Another crash, and the door splintered. Smoke and black wisps filtered through the cracks in the door and keyhole. A final blow, and the guard was in the room. An explosion sounded, and another dent appeared in the guard's breastplate. Yells, sobs, and chaos filled the space. Nemeah squeezed her eyes shut, the ringing in her ears overwhelming. Her father swung the empty rifle at the guard, but it bounced off the armor. Maeve was praying in the corner, and Orla had passed out in her mother's arms. Nemeah clenched her fists and strained each muscle in her body. The chaos in the room around her fed her anger until she felt like a tea kettle that was beyond its boiling point, just waiting for the whistle to screech.

"Stop it!" she screamed.

The force of her words blasted through the room like a gale-force wind, pushing her father back against the wall. The bed frames creaked as their legs skirted across the wooden floor. Maeve dropped to her knees, still clutching Orla. For a moment, the room was silent. No one breathed as the metal creature halted all movements. Nemeah opened her eyes to see her knight standing at attention with the mirror in its clutched gauntlet. Nemeah walked over to the figure, retrieved the mirror, and was glad to see the looking glass still intact.

"Thank you," she whispered, waving her hand as the armored creature disappeared in a swirl of air.

Turning back to her room, Nemeah found the old burlap bag lying on the floor. Nemeah waved her hand, and small air currents whirled around the room. Each gold coin floated into the air, drifting as if on invisible strings, all aimed at the burlap bag. Nemeah held it open, the sound of the gathering coins the only noise as her parents stared with wide eyes. Maeve let out a shaky sob.

"I told you, Eoghan. I told you she would have power! I told you I suspected when she was born on a pitch-black night!"

Nemeah shot her mother and father a look. "Why hide it this whole time?"

Maeve shook her head while Eoghan looked down at the floor. He had moved across the room to sit beside his wife and youngest daughter. His arms wrapped tightly around them both. Nemeah felt a small fit of jealousy bloom in her. She looked at their faces. Fear was as evident as the sun was hot. They feared her.

"I did not want to believe in such fairytales." His voice was hoarse, and Nemeah could tell he was holding back tears.

"So, pretending I was normal was the best course of action?" Nemeah tried to keep her words steady, but haste was hiding in her tone.

She wanted answers as fast as she could produce the questions. Maeve handed Orla over to Eoghan and stood on shaking legs.

"The day in the barn when Orla was born."

Nemeah thought back to so many years ago. Her mother in the stall. Blood and the neighing mare. Blankets and the heavy water jug. "What about it?"

"My waters had come early. Weeks early. I sent you out to the barn to hitch Milly to the wagon. I knew it was a big job for a small girl, but you could do it. When I finally got to the barn, Milly was running in circles, and you...you were in front of a field bursting with purple and white flowers." Maeve rubbed her stomach as she recanted the story. "It was beautiful. It was like inside our old creaking barn was a gateway to a different place. I swear I could even smell the sweet fragrance of the flowers." Maeve gave a weak laugh and looked at Nemeah.

Even though her eyes rested on her daughter's face, she could tell that her mother was not actually looking at her. Maeve's head was filled with the memory. Her eyes almost glazed over with tears before her amused expression turned to something like disgust.

"The Axis were on their way, and there was the sound of cannons coming closer. Then there was this thing. This big black mass of something grabbed you and threw you back just as one of the cannons hit the barn. It tore through the roof, and a part of the rafter hit you. The whole ordeal spooked Milly, and... well, she reared back and caught me in my side and leg. I fell, and you, you were...." Her voice cracked. "The Axis came, and they said you were dead. I yelled for them to go away. I was in so much pain." Tears streamed down her face as she turned back to Orla and her husband.

Maeve's eyes cleared as her tone became harsh. "When you came to... that thing loomed over you. It followed you with an eyeless face and clawed hands." She wiped her face. "That is when I knew you would always be cursed. Would always bring us misfortune."

Nemeah's insides twisted. Her mother and father knew she had held power since she was a little girl, and yet they had stayed silent for years, lying about what took place when the Axis came. The memory of Orla's birth came in unordered chunks, and she wished she could set it straight in her memory. The flower field, the blood, Orla's fragile little body. Then she remembered the cannons. The nervous horse. The cry of pain as her mother caught Milly's hoof in the side. Her younger self was in a trance as she mindlessly stared at the field of flowers, the sway of the petals in the wind, the dark monster made of ash and shadow. The Axis as they moved across their island. In search of something, but what? Her? The memory faded again, and Nemeah felt her head ache. She looked back up at her family. She looked around the room, her eyes finally landing on Orla's face. Her little sister was pale, and her eyes were red and raw from so many tears. She knew then that life with her family would never be the same. They would never see her as their daughter or sister again. In their eyes, she was as frightening as her metallic guardian.

"Were you glad I was not killed that day? When Orla was born?" she asked softly, her voice thick with sorrow.

"No." Her mother's voice was harsh.

Nemeah nodded, fighting back the urge to break down in front of them. "I am so sorry that I caused so much grief in all your lives."

She went to her wardrobe, withdrew a pack, and stuffed it with a few changes of clothes and the sack of gold. She moved to her nightstand and gathered the jar of herbs, a couple of books, and her ribbons. With everything carefully packed, she rewrapped the mirror in an old pillowcase and delicately placed it on top. Nemeah waved her hand again, and her armored soldier appeared at her side. Two minor dents now embellished the otherwise unmarked breastplate. The quiet shuffling of her family behind her sent a pang of mourning through her heart.

"Can you please carry this out to the barn?" Nemeah asked the soldier with her shaky voice.

With swift, graceful movements, the figure lifted the pack and slung it over its armored shoulder. Its footsteps were lighter than expected, the soft rattle of the metal fading as it descended the stairs. Nemeah stole a final glance at her family. "I will leave in the morning." She confirmed before turning away. With her heart heavy, she followed her guard down the stairs. The state of the once cozy kitchen was startling. The wasted food on the floor, the charred pie on the stove, and every dish they owned was shattered into pieces. The windows were busted, and the door was kicked in, its hinges torn from the door frame. She lowered her head as she followed her guard out to the barn. The rain started to fall as she made it past the threshold into the warm interior.

Inside, the old mare jolted nervously, whinnying in agitation. Nemeah thanked the armored figure as it set the pack down carefully beside the piled hay. The metal figure vanished almost instantly, leaving the barn quiet once more. She turned to her home, dark as the storm clouds thickened, and a thunderous crack echoed through the sky. She felt her anger flare inside of her. Her home she had loved, and her family she was devoted to, was now gone. She squeezed her nails into her palms as her vision blurred. It felt like a fire was tearing through her veins as a wail escaped her mouth. A pulse of energy boomed through the barn as another flash of lightning illuminated the dark world. Then everything went dark.

Chapter Seven

Nemeah awoke in the barn with a start, her heart pounding in her chest. Her dreams had been a whirlwind of memories, flashes of the war, fragments of yesterday's events. She rubbed her eyes, her fingers easing the lingering haze of sleep. Her head felt heavy, clouded, as she pushed herself upright. Her eyes adjusted to the dim light, and she took in a sharp breath. The barn's interior was wrecked. Broken beams and splintered wood lay around her. Hay pushed away as if an explosion had happened where she lay. The horse stall was empty, and the wagon and cart were broken beyond repair. She quickly got to her feet, the world spinning as she did so. She clutched her head and slowly lowered to a crouch.

"What happened?" She tried to remember the night before.

Flashes pulsed through her mind as she recalled her anger, though now her body felt too weak to do anything but sleep some more. The cold wind blew in through the broken barn doors, and she shivered as she looked around. Her bag was lying against the wall, its canvas side ripped as if it had been gutted. Nemeah stumbled over and pushed the contents back inside, realizing she had forgotten her coat. She looked back at her house, knowing she could never step foot inside her family's home again. *Home.* The word felt foreign now, strange and hollow.

How could it still be home when it was filled with people who saw her as the root of their suffering? They blamed her for events she could not control and mistakes she had made as a child. Her throat tightened, but she forced herself to her feet, brushing the hay from her skirt and apron. She plucked a few stray strands from her hair and crossed the barn to Milly's stall. The door was broken like every-thing else, but inside was just hay and overturned buckets. Nemeah quickly made her way outside to be greeted by the horse munching on clover. The old mare met her gaze with large, soulful eyes as if she understood what was happening. As if she knew this would be their last moment together. An ache bloomed in Nemeah's chest, sharp and unrelenting. She reached out, her hand trembling slightly, and gently scratched Milly's soft nose. The familiar gesture brought a small mea-sure of comfort, though it was fleeting.

"Be good to them," she whispered, her voice strained with worry.

Milly nudged her hand, warm breath ghosting over Nemeah's chilled fingers. Tears threatened to spill, but Nemeah blinked them away. She could not afford to fall apart just yet. She went back inside and pulled an old horse blanket from the stall wall and wrapped it around herself. The coarse fabric was scratchy but warm, a small shield against the early morning chill. The sun was still tucked below the horizon, reluctant to rise. The faint blue light of dawn bathed the world in a cold glow as the clouds thinned and the rain slackened. Her eyes wandered back to the house. The broken windows had been hastily patched with scrap wood, and a pile of splintered door frag-ments lay discarded by the entrance. The faint smell of chimney smoke hung in the air, a sign that her parents would be stirring soon. She raised her hand, and the familiar swirl of magic summoned her soldier once more. The armored figure appeared, silent and imposing, as she walked a slow circle around it.

"We cannot walk into town with you dressed like this, can we?" she murmured, twisting her hand. Magic rippled over the figure like a wave, reshaping its form.

She thought of the many people she would see at the market, all looking at her companion with eyebrows raised, the whispers that would linger in the air. She pictured the clothes her father would wear and let them guide her in the transformation. The gleaming armor melted away, replaced by a long green tunic. A hooded cloak obscured the figure's face, its features shrouded in shadow. The powerful legs were now clothed in sturdy cotton trousers tucked into weathered leather boots. Woolen gloves covered its hands, completing the disguise.

"There," she said, nodding with satisfaction. "That is better."

Now resembling a young farmhand, the figure tilted its hooded head slightly as if acknowledging her efforts.

"Can you carry the bag?" she asked, gesturing to her belongings. "Carefully? It seems to have ripped somehow."

The projection moved with quiet purpose, lifting the pack as if it weighed nothing. Though the bag's contents were heavy, the figure's posture remained steady, unbothered by the burden. It carried itself with an air of both authority and quiet empathy, a comforting presence in the otherwise desolate morning.

Nemeah studied her companion for a moment, then allowed a small smile. "You will need a name," she said softly, taking its gloved hand in hers.

She led the projection to the barn door, her steps hesitant as she looked out at the frozen trail stretching into the distance. The ground was hard and uneven, and the mud from the previous day was now crusted with frost. Unease settled in her stomach as she thought about the journey ahead. The last time she had gone into town had ended in disaster, and the memory weighed heavily on her. Her grip on the projection's hand tightened, drawing strength from its silent presence. Together, they stepped out into the frigid morning air, their breaths visible in the cold light of dawn. The path to town lay ahead, and though it was daunting, Nemeah felt a flicker of resolve. She had thought long and hard about where to go next. Her path seemed to pull her toward Fayridge, to the merchant who had bought the silver box. It was the opposite direction of the harbor that could take her away from Tirnmoor, but she felt an unshakable need for answers. Her father's demeanor had changed so drastically after that one visit to the merchant; surely, he held the key to the questions now flooding her mind.

"How about Drosen?" she asked, glancing up at her companion.

The figure remained silent, its hooded face tilted slightly in her direction but giving no indication of emotion. It stood steadfast as always. Together, they passed through the gate, stepping onto the frost-kissed road that led to town. Nemeah tightened the horse blanket around her shoulders, bracing against the chill. She glanced up at the figure beside her, her thoughts churning.

"Can you feel happiness? Or any emotion at all? Or are you... numb to such things?"

The idea of something so humanlike yet devoid of feeling stirred a quiet sadness within her. She let her eyes drop to the frozen ground.

"Can you talk?"

Her question lingered in the still air, unanswered. The figure's silence was absolute. As they walked, they passed the familiar sight of the Ashford farm. The cattle grazed in clusters on the frost-covered grass, their breath visible in the morning chill. The calves, now much larger, stayed close to their mothers, their forms barely moving in the dim light. The memory of her mother's angry face flared in her mind, unbidden. The blame and resentment in those eyes. Her father's voice was heavy with disappointment. The weight of it all pressed against her chest like a stone.

"Why would the Axis come for me?" she murmured aloud, as if speaking her questions might manifest an answer. She tried to reach into the depths of her memory, searching for scraps of what she could recall about the war.

"Said I was about the right age. Right age for what?" she trailed off, a furrow deepening between her brows.

She had been only seven when the first knights of the Axis sailed to Tirnmoor. The islanders had never imagined they would travel so far from their capital, Verdathos, practically a world away. For what purpose would anyone come to a frigid island whose main offerings were potatoes and apples? Her thoughts drifted to the stories of Haven-wood, a land abundant with figs, olives, tomatoes, and corn, wonders she had only heard of, never tasted. How could a place so rich with life attract the Axis's wrath? And why would they choose to come to this barren island of Tirnmoor? With a slight pang of frustration, she realized she understood very little of the Axis's origins or purpose. Why had they been established? Who commanded them? Did they truly leave so many villages across the island in ruin? The questions churned in her head, one after the other. Perhaps the merchant in Fayridge would have answers.

"How about Eloth?" Nemeah glanced back at her companion.

The figure's heavy footsteps fell in rhythm with hers, always a fraction behind. Though the road stretched out barren and empty, the presence of her gift kept her from feeling utterly desolate. The sun crept higher, shaking off the last vestiges of dawn, casting their long shadows onto the road ahead. She swung her arms through the air, watching her shadow mimic the motion.

"I look like an octopus," she said with a chuckle, continuing her playful motions. "Varek?" she offered another name, waiting as if expecting a response.

The quiet was her only answer. Amused, she began listing names aloud as they walked, her voice filling the stillness. Brainth, Tarvin, and Davos each met the same silence. The journey to Fayridge was swifter without the burden of the handcart dragging behind her. Her stomach growled, a sharp reminder that she had left her family's ransacked house without so much as a crust of bread. When the wooden bridge leading to Fayridge appeared in the distance, she lifted her eyes to the heavens. The sun was a dim ball of light behind nasty-looking storm clouds she hoped would carry their load a little longer.

"What about Alban?" she asked.

To her surprise, the soldier stopped mid-step. It froze as though considering the name before dropping to one knee. With deliberate precision, it raised its right fist to its chest and bowed its head in a solemn display of allegiance. Nemeah's face showed her utter shock, her heart swelling with unexpected emotion. The fear that had coiled within her since leaving the barn ebbed away at that moment. Confidence replaced it, rising like the tide. With Alban at her side, she felt, for the first time, that she could indeed do this.

"Alban," she repeated, her smile breaking wide across her face. "You like that name?"

A tear threatened to spill from her eye, but she swiped it away before it could fall. She could not cry just yet, not when so much of her resolve depended on holding herself together.

Her stomach growled again, this time sharp enough to make her wince. She glanced at Alban. "I do not suppose you are hungry, too?"

Her smile was faint but grew more potent when the scent of food drifted through the crisp air. Before they entered the town, she dug two gold coins from her bag. She was careful not to reveal more; walking around with a sack of gold was a quick way to attract trouble. The marketplace bustled with activity. Growers' stands overflowed with apples, potatoes, and cabbages. Nemeah stopped at one and bought a few apples and potatoes before heading to the bakery, where she added a loaf of bread to her haul. A shop selling outdoor wares caught her eye, and she purchased a sturdy pot, a wooden spoon, and a knife. Lastly, she grabbed a canteen and a new bag to replace her torn one. Satisfied with her supplies, she moved toward the tailor. The shopkeeper's eyebrows shot up at the sight of her draped in a weathered horse blanket, as frost still clung to the windows. After some browsing, she found a thick coat, a deep blue that nearly matched her eyes. Its sleeves were adorned with petite, embroidered stars in thread the same shade as the fabric.

"It is perfect," she said, spinning in the shop like a child in a storybook. For a fleeting moment, she felt like a princess.

She spent the last bit of her first gold coin and stepped outside, her confidence renewed. Her final stop was the antique shop, just a short walk down the bustling road. The street was alive with vendors calling out their wares, carts creaking under heavy loads, and townsfolk jostling past one another. Yet, the antique shop itself felt untouched by the commotion. She paused at the grimy window, straining to peer inside. The glass, still uncleaned from her last visit, revealed little of the shop's interior. She pressed closer, searching for a familiar flicker of lamplight or any sign of life, but saw only shadows. Her pulse quickened. The shop felt eerily still, as though it had been abandoned.

"Oh, please do not be closed," Nemeah murmured, glancing nervously at Alban. "Just, stay here. Please."

She pushed the door, surprised when it swung open with barely a groan, its rusted hinges yielding with little resistance. The dim interior of the shop greeted her with a heavy, oppressive stillness. Dust hung in the air, thick and unmoving, carrying the acrid scent of smoke. As her eyes adjusted to the gloom, unease coiled tight in her stomach. Shelves lay toppled, their contents scattered in disarray across the floor. Nemeah stepped cautiously inside, the rotten floorboards creaking beneath her weight. Broken glass crunched softly under her boots, remnants of a shattered lamp lying in a darkened pool of spilled oil. Its sharp, chemical tang stung her nose. Maps and books were strewn across the countertop in haphazard piles. Yet another smell, familiar and unsettling, caught her attention. She wrinkled her nose, trying to place it as she edged closer to the counter.

"Hello?" Her voice came out in a trembling squeak.

A sound answered her, a faint shuffle of footsteps from somewhere deeper in the shop. The hair on her arms prickled. She widened her eyes, scanning the dim corners of the room, her breaths shallow and quick.

"My father was here a few weeks ago," she called out, her voice faltering.

The footsteps grew louder. Her dizziness worsened, the fumes from the spilled oil mixed with the metallic scent in the air. Gripping the countertop for balance, she pulled her hand back almost instantly, her palm sticky with a dark, viscous substance. The smell hit her fully now, unmistakable. Blood. A low groan echoed from behind the counter, making her jump. Her body begged for her to turn and leave, but instead, she crept around the cluttered wooden counter. Papers and debris littered the floor, but her eyes locked on a shape, a body sprawled on the ground. She hesitated, her feet moving as if against her better judgment, and knelt beside the prone figure. Her breath caught in her throat as the details sharpened: a man lay sprawled on the floor, his chest heaving with shallow, labored breaths. Embedded deep in his chest was a dagger.

"Oh, chains..." Nemeah's voice wavered as she fought the urge to scream, her trembling hand instinctively covering her mouth.

The dagger's hilt caught her attention, its gilded grip wrapped in crimson leather. At its top was a crest she recognized instantly: a blazing sun.

"The Axis?" The words fell from her lips, barely audible.

Her heart raced, hammering painfully against her ribs. The Axis was here, in Tirnmoor. She glanced toward the shop's entrance, her thoughts racing. Outside, the village was alive with the sounds of trade and chatter. Merchants hawked their wares, townsfolk bustled about their errands. No one seemed aware of her discovery.

"They do not know," she whispered, her chest tightening with fear and urgency.

The faint shuffling caught in her ear again. Closer this time. She froze, her eyes darting toward the noise. The footsteps quickened. Panic surged through her as she dropped to the floor, pressing her back against the drawers behind the counter. Her hands groping blindly along the floor for something, anything, to defend herself. Her fingers closed around a slender, pointed object. Her heart leaped into her throat as a dark figure loomed over the counter, moving swiftly toward her. The sound of boots thudding against the creaking floorboards filled her ears, each step louder than the last. Before she could react, a cold blade pressed firmly against her throat. She gasped, her mind screaming for her to fight, but her body remained paralyzed.

The smell of decay and smoke radiated from the figure, overwhelming her senses as the sharp edge of the knife bit lightly into her skin. She opened her mouth to scream when a hand clamped over her mouth. It burned against her cold, trembling flesh, the heat almost unnatural, as if the figure's very touch carried the flames of a forge.

"Not so fast," a voice hissed, low and venomous. "I am just here for..." The man holding Nemeah captive let out a short, humorless laugh. "I am here for an antique. No need to alarm anyone about my... *transaction* with the shopkeeper."

Nemeah's eyes darted to the man lying on the floor. His chest no longer moved. In a swift motion, the dark figure leaped over the counter, making for the exit. Nemeah scrambled to her feet, catching a glimpse of a silver box tucked under the man's arm.

"The box," she whispered, the word slipping out before she could stop it.

The cloaked figure froze mid-step. Slowly, he turned on his heel, a wide, sharp-toothed grin stretching beneath the shadow of his hood.

"Tsk, tsk," he said, his voice deep and mocking. "You really should not have said that."

Nemeah's heart dropped. She gripped the small weapon she had found earlier, only to see it clearly now: a pencil, freshly sharpened but laughably inadequate. She winced, clutching it tighter as the assassin strode back toward her, his steps quickening.

"It seems I will have to silence you as well," he said, his tone almost cheerful. "Quietly, of course. No one must know I was here."

"Alban?" She whispered, watching the killer loom closer, his blade hissing from its sheath. Alban!" she screamed.

The air shimmered, and her soldier materialized between her and the advancing assassin. Alban's broadsword came crashing down in a swift arc, forcing the man to block. The clang of metal on metal echoed through the shop.

"So you are the one I have been searching for! Nice to meet you, shadow rat," the assassin said, his voice tinged with a twisted delight.

Blades clashed as Alban and the assassin exchanged blows, the fight confined to the narrow space of the shop. Sparks flew as their weapons collided. Then, with a burst of speed, the cloaked man vaulted through the front windowpane, shattering glass in a deafening crash before disappearing into the crowded streets. Shouts erupted outside as curious townsfolk peered into the wrecked shop. Nemeah's gaze darted to the lifeless shopkeeper and the blood staining her hands.

"We need to go," she said, her voice trembling.

Together, she and Alban slipped out the back door as calls for wardens echoed from the front. They hurried through the alleyways, putting distance between themselves and the commotion. It was not until they were far from Fayridge that Nemeah froze.

"My bag! We left the bag!" she exclaimed, turning to head back.

Alban's iron grip caught her wrist, stopping her. With its other hand, it held up her bag, the pot and canteen clinking softly against the straps. A wave of relief washed over her, mingling with a flicker of pride. They left the town behind, the fading sun dipping below the treetops as the moon's pale light began to seep into the darkening sky. The walk to Thornwatch Harbor would take two more days, and exhaustion was already clawing at Nemeah. Her feet ached, each step heavier than the last. She slowed, veering off the road into a small clearing. Branches and dead leaves cracked underfoot as she scanned the area, listening for any sign of pursuit. The forest was still.

"This will do," she said quietly. "Let us see if we can get a fire going."

"I can help with that."

The voice startled her. Nemeah spun around to see Kallemena standing beside Alban, her raven-black gown as striking as ever. She looked radiant, otherworldly, just as she had the last time Nemeah had seen her. Without thinking, Nemeah ran to her and flung her arms around her. The tears came hot and fast, all the fear, tension, and grief pouring out in uncontrollable sobs.

"There, there," Kallemena murmured, patting her back gently before wrapping her in a firm embrace. "Let us get you warm."

The fire crackled to life under Kallemena's guidance, and soon, the smell of potato stew filled the clearing. Nemeah ate in silence at first, the comfort of warm food soothing her frayed nerves. Between bites, she recounted everything: the sale of the silver box, her argument with her parents, Alban's sudden appearance, and the assassin's chilling words.

"He said he had been looking for me, a...a shadow rat?" she said, dipping a piece of bread into her stew. She blew on it, steam curling in the cool night air.

Kallemena nodded slowly, her brow furrowed. "That is a name I have not heard in many years. Shadow rat." Kallemena said it slowly, testing the words on her tongue.

She gazed into the fire, her expression distant, before turning her attention to Alban.

"He is impressive," she said, a hint of admiration in her voice. "Your powers are growing stronger." She looked back at Nemeah, her eyes sharpening. "But you will need to learn much more, and quickly, before your journey is complete."

Nemeah took another bite, too eager to eat, and immediately burned her tongue. She waved her hand frantically, trying to cool the pain.

"Like patience," Kallemena said with a soft laugh. The rain pattered on the remaining leaves in the trees and hissed as icy drops fell into the fire. Kallemena waved her hand, a glass roof covered the three, the light clinking sounded like a distant song.

"It is time I told you the story of my past. The truth of what happened long ago, before the Axis marched on the continents and before our people fell to their swords."

"Our people?" Nemeah blinked. "Ones that can make things happen with the wave of their hand?"

Kallemena nodded. "Yes, child. Now sit back and listen to history."

Part II: Kallemena

Chapter Eight

The king looked over the village far below his castle walls. The balcony he peered from gave him the vantage of seeing all the merriment that was taking place in the town center. Festive music echoed off the many frozen houses and walls and up to his majesty's ears. He let out a long sigh as he opened his eyes to the sky. Where the noonday sun should sit was... nothing. A void of light as far as the eye could see. The darkness was so thick that it seemed to devour any fragment that held any trace of illumination about it. The many cheers and shouts drew his attention back to the city below. He envied his citizens as they danced around and toasted to the celestial event happening above their heads. The Darra Convergence was usually a sign to be grateful and give appreciation to the gods above.

By sacrificing one day of light every twenty years or so, the inhabitants learned an appreciation for the sun and stars. Welcome the light with the knowledge that it could be taken away one day. As much as the king longed to celebrate with his people, he knew this day could not be filled with bliss. From deep within the castle, a distant moan echoed through the halls, followed by the cry he dreaded most, a newborn's wail. Thaloren's hand clenched into a fist, striking the icy railing. Snow tumbled from the edge, carried away by the biting wind. Behind him, hurried footsteps approached. He exhaled slowly, bracing himself.

"Your Highness."

The king turned to see one of his guards kneeling, his fist pressed to his chest, and his head bowed low.

"What is it?" Thaloren asked, his voice heavy, his gaze returning to the never-ending darkness that was now the horizon.

"It is a girl, Your Majesty. A princess."

The king's shoulders tensed. "You know what this means, then," he said, his tone laced with sorrow.

The guard hesitated but nodded. "My sincerest apologies, my lord." Without another word, he rose and left the balcony.

When Thaloren entered the royal bedchamber, the baby was already asleep. The expansive but intimate room was dominated by a massive bed draped in sashes of blue silk. The thick feather-stuffed mattress was covered with black sheets, their surface glistening with a delicate frost under the flickering glow of the fireplace. Everything soiled during the birth had already been cleaned, and the evidence of the event was erased as if it had never occurred. Beneath a thick blue swaddle, the king glimpsed the pale, delicate skin of the infant. Queen Nyssira, lying propped against the headboard, smiled faintly as Thaloren climbed onto the bed, moving carefully not to disturb the sleeping child. He kissed his wife's forehead, still warm from her exertion, and breathed in her comforting scent of sage and jasmine.

"She has your hair," Nyssira whispered, watching her husband's face as he studied their daughter.

Though it was midsummer, the castle's walls bore intricate frost patterns, and icicles hung from the ceilings of the grand halls. The palace itself was an architectural marvel encased in thick sheets of ice that shimmered like glass. Winter storms ensured the sun's warmth never lingered, leaving Glacia, the southernmost continent, in a perpetual embrace of cold. The land, stark and unyielding, was dotted with cedar trees and shifting sands carried by frigid winds from the surrounding oceans. Its people were resilient, their domed homes constructed from thick ice to shield them from the harsh climate. The citizens within the walls of the kingdom of Iskaroth were peaceful and industrious, their intellect rivaling any across the continents. They pioneered inventions and medicines that outpaced the world's understanding, trading their knowledge freely in exchange for exploration and discovery. Though untested by war, their bonds with other kingdoms were strong, and they hoped their shores would remain untouched by conflict.

"The Convergence is still within our skies," Thaloren murmured, his voice heavy with foreboding.

Nyssira's gaze drifted to the infant in her arms, her expression softening with sorrow. She knew what her daughter's birth under the blackened sky meant. Like all children born during such an event, the girl would be sent away to the Axis as soon as her gifts began to manifest. The Axis would train her, assigning her to a life of service, perhaps as a healer, scholar, or royal adviser. Yet, for all the prestige such positions carried, Nyssira's heart ached. This was her child's home, the place where she should grow up knowing her parents' love. And what of their son? Must he lose a sister to the whims of celestial fate?

"No one needs to know," Thaloren said quietly, his thumb gently brushing the baby's cheek. "We can announce the birth next week."

Nyssira turned to her husband, surprise flickering across her face. Was he truly suggesting what her heart longed for most? To keep their daughter's gift a secret and let her live an everyday life here, in the palace?

Tears welled in her eyes. "I love you," she whispered.

Twenty-two years later

"Mena! You should already be up!"

A tall woman with long white hair and pale blue eyes strode into the room, throwing open the heavy curtains. Frost coated the windowpanes, forming intricate designs across the glass. The morning light spilled into the chamber, glinting off the icy surfaces and the silver embellishments of the furniture. The woman moved with a dancer's grace, humming a cheerful tune as she crossed to the wardrobe. She pulled out a flowing dress, draping it over her arm before twirling around the room, arranging items as though she were preparing for a grand performance. She stopped at the round bed in the center of the room, its canopy adorned with thick curtains and silver tassels that shimmered in the morning sun.

"Tharos?" she called playfully, gripping the thick comforter that enveloped the bed's occupant. "Una, dohr, threin!" With a flourish, she yanked the covers away.

A sharp shriek escaped beneath the blankets as Kallemena curled into herself, tightly clutching her nightgown against the sudden chill. She pulled her legs up and shielded her face with her arms.

"Go away, Amawna," she groaned, her voice muffled.

Amawna smirked, unfazed by the princess's protests. She grabbed Kallemena's arm and effortlessly hauled her from the bed.

"I cannot have you lazing about all morning. There is too much to do! Now, up you get, *drömlithar!*"

"Sleepyhead?" Mena muttered, rubbing her face with both hands, dragging her lower eyelids down in exaggerated exasperation. "Of course, I am sleep-headed; Orentheon kept everyone up late rehearsing. I do not know why, however. Weddings are all the same. Stand by the altar, say 'I do' a dozen times, and kiss. That is it! Everyone knows the steps already."

Amawna guided the reluctant princess to the vanity and had her sit. With practiced hands, she braided Mena's long, dark hair into an intricate design, weaving in small charms meant to bring good luck.

"We will see if you are still yawning when the music starts," Amawna teased, fastening the final charm.

Mena scowled playfully, but her expression softened as Amawna helped her into a fine silk gown. The fabric was pure white, the color as pristine as the snow outside the frosted window. Against it, her onyx-black hair, like her father's, stood out in striking contrast. Her pale skin, nearly as fair as the dress itself, shimmered faintly under the morning light, a subtle sparkle woven into the threads of the gown.

In Iskaroth, it was tradition for wedding guests to wear white while the groom donned black. The bride, however, was to be a vision of vibrant color, dressed in the hues of her homeland. She was meant to be the day's most dazzling focal point, her attire drawing every eye in the room as she swayed in her new husband's arms during their first dance.

"Breathtaking," Amawna said softly, stepping back to admire her work.

Kallemena turned to the mirror, her fingers brushing the delicate fabric of her gown. Despite her earlier grumbles, a faint smile tugged at her lips.

"I suppose it will do," she said, feigning nonchalance.

Amawna laughed, giving her a gentle nudge. "*Suppose* it will do? Mena, you make the stars jealous."

Outside, the bells tolled, announcing the arrival of ships from the other continents, each bearing a royal family to witness the ceremony. Orentheon was to marry a princess from Thalasson. The tropical landmass from which the bride hailed was shaped like a massive atoll, a ring floating in the ocean, with perfect weather, abundant vegetation, and bountiful fishing. Mena felt saddened at the arrangement made for her brother and his bride. Glacia was the opposite of the tropical paradise the bride had come from. Mena had seen the bride the day before. Though she wore a veil to symbolize her devotion, Mena had caught glimpses of her features.

The girl had dark, tanned skin, like the bark of the cedar trees, and sandy-colored hair that fell in tight, playful ringlets down her back. Her deep brown eyes, the color of baby snow hares before their fur turned white, mesmerized Mena. Her brother had said that those eyes captivated him from the moment he met Princess Kivani. Her family hoped the bride would not feel out of place despite the cold, harsh land of the frozen tundra. They had decorated her room with colorful sashes in vibrant greens and yellows, colors that were rarely seen in Glacia. Mena could not help but hope that she would find comfort here one day. Hoped that she would raise a family with Orentheon, and together, they would rule Iskaroth with the same grace and dignity their parents had for the past thirty-seven years. A knock at the door pulled Mena from her thoughts. She watched in the mirror as Amawna, her attendant, danced across the room and eagerly opened the door. The queen stood in the doorway.

"It was a rough start, but I think I have managed to make the princess presentable." Amawna bowed deeply to the queen, her movements fluid and graceful, reflecting years of service to the royal family.

Mena rose to meet her mother at the center of the room. They stood in stark symmetry, their pale skin a canvas for the soft glow of the room's brilliant natural light and their deep blue eyes shimmering like twin pools of the night sky. Their features were sharp and sculpted yet carried an air of innocence, almost ethereal in their shared elegance. Had it not been for the queen's white hair and the slight creases that marked her face with the wisdom of years, one might have mistaken them for twins.

"You look beautiful," Queen Nyssira murmured, her voice a quiet melody as she gently cupped her daughter's face.

Nyssira scanned Mena from head to toe, ensuring every detail was perfect. The queen's eyes lingered on her daughter's face, softening with pride before returning to the attendant.

"Amawna, you have outdone yourself. She actually looks like a princess." A laugh was shared by everyone before the queen spoke again. "Please, give us a moment."

With another respectful bow, Amawna stepped back, her footsteps barely a whisper as the door closed behind her. In the sudden stillness, Nyssira sighed deeply, her shoulders sagging as if a weight had been lifted, though the unease in her eyes remained. She clasped Mena's hands with a tender strength, grounding herself in the warmth of her daughter's touch.

"Big day," she said, her lips attempting a smile, but it faltered, twisting into a strained grimace.

The anxiety coiled in her stomach, tightening with each passing moment. Mena could feel her nerves fluttering in her chest, a restless energy she could neither ignore nor soothe. Outside, the bells tolled again, their distant clangs announcing the arrival of yet another ship, each one bringing new faces, strangers whose sharp eyes might catch the slightest misstep. Nyssira squeezed Kallemena's hands gently, her voice soft but filled with unshakable certainty.

"You will do wonderfully, my snowdrop." Though wrapped in kindness, her words carried the weight of years spent navigating this world of diplomacy and power. "You have been preparing for this moment for years. We will come out on the other side with none the wiser."

Mena stood still, the soft, cold touch of her mother's hand grounding her as the distant sounds of the gathering echoed through the walls of the castle. She closed her eyes for a moment, breathing in the faint scent of jasmine and sage that lingered in her mother's presence, her home, her anchor. She only hoped that today, she could live up to everything they had practiced for. Yet, Mena's hands still trembled with anxiety. She had spent years training to control her Echo gift, to keep it restrained, hidden beneath a carefully constructed mask. But today, her nerves were unraveling with so many eyes bound to turn toward her. The swirl of emotions threatened to break free, and she feared the slightest slip, a burst of joy at her brother's smile, a fleeting moment of pride, could send snowflakes spiraling from her, betraying her true nature. The flutter of a single butterfly, born from her inner emotions, could expose her as the Echo she desperately tries to hide. She had worked so hard to keep it under control.

The wedding rehearsals yesterday had tested her more than she ever imagined. She had managed to keep her face impassive while her brother cracked jokes, her parents twirled gracefully on the floor with the bride and groom-to-be, and the women marveled at the bride's dress. Mena had felt the surge of emotions, the overwhelming beauty of the moment, but she had swallowed them all. The sight of the bride, a vision of sky blue and white lace spilling from the delicate bodice adorned with embroidered shells, the gown shimmering like the ocean under the sun, had almost been too much. She had to force herself not to gasp or let its beauty push her over the edge. By the end of the day, Mena had been drained, her body aching with the effort of maintaining composure. Her emotions, joy, pride, and longing pressed against the walls of her mind, eager to be released. But she had held them back, locked them away, because one slip would mean exposure. And now, facing a room full of even more strangers, she was unsure how much longer she could keep the lid on her emotions. This was supposed to be a celebration, but for Mena, it was torture.

"Maybe I should not go?" Mena's voice wavered, her words spilling out in a rush. "It would be better for you and Father if I stayed hidden here in my room. That way, I cannot mess anything up. I would hate myself if I ruined Oren's big day."

Her mother stood silent, her expression calm as Mena's anxieties poured forth.

"People could find out," Mena continued, pacing now, her movements jerky with nerves. "The Axis would be furious! We do not even know what the penalty for something like this would be." Her breathing quickened, her voice rising. "They could cancel Oren's wedding! He would never forgive me!"

The words had barely left her lips when the air in the room began to shift. Shadows crept along the walls, swallowing the light like ink spreading through water. The temperature dropped, and the corners of the room seemed to retreat into darkness. Mena's panic surged, her thoughts spiraling as her wild, untamed powers responded to her fear. The light dimmed further until it felt as though the very warmth of the room was being devoured. Her breathing came in short, sharp gasps as pinpricks of light, tiny, cold stars danced in the growing void. Her chest tightened, and her vision blurred. The panic threatened to drown her completely until warmth. A gentle hand cupped her cheek, steadying her. Mena flinched but stopped, her mother's touch cutting through the haze. Queen Nyssira leaned in, her forehead pressing softly against her daughter's. The queen began to hum a low, soothing melody that was achingly familiar. Mena's chest heaved as she tried to focus on the sound, her mother's steady presence anchoring her. Slowly, the two began to sing the words together.

"Hush now, my little light,
The stars will guide you through the night.
Close your eyes and dream away,
Tomorrow brings a brighter day."

The shadows receded, folding back into themselves like curtains drawn open to let in the light. Warmth returned to the room, and the faint stars disappeared into the ether. Mena's breathing slowed, the tension in her limbs easing as the song wrapped around her like a protective shield. Her mother pulled back, her hands still resting gently on Mena's cheeks.

"You are stronger than this fear, my snowdrop," Nyssira whispered. "And you will never face it alone."

Though Queen Nyssira could not fully grasp the weight of the stress her daughter bore, she held onto optimism. Everything would be fine. The wedding would still be a momentous celebration, uniting all nine continents in joy and unity.

"I will send for Healer Myra to bring you some silvervane tea," Nyssira said, her tone soothing but firm. "It will dull your powers just enough to get through the ceremony without incident. Afterward, you can retreat to the gardens. If your emotions overwhelm you, let them. Project freely." She gave a small, knowing smile. "Anyone who sees will think it is just the natural wildlife, snow foxes and frost birds, playing among the shrubs and snowbanks. No one will suspect otherwise."

The queen held her daughter a while longer, her fingers gently stroking through Mena's hair as she hummed the soothing lullaby one last time. When Mena's breathing steadied, Nyssira pressed a kiss to her temple before pulling away.

"I must go greet our guests," she whispered, her voice soft but reluctant.

Mena nodded, her gaze following her mother as she slipped through the door, leaving the room in stillness. Turning to the window, Mena's eyes wandered to the bustling scene below. The docks were alive with movement, ships gliding into port one by one, their vibrant sails and flags fluttering proudly in the breeze. Crowds spilled onto the snow-lined piers, every face peering up at the castle made of glass and ice, glinting in the sunlight. The royal guests were adorned in expensive silks and intricate medals, their finery catching the light like scattered stars on the icy shore. Above them, the crystal palace towered, a masterpiece of ice shimmering against the cloudless sky. Mena let out a soft sigh, marveling at the spectacle yet feeling the weight of expectation pressing against her chest.

A sharp knock broke her trance, though the door creaked open before she could respond. Healer Myra stepped inside without pause, carrying a delicate cup and saucer in her hands. Mena smirked, shaking her head at the older woman's lack of formality. Myra had always done as she pleased, rules and decorum be damned. The healer strode with purpose, her pale, sightless eyes fixed ahead as though she could see the world more clearly than anyone else. Mena watched, equal parts amused and envious.

Myra's mastery over her Darra abilities was effortless, with each movement precise and every step deliberate. It was a grace Mena yearned for, a control she had not yet found. Myra set the saucer down before Mena with a firmness that brooked no argument. Mena's eyes drifted to Myra's serene expression. She was more than just a healer; she was a guardian of secrets, a silent rebel against the rigid laws of the Axis. Myra had been the one to teach Mena how to access and hone her gift, guiding her in secrecy since the first signs of her Echo abilities. It had begun when Mena was ten years old. A vivid nightmare had wrenched her from sleep, leaving her room ablaze with illusory fire. Trapped in her terror, she had screamed for help, only for the royal guards to burst in and find nothing amiss. The fire had vanished as if it had never been. That was when her parents had called upon Myra, entrusting her with the family's carefully concealed truth.

By Axis law, every child born with Echo abilities was to be reported and sent to Verdathos for training, a practice meant to control their powers and strip them of any claim to rule. Echoes could be scholars, inventors, healers, even royal advisors, but never monarchs. The fear of an Echo ruling was ancient and deeply rooted, the idea that their power would bend kingdoms and minds alike to their will. But Myra, King Thaloren's aunt, had felt differently. She remembered too well the pain of being torn from her own family at ten, sent across the seas to serve a system that saw her gift not as a blessing but as a tool. When she discovered that sweet, bright-eyed Mena carried the same spark, Myra had wept, not with sorrow but joy.

Each Echo's ability manifested differently. For some, it was a gift of defense; for others, it enhanced their skills or brought forth creation. And in rare cases, it wrought destruction. The Axis disciples in Verdathos tested each child upon their arrival, categorizing their strengths and determining their future roles. Myra had endured that process herself, her abilities directed toward healing and sensing the unseen threads of emotion that wove through the world. Now, she used that gift to protect her family.

"As long as she does not marry a king, I see no harm in letting the princess remain with those who love her," Myra had told her nephew and his wife all those years ago. She had felt their relief, warm and radiant like sunlight breaking through clouds.

Myra's blindness had never hindered her. Through the energy that emanated from living beings, she perceived the world in a way no sighted person ever could. She could sense the subtle shifts in a person's emotions, the flutter of fear, the warmth of gratitude. It was how she gathered herbs with unerring precision, brewed her potions, and guided her steps through the icy halls of the kingdom. Mena looked up at the old healer now, her admiration evident. Myra's frail appearance belied her strength, the steel resolve that had kept Mena safe all these years.

"Thank you, Myra," Mena said, her voice soft but heartfelt.

Myra smiled faintly, the lines of her face softening. "Drink, child. The tea will steady your gift and calm your heart." She placed a hand on Mena's shoulder, the gentle pressure grounding the young princess. "But remember, no tea can replace the control you have worked so hard to master. Trust in yourself, Mena. You are stronger than you think."

Mena nodded, feeling the warmth of the tea seep through her fingers and into her soul. As Mena sipped the tea, its effects began to take hold almost immediately. The warm, sweet, earthy liquid eased down her throat, soothing her nerves with each swallow. Yet, as expected, the sharp sting of a headache soon followed, a common side effect of the silvervane brew. It was a small price to pay, a necessary sacrifice to ensure she could navigate the ceremony without betraying her secret. Any Echo was forbidden to rule, and even a hint of her abilities could invite disaster, not only for herself but for her entire family. Once the cup was emptied, Mena handed it back to Myra, who nodded approvingly.

"Steady now," the healer said softly, looping her arm through Mena's as they left the safety of her bedroom.

The sounds of laughter and lively conversation grew louder as they descended the spiraling staircase toward the grand hall. The towering ice walls reflected the light of countless chandeliers, making the entire space shimmer like a living star. Guests from across the globe filled the room, their voices harmonizing in a cacophony of greetings and pleasantries. Mena's eyes scanned the sea of finely dressed figures. Every detail seemed exaggerated under the brilliant light: the flowing gowns, the intricately tailored suits, the glint of polished medals and jewels. Hair was styled to perfection, and perfumes mingled in the air, a tapestry of floral, musky, and citrusy scents. She recognized many faces, distant cousins, ambassadors, and nobles she had met during childhood tours. Each seemed engrossed in lively conversation, their smiles wide, their laughter echoing off the high ceilings.

Myra's hand gave her arm a gentle squeeze, breaking her focus. The healer released her grip, stepping away to mingle with the guests. Alone now, Mena stood on the grand staircase, momentarily overwhelmed by the sheer magnitude of the gathering. Her headache throbbed faintly at her temples, but her earlier nerves had dissipated. She took a deep, steadying breath, feeling the lingering effects of the tea fortify her calm. From her vantage point, her gaze found Orentheon at the far end of the hall. He stood tall, his white hair contrasting against his black suit, his expression a mix of excitement and pride. Beside him was an older man Mena did not recognize, though the ornate crown resting on his head marked him unmistakably as royalty.

"Ah, here she is!" Oren's voice boomed, startling Mena with its volume, given their proximity. Heads nearby turned briefly toward the source before resuming their chatter. "King Durnovas, may I present my sister, Princess Kallemena."

Mena dipped into a graceful bow, a slight curtsy punctuating the movement before straightening to her full height. Her dark blue eyes briefly met King Durnovas' gaze before lowering in respect. The older man's weathered face stretched into a sly, wry smile, the kind that spoke of decades spent navigating courts and intrigue.

"Mena," Orentheon continued, his tone laced with an air of nonchalance that only made her more wary, "I was just telling King Durnovas here that you would be delighted to join his son, Prince Ashar, at their table after the ceremony. One of their party could not make it, leaving a seat vacant."

Mena's eyes widened for the barest second before she nodded and gave a polite smile. "Of course," she replied with a practiced elegance, inclining her head. "It would be my honor."

"There we have it," Orentheon declared, clapping his hands together as if sealing the arrangement. "Seat vacant no more. Now, if you will excuse me, my stage awaits!"

He quickly bowed and disappeared into the bustling crowd with an ease Mena envied. King Durnovas chuckled, a deep, gravelly sound that matched his imposing stature.

"Do not worry yourself, Princess," he said, his lips curling into that same mischievous grin. "My son is not one for idle chatter. You will find the conversation quite... sparse."

Mena offered a polite laugh, though her mind raced. Before she could respond, the king's sharp eyes scanned the room.

"The little rascal must be about somewhere. I would like to introduce you before the ceremony..." The loud tolling echo of the great bells cut him off.

Their resonant chimes rolled through the grand hall, their sweet melody commanding silence. Conversations ceased, and the air shifted, a ripple of anticipation washing over the gathered crowd.

"Kings and queens, lords and ladies, esteemed guests," boomed a voice from above.

All heads turned to the top of the grand staircase, where King Thaloren stood beside Queen Nyssira, their presence regal and commanding. The king's rich and measured voice carried effortlessly over the assembly.

"We thank you for traveling from the far corners of the world to bear witness to the union of my son, Prince Orentheon, and Princess Kivani."

A wave of applause erupted, the sound echoing off the icy walls of the castle like thunder.

"Please, join us in the cathedral for the ceremony," Thaloren continued, his smile warm as Nyssira's serene gaze swept over the crowd.

The applause began to die down as the cathedral doors opened, revealing the path to the next chapter of this momentous day.

The guests shuffled their way through the hall and into the cathedral, their soft murmurs of awe echoing off the high ceilings. Gasps punctuated the hum of voices as they entered the grand space. Above them, a vaulted ceiling of glass stretched to the heavens, framed by dark wooden rafters that arched elegantly over the room. The sunlight poured through, refracting into delicate patterns on the polished glass floor below. White sashes cascaded down the cathedral walls, shimmering softly in the light, while translucent seashells dangled from invisible threads, swaying gently with each passing breeze. The aisle was laid with a thick white runner, its plush fabric muffling the click of heels as the procession prepared to begin. The frosted glass pews, intricately carved and frosted with delicate swirls, glittered like ice sculptures, drawing appreciative stares from the guests. In Iskaroth, this artistry was more than tradition; it was the signature of the people.

After several agonizing minutes, the guests finally found their seats, their chatter fading into an anticipatory silence. In that quiet moment, the cello players began. They drew their translucent glass bows across crystalline strings, the music resonating with an ethereal purity that filled the cathedral. The ceremonial march began, and the bridesmaids emerged from the arched entryway one by one. Mena followed in their procession, her place just behind the bride's younger sister, a petite girl barely reaching Mena's shoulder.

The younger girl's step was light and cheerful, but Mena's was measured, deliberate, as though every step on the glass floor required a delicate balance between control and poise. Her gaze swept over the crowd, searching, but the moment she looked up at the altar, her tension ebbed ever so slightly. There stood her brother, Orentheon, his face alight with joy. His white hair was pulled back into a high ponytail, its intricate braid trailing down his back in a style that only heightened his regal presence. His tailored black suit fit him perfectly, the long tails of his coat nearly brushing the floor. On his lapel, he wore a single white shell, small and elegant, a token echoing the decorations that adorned the walls. Despite the small, practiced smile she wore, Mena's head throbbed a persistent drumming that threatened to shatter her fragile composure.

As she reached her place on the altar, Mena cast her eyes over the sea of new faces filling the cathedral. Lords, ladies, and dignitaries from distant lands sat shoulder to shoulder, their faces looking genuinely happy to be there. Her eyes sought familiar anchors amid the crowd, and she spotted Amawna seated next to her husband, a chef who worked in the palace kitchens. Mena gave them a subtle wave before continuing her scan. Her gaze drifted to the rows further in the back, catching King Durnovas scanning the congregation with an expression of mild irritation. The seat beside him remained conspicuously empty, and Mena's thoughts drifted to his absent son. Likely still wandering the castle with his servant, she mused, recalling the word *rascal* the king had used earlier. Her lips twitched in a rueful smile as she reconsidered her earlier agreement to sit next to the boy during the feast.

A "rascal" was hardly what she needed for the company after enduring the taxing effort of suppressing her powers all day. The mere thought of making polite conversation or entertaining a restless child tightened the headache already thrumming behind her eyes. *I will need an excuse,* she decided silently, *a reason to step away before the night dragged on too long.* Mena felt a pang of guilt at the thought but pushed it aside. Bottling her anxiety had left her depleted, and the ceremony had only just begun. She drew a quiet breath and straightened her shoulders, pushing her unease aside. For now, her focus had to remain on the moment, the vows her brother would soon speak, and the unbreakable unity this day was meant to celebrate. The rest could wait.

A wave of shuffling echoed through the cathedral, followed by a crescendo of murmured gasps. Mena's gaze snapped to the aisle, and her breath caught at the sight of Kivani entering on her father's arm. Her dress shimmered like sunlight over the ocean, the pale blue fabric cascading into layers of lace and frosted embroidery. Seashells and cresting waves adorned the bodice, glinting as they caught the light streaming through the cathedral's glass ceiling. Mena's eyes flicked to her brother, and a warm smile softened her features. Oren's grin stretched from ear to ear, his joy as palpable as a summer breeze. His love for Kivani was written plainly in how his gaze never left her, the world around them fading to insignificance. Kivani's smile mirrored Oren's, wide and brimming with uncontainable happiness. It was a rare and beautiful sight, two people so clearly smitten with each other, their emotions unguarded and unrestrained in the presence of so many. Mena's chest ached with envy for a fleeting moment, though she quickly pushed the feeling aside, letting herself savor the joy radiating from the couple.

As Kivani reached the altar, her father paused, his expression solemn yet proud as he offered his daughter's hand to Oren. The exchange was symbolic, a blending of families and traditions that had been generations in the making. Oren accepted Kivani's hand with a gentle nod, his smile never faltering as they turned to face the high priest of the Axis. The priest began his address, his voice carrying through the cathedral in a lyrical blend of the bride and groom's native tongue and English. The alternating languages were a deliberate gesture, a nod to the heritage of both continents coming together in union. Each word reinforced the significance of the moment, the vows they would soon exchange, symbolizing not only their love but an unbreakable alliance between their kingdoms. Mena watched, her heart full, as the ceremony unfolded before her. For all her worries about her own struggles, this moment was theirs, a bright and hopeful union destined to shape the years ahead.

The vows were brief, intimate, and perfectly suited to the moment. Each phrase was spoken with quiet conviction as the priest guided Oren and Kivani through their promises. Their voices, though steady, carried a reverence that even the most distant guests could feel. When the priest asked the fateful question, both answered in unison, their "I do" echoing softly through the glass cathedral like a harmonious note in a sacred melody. With the final vows spoken, the priest gently closed his holy book, its cover bearing the gilded symbol of the Axis. He lifted his head, his expression composed and adorned with the polished smile of one well-versed in the gravity of such ceremonies.

"By the blessing of the Axis, which binds these two kingdoms in holy union, I now pronounce you husband and wife. You may kiss your bride."

Oren turned to Kivani, his smile widening as he gently took her hands in his. Their kiss was swift but tender and left their cheeks flushed with happiness. The cathedral erupted in a storm of cheers and whistles, the walls seemingly trembling under the weight of the crowd's exuberance. Laughter bubbled up amidst the applause, and Mena could not help but let out a soft laugh herself. For this brief moment, surrounded by joy, she allowed herself to forget her anxieties. Oren and Kivani turned to face the crowd; their hands clasped tightly together as they basked in the warmth of the moment. It was a union of love and kingdoms, a day that would be etched into history.

Chapter Nine

The ballroom dazzled like a dream spun from snow and starlight. Light from countless glass chandeliers danced across the room, refracting in crystalline shards on every surface, while music from a quartet filled the air with a gentle melody that swelled and dipped like waves on the sea. Guests moved gracefully to their assigned seats, where an array of culinary treasures awaited them. Platters of fresh shellfish, still glistening from the warm waters of Thalasson, were paired with exotic delights: golden pineapples, their sweet scent mingling with the tropical tang of shaved coconut. Mena could see the wonder on guests' faces as they sampled flavors that many had only ever heard about in passing tales.

The tables themselves were draped in fabric as luminous as moonlight on frost, their surfaces adorned with intricate centerpieces. Each one was a small masterpiece of Glacian craftsmanship: glass clamshells nestled among delicate waves of clear, icy water melted directly from the castle's own reserves. Inside each shell, a snowflake hovered, suspended in pristine stasis, as though caught mid-fall in an eternal winter. The artistry honored both the icy heritage of Glacia and the sandy shores of Thalasson, symbolizing the union of two distant worlds. Mena's gaze swept across the grand room. Her brother, now the picture of marital bliss, stood at the center surrounded by a lively throng of well-wishers. His new bride, draped in delicate lace and exuding regal warmth, laughed with an ease that made it seem as though she had been born into this wintry kingdom. Across the room, Mena caught sight of her parents deep in conversation with monarchs from distant continents. Her father's broad gestures and hearty laughter were occasionally punctuated by the reserved smile of her mother, who raised a crystalline goblet in toast after toast.

Despite the joy that rippled through the room, Mena felt the familiar tug of exhaustion creeping in. The persistent throb of her earlier headache had subsided, but the mental toll of suppressing her power loomed large. She sighed as her eyes landed on her place at the table, marked by an elegant name card written in silvery ink. The name "King Durnovas" was inscribed to her left, and to her right, "Prince Ashar." Both seats were blissfully vacant. If luck held, she could eat quickly and escape to the gardens, as her mother had suggested. Taking her seat, Mena found herself surrounded by King Durnovas' entourage. She offered polite smiles and introduced herself to the group, who responded with varying degrees of enthusiasm. One woman, wrapped tightly in layers of white fabric that seemed better suited for a desert climate, managed a thin, almost pained smile. Her lips trembled slightly as she poked tentatively at a piece of shellfish, her discomfort at both the cold and the meal written plainly across her face. Mena stifled a chuckle. For all the splendor of the evening, it was a relief to find these small, human moments amid the grandeur.

The soft swell of strings and lilting notes of the orchestra filled the ballroom, creating a cocoon of sound that seemed to hush the room's idle chatter. Mena turned her attention to the center, where the first dance was beginning to unfold. Her gaze briefly caught King Durnovas, who had slumped into his chair with a huff. He rubbed his brow in a gesture that spoke of both weariness and frustration.

"My son will be the death of me," he muttered, his voice low but carrying the weight of his exasperation.

Mena felt a flicker of unexpected sympathy for the king. Though she could not fathom such public disappointment, the strain on his face was unmistakable. Prince Ashar's absence on this crucial day would undoubtedly have consequences when he returned home. For a fleeting moment, she imagined the king's frustration turning to stern words and stricter discipline, the dynamic between father and son, a world removed from her own family's closeness. Her thoughts shifted as the music grew lively, and she returned her gaze to the polished glass floor. Her brother, standing tall and radiant, bowed deeply before his bride. Kivani, the picture of elegance, returned his bow with a graceful curtsey, her head dipping low as she placed her hand in his. The two moved as one, stepping into a slow, reverent embrace that soon gave way to sweeping motions across the ballroom. Kivani's sashes and train trailed behind her, gliding effortlessly over the smooth floor as though caught on an invisible wind. The music dictated their steps, a melody that wove itself around the couple, sealing them in a moment that felt as eternal as the stars.

The look on their faces caught Mena's breath. Peace and love radiated from them as though their hearts beat in perfect synchronization. The tension in Mena's chest softened, and she allowed herself to be drawn into the music's gentle pull. Each note seemed to unravel her thoughts, replacing them with the rhythm of the strings, the soft calls of the woodwinds, and the delicate, crystalline chimes of the piano. The melody was alive, vibrant, and full of longing. Mena felt it tug at her soul, each note like a thread teasing the edges of her power, beckoning it to life. Her fingertips tingled with the urge to create her mind aflame with shapes and light that begged to take form. Every pluck of a string, every haunting rise of the flute, seemed to speak to something deep within her, a magic that stirred just beneath the surface, aching to be freed. She closed her eyes for a moment, letting herself be carried by the music, each wave of sound lifting her higher into a state of ethereal bliss.

A simultaneous gasp rippled through the room, sharp and breathless. Mena's eyes snapped open. The world around her had dissolved into darkness. Stars filled the space overhead, twinkling against the void like a thousand tiny pinpricks of light. She looked down, and the glass floor had vanished, replaced by the mirrored reflection of the celestial sky. It was as if the dancers were floating on the surface of a still, midnight sea, the world above and below blending seamlessly into one. Her brother and Kivani, still in the midst of their first dance, moved with an ethereal grace. Their bodies swayed in time with the music, but it was the starry backdrop, the strange and beautiful distortion of the room, that held Mena's gaze. The scene was breathtaking, as if the very fabric of reality had bent to their love. As they reached the end of their dance, they kissed, just a light, tender meeting of lips, but in the shadow of that celestial spectacle, it felt like a vow, timeless and unbreakable.

The applause that followed snapped Mena back to reality. The darkness lifted, and light flooded the room once more, restoring the ballroom to its warm glow. The crowd buzzed with murmurs as if in collective disbelief at the beauty they had just witnessed. Mena's heart was racing. She glanced at her mother, who sat nearby, her brow furrowed with concern. Mena could see the unspoken question in her mother's eyes: *did anyone suspect her?* The atmosphere shifted as a new round of applause filled the air. Mena turned to see her great aunt Myra step forward, her graceful movements drawing the crowd's attention.

"A most gracious thank you to our wonderful healer, my great aunt Myra, for her amazing Echo ability to make my first dance with my new wife even more memorable," Oren announced, his voice full of warmth.

He placed a gentle kiss on Myra's cheek as the blind woman lifted her hand in acknowledgment. The crowd cheered, but Mena's attention was already drifting. *That was too close.* She felt a wave of heat wash over her, followed by a cold sweat as she scanned the room. Her eyes settled on the high priest of the Axis, sitting at a nearby table, his face still framed in the pleasant smile he wore while conversing with his companions.

Trying to regain composure, Mena stood, her chair screeching behind her. "Please excuse me, your majesty. I think my mother is..."

Her words faltered when she was interrupted by a flash of white, silver, sharp against the warmth of the ballroom, invading her vision. Mena froze. Standing before her was a tall and imposing man, his appearance far different from what she had expected. His sharp, irritated gaze met hers, and a small grimace tugged at the corners of his mouth as he quickly gave a shallow nod and lowered himself into the chair beside her. King Durnovas' voice cut through the tension.

"Better late than never, I suppose," he muttered, his tone tense with barely contained frustration. "Princess Kallemena, this is my son. Prince Ashar."

Mena's eyes flicked between the king and the young man before her. He was nothing like the boy she had imagined. This was not the carefree prince of adolescence she had expected but a man with a demeanor that spoke of impatience, of authority that had yet to be earned. His sharp eyes, dark and cold, swept over her, barely concealing the irritation that pulsed beneath the surface. She took a breath, met his gaze, and immediately felt the weight of his presence, something unsettling and yet strangely magnetic. But before she could process her thoughts, King Durnovas cleared his throat loudly and stepped toward his son.

"That is no way to greet our host's daughter," the king scolded while grabbing Ashar by the arm and pulling him back to his feet.

Ashar rolled his eyes, clearly unbothered by the rebuke, and straightened his suit jacket with an air of practiced indifference. His hand extended toward Mena as he forced a smile stretching awkwardly across his face.

"It is a pleasure to meet you, Princess."

Mena hesitated, her gaze darting between the king and the prince. The tension in the air thickened as though the very atmosphere around her had become charged. Before she could gather her thoughts, King Durnovas reached for her wrist, placing her hand into his son's, forcing a connection that burned through her skin like fire. At the touch, Mena's heart skipped a beat. The heat was immediate, intense, almost unbearable. Her skin felt as though it were catching fire, the sensation crawling deep into her bones and wrapping around her pulse. She jerked her hand away in instinctive panic, her breath quickening as she stared wide-eyed at Ashar.

"I-I am so sorry," she blurted, quickly ducking her head into a clumsy bow. "I have to go."

Without another word, she turned and glided across the room, her steps a blur as she moved toward the mirrored glass doors. She needed to breathe fresh air; she needed distance between herself and the hundreds of bodies crammed into the ballroom, and before the burn of that touch consumed her completely, she needed to run away.

The evening air carried a chill, and as Mena stepped into the garden, she felt the weight of the cold seep into her skin. Light snowflakes began to drift lazily from the sky; each one a tiny, delicate marvel against the velvet dusk of sunset. The crisp, icy air hit her feverish skin, sharp and refreshing. It was as though the cold had a purpose: to cleanse, to settle the heat that still burned beneath her flesh. Her lungs could finally expand, drawing in the cool, oxygen-rich air after the suffocating pressure of the crowd. She looked down at her hand, the one that had touched Prince Ashar's. The sensation of his skin against hers lingered like a phantom burn. The warmth had been unlike anything she had ever known, more intense, more invasive than the heat of the furnaces or the fires in the hearths of the castle. It was not the sting of a scalding pot nor the sun's gentle warmth after a long winter. It was a heat that seemed to flow through her entire being, a kind of fire that did not scorch but pulsed with an unsettling rhythm as though it were alive inside her. She could not find the words to explain it, nor could she fully understand it.

"Excuse me?"

The voice sliced through her thoughts like a blade, startling her so much that Mena spun too quickly. Her foot slipped on the snow-dappled stone, the icy surface betraying her balance. For a breathless moment, the world tilted, and she braced for the sting of a fall, but it did not come. Strong hands caught her, steadying her, their warmth startlingly vivid even through the layers of her gown. Those hands. That same burning sensation. The touch sent a jolt through her, sharp and electric, her breath hitching as her eyes darted upward. The prince. His dark gaze bore into hers, filled with something she could not quite name: curiosity, irritation, or perhaps something more guarded. Panic surged in her chest, and she tore herself from his grasp, stepping back as her heart slammed against her ribs. She fumbled with her gown, smoothing the fabric with trembling hands, then brushed stray tendrils of hair from her face. Heat crept up her neck and into her cheeks, an unwelcome flush she cursed as much as the clumsy laugh that escaped her lips, a brittle, hollow sound.

"I am sorry if I frightened you," Ashar said, his voice deep, laced with an uneasy sincerity.

Mena forced a smile, though her nerves betrayed her. The edges of her mouth twitched, refusing to cooperate. "It is fine. Truly."

The prince shifted his weight, his broad shoulders stiff against the biting cold. He rubbed the back of his neck, glancing at the shimmering glass statues that surrounded them. In the day's dusk light, the sculptures glistened with frost, their fragile elegance contrasting sharply with the awkwardness thickening the air between them. Silence stretched, taut and unbearable, as if even the snowflakes paused to watch their faltering interaction.

"It was a lovely ceremony," he finally ventured, his tone measured as though trying to tread lightly over a breaking bridge. "Your brother seems... very happy."

Mena dared a glance at him, studying the sharp angles of his face and the guarded expression that betrayed nothing of what he truly thought. She nodded, folding her arms tightly across her chest, the cold air seeping into her skin despite the lingering warmth his touch had left behind.

"Yes," she said softly, casting her eyes downward. "He loves Princess Kivani deeply."

Her gaze flitted to a nearby glass sculpture. Its glistening surface seemed to pull her toward it, a welcome distraction. She inched closer to the sculpture, her movements slow and deliberate, hoping the prince would catch the hint. Yet, instead of retreating, Ashar remained where he was, his presence a constant, weighty thing that prickled at her composure. Mena let out an irritated sigh as she sensed his heat beside her again, unshakable and persistent. They stood in silence, their gazes fixed on the glass statue before them. She knew the figure represented one of her ancestors, though she would be hard-pressed to remember which one without the aid of the weathered plaque at its base. The translucent woman was a vision of quiet power, standing tall with a feather delicately held between her fingers. The artistry was undeniable; the feather looked as if it could float out of the woman's hand at the slightest breeze.

"Beautiful," Ashar murmured, his voice breaking the silence like a sudden gust of wind.

Mena stiffened, her chest tightening as she sucked in a sharp breath of icy air. The chill clawed at her throat, and before she could stop it, the sudden intake tangled with her spit, triggering a violent coughing fit. She doubled over, choking and rasping as heat surged to her cheeks, deepening the flush already rising from his nearness.

"Are you all right?" Ashar asked, his voice tinged with genuine concern.

He waved his hands awkwardly, unsure whether to pat her back, fetch help, or stand perfectly still. Mena held up a hand, desperately trying to silence him as she fought to stifle the choking spasms. Her attempt to hold her breath only made it worse, and her face burned hotter with each ragged cough that escaped. He took a step towards her, his hand poised and ready to slam down on her back. She shook her head and waved him off, finally allowing herself the deep, guttural coughs her body demanded. The sharp edge in her windpipe began to fade, leaving her throat raw but no longer rebelling against her. She kept her back to him, willing herself to cool the mortifying heat on her face. Her fingers brushed her brow, wiping away beads of sweat that had already started to chill and crystallize in the frigid air.

"Are you all right?" Ashar asked again, his tone laden with apology. "I am so sorry, I did not mean to! I was... complimenting the woman."

Mena turned slightly, catching the nervous motion of his hands as he gestured toward the statue.

"The statue of the woman, I mean. Not you. Well... you too, of course," he fumbled, his words tangling like threads caught in a thorn-bush. "And her. The woman made from glass. The craftsmanship, yes! That is all I meant...Chains!"

He pinched the bridge of his nose between his thumb and forefinger, muttering a low curse at himself under his breath. Mena bit her lip, torn between sympathy for his floundering and amusement at the sheer absurdity of the moment. She kept her back turned, her shoulders trembling as she fought to contain the bubbling laughter threatening to escape. But the effort was futile. A snort slipped out, breaking the dam, and a howl of laughter burst forth. She spun around, clutching her stomach as the prince's wide-eyed look of pure shock and horror only fueled her mirth. Ashar blinked, stunned initially, but her infectious laughter soon pulled him in. A chuckle escaped his lips, then another, until he was laughing alongside her. The once tranquil garden now rang with the sound of their hearty, unrestrained mirth echoing off the ice-laden walls. Tears streamed down their faces as they doubled over, their laughter bordering on delirium.

"Stop... please!" Mena gasped, clutching her sides as though her ribs might break.

Even as their laughter finally subsided, their smiles lingered, soft-ening the tension between them. When their eyes finally met, the air seemed to shift. He noticed her pale skin, luminous in the fading light, and her deep blue eyes, which seemed almost black, as though they were tiny galaxies housing a thousand stars. Her smile was disarmingly perfect, carrying an innocent and alluring charm.

Mena held her breath as she took him in, the pine green and brown of his eyes flecked with streaks of amber, his warm, rich complexion framed by waves of dark brown hair. There was a natural strength about him, his height towering over hers despite her own Glacian stature. Ashar extended his hand, his expression soft but earnest.

"I owe you a proper introduction." His voice was steadier now, tinged with warmth. "Ashar Durnovas, prince of Highspire."

She hesitated momentarily, then laid her hand lightly on his. His touch was warm, almost unnervingly so, against her chilled skin. He raised her hand to his lips and kissed her knuckles with a respectful bow of his head.

"Kallemena Vaelora. Princess of... well, here." She gestured vaguely toward the towering castle behind them.

Ashar turned, his gaze tracing the snow-capped spires and shimmering glass walls.

The last rays of sunlight painted the castle in hues of pink and gold, the icicles catching the light as if they were tiny crystals dancing in the breeze. Mena pulled her hand back abruptly, rubbing the spot where his touch had left a lingering warmth.

"Do you feel it too?" he asked, his tone low and cautious, but his gaze locked firmly on hers.

Her body stiffened, and she lifted her eyes to meet his, searching for the meaning in his words.

"When I touched your hand the first time," he continued, rubbing his fingers absentmindedly, "it was like my skin froze instantly. It was not as intense this time, but before... it was almost painful."

Mena looked down at her own hand, flexing her fingers. "No... it felt like burning to me. As though your touch seared my flesh to the bone."

They both fell silent, their eyes drifting to their own hands, then to each other's, as if the answers might reveal themselves in the space between.

"It also was not as painful for me this time," Mena murmured, her voice uncertain. "I have never..." She hesitated, searching for the right words. "I have never felt anything like that before."

"Me neither," he admitted, his voice carrying an odd mix of relief and curiosity.

Their shared unease hung between them like an invisible thread, tethering them together even as it raised more questions. Slowly, Ashar stepped closer, his movements tentative. He raised his hand, hovering it inches from her arm. Mena could feel the heat radiating from him, an energy that seemed to pulse in the space between them. Neither dared to move, their breaths mingling in the frosty air.

"What is this?" she whispered, her voice trembling as much from the sensation as the question itself.

Ashar did not answer immediately, his expression darkened by the same confusion that clouded her own.

"I do not know," he admitted at last, his words barely louder than a breath.

"Mena!" Oren's voice sang through the frosty night, bouncing off the snow-laden walls, shattering the moment. Both she and Ashar were startled like guilty children caught in mischief.

She turned to see her brother, his face alight with shenanigans, a smug smile plastered across his features.

Ashar quickly withdrew his hand, running it nervously through his hair as he stepped aside, suddenly far too interested in the snowy ground.

"I am about to cut the most delicious cake you will ever taste, and I get to do it with the most beautiful woman who is now calling herself my wife!" Oren exclaimed, his excitement bubbling over as he bounced on his toes like a boy instead of a grown man of twenty-seven. "Come on!" He waved her over with exaggerated enthusiasm, still practically vibrating with energy. "It towers above us all; how the cooks made such a majestic masterpiece is beyond me, but oh, I do love wedding cakes! I love love! I love being married!"

Mena hesitated, smoothing her dress and giving Ashar a small, polite curtsy. "Your Highness," she murmured, her voice a little too formal for the moment.

Ashar nodded, his lips parting as if to say something, but the words did not come. Instead, he watched her go, his gaze lingering as she turned and made her way to Oren. Her brother's arm looped around hers as he led her toward the grand hall. His grin was as wide as the sky, and his steps were as uneven as the tide. The smell of ale wafted strongly from him.

"What is that look for?" she asked, nudging him playfully back upright.

Oren pointed to his face, mimicking a sly grin. "Oh, this face?" His words slurred. "This is the face of a man who knows how to match them," he said with exaggerated wisdom as though he were an ancient oracle. "I knew you would like him."

Mena froze mid-step, her mouth falling open in disbelief. "I do not!" she blurted, her voice louder than she intended.

Oren's grin only widened as he lazily slipped back into the ballroom, closing the mirrored doors behind himself, leaving her flustered and alone in the dimly lit hall.

Frustration bubbled in her chest, a mix of embarrassment and indignation that made her cheeks burn. How dare he tease her like that? Her, like a prince? Knowing the match could never be. She was doomed to be a spinster. Forever alone. She huffed as she leaned against the cold wall. "And yet..." Was she truly angry with Oren? Or was she angry that the idea of Prince Ashar was not as off-putting as it should have been? She allowed herself a brief daydream of being happily married with a family of her own. Her brother's smug face flashed in her mind, and she felt the sting of humility that only a younger sibling could endure. With a growl of frustration, Mena slid to the floor, the cold greeting her skin as she buried her face in her hands.

Her power stirred in response to her emotions, seeping out like a slow, deliberate breath. A delicate butterfly materialized on the stone floor before her, its silver-frosted coloring shimmering faintly in the flickering light. It fanned its wings lazily, oblivious to her turmoil. Mena exhaled, her irritation ebbing as she focused on the small creature. She waved a hand, and another butterfly appeared. Then three. Then seven. Soon, the space around her came alive with movement as dozens of butterflies emerged, their wings creating a mesmerizing dance. They flowed together in a synchronized wave, a soft, silken ripple that swept through the air and across the floor in an elegant ballet.

"You...you are an Echo."

The voice was soft but firm, cutting through the quiet like a blade. Mena froze, her hand still raised mid-summon. The butterflies scattered, their delicate forms dissolving into the cold air, leaving nothing but silence and the faint shimmer of frost on the floor. She turned, her heart pounding in her chest, to see who had spoken. She had forgotten herself, forgotten that the castle was filled with strangers, any one of whom could bear witness to her secret. And now, standing just down the hall, was Ashar, frozen in place, his expression a mixture of shock and disbelief.

"I... I can explain," she stammered as she stumbled to her feet, her voice trembling as much as her hands. "It is not what it looks like. Well, it is, but please, do not tell anyone."

Her stomach twisted into knots, and nausea threatened to erupt up her throat. She had been a fool, an absolute fool. This was why Oren teased her, why her parents still hovered over her like watchful sentinels. She was too naive, too reckless, too inexperienced to control herself. Before Ashar could respond, the glass doors leading to the ballroom flew open with a burst of light and sound.

"Mena! You are missing the cake!" Amawna's voice rang out in delight, her tone oblivious to the tension hanging in the air.

She swept into the hallway, her smile radiant, her movements lively, and she was utterly unaware of Ashar's presence. Before Mena could react, Amawna grabbed her arm with the easy confidence of an old friend. "Come on!" Mena had no choice but to follow as Amawna pulled her back toward the ballroom, the doors closing behind them with a finality that left the hall in silence once more. Ashar remained rooted to the spot, his mind racing. The image of Mena surrounded by frost-kissed butterflies played over and over in his head, each detail more vivid than the last. What he had seen was nothing short of re-markable and dangerous—a royal Echo. The thought sent a chill down his spine. The law was clear: no Echo could remain part of a royal fam-ily. Yet here she was, Kallemena Vaelora, defying the very tenets of the Axis. It could not be a secret; her family must know.

He realized they had all been hiding the truth, the implications settling heavily on his shoulders. Then, another thought struck him, a revela-tion that made his heart beat faster.

She is an Echo, just like me.

Chapter Ten

Mena was a bundle of nerves and confusion. She had spent the entire week of celebration carefully avoiding Prince Ashar, determined to keep their paths from crossing until the last of the guests could finally leave. She would feel his eyes on her when everyone would take their meals in the banquet hall. Even from across the yard, through the bustle of the entertainment that dazzled when the weather was nice in the frozen tundra she called home. Acrobats from across the nine great continents would perform for all the guests, doing daring acts that made the crowds gasp every few seconds.. Yet, as she awoke each morning, a knot of dread formed in her stomach. She wondered if today would be the day the Axis would swiftly arrive at her door and drag her away to Verdathos.

Every footstep outside her chambers would send her spiraling into panic, forcing her to burrow under the covers like a child trying to escape a scolding they have no doubt earned. Amawna had noticed the subtle shift in her demeanor, the increasing tension that seemed to cling to her like a second skin. She had even sent for Myra, assuming Mena was coming down with some fatal illness.

"I promise I am not sick," Mena muttered, her voice small as Myra's cool fingers pressed against her forehead. Then, she gently traced the lines of her temples. "Amawna is overreacting. I am as right as the snow."

Myra let out a soft breath, her blind eyes scanning Mena's face before moving down to her neck and pressure points. "You are a bit warm."

She continued her examination with gentle care, but their silence spoke volumes. Myra nodded more to herself than anyone else, but Amawna caught it as a sign to call herself to action. The loyal attendant, whose anxiety was written all over her face, watched with hawk-like eyes as the examination continued. Mena could see her attendant's thoughts racing. She knew that at any moment, Amawna could be off on a frantic search for remedies, no matter how outlandish or ridiculous, to cure her beloved princess.

"Is it a fever?" Amawna asked eagerly. "Her face is pink."

Gently, resting her palm on Mena's forehead again, Myra's voice was a calm murmur. "Any pain?"

"If it is fever, I can fetch you some willow bark. Or would you prefer elderflower? I can mix it with peppermint." Amawna's voice was frantic as she ticked off the ingredients on her fingers.

"No," Mena groaned, unable to hide the irritation in her voice. "It is not a fever." She sat up slightly, still feeling the weight of the tension in her chest.

Amawna was already ready to spring into action, her eyes lighting up. "Oh! Is it that time of month? I could fetch the hot water bottle, some ginger, and clove," She clapped her hands together. "And your favorite lemon tarts!"

Mena rolled her eyes as she let out an exaggerated groan and fell back against the bed in frustration. "No, Amawna," she gritted her teeth. "It is not that either."

She wished she could explain that it was not sickness she was hiding from. It was something else entirely, a storm of emotions, a quiet dread that gnawed at her, making her skin prickle with the fear of being discovered. Ashar's touch, the overwhelming connection she felt, the impossible sensation of something more, his knowledge of her gift, her world was shifting, and she was not sure she could stop it. She pulled her pillow over her face and wrapped her arms around the silky case that smelled of her hair soap. Myra chuckled softly as she sat at the edge of the bed, her hand waving dismissively through the air. The light in the room dimmed, and a sudden chill crept through the space, the crisp air a welcome relief to Mena's burning flesh. She could hear Amawna's footsteps retreating from her room, growing fainter with each passing moment. Mena glanced toward the door, watching as the mirrored panel slid slowly shut, its metallic latch clicking softly into place.

"You sent her away?" Mena's voice was tentative, a mixture of curiosity and lingering anxiety.

Myra's lips curved into a knowing smile as she nodded, her eyes twinkling with a touch of mischief. "You needed privacy, did you not?" she said, her voice light yet knowing. Mena exhaled slowly, the relief almost palpable as her shoulders relaxed.

"So, who was it?" Myra's voice shifted, more serious now, as her hand gently rested on Mena's.

"Who was who, Aunt Myra?" Mena's heartbeat picked up, an unease stirring in her chest despite the comfort of the room.

"The one who saw you use your gift." Myra's fingers flicked as if dispersing the very tension Mena was trying so hard to hold in. "Your fear and anxiety have filled the room. That could only mean one thing." She fixed Mena with a steady gaze, her expression both calm and expectant. "So, who saw you?"

Mena swallowed hard, the air feeling thick around her as she leaned against the headboard. Her fingers twisted nervously around the blanket's tassels, the fabric catching between her fingertips. "The prince," she whispered, the weight of the words feeling heavier than she anticipated. Prince Ashar Durnovas of the continent of Kalyra."

She covered her face with her hands, bracing herself for the scolding she knew was coming. The silence stretched out, amplifying the sound of her racing pulse. When no reprimand came, she hesitantly lowered her hands, peering through her fingers. Myra sat with her eyes closed, her face unreadable as her hands moved in the air, fingers spread wide in concentration. Her expression shifted slightly, a smile tugging at the corner of her mouth as her eyelids fluttered. Mena watched in silent anticipation, sensing that Myra was looking for something, something important. It was only when Myra's hands fell that Mena dared break the silence.

"What did you see?" Mena asked, eager to know her fate.

She leaned forward, unable to contain the curiosity that burned inside her. Myra opened her eyes slowly, and Mena was stunned by their appearance. They were both striking pale blue with flecks of silver swirling within her irises. Her pupils were nearly nonexistent, making her gaze all the more intense.

"What was it?" Mena pressed.

Myra patted her hand one last time before rising to her feet, her expression thoughtful. "I will send Amawna back in to help you get dressed. We need to have a conversation with your mother and father."

Mena's stomach churned at the mention of her parents. She could only imagine what that conversation would entail. Amawna hummed softly as she worked to untangle the princess's tangled locks, carefully separating the hair with patient hands and weaving it into perfectly styled layers. The rhythmic motion and the feel of the brush glide through her hair were soothing, but it did little to calm the storm of nerves raging inside Mena. She absentmindedly sipped the chamomile tea Amawna had brought for her, though it did nothing to settle her roiling thoughts. Her mind kept returning to the conversation she knew awaited her, the one with her parents. The weight of the secret is now out in the open, no longer just her family's burden to carry. What would they think when they learned someone else knew? A scolding, she decided, and a harsh one at that.

Once Amawna had finished, she took the empty cup and hurried from the room, her soft footsteps echoing in the distance. Mena remained at the vanity, staring at her reflection, the worry evident in the tightness of her face. Her reflection felt foreign to her now, like a stranger she had to face. With a long, shaky breath, she forced herself to stand. Her feet felt heavy as she walked toward the door. She stole a quick glance back at her bed, wondering if anyone would really notice her absence. She gave a defeated sigh and opened the door. She slipped into the hallway. The silence of the corridor seemed almost suffocating, the emptiness eerie considering the number of guests still staying at the castle. She moved quickly, her steps echoing in the stillness, heading toward the stairs. She could find her parents amid the remaining guests, but if Myra had sent for them, it was likely that the study would be the most direct place to speak. That was where they would have the most privacy.

"Ah, if it is not one of the ladies of the house."

Mena felt herself tense. Heavy footsteps echoed against the glass floor as a tall figure approached. She turned, curtsied, and found herself face-to-face with High Priest Vallorith. Cloaked in a crimson robe with a golden sun embroidered on his chest, he exuded an air of authority. In his pale, uncalloused hands, the hands of one who had never toiled, he held the holy book of the Axis, its leather cover worn from years of handling. It was a symbol of his life within the Axis's towering, insulated walls, where knowledge of every kind was hoarded and protected. It was a life devoid of labor, of contact with the outside world. A life, Mena thought, that was far too foreign to hers.

"Good morning, High Priest Vallorith. I trust you have been enjoying your stay here in our kingdom?" she asked, keeping her voice steady despite the unease that racked her brain.

The high priest gave a small, tight nod, then offered his arm. Mena hesitated before slipping her arm through his. Instantly, she felt trapped, like a mouse caught in a cat's paw. The familiar surge of unease rose within her, an ache behind her eye, a swirl of fear that threatened to spill from her. She had to keep it under control... keep her gift contained. She focused on her breathing, blocking out the storm of emotions building beneath the surface.

Vallorith continued talking as they made their way down the hall. His voice was smooth and calm, "Despite the cold, it is quite pleasant here. I assume you natives have built up a tolerance to it. I could never build up such a barrier; I, myself, love a good summer's day. We open the windows in the towers and allow the hot, dry air to greet us in our studies. It really is quite a sight. You and your family should come to visit sometime. However, I am unsure how cold-natured people like yourselves would fare in the summer heat. Too delicate." He chuckled as if he had just told a joke. "You might melt." Another bout of laughter escaped him.

Mena blinked, only just catching the end of his words. "I am sorry?"

The high priest stared at her resignedly as if greatly offended by not being heard the first time.

"We were discussing this dreaded cold," he said, his voice snappish as they began to descend the stairs into the grand hall. "You must admit that being perpetually cold is rather dull."

"Yes," Mena replied, forcing her voice to remain calm, "I suppose it can seem monotonous."

Vallorith pulled her closer, and the pressure on her arm intensified. Her discomfort grew. His velvet robe pressed against her skin, thick and heavy like a weight she could not shake. She struggled to maintain her composure, each step feeling like a battle. She tried to take a deep breath, hoping it would do her shakiness good, but immediately regretted that decision as she smelled the scent that now encompassed them. The high priest smelled of soiled flesh and harsh herbs. The smell of someone who had not bathed in days, maybe even months. She exhaled the air that was trapped in her lungs, not wanting it to taint her bloodstream. She would rather pass out than smell that scent again.

"I am glad I have spent this time here, though." Vallorith went on, his gaze fixed on her, "Your family is lucky to have such a talented healer such as your aunt in your household. Her gift is quite strong, for even now, I can feel her presence throughout the entirety of the castle. Her ability looms everywhere." He smiled down at her. "I have never had the pleasure of meeting such a strong Echo before."

"Mena!" voices called after her, but she did not stop. Each cry of her name spurred her forward – faster – until their voices faded behind her.

She tore up the grand staircase two steps at a time, her gown bundled in her fists. Her lungs and throat burned with exertion and emotion as she reached the door leading to the west tower. She pushed it open and began to climb. Up and up, she ascended the spiraling steps, her breath coming in ragged gasps. Her legs ached, but she refused to slow. At last, she reached the top. The room at the pinnacle of the tower was her sanctuary. Light poured in from all sides, streaming through tall windows that framed a breathtaking view of her homeland and the snowy peaks beyond. The space was warm and alive, its air lightly scented with the fragrance of greenery.

Vines wound their way up the walls, their leaves reaching skyward as if defying the glass confinement. A soft blue chaise rested on a plush rug the same hue as the endless heavens beyond the glass. Usually, this place brought her solace. But not today. Mena stumbled into the center of the room, her chest heaving, her vision blurred by tears. The warm, inviting air could not soothe her. The sight of the familiar, comforting plants only deepened the ache in her chest. Then, without warning, a scream tore from her throat. Raw, primal, filled with all the anguish and fury she could no longer contain.

Darkness rushed outward from her in an unstoppable wave, swallowing the light. The entire room was consumed by her power, encased in an impenetrable void of black. Her barrier, her refuge, sealed her away from the world outside. The air turned icy in an instant. Goosebumps prickled her skin as the warmth drained from her sanctuary. Tears streamed down her face, freezing into delicate crystals on the now sightless floor. Her sobs echoed in the emptiness, ragged and broken, filling the void with her despair. What was her father thinking? Her mind raced, the question burning like a flame she could not extinguish. She had trusted him to make things right, to protect her. All of them. Her mother, brother, and even Myra.

Instead, they had betrayed her, deciding her future without her consent. To marry her off, send her away to strangers in a distant land, how would that protect her? How would that make her safe? She curled into herself, her arms wrapping tightly around her knees as she sank to the cold floor. The darkness pressed closer, wrapping her in its suffocating embrace. She did not want to go. She did not want to leave the safety of her glass castle, the only home she had ever known. Her sobs quieted, replaced by the heavy stillness of her void. She sat there, frozen in anguish, her mind swirling with fear and betrayal, unable to imagine what awaited her beyond the darkness. Beyond Glacia. And what of her gifts? Would strangers be so willing to look past what she was? An Echo? Would she be safe?

"Kallemena?"

The voice cut through the stillness; she did not need to look to know who it was intruding on her wallowing. Yet, her heart still began to race. She cursed her betraying emotions, as Ashar stood just inside the room. Tall and cautious, his hands outstretched in a placating gesture, trying to navigate the dark that encased him. Each step he took forward was deliberate, his boots barely making a sound against the floor. Vexation flared within her like a sudden fire. He had followed her again. He had seen her ability before, and now he was witnessing it in its raw, uncontrollable state. Her jaw clenched as she raised her hand. With a flick of her wrist, the faint light from the open door behind Ashar was swallowed by her darkness. The void enveloped him completely, and she heard the sharp gasp of surprise, followed by the thud of a body hitting the floor. Mena smirked, a slight sense of satisfaction creeping in. Let him feel her power. Let him know she was not to be trifled with. She was not some sweet girl who could get passed off so easily.

A flicker of light disrupted her darkness, catching her off guard. At first, it was small, barely more than a pinpoint, but it grew quickly, multiplying until thousands of tiny orbs filled the room. Each one glowed with a soft, golden warmth, their light flickering like tiny

His smile was cold. His emerald eyes gleamed with something unsettling, almost predatory, as he looked at her. His teeth, unnervingly straight with pointed cuspids, gleamed in the soft light of the hall. He towered over her, a silent giant in his imposing robe. She could feel the weight of his presence like a heavy shadow pressing in on her.

"Kallemena, come see what yuh bredda bring mi now, eh!" Kivani's deep islander accent was a welcome intrusion, breaking the tension.

Mena quickly withdrew her arm from Vallorith's grip and respectfully bowed, giving a polite, formal smile. "I do hope you have a safe journey back to your home continent, High Priest Vallorith."

The priest gave a curt nod to both women before turning on his heel, making his way toward the door with measured steps. He disappeared into the morning sunlight, likely seeking warmth from the lingering cold inside. Kivani smirked as she nudged Mena's arm. "Mi save yuh skin, sista," Kivani said with a mischievous grin, fixing a stray curl from her head. "Dat man bring bad juju, mi can feel it anytime his eyes are upon me."

Mena shivered at the thought of her arm entwined with Vallorith's. "He smelled horrible, and he is very pompous." She glanced around, grateful the hall was empty. "What was it you wanted to show me?"

Kivani's smile grew wider, her eyes gleaming with playful mischief as she strode confidently down the hall. "Nuttin, mi was just making up a little fib. Just needed to get yuh away, dat's all." She winked at her new sister-in-law.

Both girls laughed, the sound light and carefree, but it quickly stilled when a dominating figure entered the hall. King Thaloren, his expression serious, stared down at Mena with the weight of authority. Mena knew instantly that Myra had spoken to him, and now it was time to face the consequences.

"We need to talk," Thaloren's voice was firm, the words carrying a quiet command.

Without another word, he turned and walked away, and Mena, though reluctant, knew she had no choice but to follow. She gave a small, fleeting wave to Kivani, who stood alone in the grand hall, her island beauty contrasting against the gleaming white and silver walls. The room seemed to magnify her, leaving her standing like a lone beacon amidst the opulent emptiness.

Mena hurried to catch up with her father as he entered the study, swiftly shutting the door behind him. Inside, she saw the familiar faces of her mother, brother, and great-aunt Myra. King Thaloren sat behind his large, dark wooden desk, crafted from imported timber from a distant continent. The study was the darkest room in the castle, its walls draped in rich fabrics and paintings that obscured any view of the outside. The dim light flickered from two lamps mounted on the walls and a few scattered candles on the desk, their wax trailing down and pooling on the glass floor, carpeted in deep hues of green and gold. All the windows were shut tight, their curtains were drawn, and King Thaloren spoke in a low, hushed tone as if fearing even the walls might overhear what he was about to say.

"Myra has told us of your predicament." The king settled deeper into his worn chair, his voice stern yet controlled.

Mena glanced around at her family. Their faces showed no signs of strain, no furrowed brows of concern.

Thaloren continued. "Ashar has not spoken of your gift to anyone else. Myra has sensed this from him."

Mena shot a glance at her great aunt. Myra's eyes, pale and eerily glowing in the dim room, locked with hers. Mena turned back to her father, confusion rising within her.

"Well, that is good, is it not?" she said, trying to ease the tension in her chest.

The king's expression remained unreadable. Mena had expected either fury or relief but found only a quiet, impenetrable calm.

"Since he has kept your secret these past few days, that tells me one thing," Thaloren said slowly, "and there is only one thing to be done." He reached for a small silver bell beside him and rang it three times.

The sound echoed in the room, and within moments, an attendant appeared, bowing low. "Yes, your majesty?"

"Bring me King and Prince Durnovas of the continent of Kalyra," the king ordered, his voice firm but with a hint of merriment hidden deep within.

The servant bowed again and quickly left, closing the door behind him. Mena jumped to her feet and paced in frantic circles.

"What do we need with them? If Ashar has kept my secret, then surely we are safe. Perhaps he has even forgotten what he saw." She snapped her fingers, suddenly struck with a thought, and grasped the back of her mother's chair. "We could say he was inebriated, overwhelmed by the ale he drank. His senses were clouded, drunk!"

She felt a surge of triumph, cursing herself for not thinking of this sooner. Instead of hiding in her room, she could have been planting the idea in Ashar's mind. Maybe she could have convinced him by now. Before anyone could respond, a loud knock echoed from the door, making everyone jump in their seats.

"Enter," King Thaloren commanded as he rose from his seat.

The door swung open, and King Durnovas and Prince Ashar were ushered into the room.

"Refreshments, my king?" the attendant asked, pausing as the guests settled into their seats.

"Bring us the royal ale," Thaloren said, his tone carrying an air of finality. "We are to celebrate."

The words sent a jolt through Mena, her clever demeanor now fading into confusion. Celebrate? Celebrate what? Her father knew their secret had been compromised, yet he seemed poised to rejoice. The attendant bowed and exited swiftly, leaving a heavy silence in his wake. Mena's thoughts churned, her pulse thundering in her ears. Her father stood tall, his commanding presence filling the dim room.

"King Durnovas," Thaloren began, "I have accepted your proposal. Kallemena will wed Prince Ashar."

"What?"

The exclamation burst from both Mena and Ashar simultaneously, their shock mirrored in their wide eyes as they turned to each other, then back to King Thaloren. King Durnovas erupted in laughter, clapping his hands together with enthusiasm. Nyssira gripped her daughter's hand as tears welled in her eyes. As Mena looked down at her mother, expecting sobs of sadness, she was surprised to see a smile on her face. These were tears of joy. Mena was horrified as she took her seat, the room began to spin around her.

"Ah, wonderful news! The kingdom will rejoice at this union. Preparations will begin the moment we dock at Highspire." King Durnovas slapped Ashar on the back, his grin broad and triumphant. "A wedding!"

Mena's chest constricted as her mind spun, her breath shallow and quick. A wedding? A proposal? This cannot be happening. Before she could speak, the attendant re-entered, wheeling in a cart laden with five bottles of Iskaroth's finest royal ale and an array of delicately crafted finger cakes and puffed pastries. He moved with practiced efficiency, pouring drinks and handing them out. Mena accepted the glass mechanically, her fingers trembling as she held it. She glanced at Ashar, whose face was blank. Was he taking the news as hard as she was?

"A toast!" Her brother, Oren, rose from his chair with that same mischievous smile resting on his lips. "To a bond that will strengthen our households and our people." His eyes gleamed as he turned to Mena. "Little sister, I am so happy for you. Lúvaren!"

The others followed suit, their voices ringing with pure joy as they sipped from their flutes. Mena and Ashar, however, remained motionless. The weight of their silence contrasted sharply with the celebratory murmurs around them. Mena's hand trembled as she placed her untouched drink heavily on the cart. The clang of the glass against the silver tray echoed like a sharp protest. Without a word, she turned and bolted from the room.

"Mena!" voices called after her, but she did not stop. Each cry of her name spurred her forward – faster – until their voices faded behind her.

She tore up the grand staircase two steps at a time, her gown bundled in her fists. Her lungs and throat burned with exertion and emotion as she reached the door leading to the west tower. She pushed it open and began to climb. Up and up, she ascended the spiraling steps, her breath coming in ragged gasps. Her legs ached, but she refused to slow. At last, she reached the top. The room at the pinnacle of the tower was her sanctuary. Light poured in from all sides, streaming through tall windows that framed a breathtaking view of her homeland and the snowy peaks beyond. The space was warm and alive, its air lightly scented with the fragrance of greenery.

Vines wound their way up the walls, their leaves reaching skyward as if defying the glass confinement. A soft blue chaise rested on a plush rug the same hue as the endless heavens beyond the glass. Usually, this place brought her solace. But not today. Mena stumbled into the center of the room, her chest heaving, her vision blurred by tears. The warm, inviting air could not soothe her. The sight of the familiar, comforting plants only deepened the ache in her chest. Then, without warning, a scream tore from her throat. Raw, primal, filled with all the anguish and fury she could no longer contain.

Darkness rushed outward from her in an unstoppable wave, swallowing the light. The entire room was consumed by her power, encased in an impenetrable void of black. Her barrier, her refuge, sealed her away from the world outside. The air turned icy in an instant. Goosebumps prickled her skin as the warmth drained from her sanctuary. Tears streamed down her face, freezing into delicate crystals on the now sightless floor. Her sobs echoed in the emptiness, ragged and broken, filling the void with her despair. What was her father thinking? Her mind raced, the question burning like a flame she could not extinguish. She had trusted him to make things right, to protect her. All of them. Her mother, brother, and even Myra.

Instead, they had betrayed her, deciding her future without her consent. To marry her off, send her away to strangers in a distant land, how would that protect her? How would that make her safe? She curled into herself, her arms wrapping tightly around her knees as she sank to the cold floor. The darkness pressed closer, wrapping her in its suffocating embrace. She did not want to go. She did not want to leave the safety of her glass castle, the only home she had ever known. Her sobs quieted, replaced by the heavy stillness of her void. She sat there, frozen in anguish, her mind swirling with fear and betrayal, unable to imagine what awaited her beyond the darkness. Beyond Glacia. And what of her gifts? Would strangers be so willing to look past what she was? An Echo? Would she be safe?

"Kallemena?"

The voice cut through the stillness; she did not need to look to know who it was intruding on her wallowing. Yet, her heart still began to race. She cursed her betraying emotions, as Ashar stood just inside the room. Tall and cautious, his hands outstretched in a placating gesture, trying to navigate the dark that encased him. Each step he took forward was deliberate, his boots barely making a sound against the floor. Vexation flared within her like a sudden fire. He had followed her again. He had seen her ability before, and now he was witnessing it in its raw, uncontrollable state. Her jaw clenched as she raised her hand. With a flick of her wrist, the faint light from the open door behind Ashar was swallowed by her darkness. The void enveloped him completely, and she heard the sharp gasp of surprise, followed by the thud of a body hitting the floor. Mena smirked, a slight sense of satisfaction creeping in. Let him feel her power. Let him know she was not to be trifled with. She was not some sweet girl who could get passed off so easily.

A flicker of light disrupted her darkness, catching her off guard. At first, it was small, barely more than a pinpoint, but it grew quickly, multiplying until thousands of tiny orbs filled the room. Each one glowed with a soft, golden warmth, their light flickering like tiny flames encased in glass. They danced and swirled around her, illuminating the space in an otherworldly glow. Mena froze, her agitation melting into awe. Once cold and impenetrable, her void was now alive with light and warmth. She turned slowly, her now wide eyes blinking in disbelief.

"I did not do this..." her voice barely above a whisper.

Her gaze found Ashar. He was no longer on the floor but standing again, his expression calm, his eyes locked on hers. In his cupped hand, a single orb hovered. He brought it to his lips, exhaling gently, and the orb sprang to life, filling with flame and floating upward to join the others.

"You?" Her voice was incredulous. "You are an Echo, too?"

Ashar's silence was answer enough.

* * *

Far below, in the castle courtyard, the festivities were in full swing. Acrobats and jugglers entertained the gathered crowd, a kaleidoscope of motion and color. Performers in sparkling costumes flipped and balanced atop glass balls stacked precariously high. A table to the east groaned under the weight of food and drink, the sunlight glinting off the golden goblets and polished platters. Though the air was crisp, the sun's warmth made the day pleasant, and the crowd's laughter and applause echoed against the castle walls. A snow leopard roared, drawing cheers from onlookers. A trainer crouched before the beast, placing a small treat on its nose. With a quick command, the leopard flicked its head, sending the treat into the air. It leaped after it in a graceful somersault, catching the morsel mid-flight and landing on its hind legs with the crowd erupting into another thunderous applause. Among the spectators stood High Priest Vallorith, his sharp eyes taking in the scene.

Watching a woman dressed in a suit of reflective plating that flowed from her in sheets of tulle, she balanced a sword carefully on her nose, the double-sided weapon so sharp it was hard to tell if the woman was in pain or just concentrating. She danced to a violinist's song as he danced around her, together making an intimate display. Vallorith's eyes were fixed on the weapon's hilt, almost willing it to tilt to the side just enough to fall. His attention, however, was soon drawn upward. High in one of the castle's towers, something peculiar caught his notice. A room that had looked translucent before had turned pitch black in an instant as if swallowed by shadow. Moments later, as suddenly as it appeared, the phenomenon vanished. He snapped his fingers, summoning an attendant.

"Are there any other Echoes in the service of the king and queen besides Healer Myra?"

The attendant furrowed his brow, clearly perplexed. "None that I am aware of, High Priest."

Vallorith's lips curled into a smile, a thin, knowing expression. "Very good," he said, dismissing the man with a wave.

His gaze found healer Myra amongst the crowd. He spotted King Thaloren and Queen Nyssira as well, but precious princess Kallemena was missing from the festival. His eyes lingered on Myra, sweeping her hand down the silky fur of the leopard. A gleam of intrigue twinkled in his eyes before he turned back to the performers, his amusement no longer forced.

Chapter Eleven

The void vanished. Sharp and sudden sunlight poured back into the room, forcing Mena and Ashar to shield their eyes. When Mena opened hers again, Ashar held out his hand, his expression one of cautious sincerity, as if he wanted to offer answers as much as he sought them. Mena hesitated, then placed her hand in his. Warmth radiated from his palm, seeping into her cold fingers. He gently led her to the chaise, where they sat silently facing one another.

Questions swirled in Mena's mind, colliding and spiraling until she could only manage a soft "Hello."

Ashar's lips curved into a small, reassuring smile. His hand covered hers, steady and warm, as his eyes searched her face.

"Are you..." Mena began hesitantly.

"No," Ashar interjected quickly, shaking his head. "I am not like you." He froze, his words hanging awkwardly between them. "Not that what you are is bad!" he added hastily, his gaze dropping to the blue rug beneath them.

The toe of his boot scuffed at the plush fibers as he took a deep breath and began again. "I was born on the Day of Zenith when all the stars align in their celestial cycle and shine so brightly that you can see them during daylight. There are thousands of lights in the sky when there should only be one. Our sun." He held up his hand, and the glow of a flame appeared, small but bright. "It does not occur as often as the Darra Convergence. Zenith only happens once every sixty years or so. Sometimes falling on sixty-three years and sometimes only fifty-nine."

He turned his palm over, the small flame dancing to the back of his hand as if alive and needing to climb higher and higher. Mena watched, mesmerized.

"How did you know I was not born on the Day of Zenith?" she asked, curiosity lacing her tone. "Are we not both Echoes?" She waved her hand, and a delicate silver-winged butterfly appeared, glowing softly as it perched on her palm.

Ashar's smile deepened as he extinguished his flame and watched the butterfly crawl from her hand to his. "I cannot create like this," he said gently. "That is the difference between you and me. Total opposites."

Mena frowned, confusion clouding her features.

"I am a Cairn," Ashar explained. "Born under the stars' brilliance, gifted with their power. I can wield fire, heat, light... but I can only destroy. I cannot create like you. A Darra. You were born during the Convergence when the void shrouded the world, and not a single ray of light could break through. Total darkness."

His gaze grew distant. "I remember it. I was two years old when the first one occurred during my lifetime, and I thought the world was ending. I cried for days."

The thought of a tiny, inconsolable Ashar drew a soft laugh from Mena, and his lips quirked upward in response.

"The last one, two years ago, I was well... old enough to understand what was happening. I was in awe that something could block out all the light. Even my own flame was not as brilliant."

She thought back to two years ago. When the day was as dark as the depths of an icy well, she had felt her gift begging to be released and be allowed to create and project whatever she could. She had stayed in her room watching from her window as the town celebrated with her parents and most of the castle's workers. She was too afraid she would have gotten lost in the moment and revealed herself to hundreds of people. What would they have done if they had discovered their beloved King and Queen had hidden such a secret from their loyal citizens? Would their loyalty survive such a scandal?

"How do you know so much about this?" she asked, tucking a strand of black hair behind her ear.

Ashar hesitated, momentarily flustered by the motion. He stood abruptly, moving to one of the towering windows. Beyond the glass, the castle grounds sprawled below, a kingdom alive with movement. Though the view was breathtaking, the dizzying height made him take a cautious step back.

"My mother," he said quietly. "She made my father promise to teach me about the celestial cycles, about my gift and, well, hers."

"Hers?" Mena's voice softened. "So... she was an Echo also? Like me or you?"

A shadow crossed his face. "She was a Thorn, able to move earth and grow plants. My father said her gift was beautiful, but unfortunately, I did not have the chance to see it. Right after I was born, she passed." He shrugged, absently poking at one of the climbing ivies on the wall. "She made my father promise not to let the Axis take me. She did not want to die knowing my father would be left alone with strangers raising her only child. So, he hid my gift from the kingdom and the Axis. My birth was announced a week later... and her death the following day."

Mena lowered her head, her heart heavy with unspoken grief. She could not imagine growing up without her mother, never holding her hand, never hearing her sing lullabies that anchored her soul through the years.

"I am so sorry," she murmured, blinking back tears. She cleared her throat, forcing herself to focus. "Why can I create if you cannot?"

Ashar rubbed his forehead as if sifting through a distant memory. "The way the books explained it, Darras create like dreams, fleeting, ephemeral, but more real than anything in the waking world. Cairns do not dream. We burn."

Mena stood, her steps light and deliberate as she crossed the room to join him by the window. She hesitated, her gaze flicking to his. "Do you think... a Cairn and a Darra can get along?"

"You mean the marriage?"

Both of them flushed scarlet, quickly averting their gazes. Now, Mena fiddled with an ivy leaf while Ashar rubbed the back of his neck, the unspoken question hanging between them like a weight. Ashar racked his brain, searching for anything he had read about two Echoes living together, marrying, or even... He shook his head sharply, banishing the thought before it could take root. Mena cleared her throat, her own cheeks glowing crimson.

"Friends first?" she offered, extending her hand.

Ashar hesitated, then took her hand in his. Her touch was cold, her fingers like frost against his warmth, but he squeezed her hand firmly, offering a tentative smile.

"Friends first," he agreed.

***

The next three days passed in a blur of howling winds and icy rain. A fierce summer storm had swept in from the mountains, bringing blinding sleet and freezing temperatures. The thick ice walls of the castle grew even denser, encasing the structure in a crystalline shield. On the docks, some guests, desperate to escape the continent, attempted to rally their crews. Their efforts were futile; belongings were drenched, and the abandoned items were soon frozen under sheets of ice. Within the castle, however, the furnaces roared, and hearths blazed, filling every room with a comforting warmth. Mena found herself spending much of the storm in the library with Ashar, who had unearthed a small trove of books and scrolls on every celestial event.

Mena felt a pang of foolishness for never venturing to the library herself. She had avoided learning more about her abilities, always treating her gift as something to suppress and conceal. But now, the idea that her betrothed was an Echo and someone who celebrated their abilities sparked a thrill of possibility. Would she finally be free to wield her magic openly? The idea was intoxicating. Her thoughts drifted to stories she had heard of Kalyra: endless plains, scorching deserts, towering mountains, and forests so dense they were said to house ancient tribes. It was a vast world, one she had never imagined exploring before.

"Here is something," Ashar said, interrupting her musings as he dropped a hefty book onto the table. He flipped it open to the middle and pointed to a passage with an eager grin. "Look at this: a Darra who used his gift to help build the sanctuaries on Verdathos before the Axis existed! He created the walls and ceilings with nothing but his abilities. They still stand today. And here, a Thorn and Zeph that created floating islands on Aetheria that are still inhabited."

Ashar's excitement was infectious. His face lit up with childlike wonder like a boy discovering tales of conquering heroes. His thirst for knowledge, the way he devoured every story and turned to Mena with a spark in his eyes, made her heart stir. He looked at her as though she were a treasure discovered after centuries. Mena felt the tight armor she had built around her gift for the first time begin to loosen. She wanted to show him what she could do, what she could create. With the library doors firmly shut and locked and Myra, ever the dutiful chaperone, stationed to ensure propriety, Mena let her defenses fall. She started small. A delicate silver butterfly flitted into existence, its wings shimmering as though woven from moonlight. A fox followed, then a bird, and finally a towering polar bear. Each projection felt like a fragment of her soul brought to life. Ashar watched, captivated. His gaze followed her every movement, his amazement unguarded and his admiration evident. She was a revelation to him, a woman who had thought her gift a curse, now embracing it with grace and wonder.

Myra, standing quietly in the corner, felt the shift in the room. She could sense the growing strength of Mena's magic, the way her creations began to take on a life of their own. These were not mere figments or extensions of Mena's will. They moved with purpose, their eyes glinting with intelligence. This power was unlike anything Myra had witnessed in her ten years with the Axis. It was said that such abilities had been long extinguished, that Echoes now wielded magic only as an extension of their natural skills. Myra's own gift, born from blindness, had allowed her a kind of vision that helped her navigate the world. But she had never imagined the power to create life as Mena did now. She had known of the void Mena wielded when her emotions overwhelmed her, her anxiety digging deep, an empty space where the princess could retreat and feel neutral, untethered. But this was something entirely different. This was not an escape; this was creation. Mena's face glowed with an emotion Myra could not quite place. Freedom, perhaps. Or joy. Watching her, Myra could not help but feel that this moment marked a turning point, not just for Mena but for all of them.

"Can you see it, Myra?" Mena whispered, her voice soft, as though afraid to disturb the fragile beauty she had conjured.

Myra raised her hands, her unseeing eyes searching the space. A wave of sensation washed over her, brushing against her skin like a ripple through still water. She could feel the essence of the room shifting, expanding beyond its walls. Mena stood at the center of it all, her presence like a beacon, while Ashar hovered close beside her. Their auras burned brightly, radiating an intensity that seemed to grow stronger when they were near one another. As the wave flowed outward, Myra turned her attention to the objects it touched: the bookshelves, the tables and chairs, the couch, the crackling fireplace, and then something far beyond. A new space unfolded in her mind, vast and alive. Myra's breath caught in her throat as she sensed rolling hills stretching endlessly, with towering mountains rising in the distance. The warmth of a radiant sun pressed against her skin, its energy embracing her like a golden cloak. She felt the breeze rustle through unseen trees, their towering trunks, and sprawling branches alive with the rustle of falling leaves.

"What..." She clasped her hands over her mouth, overwhelmed by the vision. "Mena? How?" Her voice trembled. "Where is this?"

Ashar stepped closer, his eyes flicking between Myra's awestruck expression and Mena's pale face. The strain of such immense creation was visible now. Mena swayed on her feet, her breathing shallow, the weight of her magic pulling her down.

"Mena, you should sit," Ashar said gently, his hands steadying her as he guided her to the couch where Myra now sat, still trembling from the vivid wonder she had experienced.

Myra reached out, her fingers brushing against Mena's. "This... this is more than magic," she said, her voice hushed with reverence.

Mena managed a weak smile, though her exhaustion was evident. Beads of sweat glistened on her forehead, and her chest rose and fell heavily.

"I will get you some water," Ashar said, his voice steady but filled with concern.

Before leaving, he glanced back at Mena, worried by her exhausted appearance. The room was quiet again, save for the crackle of the fire and the whisper of leaves Myra could still feel in the edges of her mind. She could feel Mena's heartbeat pounding strongly beneath her finger-tips, each pulse echoing the strain her great-niece's body had endured. Concern etched across her face, she placed a steady hand on Mena's wrist, letting her power flow gently through the girl like a soothing balm.

"Take a break," Myra urged.

The vivid energy that had filled the room began to recede. Myra felt the pulse of Mena's magic dim as the conjured landscape dissolved, leaving the cold reality of the library behind. Myra reached for Mena's forehead, her palm brushing against the damp skin. A frown deepened her features.

"You have depleted yourself," she said firmly, though her tone held a note of tenderness. "You must be careful not to make this a habit."

Her hand returned to Mena's wrist, pressing lightly as she spoke. "Your body is too weak to keep itself warm. You are catching a cold." Myra slipped an arm around her, helping her to her feet. "Come, let us get you closer to the fire."

As Mena stood, a wave of dizziness crashed over her. The room spun in a whirl of shifting shapes and shadows before everything went dark.

When she opened her eyes again, she was lying in her bedroom. The soft light of a single candle danced on the walls, casting long shadows that flickered like whispers. Her mother, Nyssira, sat on the edge of the bed, her hands deftly working a silver needle through some fabric. The blue thread wove in and out, forming the delicate petals of a flower, its shape slowly emerging with each pass of the needle. Nyssira's eyes lifted to meet her daughter's, a mixture of concern and reproach shining in their depths. The look alone spoke volumes, and it was clear to Mena that she was in trouble. She pushed herself upright, her back pressing against the headboard as she gathered the thick blankets around her. Every muscle in her body ached, and her limbs were leaden with fatigue. She drew the covers higher, the cold seeping into her bones sharper than she was accustomed to. Nyssira's gaze softened, her fingers momentarily stilling in their work.

"You are finally awake," she said gently, though the undertone of disapproval remained. "Myra said you outdid yourself. You created an entire world."

Nyssira set her needlework aside and turned fully to her daughter, her expression a careful balance of pride and concern. "She also said exerting that much energy at once could be dangerous. What were you thinking?"

Mena blinked, her thoughts swirling back to the moment. She recalled the vivid images in her mind, the drawing in the book Ashar had found, the way she imagined the scent of the trees, the feel of the grass beneath her feet, and the hum of distant life.

"I made a portal to another place," Mena whispered, a note of awe lacing her voice.

A smile stretched across her lips, and she glanced at her mother, who wore a similar expression. They both burst into laughter, the sound of shared relief echoed through the room. Excitement coursed through Mena's veins, replacing her fatigue, if only for a moment. If she could do that, what else could she be capable of with time and practice?

"Ashar!" she exclaimed suddenly, sitting up straighter. "He left to get me water. Does he know I am all right?"

"Him di one who carry yuh here, yuh know."

Startled, Mena turned her head to the opposite side of the bed. There, seated with perfect stillness, was Kivani. She wore a stunning green and gold dress, the fabric shimmering like sunlight filtering through tropical palm leaves. It reminded Mena of the drawings she had seen of lush island paradises, breezy and vibrant. Mena's gaze darted between her mother and Kivani, confusion spreading across her face.

"You know?" she asked, her voice tight with worry, the reality of her secret clawing at her exhaustion. "She knows? Kivani knows?"

Kivani's lips curved into an amused grin. "Mi did know de whole time, even before me and yuh bredda get married." She laughed, a warm, lilting sound. "Yuh mother thought it only fair for mi to understand fully what mi was marrying into. But," she added with a playful smirk, "Mi give dem a shock of mi own when dem realize dem never had nutten to worry about."

With a flick of her wrist, Kivani held up her hand.

A spiraling droplet of water grew and grew, its tiny waves dancing around until it was a stream of water that wrapped around Kivani's body, illuminating a faint blue glow.

It flowed like a river, yet was delicate enough to look brittle as a thin piece of glass. It swirled back to Kivani's palm before she released her power and spread a dense mist throughout the room.

Mena's jaw dropped. "You? You are a Talon?" She brought her hands to her mouth. "First Ashar, and now you?"

The mist settled as Kivani blinked in surprise. "Hold on, wah?" She spun to Nyssira, wide-eyed. "Ashar is a Talon?"

"No," Mena smiled. "He is a Cairn."

Laughter erupted from Kivani as she twirled around the room, her joy infectious.

"Mi tell you! Mi tell you there are more of we than we did tink!" Kivani told Nyssira.

"More of us?" Mena echoed, her mind spinning as she watched Kivani dance across the room.

"Yes!" Kivani exclaimed, pausing to grin at Mena. "Di royal families like your own, there are more, families who keep dem babies home, instead of sending dem off to that godforsaken Axis. Dis a new age, Mena. We need to show di world the Echoes can be more than just di helpers. We more powerful than dem could have ever imagined."

Mena felt a surge of joy as the three of them laughed, but then something else settled in: a gnawing sense of regret. She could not understand why at first, but then it hit her. The laws. The Axis's restrictions on royals being Echoes. What could other Echoes do if she could create portals to whole worlds with her power? Others who had been taken from their families were robbed of a chance to live freely with their loved ones, to be the successors their parents had dreamed of—people like her great-aunt, Myra.

"No." Mena's voice came out harsh. She was not sure the others heard her until the cheering died down.

"No?" Kivani raised an eyebrow. "Wa yuh mean, no, Mena? Dis is our time to shine. To bring back glory to being an Echo and show di world that we can be more dan dem tink. Yuh do not want dat?"

Mena stared at Kivani, her body desperate for sleep but her mind a whirlwind of thoughts. She hated seeing the disappointment on Kivani's face, but they could not do what she was suggesting.

"The Axis has these laws because they feared an Echo becoming too powerful and taking over. If I could create a doorway to a distant land that I had never seen before today, what could someone with evil intentions create? What could they do to people like the Axis?"

Kivani scoffed. "Whateva dem damn well please."

"Exactly." Mena's voice grew firmer. "They could kill them. And what is to stop them from going further? What is to keep them from harming innocent people or even other Echoes who go against them? If we act recklessly, we will spark a war."

Kivani's face grew serious as she processed Mena's words. They all knew she was right. If Echoes went public and wielded their power freely, what was stopping them from becoming unstoppable? No normal human could stand against a fully trained Darra, capable of creating anything from nothing. And Cairns, Ashar had said he could only destroy.

How much and how far could that power reach? How much devastation could a rogue Echo cause if they turned against the Axis or the kingdom they served?

"So yuh say wi just... keep on hiding?" Kivani's voice was laced with frustration.

Mena glanced at her mother, then back at Kivani.

"I am saying we figure out how to do this the right way," she said, her tone resolute. "Without causing a surge of angry Echoes and bloodshed. There has to be a way. A peaceful way."

That night, after Nyssira and Kivani had left, Mena lay awake, staring out her window. The moon's glow was hazy, distorted by the frost clinging to the glass. A faint prickle of unease lingered on her face and neck, the only parts of her body left exposed to the frigid air. Her throat was raw, and a sneeze hovered just at the edge of her sinuses, teasing her. The thought of falling ill while Ashar was still at the castle filled her with dread. Once the mountain storm cleared, he and the other guests would sail back to their kingdoms, leaving her behind. Her heart clenched at the idea of not seeing him again until the wedding. The realization startled her, and she sat up straighter in bed. Had her feelings truly changed this much in a single week? Only days ago, the thought of marrying Ashar had felt like a dagger twisting in her gut. But now, she could not shake the memory of his face, how concerned he had looked when he carried her to the couch after her magic had left her drained and weak. Could he feel the same way she did? Her gaze drifted back to the window, and with a deep breath, she slid out from under the covers. The bitter cold bit into her skin as she padded across the room to the frosted panes.

It took several attempts to unlatch the window, but she finally broke it free from the ice's grip. Leaning out, she scanned the dark facade of the castle. Most of the windows on this side were unlit, except for one.

Counting carefully, she traced two rows down and five windows across. If she was correct, that was Ashar's room. And if she was wrong? Well, she would deal with the consequences later. She raised her hand, focusing on the magic within her. At first, nothing happened, a jolt of panic shooting through her.

But after a moment of concentration, silvery white wings began to form, accompanied by deep golden eyes that stared back at her. A snow owl emerged, perched delicately on her outstretched hand. Its taloned feet pressed lightly against her skin as if aware of its fragile creator. Around its leg was a note secured by a delicate strand of yarn. Mena dropped her hand, and the owl took flight, its silent wings gliding effortlessly through the still night. It swooped down and passed in front of the lit window once, twice, and then a third time, letting out a soft screech before returning to Mena's hand. She stroked its feathers, marveling at the creature's beauty when she heard the faint crackling of ice. Peering down, her heart leaped at the sight of Ashar leaning out onto the ledge beneath his window. His hair was tousled, and he looked up at her with a tired but warm smile. He waved, and Mena returned the gesture, her body feeling weaker by the minute.

"Go," she whispered, and the owl took flight once more, gliding gracefully down to Ashar's outstretched hand.

She watched as he untied the note from the owl's leg when a sudden gust of wind bit into Mena's exposed skin. The icy blast drained the last of her energy, and with a final wave of her hand, the owl disappeared in a wisp of silvery light. Ashar glanced back up in time to see Mena pull herself back inside. Alarmed, he quickly threw a robe over his pajamas and rushed out of his room. Within minutes, he was outside Mena's door, his breath coming in short gasps from the sprint through the cold halls. He hesitated, torn between propriety and urgency. Should he find a guard? Nyssira? He glanced back down the hallway, unsure of where the royal chambers were located. A soft thud sounded from inside Mena's room, and his hesitation evaporated. Hastily, he turned the handle and pushed the door open. The room was dark except for the faint glow of a dying fire.

"Mena?" he whispered, his voice low.

For a moment, panic seized him. What if this was not her room? What if he had miscounted? But then he heard her faint voice.

"Ashar."

He rounded the bed instantly, finding Mena slumped on the floor, her body trembling. Sweat glistened on her pale forehead. He scooped her up without hesitation, placing her gently back in bed. He pulled the thick comforter over her before turning back to the fire. Rubbing his hands together, he concentrated. Steam rose from his palms, quickly turning to smoke. With a practiced motion, he waved his hands over the embers, coaxing the fire back to life. Flames sprang up, devouring the logs with renewed vigor, casting warmth and light across the room.

"Did you read my note?"

Ashar turned to see Mena propped up weakly against her pillows. Her face was pale, and her eyes were sunken and bruised. Her once luminous irises now looked dull, and her face held the strain her powers had taken on her body. He pulled the note from his pocket, still tied shut with string.

"Not yet," he admitted. "I saw you close your window, and your owl disappeared. I was worried."

Her face fell slightly. "Do not bother. It will seem dumb now."

Ignoring her protest, Ashar untied the string and unfolded the parchment.

"Hello?" he read aloud, chuckling softly. "That is all it says?"

Mena's cheeks flushed, whether from fever or embarrassment, she could not tell. "It is just... what I said to you after the marriage announcement."

"I remember," Ashar said gently, his smile easy and warm.

He hesitated for a moment, then sat on the edge of her bed. His hand hovered near hers, unsure of what was appropriate. But when he saw her shivering again, he made his decision. Sliding under the covers, he drew her close, focusing his energy to raise his body temperature.

"Thank you," Mena murmured, her voice barely audible. "You are so warm."

Ashar adjusted until her head rested in the crook of his shoulder, her icy hand tucked safely in his. Her cool touch was strangely comforting against his warmth. He pressed a soft kiss to the top of her head, breathing in her hair's fresh, wintry scent. The room fell silent, the crackling fire their only companion as both drifted into a deep, peaceful sleep.

Chapter Twelve

Mena awoke to hushed whispers and the faint rustling of fabric. The warmth at her back consumed her as she nestled closer to its source. A soft, even breath warmed the back of her neck. She froze. Turning her head slightly, she was greeted by the sight of Ashar, his arm tucked beneath her head, his face peaceful in sleep. Her breath caught. Heat rushed to her cheeks as she realized the predicament they were in. Carefully, she edged away to the edge of the bed, her movements deliberately slow to avoid waking him. The whispers grew louder with laughter being stifled. She stood to see her attendant bowing, a mischievous grin stretching across her face. Myra was frowning, her hands resting on the edge of the footboard as panic surged through Mena. How had she ended up in this situation? How much trouble would she now be in? The disgrace that would be brought to both their families? She scrambled for her wardrobe, the thin fabric of her nightgown now feeling sheer in her shocking predicament. The loud squeak of the wardrobe door made her insides squirm as she hastily tugged on her robe. Behind her, she could hear Ashar stirring, a yawn escaping his lips as he sat up in the bed, shocked to see so many pairs of eyes assessing his appearance.

"Ladies," his voice croaked, rough with sleep, as he hurried to his feet. His disheveled hair and rumpled robe betrayed his attempt at composure.

Mena's eyes locked with his, and their awkwardness deepened. She noticed the faint blush creeping up his neck as he attempted to straighten his robe and head for the door.

"Not so fast, young prince," Myra's voice boomed, commanding and firm.

Ashar stopped mid-step, his shoulders tensing. Mena winced, her mortification doubling as Myra gestured for them both to sit.

Amawna, who was clearly enjoying the spectacle, giggled. "I will ensure no one has noticed the young prince's absence."

"Yes, thank you, Amawna," Myra said curtly, her expression hardening. The younger woman left with a spring in her step, the door clicking shut behind her.

"Now," Myra began, her unseeing eyes somehow pinning them in place. "What did you do to her?"

Ashar inhaled sharply. She wasted no time. Last night flashed through his mind, all harmless when you were not caught the next morning.

"Nothing!" he blurted, raising his hands defensively. "I swear to you on my mother's grave. She was freezing and shivering uncontrollably. I feared she was catching a cold; she looked really pale, and I knew she needed to get warm, so I warmed her. I just wanted to help." His plea was innocent.

Myra's hand shot up, silencing his frantic confession. Her brow furrowed, her fingers pressing against her temple as if warding off a headache. "You *warmed* her? How?"

Ashar's throat went dry as she extended a hand toward him, her pale, unseeing eyes narrowing. Was she testing him? Reading his thoughts? Could she do that? He swallowed hard, sweat gathering beneath his nightclothes.

"I just used my gift," he admitted, his voice trembling. "I warmed myself and lay beside her until she stopped shaking. Then, I guess... we fell asleep?"

He rubbed the back of his neck and glanced at Mena, whose nervous expression mirrored his own.

"He is telling the truth, Aunt Myra. Nothing happened," Mena interjected.

"Shush!" Myra snapped, silencing her.

Her outstretched hand hovered toward Ashar before she extended the other toward Mena, her blind eyes darting as though scanning for something in the room.

"You healed her," she murmured, her voice low and uncertain. "I do not know how your gift did it, but it did. This... this is unknown to me. We were never taught this at the Axis, of course, why would we have? Everyone was forbidden to learn of the other Echo's abilities; how could we have known?"

Her words hung in the air as if waiting for an answer. Ashar's brow furrowed in confusion. He opened his mouth to speak but found no words. Mena turned to him, her eyes wide with questions, just like his.

"What do you mean, he *healed* me?" she asked.

Myra stepped closer, placing a cool hand on Mena's forehead. Her fingers lingered there, motionless, before she pulled away.

"Yesterday, after you projected that... portal, your body was stripped of all its energy," Myra explained. "I could feel your gift fading, overtaken by a deep-rooted sickness I have never come across before. I did not want to alarm you, but I had never seen it happen before when an Echo exhausts their abilities completely." She sighed, her voice softening. "I sent inquiries by messenger bird late in the night. I have already received two replies. Neither was helpful." She waved the comment away like a pestering fly.

Mena's stomach dropped as Myra cupped her face, her expression both relieved and grim.

"I was afraid your gift would be lost forever," Myra whispered.

She turned abruptly to Ashar, her tone sharpening. "But whatever you did last night restored her. You did not just stabilize her; you reenergized her abilities. She is whole again, without flaw."

Mena's mind reeled. She had almost lost her gift? *Her gift!* Her hands trembled as the weight of the revelation crashed over her. She had been reckless, untrained. The portal had drained her completely, and now she was lucky to still have her abilities at all. She looked up at Myra, shame and determination warring in her chest.

"Can I overcome that? Could I strengthen my ability so that it never happens again?"

Mena's voice was steady, but her hands trembled. She balled them into fists at her sides, willing herself to appear resolute. Ashar's head snapped toward her, his eyes wide with disbelief.

"You want to attempt that again? It almost cost you your gift!" His voice cracked as he looked from Myra to Mena, desperation coloring his tone. "Tell her she cannot be so foolish!"

Myra remained silent; her mind working through the jungle of knowledge in her brain. Finally, she spoke, her voice calm but charged with meaning.

"With practice," she began, "I think you could surpass what we have ever known." Her gaze turned toward Ashar. "Both of you."

Ashar froze, his pulse hammering in his ears. The room felt unbearably warm, and sweat trickled down his back and legs, clinging to his clothes and skin. He shook his head, his voice trembling.

"Cairns only destroy. I already know everything about my ability."

Myra moved with startling swiftness, seizing his wrist in a vice-like grip. Ashar gasped as a jolt of energy surged through him. It slithered through his veins, coiling around his muscles like a living thing. His eyes widened as he stared at her, the faintest hint of a smile curving her lips.

"Are you so certain, young prince?" Her question was a challenge he was unsure whether to accept.

Before Ashar could respond, a sharp knock on the door interrupted the charged moment. Amawna breezed in, a tray perfectly balanced in her hands, laden with enough food for two.

"I told his guard and servant that the prince left early this morning with the princess on a riding trip to see some of the wonders Glacia has to offer. No one suspects a thing."

She set the tray on the table by the window and skipped to the door, her grin as sly as ever. "I will bring some clothes for the prince once the coast is clear."

Without waiting for a reply, she slipped out, humming under her breath. Myra watched her go before crossing to the door herself. She paused, her hand resting on the polished glass as she turned back to Ashar and Mena.

"Tell no one what we have discussed. I must learn more and consult my books." Her expression darkened as her blind eyes seemed to fix on Ashar. "A fire in a forest seems to destroy it, but it paves the way for new life."

Puzzled, Ashar looked to Mena before turning back to the wise healer. Myra did not wait for him to respond. She was gone, the door clicking shut behind her. Thick and suffocating silence filled the room. Ashar turned to Mena, his face filled with concern.

"What does she mean by that?"

Mena only shook her head. They both stared at the tray of untouched food, minds racing with questions they never knew to ask.

***

High Priest Vallorith savored the last bite of his spiced quail, the taste mingling perfectly with the sharp tang of his dark ale. A swift knock at the polished glass door interrupted the tranquil silence of his retreat from the Glacian cold.

"Enter," he commanded, his voice smooth but laden with authority.

A short man in a white robe that mirrored Vallorith's own stepped in, bowing low. In his hands were several scrolls. Vallorith rose from his chair with deliberate ease, setting down his goblet before crossing the room. He snatched the scrolls greedily, like a child claiming a coveted prize.

"Written by her own hand?" he snapped, unrolling the first parchment with a practiced flick of his wrist.

"Yes, my lord," the disciple replied, his head bowed even lower.

Vallorith's eyes darted over the first scroll, his cunning smile quickly dissolving into a deep scowl. He tossed it aside and moved to the second, then the third. The more he read, the darker his expression grew. With a smooth motion, he rolled the scrolls back up and twisted them in his hands. He paced back and forth, his mind whirling with the information he had just read. The wind howled outside as he stalked to the window, his breath fogging the glass as he stared out to the frozen shore, his ship bobbing on the waves. Then, with a sharp exhale, he turned on his heel, his lips curling into a crooked grin.

"She is stronger than I imagined. Have the ships ready; we will leave tonight," he said, his voice calm yet chilling. "Send word to the Axis to prepare for a new arrival. A Darra. No need to test her, I can feel what she can do already."

The disciple nodded quickly, his head still bowed. Vallorith waved his hand, and a long mirror shimmered into existence before him. His sharp green eyes scrutinized his reflection. He spotted a single stray crumb on his crimson robe and brushed it away with a quick, irritated motion. A strawberry seed lodged between his teeth earned a click of his tongue as he dislodged it, smoothing back his blond hair with a swift gesture.

"And get me an audience with the King," he added, his tone nonchalant as the mirror vanished.

The disciple hesitated, his voice trembling. "Which king, my lord?"

The world seemed to shift beneath the guard's feet. The glass floor his feet stood upon shimmered and then vanished, replaced by a swirling abyss of black water. The deafening roar of the vortex filled the room as icy sprays lashed at the edges of the man's robe as his body dangled above the deathly waters. The disciple clawed desperately at the now slickened surface, his nails scraping futilely against the floor that remained solid under Vallorith's feet. Vallorith took a slow, deliberate sip of his ale, watching the man's panic with a smirk.

"Which king?" Vallorith repeated, his words dripping with mockery. His bellowing laughter echoed through the chamber. "You are a funny one. You really have a talent for testing my patience! Which king do you think?" He threw his arms out as he circled the broken hole in the floor. "Whose castle are we in, Rhez?"

The disciple clung to the edge, his face pale, tears streaming as his grip was slipping, the bottom of his robe now being pulled by the water's strong current.

"Th-Thaloren Vaelora! Please, my lord, spare me!" The disciple's hands gave way, and he felt himself falling.

His body hit the polished floor with a thud that knocked the wind from his lungs, his robe dry, and the floor intact. He stumbled to his feet and composed himself. With his breath trembling at every gasp and his eyes on the verge of more tears, he bowed his head, his shaking hands confirming his lingering terror.

Vallorith downed the last of his ale, his smirk never wavering. "Good. Now, get out of my sight."

The man stumbled on his feet, eager to escape the madman in the room. Vallorith grabbed his holy book from the table and strode to the door. He began whistling a low, haunting tune that echoed eerily as he disappeared into the corridor.

Outside, King Thaloren strolled through the palace gardens with a group of departing guests. Snow dusted the hedgerows, and the crisp morning air carried the faint aroma of pine and frost-covered roses. His easy demeanor masked the exhaustion from days of hosting dignitaries. Endless banquets and jokes he had heard a thousand times over. He was relieved the last of them would be departing this evening. Hurried footfalls disrupted the peaceful atmosphere as a short man in a white robe quickly approached. One of Vallorith's disciples, pale and sickly looking, bowed deeply as he handed the king a sealed note. The King eyed the man before breaking the wax and skimming over the letter. The disciple bowed again, his head nearly hitting his own knees before straightening and quickly fleeing the king's presence.

"Excuse me, everyone," Thaloren said, tucking the note into his coat. "It seems I have been summoned." He offered a polite smile and inclined his head before making his way toward the castle.

In the study, the king froze at the sight of the High Priest seated at his desk. His boots kicked up on the polished wood as Vallorith treated himself to one of the king's cigars. A deep inhale made the cigar glow bright before a cloud of sweet vanilla and cedar filled the room. A flicker of irritation passed behind Thaloren's gray eyes, though his face remained composed. Vallorith's expression, however, betrayed none of his thoughts, only the sinister curve of a smile that never quite reached his sharp green eyes.

"Ah, my dear friend." Vallorith rose, his crimson robes trailing behind him as his hand skimmed the polished desk's surface. "I was just admiring the craftsmanship of your desk. Remarkable work."

Thaloren stepped forward, his gaze falling to the desk. The wood-grain shone with the luster of countless polishings, though faint scuffs marred its perfection, reminders of heavy ink jars and the occasional misplaced wine glass.

"Indeed," the king said coolly. "It was a gift from far overseas. But I doubt you came to discuss furniture, High Priest."

Vallorith's eyes gleamed like a predator sizing up prey. He circled the desk with slow, deliberate steps before stopping in front of a chair opposite the king. Thaloren lowered himself into his own seat, motioning for the priest to do the same.

"I received your note," Thaloren began, ringing the silver bell on his desk. An attendant entered almost immediately. "Wine?"

The priest shook his head. "I would prefer a glass of your famous royal ale, the kind you served at the wedding. One last indulgence before I leave your...beautiful continent."

His tone dripped with disdain as he took another drag of the cigar, ashes falling to the carpet. His final words rang like a snake's hiss as he kept his eye unblinkingly on the king. Thaloren nodded to his attendant, who bowed and disappeared.

"The castle will be quieter once all the guests have left. I trust your journey back to the Axis will be swift and uneventful. No doubt they will be desperate for their High Priest's guidance."

The priest's lips curled, though his eyes remained as calculating as ever. When the attendant returned, pouring the ale into a silver goblet, Vallorith raised the glass with a slight smirk.

"To safe travels," Thaloren said, lifting his glass.

Vallorith mirrored him, but just as the king was about to drink, the priest added, "And to your daughter finally joining the Axis."

The words struck like a dagger. Thaloren choked on the spiced liquid, coughing as he set the goblet down with a trembling hand. His eyes reddened, and his throat burned as he gasped for air.

"I am sorry, old friend," he said, his voice hoarse. "I must have misheard you." He patted his chest and gave a strained laugh. "My daughter, join the Axis?"

His bark of laughter filled the room, though the sound was hollow. Without missing a beat, he rang the silver bell again. The attendant reappeared, his expression tense at the king's sudden shift in demeanor.

"Bring Healer Myra and King Durnovas here immediately," Thaloren ordered, his voice steel.

The attendant bowed and hurried off, leaving the two men alone once again. Vallorith leaned back in his chair, taking another leisurely sip of his ale. The cigar, now a stub, sat resting on the edge of the king's desk.

"You heard me perfectly, Thaloren. Your daughter will serve the Axis. After all, the stars have been watching her for quite some time."

Vallorith raised his hands in a gesture of mocking peace, his smile razor-thin. "Dear Thaloren," he began, his tone saturated with condescension. "I am well aware that your aunt is not the only Darra in this palace." His piercing green eyes narrowed, daring the king to refute him.

Thaloren's silence was damning.

"As you know, it is my sacred duty as High Priest of the Axis to root out any *undocumented* Echoes and ensure they are brought to Verdathos for proper training." Vallorith clicked his tongue and shook his head as though speaking to a misguided child. "Young Kallemena will be a bit behind her peers; of course, it is your fault entirely for trying to hide her all these years, but no matter. She will receive the finest education and the best discipline. Is that not all a father wants for his children? To see them succeed?"

Thaloren's knuckles turned white as his fist pressed into the desk. His jaw clenched, his voice low and dangerous. "It is. As any parent would have it. And I will see my daughter succeed... under my roof. Kallemena will not going to Verdathos."

The door opened, cutting through the rising tension. Myra entered on King Durnovas' arm, her soft steps hesitant. Vallorith's grin widened like a predator spotting fresh prey.

"And here is the woman who assisted me in obtaining undeniable proof," Vallorith announced, gliding across the room to intercept Myra. He reached for her hand, but she recoiled as though burned by his touch.

"Proof?" Thaloren's voice sharpened. "What proof?"

Vallorith moved with theatrical flair, dancing around the room with childlike glee. "Oh, I am so glad you asked."

He snapped his fingers, and three parchments materialized, hovering in midair. Their edges glowed faintly as though imbued with some unholy magic.

"Shall I read them aloud?" Vallorith teased, his voice mocking. He turned to Myra, his smile cruel. "Or would you prefer to enlighten the room? No? Of course not, silly me. You are as blind as a bat."

He cleared his throat dramatically, plucking the first parchment from the air.

She has shown great progress, controlling her gift; she can now make simple creatures, butterflies, and moths. Vallorith gasped theatrically, his hand flying to his cheek. "Goodness, such control!"

He snatched the second parchment.

"She can now emit a void-like presence, a defense for when she feels vulnerable. How far can it reach? Oh, how intriguing."

Finally, he retrieved the third, his voice dropping to a whisper for effect.

"Can her ability grow beyond her control? Danger? Look for older texts predating the establishment of the Axis. Power of the gods?"

Vallorith turned to Myra, his grin splitting wider. "Fascinating questions, do you not agree?"

Myra paled, her voice trembling. "There is no name written, of whom do you think I speak of?"

With another snap of his fingers, the parchments vanished. Vallorith's expression turned venomous.

"I know of whom you speak!" He turned to look at Thaloren. "A kingdom hiding its Darra princess, all in hopes that she might one day rule," he sneered, his voice brimming with disdain. "Did you think the law would simply overlook this? That your defiance would go unnoticed?"

He opened his holy book with deliberate precision, flipping through its pages until he found the desired passage. His voice took on a sermon-like cadence as he read:

"All Echoes born to a royal family must be sent to Verdathos, where they will undergo training in select skills to preserve peace across the continents. Any ruler who defies this mandate forfeits their kingdom's treaty with the Axis, thereby losing all trade and military aid. Said kingdom will face exile, starvation, and war."

Vallorith snapped the book shut with a loud *thud*, savoring the sound. "Now, I am willing to let this... unfortunate lapse in judgment pass without consequence," he said, his grin sickening. "Provided it is corrected today. Kallemena will leave with me tonight. She will train with others like her and be enlisted as a servant to the Axis."

Thaloren's anger was evident in his face, but he remained silent.

"And, as an added courtesy," Vallorith continued, his tone syrupy with mock generosity, "I will refrain from imprisoning Healer Myra for her reckless behavior. She will be sent to Morbessa to live her remaining years under the watchful eyes of the Morin. She will repent for her treasonous acts. You should really be thanking me; an unchecked Echo is a dangerous liability, after all." Vallorith folded his hands neatly, waiting for a response.

"No!" Myra cried, her voice cracking with desperation. Tears welled in her eyes as she stepped forward. "No, she cannot go. She *will not* go! That place is the ruin of an Echo! It strips them of their power, of who they are! Mena's gift could flourish here, in her own kingdom, on her own land." Her voice broke as her gaze darted toward Vallorith. "That place will destroy her! The treaty, the Axis's so-called protection, it can all go to hell!" She spat the last words in Vallorith's direction, her shoulders trembling with rage.

King Durnovas stepped forward, his arm steadying Myra. His gaze was firm as it shifted to Thaloren. "Prince Ashar and Princess Kallemena are betrothed," he said with measured authority. "As King of the continent Kalyra, I will ensure trade continues with our distant friends of Glacia. Your people will not starve, nor will they be abandoned to harm."

Thaloren met Durnovas' eyes, and a mutual understanding passed between them. Myra felt a swell of hope in her chest, but it caught in her throat as Thaloren turned to Vallorith.

"My daughter will not be going anywhere with you." his voice was low but unwavering. "If this removes Glacia from the treaty, so be it. Perhaps it is time for the Axis to be restructured. These are not the same lands as when the Axis was first formed. Kingdoms have grown. People no longer see the Echoes as gods; they embrace them as their own. Normal people just trying to live their lives." Thaloren glanced briefly at Durnovas and Myra before his gaze returned to Vallorith. "Maybe it is time for the ways of the Axis to go to the past?"

A flicker of something dangerous crossed Vallorith's face, anger or perhaps contempt, but he quickly masked it with a thin smile. His fingers tightened around his holy book, the spine creaking under the strain. For a fleeting moment, a scene played out in his mind: The room filled with water, thrashing limbs, the satisfaction of watching them all drown in silence. How easy it would be. To remove those who say such things? He was the head of the Axis. A powerful Echo that was not to be crossed! Instead, Vallorith exhaled slowly, his hand smoothing back his already perfectly smooth hair.

"I see we are at an impasse." His voice was calm, almost soothing, but the tension in the air only thickened. "Very well. I will leave tonight and arrange for an audience with the Nine Continent Kingdoms as soon as possible."

He inclined his head in a shallow bow, his eyes lingering on each of them before turning toward the door. "May the gods guide your choices," he said quietly, though the venom in his tone belied the sentiment.

The door shut behind him with an unsettling gentleness. Myra turned to Thaloren, her face grim and pale.

"He is plotting something," she said, her voice almost a whisper. "I could feel it, his energy, before he left. He was furious but suddenly... content. Watch him, Thaloren. Keep guards on Mena. He will not let this go."

Thaloren nodded, his expression dark. "Then we will be ready."

The king doubled the guards at every door and station, issuing silent orders to keep a close watch on every remaining guest. Yet despite the precautions, an uneasy tension gripped the castle as night crept closer.

Thaloren stood with his wife, Nyssira, from the balcony of his chambers, watching the commotion below. The High Priest's men worked tirelessly, hauling crates and goods onto the ship moored at the icy docks. Their movements were hurried but methodical, their torches cutting through the growing darkness. Nyssira's soft voice broke the silence.

"The High Priest is greedy," she said, her gaze fixed on the endless line of provisions yet to be loaded. "Let him take what he wants. None of it matters as long as he is off our land and far from our family." She laid a hand on Thaloren's chest and kissed his cheek, her touch warm despite the chill in the air. "Come to bed. By morning, he will be gone."

Thaloren lingered a moment longer, his sharp eyes scanning the docks. It was not until he saw Vallorith himself board the ship, his long robes trailing like shadows in the torchlight, that he allowed himself to breathe. Only then did he turn away, closing the balcony doors behind him as the night deepened.

***

Mena lay awake, staring at the shadows that danced across her ceiling. Her heart ached for time, just a little more. Another week, a month, anything to delay the moment Ashar would sail back to his homeland in the morning. The day they spent together played on repeat in her mind, each moment both a comfort and a torment. A guard, her mother, or even Kivani and Oren had been nearby at every turn, their watchful presence a constant reminder of her status. Kivani and Ashar had spent much of the afternoon comparing the Cairn's abilities to a Talon, their rivalry playful. When Kivani's water snake doused Ashar's phoenix flame, she let out a roar of laughter that echoed through the halls. Mena smiled, watching the two bond over their powers, which had been hidden from the world like hers. When Oren was called away, Kivani followed, leaving the prince and princess alone for the first time.

They had toured the glass gardens, their reflections shifting in the translucent panes as they marveled at the intricate designs. In the village, Mena led him to the workshops where gifted artisans sculpted raw sand into flawless works of art. She loved the way his expression lit up as he watched the process, asking questions and marveling at their skill. Later, they rode through the snowy plains surrounding the castle, the evergreens standing tall and silent against the frostbitten landscape. Yet, despite the beauty of Glacia, Ashar's attention never wavered from her. Mena could feel his gaze on her as they walked, his eyes tracing her movements, lingering on her smile. Each time she caught him watching, his cheeks would flush crimson, and he would quickly avert his gaze. But she could still feel the warmth of his admiration, as steady and undeniable as the sun. Her heart tightened at the thought of him leaving.

The months until she joined him in Highspire seemed endless, and though their union had been arranged, she could not help but hope that his feelings for her ran as deep as the ones growing within her. She could feel her face flush as she thought of him, the way her chest fluttered when he spoke, the way her stomach flipped when he smiled at her. She did not have much experience with love, but she was sure this was it. The start of something real. Ashar made her feel as though she were the only star in his sky. When they met hers, his eyes held a quiet longing, like a traveler seeing the first glimpse of home after a long journey. Mena tossed and turned in her bed, torn between wanting the sun to rise and begging it to stay hidden. Every passing hour brought her closer to seeing Ashar again and closer to his departure.

She pressed her face into her pillow, whispering into the silence of her room, "Just one more day."

A soft knock pulled Mena from her hazy, restless doze. She sat up, blinking into the shadows of her room, unsure if she had imagined the sound. Then it came again, faint and almost hesitant, tapping lightly against the glass door. Her heart quickened. She squinted at the dim silhouette framed by the hall's weak light spilling under her door. She was not dreaming. Hastily, she pulled on her robe, tying the sash tightly around her waist as she padded to the door.

"Who is it?" she whispered, her voice barely audible.

There was no answer, only another light knock. With a sharp breath, she eased the door open, her room flooding with the muted glow from the hall. The sudden brightness stung her tired eyes, and she blinked to focus. Ashar stood there, wrapped in his robe, a slight grin tugging at his lips. He held two cups in one hand and a bottle of ale in the other.

"Ashar!" she hissed, quickly grabbing his arm and tugging him inside.

Her pulse raced as she peeked into the corridor to ensure no one had seen him. Satisfied they had not been discovered, she shut the door and turned to him.

"What are you doing here? And where are my guards?" she demanded in a breathless whisper, though the corners of her lips betrayed her amusement.

Ashar did not answer but instead playfully pressed his finger over his lips, signaling that she should remain quiet. He moved toward the small table by her window, setting down the cups and uncorking the bottle. The rich scent of spiced ale wafted through the air as he poured the purplish liquid carefully and handed her a glass. His smile widened as he raised his glass in a mock toast.

"What is this for?" she asked, unable to hide her smile as she accepted the drink. "What are we drinking to?" she teased, tilting her head.

He still did not reply, only clinking his glass lightly against hers before downing the ale in one long gulp. Amused, Mena giggled and followed his lead, the sweet, spiced warmth coating her tongue and sliding down her throat like a velvet ribbon. The room suddenly felt colder in contrast, and she shivered, glancing at the hearth where the fire had dwindled to faint red embers.

"Can you relight it?" she asked, wrapping her arms around herself.

Ashar nodded and crossed the room. Kneeling before the hearth, he carefully stacked fresh logs onto the glowing embers. Instead of using his abilities, he bent low and blew softly, coaxing the faint heat back to life. Mena watched him, sipping the last of her ale as a smile tugged at her lips. He could have easily relit the fire with a simple wave of his hand, yet he did not. There was something endearing about his effort, about the immense patience he poured into the task.

"You are being ever so quiet," she said with a laugh, setting her empty glass on the table and walking over to him.

She wrapped her hands around his arm and pulled him gently to his feet.

"You could have just waved your hand," she murmured, her voice soft as she lifted his palm in her hand and traced the lines with her fingers. Her touch light and airy.

Her cheeks blushed as she gazed into his eyes, trying to remember every little detail. The shape of his nose, the curve of his jaw. His perfect smile on his lips. If this was their last night together, she wanted it to be worth remembering. Something she could hold onto, day and night, knowing he was thinking about it too. A kiss. Something so small yet so meaningful for him to remember her by. Her heart raced as she gazed into his green eyes, her thoughts a whirlwind. They had agreed to take things slowly. Friends first, right? But her feelings for him had grown far beyond friendship, so quickly and profoundly that it left her breathless. Butterflies filled her stomach as she watched him, searching his expression for any sign of hesitation. And then, she acted. Pressing her lips to his.

The world around her melted away as Ashar wrapped his arms around her, pulling her closer, returning her kiss. The flutters in her chest erupted into a storm, her mind reeling with joy and longing. She wanted this moment to last forever, to burn itself into her soul like a warm, unending fire. But something was wrong. His lips were cold. Freezing, like ice pressed to her skin. His hands chilled her through her gown and robe, frigid as winter frost. Her elation turned to confusion, then dread. She pushed him away, recoiling as a rancid, foul stench hit her nose, a smell so putrid it made her stomach turn.

"Ashar?" The name a question on her lips.

The man before her smiled, but it was not the warm, boyish grin she had grown so fond of. It was sharp and cruel, twisted with malice.

"I will admit," he said, envy coating his words, "I find myself jealous of the young prince. You are quite the beauty, princess. And with what I have felt of your... gift, you would make a most suitable match for me."

A shiver ran down her spine as he circled her, his steps slow and predatory, like a wolf cornering its prey.

"Guards!" she screamed, backing away toward the door, her voice high and panicked.

The man smirked, his features shifting before her eyes. His dark hair lightened to a stark silver blond, and his robe deepened to black crimson, the golden insignia of a sun now gleaming on his chest. It hit her like a blow. Ashar's eyes were hazel, warm and kind, not this unsettling green that glowed faintly in the dim light. How had she not noticed sooner? Blinded by her own foolish desires. Her stomach plummeted, her fear bubbling over.

"Guards!" she screamed again, her voice echoing through the room. But as she opened her mouth, a stabbing pain lanced through her skull.

She stumbled, her hand shooting to her temple as her vision blurred. Her breathing quickened as the pounding headache worsened, spreading like wildfire.

"No..."

Her gaze darted to the empty glass on the table. It was not the ale. She had drunk ale countless times before; a single glass had never left her like this. But this sensation, this oppressive, creeping fog overtaking her body and mind, was horribly familiar. The realization clawed at her, threatening to suffocate her. Silvervane. Her gift, the very essence of who she was, was slipping away, buried under its bitter grip. She staggered back, her legs trembling as the High Priest stepped closer, his green eyes gleaming with cold amusement.

"Silvervane," she gasped, panic tightening her chest.

"Yes, well, we could not have you misbehaving on the long journey," Vallorith said smoothly, brushing an invisible speck of dust from his sleeve before folding his hands behind his back. His calm, measured tone made her stomach churn. "Grab a few belongings, Princess. Let us go. My ship is waiting."

"Guards! Help!" Mena screamed, her voice piercing the quiet room as she bolted for the door.

Before she could reach it, Vallorith's hand shot out and grabbed her by the arm, throwing her back with alarming force. She collided with the footboard of her bed, a sharp pain radiating through her spine as she crumpled to the floor. Every breath burned in her ribs, and her head throbbed with the pounding weight of the tainted ale.

"Do not do that!" Vallorith hissed, his composure cracking for a moment. He loomed over her, his watchful eyes flashing with anger. "I am being polite. Do not make me regret it." He inhaled sharply, his voice softening into something chillingly calm. "Now, gather your belongings before I change my mind and drag you out of here with nothing."

Mena's hands shook as she pressed against the floor, trying to stand, but the pain in her back was too much. Instead, she scurried on all fours toward the window, desperation giving her strength. Her breath fogged the glass as she fumbled with the clasp and shoved the pane open, letting the frigid night air sweep into the room. Vallorith tilted his head, watching her with a bemused expression.

"Oh, this is *hilarious*. What is your plan, Princess? Throw yourself from the window? It is quite the drop."

Ignoring him, Mena leaned against the window frame, her chest heaving as she tried to push past the pain.

Vallorith turned his attention to the embers in the hearth, his lips curling into a sinister smile. "You told me to just... wave my hand." He lifted his hand, making a grand, theatrical gesture over the logs. Nothing happened. His smile widened, and a sharp laugh burst from his lips. "Are you telling me that your betrothed is a Cairn?" He clapped his hand to his forehead, shaking his head in disbelief. "An *Echo* engaged to an *Echo*, oh, how poetic." His gaze snapped back to her, the taunting in his expression hardened into something darker. "And a *royal* Cairn at that. A prince to the Kalyran throne." His eye twitched as his voice dropped to a venomous whisper. "Well, is that not... *convenient?*"

Mena pressed herself tighter against the window, her breaths quick and shallow, the silvervane making its way through her veins.

Vallorith's lips curled into a sneer. "Time is up."

He closed the distance between them in two strides, yanking her to her feet. Pain lanced through her back, and she let out a strangled cry, her legs buckling beneath her. His grip was like iron as he dragged her toward the door, ignoring her protests.

"No!" she screamed, thrashing against him.

She clawed at his hand and dug her heels into the floor, anything to slow him down. With a grunt of frustration, he released her, sending her stumbling into the table. She caught herself just in time, her hand curling instinctively around the bottle of ale. Without hesitation, she swung it with all her strength. The bottle shattered against Vallorith's face with a sickening crack, shards of glass and ale spraying across the room. For a moment, there was silence, save for the sound of liquid dripping to the floor. Vallorith staggered back, clutching his face. When he lowered his hands, Mena saw where the blow had landed. His jaw hung grotesquely slack, blood dripping in thick rivulets down his chin. His eyes burned with fury, the cold, calculated veneer gone, replaced with raw rage.

"You *wretch*," he spat, his words garbled and wet.

Mena did not wait for his retaliation. She stumbled toward the window, every movement agonizing, and thrust her hand into the frigid night air. With all the strength she could muster, she summoned her snow owl. The effort was excruciating. Her head felt as though it might split in two, the silvervane's suppressive power clawing at her mind. But then, in the distance, she heard the familiar rustle of wings.

The owl appeared silently, its pale form a blur against the dark sky. It soared away from the castle, circling once before letting out an ear-piercing screech that echoed through the night. Relief surged through her for a brief moment. Someone would hear. Someone would come. But the strain was too much.

The throbbing in her head intensified, and her vision blurred. Mena clutched her temples, sinking to her knees as the world tilted around her. Above her, Vallorith loomed, his bloodied face twisted with unknown emotions. She watched, horrified, as he clutched his dislocated jaw with both hands and wrenched it back into place with a sickening pop. The squelching sounds churned her stomach, bile rising in her throat. His pale fingers wiped the blood smeared across his chin, his eerie green eyes locking onto her with a venomous glare. Her head throbbed, her heart hammering against her ribs as she stumbled back. The owl's distant screech echoed through the night, a fleeting cry of freedom. Vallorith staggered toward her, his movements slow but deliberate. The sheer rage in his gaze was enough to freeze her in place. He grabbed her arm with an iron grip, pulling her close. She gagged at the stench of blood on his breath as he spoke through clenched teeth, his words slow and deliberate, his jaw barely moving.

"You... will... *pay*... for that."

His fingers dug into her arm, icy and unrelenting, sending sharp pulses of pain through her. She felt the silvervane's effects sinking deeper into her body like chains dragging her down. Her strength waned; the magic tethering her to the snow owl snapped, and its screeching abruptly ceased.

"No," she gasped, her voice breaking as her breathing became labored.

Vallorith yanked her roughly toward the center of the room, dragging her like a rag doll. She twisted and struggled, but her limbs were weak, her body betraying her. He paused before the door and raised his free hand. His long fingers fluttered through the air with a lazy wave, and the room around them began to warp. The edges of Mena's vision blurred, her surroundings hazing into a swirl of shifting light. A sickly pressure built in her head as a new scene took shape before her: the wooden deck of a ship, creaking underfoot, surrounded by the vast, roiling sea. Her skin prickled as they passed through the portal, the sensation like a bubble popping against her body. A gust of wind slammed into her, whipping her hair and the thin fabric of her gown and robe. The sharp tang of salt filled her nose as sea spray clung to her face and clothes.

"Mena!"

Her name tore through the chaos, cutting like a knife. She spun toward the sound, Vallorith's crushing grip still locked on her arm. Her eyes darted frantically back toward the portal. It was shrinking rapidly, but she caught one final glimpse of her room. The blood and ale splattered across the floor, shards of glass glittering in the dim light... and then *him*. Ashar. He stood frozen in the doorway, his hazel eyes wide and fixed on hers.

"Ashar!" she screamed, her voice desperate.

But before he could move, the portal dissolved, erasing her tie to home. Her knees buckled beneath her, but Vallorith did not loosen his hold. The ship's deck blurred as her vision swam with tears. She blinked hard, forcing herself to focus on her new surroundings. Dozens of crew members and armed guards stood scattered across the deck, their gazes drawn to the scene Vallorith had dragged into their midst. A man in a pristine white robe approached, his expression grim as he held out a clean rag. Vallorith snatched it from him with a vicious swipe, pressing it against his bloodied face.

"Lock her below," Vallorith growled, his voice colder than the air around them.

He shoved Mena forward, and she stumbled into the robed man, who grabbed her cautiously by the shoulders.

"And Rhez, make sure the only water she gets is laced with silver-vane," Vallorith added, dabbing at his jaw as his lips twisted into a cruel smile. "It would be best for everyone that way."

Mena's heart sank at the name, its weight like a stone in her chest. She barely noticed as the man in white led her toward the ship's hold, her mind reeling. Weak. Helpless. And at the mercy of her captor. Vallorith wiped at his still bleeding face with the rag as he stalked to the captain's quarters, his heavy boots echoing on the wooden deck. Without a glance back, he slammed the door shut behind him, the sound reverberating like a gavel sealing her fate. The man in the white robe turned to Mena, his expression blank but his movements careful as he reached for her arm. His grip was gentle, almost hesitant, as though he feared breaking her further. He guided her below deck, each step down the creaking stairs plunging her deeper into the ship's cold, dark belly. The chill was biting, even without the wind. Mena's damp clothes clung to her skin, leeching away what little warmth she had left. She shivered uncontrollably, her teeth chattering as they descended two levels into the ship's hold.

The air was heavy with the mingling scents of damp wood, sea salt, and the faint tang of dried herbs and oils, supplies from her homeland packed away in crates that lined the cramped space. But amidst the crates stood a small, barred box. Mena felt her heart sink. The cage was barely large enough to hold a person, its iron bars dulled by rust and worn smooth where countless hands must have gripped them before. It looked like something used to transport livestock or captured beasts, not a human being. Her knees quivered as she approached, ducking her head to step inside. The bundle of straw in the corner offered little comfort. She sank onto it, tucking her knees close to her chest in an attempt to conserve heat. The hay was rough against her bare feet as she tried to drape it over them, a futile shield against the biting cold. The man in the white robe slid the cage door shut with a metallic clang, threading a heavy padlock through the latch. For a moment, he lingered. His eyes flicked to hers, something unreadable in their depths: guilt, pity, or perhaps resignation. But he said nothing. He lowered his head and turned away, the soft rustle of his robes fading as he climbed back to the deck.

Now, she was alone. The ship swayed and creaked, the rhythm of the waves making her stomach churn. Each shift of the vessel felt like a reminder of how far she was being taken from everything she had ever known. Her great-aunt's words echoed in her mind, a cruel warning she could no longer ignore: *Verdathos is like a living hell.* She clenched her arms around her knees, the ache in her ribs and back a constant throb against the sharp chill of the air. Her head still pounded from the silvervane, the fog in her mind making it hard to think, to hope. The despair was suffocating, creeping into every corner of her being. Tears welled in her eyes, hot against her cold skin.

She stared at the floor of the cage, tracing the faint grooves in the wood as her thoughts spiraled. *What would Ashar think if he saw her like this? Would he even know where to find her? Would her parents come looking for her? Would they be safe from Vallorith's wrath?* The ship rocked harder, the motion almost violent, as if even the sea was unsettled by the cruelty on board. Mena shut her eyes tightly and buried her face against her knees, trying to block it all out: the cold, the fear, the crushing weight of the unknown. But no matter how tightly she curled into herself, the cage around her remained.

Chapter Thirteen

"Mena!" Ashar's voice echoed through the now-empty room, bouncing off the cold, smeared walls.

The portal had faded along with Mena, leaving behind only darkness and silence. The stillness swallowed his cry, and the adrenaline that had surged through him moments earlier began to ebb. He had heard the owl's screech outside his window and thought it was her, a sweet reprieve in the dead of night. He had crawled out of bed, running a hand through his hair and straightening his robe, imagining her wanting to see him just one last time before he left. He had spent half the night lost in thoughts of her: how they could steal another moment together, how he might delay his departure, perhaps even delay long enough for another mountain storm to encase their ship in ice, anything to linger by her side a little while longer. So when her owl's familiar call pierced the night, his heart had soared. She must have been thinking of him as well. He opened the window, watching as the owl swooped lower, its wings cutting through the cool air, only to vanish into the void without a sound. Then, he heard the shouts.

Flinging open his door, he tore down the halls, yelling as he ran. "Quick! The princess is in trouble!"

But the guards, doubled in number for her safety, now sat slumped against the walls. Some were fast asleep, others rubbing their temples in confusion. None followed. Ashar's chest tightened. He took the stairs two at a time, his mind racing with dread. When he reached her chambers, he burst through the doors. And froze. Mena stood there, her face etched with terror, her dark eyes wide and glistening in the moonlight. Her skin, pale as porcelain, seemed to glow from beyond the portal.

"Mena!" he shouted, but she was gone before he could reach her.

Silence replaced the crash of waves and torrential wind. Ashar's gaze darted around the room, alarm clouding his thoughts. He stepped forward cautiously, the faint light from the hall casting long shadows across the chaotic scene. With a wave of his hand, glowing orbs blinked into existence, flooding the room with soft, golden light and revealing the full extent of the destruction. The neck of a shattered bottle lay discarded on the floor, its jagged edges glittering ominously. Pieces of glass were scattered everywhere, catching the glow of his magic. Ashar tread carefully, his bare feet brushing against cold slivers of debris. The table was overturned, its top cracked clean in two, and two cups lay smashed beneath it. Ale was splattered across the glass floor and smeared along the walls, its citrusy fragrance lingering in the air, mingling with a darker, metallic tang. Blood. Ashar's stomach churned as his eyes fell on the dark pool spreading before the broken table.

Crimson drips trailed across the floor, stark against the pale sur- faces. His chest constricted, and his thoughts spiraled. Whose blood? Was she hurt? How badly? He lowered himself onto the edge of Mena's bed, burying his face in his hands. Closing his eyes, he tried to piece together every detail, every clue that could explain what had hap- pened. Two cups. A bottle of ale. She had not been alone. Someone had been here with her, drinking. Jealousy flared hot and fast, burn- ing through his core. He spotted the table that was now broken on the floor. Blood and shards of broken glass were everywhere. A fight. His fists clenched, and he felt the heat rising to his skin, his powers threatening to surge uncontrollably. He forced a deep breath, steady- ing himself when a faint memory surfaced.

The scent. Amidst the ale and blood, there had been something else, salty, briny, like the sea. And the wind. He remembered how it had rushed through the room, carrying that sharp, foreign smell. Ashar's eyes snapped open.

"A ship," His voice angry as he strained to recall more details before his fury consumed him.

Mena's face flashed in his memory, her features twisted in shock, tears streaming down her cheeks. She had been in distress, terrified. A tall figure had a firm grip on her, his hands digging into her frail arms. Though the man had been turned away, Ashar remembered the dark crimson robes and the blond hair that was flat and smooth.

"Vallorith," he spat, disgust dripping from the name as his body tensed.

Flames erupted from his hands, surging uncontrollably. They shot across the room, licking the walls and consuming the air. The acrid scent of scorched wood and the burnt sugar of spilled ale filled his lungs as curtains and rugs ignited. He wanted more destruction, to let the flames consume everything, to explode with the fury ripping through him. But through the haze of rage, he forced a breath. Closing his eyes, he inhaled deeply, then exhaled, steadying himself. Slowly, the fire receded, retreating into his hands until nothing remained but blackened fabric, soot lining every surface. Footsteps pounded down the hall. Armed guards burst into the room, their swords gleaming in the glow of the still-burning embers. The tips of their blades hovered at Ashar's throat.

He raised his hands in surrender. "Wait."

Before he could explain, another set of footsteps approached, heavier and more deliberate. King Thaloren stepped into the room, his face dazed from being woken in the middle of the night. His tired gaze swept over the disarray, the bed, the shattered furniture, the scorched remains of the once-lavish furnishings. Then his eyes landed on Ashar.

"Put down your weapons," the king commanded, his voice trembling as he fought to maintain composure.

The guards hesitated before lowering their swords. Thaloren's gaze turned to Ashar, disbelief and anguish flickering across his face.

"It was the High Priest," Ashar said, gripping the king's arms. "It was Vallorith. I saw him take her."

Thaloren's expression darkened, his brows furrowing as he tried to make sense of it all. Before either could say more, a wail pierced the heavy silence. Queen Nyssira collapsed to her knees in the doorway, her sobs wracking her body. She clawed at her chest, gasping for air between cries.

"Mena!" she screamed, pounding her fists against the floor.

Thaloren was at her side instantly, wrapping his arms around her trembling frame. Tears streaked his face as he held her close, her muffled voice breaking against his robes.

"My baby..." Nyssira's voice cracked as she clung to her husband.

The guards shifted uneasily, their silence amplifying the tension in the room. Thaloren looked up, his expression hardening as he directed his fury at the soldiers. "How?" he demanded, his voice rough with sleep. "How did he get past all of you?"

One guard stepped forward, his face pale and his posture rigid. "It was Prince Ashar, my lord. We did not see the High Priest."

Thaloren's sharp eyes snapped to Ashar, narrowing dangerously. The guard hesitated, then continued, his voice faltering. "The prince... he walked past us, but as he did, it was like the air was stolen from the room. We could not breathe. Some of us fainted. The rest of us... we could not think clearly, could not move." He swallowed hard. "Then we heard the commotion from the princess's room. We tried to respond, but we were still dazed. That is when we saw..."

His gaze darted nervously between Ashar and the king.

"That is when we saw Prince Ashar again, racing through the halls toward the princess's room."

The room fell deathly quiet as Thaloren stood, turning to each person in the room, looking for answers. "Someone explain this to me, now!" the king thundered. "Where is my daughter?"

It all made sense to Ashar now; his stomach dropped like a stone. She had thought it was him. She had opened her door for him.

"A portal," Ashar murmured, taking a step forward. "It was not just an illusion; it was a portal like the one Princess Kallemena conjured in the library." His voice trembled as he met the broken expressions of her parents. "He must have disguised himself as me. I have heard of Darra wielding such gifts, but I always thought the stories were exaggerated."

He turned to King Thaloren, his jaw clenched. "It was a ship. I could smell the saltwater and feel the wind. She is on a ship, probably headed for Verdathos."

Before the weight of his words could fully sink in, King Durnovas rushed into the room. His eyes widened in shock as he took in the scene: the scorched walls, the blackened curtains, the scattered splatters of blood and ale. His gaze found his son, and in that moment, Ashar's composure faltered. Durnovas pulled him into a tight embrace, his voice trembling with conviction. "We will get her back," he whispered.

Thaloren knelt beside his grieving wife, gently stroking her long white hair. "We will get her back," he repeated softly; his words meant as much for himself as for Nyssira.

Ashar felt hot tears streak down his face, anger bubbling under the surface. He gritted his teeth, fighting the surge of power building within him. The pressure mounted like a volcano threatening to erupt. But then, an icy touch rested against his back, and a sudden calm washed over him. He spun around, expecting Mena, but he was met with glowing pale blue eyes instead.

"Myra," he breathed.

The woman's expression was strained as she took his hand, a wince flickering across her face. "I can still feel her," she whispered, her voice tight with anguish. "She is so scared."

She stepped further into the room, her gaze sweeping over the destruction. Her face grew increasingly troubled as she approached the bloodstains mingled with the spilled ale. Slowly, she knelt, dipping her fingers into the dark liquid.

"This is his blood," she murmured, a small, grim smile tugging at her lips. "Even with her powers hindered, she fought well."

"Hindered?" Ashar blurted, his anger gathering its second wind. "What do you mean, hindered?"

"Silvervane," Myra said. Turning towards the others, she held up her fingers, coated in sticky charred ale. "He used it to weaken her. She is powerless right now."

The room fell silent, Myra's words hanging heavy in the air. Thaloren stepped forward, his commanding presence returning.

"Wake every guard. Ready the ships." He turned to Myra. "You can still feel her?"

Myra closed her eyes, reaching out with her magic. "Yes," she whispered. "She is still within my reach."

Without another word, Thaloren strode from the room. Nyssira scrambled to her feet, rushing after him. "What are you going to do?" she called, her voice full of desperation.

"I am going to bring our daughter home," Thaloren replied, his tone resolute.

The ships were ready within the hour. King Thaloren and King Durnovas stood at the helm of the lead vessel, their expressions set with determination. The crew lined up in perfect formation, their polished glass armor gleaming in the moonlight. Thaloren stepped forward, inspecting his soldiers. Pride swelled in his chest as he looked upon their unwavering focus. Their weapons remained sheathed, but their resolve was unmistakable.

"We are a peaceful people," he began, his voice steady but firm. "We will do everything in our power to bring Princess Kallemena back without bloodshed."

He paused, his gaze sweeping over the rows of disciplined soldiers, their dark blue tunics visible beneath their translucent armor.

"But if we must raise our swords," he said, unsheathing his blade and holding it high, "We will strike with power and dignity. Let us catch this coward!"

A unified cry rang out from the soldiers. "For the princess! For Glacia!"

The boatswain's voice bellowed over the deck. "Raise anchor! Make ready the sails! All hands aloft! We have prey to catch!"

The crew moved with precision, hoisting the massive sails. The canvas unfurled, momentarily blotting out the moonlight, but the sailors navigated the ship with the ease of muscle memory. Every board and every rope was familiar to them, their hands moving swiftly to secure their vessel. The boat lurched forward, cutting through the icy waves with its keel. Thaloren stood at the prow, spyglass in hand, scanning the dark horizon. Behind them, six ships followed in formation, their sails catching the wind. Thaloren felt the weight of responsibility settling on his shoulders. He glanced back, his eyes finding Nyssira's silhouette on the docks. She stood beneath the glow of the ice castle, her figure a fragile beacon as she waved them off. Turning to Durnovas, Thaloren saw the other king still peering through his spyglass. Both men shared the same belief: they would catch up. They had to.

"Is this the right thing to do? Am I being too hasty?"

King Durnovas lowered his spyglass, his weathered face calm but firm. "Thaloren, you do not have much experience with war," he said, clapping his old friend on the back. "But your daughter was stolen in the night. Kings have waged wars for far less. The fact that you still seek peace through all of this is proof of your strength, not weakness." He glanced toward the horizon, his expression hardening. "Do not let inexperience keep you from doing what is right for your family and your kingdom."

Durnovas' gaze fell to the deck below, where Ashar stood, scanning the waves with restless energy. "If he had taken Ashar..." His voice dropped, and his fists clenched as fury rippled through him. He slammed one hand against the railing, the wood groaning beneath the blow. When he looked back to Thaloren, his expression was fierce. "I would be calling for his head."

They sailed on through the night, the hours dragging with no sign of their quarry. When dawn broke, sunlight spilled over the water, warming the air. Ashar stood at the bow, the salty spray of the sea his only defense against the fatigue weighing down his eyelids. Beside him, Myra stepped forward, her arms outstretched as she reached for something only she could sense. Her glowing eyes scanned the horizon, her expression growing heavier with each passing moment. Finally, her hands fell to her sides in defeat. Ashar placed a reassuring hand on hers, giving it a gentle squeeze.

"We still know where they are heading," he said, his voice steady. He glanced back at his father, who remained vigilant at the helm, spyglass in hand. "We are still on course for Verdathos. Whether it is on the ocean or land, we will get her back."

Myra ran her hand up his arm, her fingers tracing the cold metal of the armor he now wore. Her cold palm cupped his cheek while her other hand rested lightly on his wrist. Her glowing, pupil-less eyes darted across his features, her expression unreadable.

"Deception is close," she whispered suddenly, her grip tightening like a viper's coil as Ashar instinctively tensed.

He turned to go, ready to warn his father, but Myra clung to him. "The Darra is not who he claims to be. Be wary of the one who fell, for the reflections will consume you, though it will not be the end."

Ashar froze at her cryptic words. Her trembling hands released him as she staggered back, clutching her head. A single tear slipped from her glowing eyes as she shook her head.

"Healer Myra, are you all right?"

"There!"

King Durnovas' voice cut through the air like a horn. The crew erupted into motion, rushing to the railings. On the horizon, three dark shapes emerged, their sails crimson against the golden glow of the rising sun.

"Rows ready!" the boatswain bellowed.

Long oars plunged into the water with synchronized precision, cutting through the waves with powerful strokes. "Row true and strong!"

The crew's chant was not made of words but a rhythmic hum that resonated through the ship, unifying them purposefully. The vessel surged forward, its speed mirrored by the six others in formation. Together, the fleet bore down on their prey, their prows slicing through the icy waves. As they closed in, the High Priest's fleet came into sharp focus, three ships flying the crimson banners of Verdathos. For each Verdathos vessel, two Glacia ships moved to flank them, boxing them in.

"Board!" Durnovas roared, his voice carrying across the water.

Hooks flew through the air, their iron claws biting into the enemy decks. The crews worked swiftly, dragging the ships closer until they were bound together like stitched fabric. The Glacian and Kalyran soldiers surged forward, ramps slamming down to bridge the gaps between the vessels. They charged aboard the crimson-sailed ships, glass armor glinting like shards of sunlight. The Verdathos crews, a collection of robed men and women, were missing from the decks. All the soldiers found were scarce supplies and vacant cots. The emptiness of the ship left unease growing in everyone's stomachs. Within moments, the charge subsided, replaced by tense silence. The Glacian and Kalyran soldiers formed ranks, lining up in tight, neat rows. King Thaloren strode across the captured deck, his boots thudding against the planks. His detailed gaze swept the ship, scanning every shadow, every corner.

"Where is he?" his voice was filled with irritation as he clenched his fists. He turned to a soldier standing nearby. "Find my daughter. Now!"

The soldier nodded, patting their fist to their chest before disappearing below deck. Thaloren's chest tightened as he looked across to his crew. His eyes burned with unspoken questions, but his resolve never wavered. Somewhere on this ship, Kallemena was waiting, and he would not leave without her. As the armored woman descended swiftly below deck, her footsteps echoing down the narrow wooden staircase, Ashar and Myra followed close behind. The prince's hand steadied the healer as she moved cautiously down the dark staircase. Above, King Durnovas marched aboard the second ship, his piercing gaze sweeping over an equally desolate ship deck. The faces of his soldiers looked to one another for any clue or answer to where the enemy crew had gone.

"Where is Vallorith?" Durnovas demanded, his voice sharp as steel.

Thaloren stood on the central ship's deck, echoing the same question with more measured tones. "Where is he? Show yourself, you coward!"

No one answered. The silence hung heavy in the salty air, broken only by the creak of the ships' hulls swaying in the waves. The soldiers exchanged nervous glances, their eyes filled with dread, but none dared speak. Thaloren's jaw tightened. He looked out to the sea, the rising sun blinding on the open water. "Where?" he implored. "Where could he and all of his crew go? How do empty ships sail themselves?"

From the third ship, a soldier's voice rang out. "Vallorith is not here, my lord!"

King Durnovas emerged from the captain's quarters of the second vessel, his expression dark. "Nor is he on this one," he called, his voice tinged with frustration. He gestured to his men, clad in gleaming silver armor crowned with green-feathered helmets. "Search every corner. Leave nothing unchecked."

King Thaloren paced the deck of the central ship, his expression etched with worry. His thoughts churned, but before he could speak, a soldier shouted from below.

"In here, my lord!"

Thaloren's heart leaped. He strode toward the entrance to the ship's lower quarters, his long coat sweeping behind him. As he descended, the air grew thick, the scent of damp wood and tallow filling his nostrils. He stopped before a cabin door, slightly ajar, its dark interior barely illuminated by the flickering light of a single candle. With a steadying breath, Thaloren pushed the door open. The cabin was sparse but eerily familiar. A sturdy desk stood in its center, its surface cluttered with parchment and a quill. The single candle burned low on the desk's corner, casting shadows that danced along the walls. It was a room meant for quiet study, a space that reminded Thaloren of his own chamber back at the castle. His eyes darted across the room, taking in every detail. Papers covered in hasty scrawls littered the desk. Maps were pinned to the far wall, their edges curling from the moisture in the air. A faint metallic tang hung in the room, mixing with the lingering scent of burnt wax. And then he saw him. Behind the desk, shrouded in the soft glow of candlelight, sat a man garbed in crimson robes. His face was pale, his smile sharp as a knife. He leaned back in the chair as though he had been anticipating this very moment.

"King Thaloren," the high priest said, his voice smooth and taunting. "Welcome."

***

Below deck, Ashar charged deeper into the dim, narrow corridors until he reached a compartment packed with crates and sacks. He flung his hand forward, summoning glowing orbs of light that illuminated the space. Stacks of wooden boxes towered to the ceiling, burlap bags slumped against the walls, and at the far end, a single cage loomed, its occupant slumped motionless on the floor. Ashar's heart surged. He sprinted to the cage, dropping to his knees and pressing his face against the cold iron bars.

"Myra! She is here!" he shouted, his voice trembling with urgency. He scanned the lock, his mind racing. "I need a key!"

Desperation clawed at him as he drew his sword and struck the lock with all his strength. The blade clanged against the iron, leaving only faint scratches.

"I will get you out, Mena," he vowed, gritting his teeth. "Just hold on."

He wedged the tip of his blade between the bars and pulled, straining against the unyielding metal. The sword bent under the force, but the lock refused to give. Frustrated, he hammered at the lock with his hilt, each blow echoing hollowly through the hull.

"Myra!" he called again, hysteria rising in his voice.

Gripping the bars tightly, he closed his eyes and focused, channeling energy into his hands. Heat surged through his veins, and soon, the metal began to glow orange, then white-hot. The metal melted, molten rivulets pooling dangerously at his feet and threatening to ignite the wooden floorboards. Quickly, Ashar absorbed the heat back into himself, the molten metal solidifying and blackening once more. He shoved the bars aside and slipped into the cage, kneeling beside the still figure.

"Mena," he whispered, his voice breaking as he cradled her limp form in his arms. Myra arrived, crouching beside him, her sightless eyes wide with alarm. Her hands hovered over the figure, trembling as she worked.

"No," she breathed, her voice strained. "No, no, no!"

Ashar's heart plummeted. He grabbed her shoulder, his voice a frantic plea. "What is it? What is wrong with her?"

"It is not her!" Myra's voice pleaded as she swept her hand over the figure. A shimmering wave spread across it, and in an instant, the illusion shattered.

Ashar looked down in disbelief, the weight in his arms now nothing more than a sack of grain. He froze, staring at the lifeless burlap.

"Myra, what..."

But she was already moving. Her hands worked in frantic, fluid motions, weaving a shimmering bubble around him. The air grew colder, biting at his skin as the dim light around them grew brighter. He felt the sting of snowflakes hit his face, and a blistering wind at his back. From under him, the world opened, and he fell. Snow enveloped him as he got to his feet and looked around—the glass towers of Iskaroth's castle stood tall in the distance. The biting cold brought water to his eyes as he peered up to see a portal hovering above his head.

"Find her!" Myra's voice was hoarse, her words barely audible over the rush of energy surrounding them. "And remember, the reflections are not the end."

Before Ashar could respond, the portal faded, and he was alone in the snow. Anger flashed through him, "No!" He released his energy, flames enveloping his body. Flames flashed through the sky, a hiss of ice melting beneath the heat, leaving behind an intricate scorch mark on the sand that hid below the layers of snow. Steam rose from the ground as he fell to the blackened earth, his cries of frustration echoing on the wind.

***

Vallorith's smile glinted in the candlelight, his eyes and teeth catching the flickering glow of the flame. He slid his hand leisurely across the desk, his gaze never wavering from Thaloren.

"I must say, I did admire your desk. I am considering commissioning one for myself." His voice was calm as he snapped his fingers. The door behind Thaloren slammed shut with a thunderous bang.

"What have you done with my daughter? Where is Mena?" Thaloren spun around as his pulse quickened. The room felt smaller, the air now heavier. "Where is my guard?"

Vallorith's grin widened as he rose to his feet, his dark robe cascading behind him like a shadow. He circled the desk, his movements deliberately slow and unhurried. "Your guard, my lord? He is here." His voice shifted deeper, darker.

"It was you." Thaloren's chest tightened as dread clawed at his mind.

He had been tricked, and his heart thundered in realization. He turned to the door, but it had vanished, leaving only an unbroken wall of polished wood. When he looked back, Ashar stood before him, his expression eerily calm.

"Do not worry," Ashar said, his voice laced with something foreign. "I will take good care of your precious Mena."

Thaloren blinked, and Ashar's face melted away, replaced by Vallorith's sinister grin.

"How do you know this power?" Thaloren demanded, gripping the hilt of his sword. "The Axis does not teach it. This magic is reserved for the gods!"

Vallorith chuckled, his laugh too loud for the small space. "Oh, dear king, your naivety is almost endearing. Darra Echoes, like me and your precious Mena, are limited only by our imaginations. And as far as gods go, well, I intend to surpass what they intended for their *chosen ones*."

With a wave of his hand, the room shifted back to its original form. The ship rocked gently once more as if the moments before had been a cruel illusion.

"You have overstepped, Vallorith," Thaloren spat, his voice trembling with fury. "The council will hear of this. Mark my words!"

Vallorith's grin stretched wider, a devilish glint in his eyes. "Still clinging to that feeble hope, are you? I meant every word I said in your office. Mena will be trained at Verdathos. She will embrace the Axis, and your kingdom will pay the price for your defiance."

Thaloren stepped forward, his grip tightening on his sword.

"But you fail to grasp the full scope of my vision," Vallorith continued, tilting his head. "There will be no more council, no more kingdoms, and no more monarchs. There will only be me, ruling over it all." He paused, savoring the moment. "With your daughter by my side."

"No!" Thaloren lunged, his blade aimed for Vallorith's chest.

Black smoke filled the air, a dense fog that sucked the air from the kings lungs. He swung his sword over and over until it struck the wall of the cabin. The haze thinned, and Thaloren could see a small portal. Through the narrowing gap, Vallorith's grin lingered like a taunt.

"Do give my regards to the flames," Vallorith said, raising his hand one final time.

The ship shuddered violently beneath Thaloren's feet as an explosion roared from below deck. The floorboards splintered, the force throwing him backward. Screams and cries of his soldiers filled the air, blending with the deafening cacophony as another blast erupted, and the king hurried back to the ship deck. Thaloren staggered on his feet, his ears ringing. The ship groaned as it began to split apart. Flames licked at the timbers, and bodies were strewn across the deck. His heart stopped as he remembered. Ashar was below deck. He had gone to find Kallemena. Thaloren stumbled to the railing, his vision swimming. Across the burning wreckage, he spotted King Durnovas standing at the helm of his sinking ship. A jagged shard of the mast pierced his chest, and blood soaked his silver armor. Durnovas locked eyes with Thaloren and mouthed something, silent words that rang louder than the explosions.

"Save them."

Thaloren slammed his fist to his chest in a solemn salute. His voice trembled as he vowed, "I will find them both."

The ships burned around him, sinking into the icy sea.

Part III: The Axis

Chapter Fourteen

Mena could not tell how many days had passed since she had been locked inside the barred crate in the ship's damp, shadowy hold. Time blurred into an endless rhythm of creaking timbers, sloshing waves, and the occasional heavy footsteps of the crew above. Every motion of the ship sent her body crashing against the iron bars of her tiny prison. The bruises on her shoulders and back throbbed with a relentless ache, her body battered by each mountainous wave that heaved the vessel skyward, only to slam it back down with bone-rattling force. The first few hours had been the worst. She would cling to the bars in a desperate attempt to stay steady, but the ship's violent rocking was unrelenting. Her stomach churned with every lurch until she retched the remains of her laced ale onto the damp wooden floor beneath her.

The stench lingered, mingling with the acrid tang of saltwater and mildew, creating an oppressive atmosphere that clung to her skin and hair. Day and night lost all meaning in the never-ending darkness. The only indication of time's passage was the arrival of her meager meals: a thin strip of smoked meat crumbled at her touch and a stale crust of bread too hard to chew without soaking it in the water they gave her.

She hesitated to drink it, knowing full well that the bitter taste of *silvervane* infused the liquid. She could taste the telltale herbal bite that lingered on her tongue and feel the dampening of her power's energy with every swallow. Yet thirst always won. No matter how much she tried to resist, her trembling hands would seize the cup and down its contents greedily, the cool liquid easing the fire in her throat even as it sparked a new kind of pain. The headaches began shortly after each drink, sharp and merciless, as if needles pierced through her temples. She would curl into herself, cradling her head as tears spilled freely down her cheeks. Her thoughts always turned to her family during these moments. Were they still safe? Or had the Axis come for them, too? The ache in her chest was unbearable, a clawing grief that would not let go. Gnawing at her sanity until it gave way to the loneliness. The ship's belly echoed every sob, the sound bouncing off the walls and returning to her like a cruel reminder that she was utterly, inescapably alone.

The groans of the ship's timbers became her only lullaby, and even those could not keep the nightmares at bay. Each time she drifted into an uneasy sleep, the horrors of her last hours in Iskaroth replayed in relentless detail. She saw Vallorith's grin. The blood dripping down his chin as he spat his words at her. She heard his voice, cold and vengeful, promising that she would pay. The memory of his unholy stare sent shivers down her spine, even now. Then came Ashar's face, his wide, horrified eyes as he called for her, just a second too late. The portal's swirling magic swallowed her whole, leaving her last glimpse of him burned into her mind: his hand outstretched, his lips forming her name. Mena woke with a gasp, her heart pounding in her ribs like a caged bird. Her cheeks were wet, her matted hair clinging to her skin in sticky tendrils. The feeling was now routine, having woken this way many times before.

Mena braced herself for the familiar sway of the ship, for the relentless rocking and crashing that had gone on for days or weeks, perhaps. But today, it did not come. The ship was steady. She blinked in the dim light of her prison, her senses alert to the change. The air felt warmer, no longer damp and bone-chilling as it had been before. Straining her ears, she caught something faint and unfamiliar. Singing. Her heart quickened as she lifted herself from the damp wooden floor. She tilted her head, listening intently. The sound was faint but undeniable, low and high hums interwoven into a soft, lilting chorus. It drifted down from above, wrapping around her like a fragile thread of hope. Tears welled in her eyes as she crawled toward the edge of her cage. People. She could hear *people*. The singing stirred a flicker of something she had not felt in what seemed like ages, a strange ache, a longing for something she could not name.

Her gaze fell to the plate of food sitting just outside the bars. A piece of smoked meat, stale bread, and the dreaded cup of water, its clear liquid glinting faintly in the dim light. Her stomach churned at the sight of it, and a dull throb began to creep into her temples. Even before she took a sip, she could feel the phantom effects of the *silver-vane* coursing through her body. Swallowing hard, she pushed her head against the bars, desperate for clarity, for answers. The singing was still there, soft and distant, accompanied by faint, rhythmic footsteps on the floor above her.

"Help!" she called out, her voice hoarse and cracked from disuse.

The sound startled her. It felt foreign to her ears as if it belonged to someone else. She clenched her hands around the bars, the cool metal a relief against her chapped skin. Her heart was a mixture of fear and desperation surging through her. Would they hear her? Would they care? Mena had stopped trying to talk to the disciple days ago. After the third or fourth time he had brought her food, she realized there was no point. The man in the white robe, the one who always lowered his head in quiet reverence when Vallorith was near, was gentler, yes, but he still avoided her gaze and kept his distance. He knew better than to talk to her, even if his demeanor was softer than his master's cruelty. And so, she had given up, retreating into silence and letting her thoughts fill the void. The only sounds that had accompanied her silence were the groaning of the ship, the echo of her sobs, and the occasional sloshing of waves against the hull. But now, there was something else. The singing. It seeped through the wooden planks and into her cell, a faint melody that felt like a lifeline.

"Help!" she shouted again, louder this time, her voice an unfamiliar screech.

The footsteps above faltered for a brief moment, then continued. Her breath hitched as she pressed her face harder against the bars.

"Please!" she yelled. "Someone... anyone!"

Mena licked her lips. They were dry and cracked, and her tongue felt coarse, rough like a cat's rasping tongue. Her eyes flickered to the cup of water, the liquid glinting faintly in the dim light. She hesitated, her stomach twisting. The silvervane that tainted the water would only make her weaker. If she could hear people above, then surely they could hear her also. Maybe, just maybe, she could escape. But to have any chance, she needed a clear mind. Shaking her head, she pushed the cup aside and leaned forward, extending her hand through the bars of her cage. She closed her eyes, summoning every ounce of focus she had. In her mind, she conjured the image of her owl. She visualized its speckled feathers, the piercing depth of its round eyes, and the sharp curve of its beak and talons. Her heart raced as she willed it into existence. Nothing happened. The magic within her stirred faintly, like an ember buried under ash, but it refused to ignite. She clenched her teeth, her breathing ragged. Tears pricked her eyes, and frustration surged in her chest.

"No," she shook her head, willing herself not to crumble. "I am stronger than this."

She focused again, her hand trembling as she imagined the owl's graceful wings and haunting call. Her body shuddered with the effort. Her head throbbed with a sharp pain that radiated through her temples and blurred her vision. Still, her hand remained empty. Defeated, she slumped forward, resting her forehead against the cool iron bars. The chill seeped into her burning skin, a fleeting relief from the fire raging inside her. Exhaustion tugged at her limbs, but her thoughts raced. Myra's warnings echoed in her mind: *Do not overreach. Do not drain yourself completely.* What would happen if she did? Could she lose her abilities altogether? For a fleeting moment, the thought tempted her. If the Axis had no use for her magic, would they finally release her? Could she go home? But then another thought struck her, cold and cutting. Did she truly want that? To let them win?

These were the people who had torn her from her family, who had locked her in this cage and treated her like an animal. She thought of her parents, of Oren and Kivani and Ashar. Would they want her to surrender a piece of herself to survive? Her stomach growled a deep ache that ate at her insides. She crawled toward the pathetic plate of food. Her hand hovered over the plate before pulling back. She could not bring herself to eat. Instead, she curled into a ball, wrapping her arms around her knees, pressing her back against the bars. Her mind drifted, consumed by hunger and fatigue. She shook her head, knowing it was futile, yet her hand rose again, trembling as she focused on something small. *Delicate. Light as a feather,* she thought, clinging to the fragile spark of hope buried deep within her.

At first, there was nothing. Then, a flicker. A faint blur that sharpened and grew. A butterfly. It perched on her palm, fragile and luminous, its glowing wings fanning slowly. Mena's breath released as she stared at it, the soft light blinding after so much time in darkness. She could not remember how long it had been since she had seen sunlight. Her gaunt frame felt foreign to her, her ribs and spine sharp beneath her thin skin. The butterfly stayed with her, its presence fragile and fleeting, a testament to her resilience. She held onto it for as long as possible, savoring the tiny victory against the oppressive silvervane. But her body trembled, exhaustion creeping in like a tide. Her vision blurred as she let the butterfly go, watching it drift away before vanishing into nothingness. She slumped back against the bars; her breathing labored, the cool iron soothing her fevered skin. The singing continued above, distant and haunting. Its melody threatened to lull her into a restless sleep when a slow, deliberate clap shattered the quiet. Mena's eyes flew open. Her heart raced as she scanned her cage, her pulse pounding in her ears. Out of the shadows, a figure emerged. His dark robes blended seamlessly with the gloom of the ship's hull. He stepped forward, towering even in his crouched posture to avoid hitting his head on the low beams. Mena's throat tightened as his presence filled the confined space.

"I knew you were strong." Vallorith's voice was like scraping metal against stone, grating against her ears. "Yes, a perfect pupil for the Axis."

He stepped toward the stairs, his boots thudding against the wooden planks, before turning back to her. His eyes glinted in the dim light, a predatory gleam that made her stomach twist.

"We have docked. Drink up, and maybe, just maybe, I will let you out to see your new home." His lips curled into a smirk as he ascended the stairs, his robes whispering against the narrow walls.

Mena sat frozen, her heart pounding in her chest. The moment he was gone, she pulled her tattered gown tighter around herself, wrapping her arms around her body as though she could shield herself from his gaze. *How long had he been sitting there? Watching her?* She felt sick and violated in ways beyond the physical. He had seen her. Her willingness to go against his plan, her power, the fleeting flicker of magic she had willed into existence. Her chest burned with humiliation and fury. She did not want him to see her. She did not want him *near* her. And now he knew. He knew she could still project, even with the cursed silvervane running through her. The sound of hurried footsteps broke through her spiraling thoughts. She squinted through the dark, her heart sinking as the familiar figure of the disciple descended the stairs. His pristine white robes seemed to glow faintly in the dim light, but he was not alone this time. Five others followed behind him, their expressions cold and their movements rigid with authority. The air shifted, thick with the promise of violence.

"Drink," one of the men ordered, his voice sharp and commanding. "Or you will stay in there."

Mena's eyes darted to the kind-faced man. His expression was heavy with sadness, his gaze flickering with unspoken apology. He gave her a slight, almost imperceptible nod, a silent confirmation of the other man's words. Her throat tightened as she weighed her options. She did not want to obey them. She did not want to submit to their control. But the thought of staying in this cage, hunched and suffocated within the ship, made her stomach knot. Her limbs ached for movement, and her lungs yearned for fresh air. She needed strength, sunlight, and anything that could help her escape. Her eyes fell on the meager plate of food and the dreaded cup of water. Her thoughts raced. Could she project something strong enough to free herself? Could she summon the strength to fight? Her hunger gnawed at her defiance, and the ache in her stomach was a relentless reminder of her fragile state. She needed energy. She needed to survive. With trembling hands, she reached through the bars and grabbed the cup. The water felt cool against her parched lips, and she forced herself to drink, her body screaming in protest. The familiar earthy taste of the silvervane coated her tongue, and she swallowed it down, bracing for the pain she knew would come. Another disciple stepped forward, a second cup in hand. His lips curled into a cruel smile as he shoved another full cup toward her through the bars.

"And this one," he said, his tone commanding. "The High Priest wants to ensure you do not cause trouble."

Mena's hands shook as she stared at the second cup. Her pulse quickened, panic surging through her tiny frame. She glanced at the kind man, but his gaze fell to the floor, unable, or unwilling, to meet her eyes.

Mena's heart shattered as she stared at the second cup of silvervane. Two cups. She had never endured so much before. Her head already throbbed from the first, each beat of her pulse sending a fresh wave of pain behind her eyes. The second cup would render her useless, unable to think or wield her abilities. Tears slid down her face, silent and unchecked. Her trembling hands took the cup, and she forced herself to drink, choking back the bitterness. The pain blossomed immediately, spreading from her temples and wrapping around her skull like an iron band. She clutched the side of her head, her breath shallow and ragged as a faint gasp left her lips. The sharp clink of a key in the lock was barely noticed. The screeching sound of the cage door swinging open sent an involuntary jolt down her spine. A rough hand gripped her arm, yanking her from her confined space. Her muscles screamed in protest as she stood, her legs wobbling beneath her like those of a newborn foal. Another hand, gentler, steadier, took hold of her other arm. She knew the touch. The kind one. Together, they hoisted her upright, guiding her toward the stairs. Each step felt insurmountable, her body trembling with exhaustion. Her lungs burned like she had just run the entire length of her castle's corridors. Just when she thought her legs would buckle beneath her, they emerged onto the ship's deck.

The sunlight was blinding, piercing her closed eyelids. She squeezed her eyes shut tighter, the warmth of the sun on her skin a sharp contrast to the cold, damp darkness below. The air here was dry, hot, and entirely unlike the misty coolness of her homeland. It was fresh and clean, and she welcomed it despite the heat. She gulped down breaths of the salty, floral-tinged air, desperate to rid herself of the ship's stagnant, rotting stench. Her bare feet touched the sunbaked wooden boards, the heat melting into her skin as her body swayed unsteadily. Mena blinked, trying to adjust to the light. At first, the world was nothing but a searing blur of brightness. But as her eyes began to focus, the sight before her stole the air from her lungs. It was beautiful.

A massive stone wall stretched endlessly in both directions, its surface weathered and ancient yet imposing. Stairs carved from the rock spiraled upward, leading to a place hidden from view. The brilliant blue sky blanketed the horizon, its clarity unmarred by even the faintest wisp of cloud. Branches of green spilled over the top of the wall, cascading like a living waterfall. Leaves rustled gently in the breeze, their sound mingling with the rhythmic crash of waves against the shore. The ocean sparkled like a field of gemstones, its surface dotted with the shadows of massive white birds. She watched as one of the birds hovered on an invisible current before diving sharply into the water. It reemerged moments later, a shimmering, red-scaled fish writhing in its talons, nearly as large as the bird itself. Mena's heart ached at the sight, and the sheer marvel of the world above deck. It was a cruel reminder of how far she was from her home.

The gentle man tugged her arm, pulling her toward the ramp fastened between the dock and the towering stone wall. Her legs stumbled to follow, her body weak with every step. From somewhere high above, the ethereal singing grew louder, the angelic chorus echoing off the stone walls and vibrating in her chest. The sound was hauntingly beautiful, so pure and layered that it brought fresh tears to her eyes. She did not know if it was the pain in her head, the exhaustion in her body, or the vast overwhelming nature of this place, but she felt her soul crack. Her breathing hitched as she let herself be led toward the ramp, the melody following her like a ghost.

"Where are we?" Mena's voice was strained by the intense pain that lingered behind her eyes.

The disciple behind her huffed impatiently, shoving her forward. The kind man stayed close by her side, his steady presence grounding her as she gripped the handrail of the ramp. Slowly, painfully, she made her way off the ship. The relief of her bare feet touching the cool stone, shaded from the blazing sun, was almost enough to make her forget the ship entirely. She never wanted to return to that cage. Never again. Her gaze fell on the many steps leading up the wall. The climb looked impossible, but the thought of returning to the ship was worse. She looked out to the water, the waves crashing against the stones that jutted straight up from the sea. It was as though the wall had risen from the ocean's depths. She had never seen construction like this, and given her short life spent primarily on Glacia, that was not a small statement.

"Move." A stern command from another robed man made her trip, her shin meeting stone.

She cried out in pain as the kind man hoisted her back to her feet. The man's hands held her steady and close as she limped up the stairs.

It was slow going, each stair smooth and cool beneath her bare feet as she climbed higher and higher. The air grew drier, and her body ached with every step. By the time they reached the top, she was level with the ship's mast, far below. Mena's eyes struggled to take in the sheer magnitude of what lay before her. It was all too glorious to absorb at once. Everywhere she looked, there were trees, their long branches swaying gently in the breeze rushing off the water. Pathways carved with clean, graceful lines seemed to flow naturally with the land, never intruding upon it. In the distance, brown mountains rose from the earth, their slopes covered in a patchwork of green and yellow trees. The sun hovered high above, casting long shadows beneath the forest canopy. The courtyard ahead bustled with people. Despite their movements, the area was bare, save for one imposing statue at the center. Mena's gaze locked on it, her unease growing as she took in the figure of a woman. She was tall and slender, with hair that flowed from her scalp like a waterfall down her back. Her arms were wrapped in vines that clung to her skin. Her cupped hands were held up to the sky as if offering to something or someone. Around her feet, flowers and saplings took root.

Upon her head was a crown that looked like it had been made of antlers from deer. She was masterfully sculpted in every sense, perfectly proportionate. The gown she wore looked like it had been made of the Ardorian wilderness and would grow green with a passing rain. A plaque was badly worn at her feet and appeared to be unreadable. The symbolism of the whole statue was lost on

Mena, but the sight of it made her feel small and unworthy of being in its presence, dressed in such filth.

Before she could become embarrassed by her own appearance, her eyes were drawn to the building looming before her. She had some-how missed it earlier, but now it was all she could see. Towering, black walls made of slate as dark as the void itself. It stood in stark contrast to the bright, colorful landscape around it. The building was so tall that she had to tilt her head back to glimpse the top, her neck straining with the effort. On the wall above, an insignia gleamed, a large, golden sun, its rays radiating outward like a symbol of power and unity.

The same golden sun adorned the patches of the high priests' robes. It was a symbol meant to be worshipped, and Mena knew, even before the guards nudged her toward the doors, that this was the heart of their authority.

Vallorith stood at the door, his presence imposing as he surveyed the gathering around him. A satisfied smile crept across his face as every head lowered in obedience.

"Bring her to the nursery," he commanded, his voice rich with authority. "Get her cleaned up, she smells like a damn pig."

With a single push, he sent the massive black doors creaking open, his laughter filling the air as he strode inside. "Welcome to your new home, princess!" The sound of his voice mingled with the distant chorus of angelic singing.

The kind man handed Mena off to an older woman dressed in pristine white robes. Her white hair was braided down her back. She took Mena's frail hand, guiding her gently through the hall, her touch light but firm.

"Wait!" She tried to pull away, the darkened hall engulfing her vision. "What was his name?"

The woman looked behind them, the man staring after them with longing eyes.

"His name is Brother Rhez." The woman's voice was soft as she continued to guide Mena down the hall.

Mena's bare feet padded softly along the black stone floors, each step echoing in the vast, empty space. The singing grew louder the further they went, filling the air with its sweet, harmonious tones. High above, various-sized wind chimes played and clanged in a sweet melody. With each passing breeze from the sea, the ceiling would harmonize and tweet as if thousands of voices were singing in unison. Above them, a massive sun had been carved into the roof, its golden rays radiating outward, casting an unnatural, almost otherworldly light upon the space. The hall stretched endlessly before her, its dark walls absorbing the sound and light. At the far end, the hall split into four smaller corridors, each leading to different wings of the building. The massive size of the place overwhelmed her senses, making it hard to focus on any one detail. She tried to track their path as they turned through various doorways, but the halls all seemed to blur together in her mind, their black stone and clean angles disorienting. The woman beside her moved in eerie silence as though gliding, her footsteps barely making a sound against the stone floor. Mena felt small, lost, and unsure.

"Where are we going?" she asked, her voice too loud in the cavernous space.

The words bounced off the walls and echoed back to her, making her feel like an intruder in a place where she had no right to be. The woman's pace did not falter. Mena waited several minutes before she asked another question, "Is this the continent of Verdathos?" The older woman did not respond, her expression unreadable as she continued to lead Mena deeper into the building. The singing swirled around them and, as beautiful as it was, offered no answers. The silent woman did not speak as they ascended yet another set of stairs, steeper and longer than the first. Mena's muscles groaned with the effort, and she struggled to keep pace, her limbs weak and trembling. They climbed and climbed, each step feeling heavier than the last. Mena's breath came in shallow gasps, and the world around her began to blur. She thought, briefly, that she might collapse, but finally, they reached a doorway.

The wood was a lighter brown than the rest of the ministry's blackened walls, its warmth starkly contrasting the surrounding darkness. The woman produced a key and unlocked the door with a soft click.

On the other side, Mena's expectations were shattered. Instead of the cold, stone halls of the ministry, she found herself facing a second courtyard, bathed in soft sunlight. Hanging trees draped over the edges, their branches swaying gently in the breeze, casting patches of shade on the smooth, sandy pathways. A shorter wall encircled the space, and at the far end, a building stood, its stone walls gray and brown, with a tiled roof that gave it an almost rustic, homely feel. Mena could hear the faint sound of children's voices, their words flowing in unison, reciting something that sounded like a prayer. The woman locked the door behind them, the click of the lock was a stab to her heart, before she led Mena toward a smaller building on the west side of the courtyard. As they moved, Mena's gaze wandered, her eyes not knowing what to focus on first.

From this height of this level, she could see the entire courtyard below, the distant statue in its center, the grand, black-roofed ministry stretching far below, and even the ship that had carried her here. It was as though she was perched on the side of a mountain, the world sprawled beneath her. The only way to reach this secluded place had been the swirling tower they had just climbed, its dizzying height adding to the disorienting sense of isolation. The woman cleared her throat and, without a word, opened a door to the smaller building. Inside, the sight took Mena by surprise; rows of small bunk beds lined the walls. The bunks were child-sized, a far cry from what she had expected. Down a narrow hallway, Mena found the baths, hot springs that steamed gently, bubbling with warmth. The air was thick with the scent of minerals, soothing to her senses after the exhaustion of the climb. The woman rummaged through a cupboard, her movements brisk and efficient, before pulling out a towel, a plain bar of soap, and a freshly laundered white robe. She handed them to Mena with an almost impersonal gesture.

"Clean yourself up," she said, her voice flat. "Meet us in the church. There, we will have our final meal of the day. Hurry along now; you smell awful."

The woman left and Mena was finally alone, free from her cage. Her legs buckled beneath her, and she collapsed to the floor, the weight of everything crashing down on her. Sobs wracked her body, each breath a sharp intake of pain. She was drowning in the gravity of her circumstances, this place, these people, everything that had led her here. The sound of the water in the bath hall, gentle and serene, only made her feel more lost. The steamy mineral smell of the spring mingled with the stagnant scent of her own body, and Mena realized just how filthy she was. Once a silken white, her nightgown had dulled to a yellowish-brown, stained beyond recognition. Her hair, matted with bits of hay and dirt, hung limply around her face. Her skin was grimy and gray, caked with who knows what. The realization made her shudder and she could not bear to think about it any longer. With trembling hands, she peeled off the tattered remnants of her gown and sank into the hot, crystalline waters.

The heat seeped into her bones, loosening the tension in her sore muscles. She scrubbed at her scalp, gasping as she found a few bugs nestled behind her ears. Horror bloomed in her chest, but she did not stop. She scrubbed her skin with the coarse soap until it burned, her flesh pink and raw. The robe waiting by the pool seemed like an insurmountable task, but she could not stay in the water forever. Reluctantly, she climbed out, the warmth of the spring retreating as she dressed. The heavy fabric of the robe clung to her skin, its weight a constant reminder of her new reality. She tried to braid her hair the way Amawna had done, but the result was uneven and lumpy. Her fingers shook as she finished, and she sighed deeply. Slippers, slightly too large for her feet, were waiting just outside. She slipped them on, grateful for the soft, cozy insides.

Taking a deep breath, she ventured back outside to the courtyard. A house sat across from hers, a mirror image of the one she had just left. She wondered briefly how many more of these buildings were hidden in the shadows of the tower. The sounds of voices echoed from the church, and Mena hesitated before pushing open the door.

The room fell silent as soon as she entered. Her eyes widened at the sight before her. Children. There were so many of them, no older than twelve, all wearing identical white robes with a sun embroidered on the shoulders. Rows of seven tables lined the floor, each surrounded by small, quiet faces. Mena estimated that nearly a hundred children were all sitting in perfect stillness as if awaiting something. How could so many parents send their children away, knowing the Axis's cruel demands? Sadness filled Mena's chest; she longed for her home, for something familiar. At the front of the room stood a woman in a crimson robe, her hands clasped in a prayer-like fashion. She did not look up when Mena entered, but the weight of her presence filled the room. Mena stood there, frozen for a moment, as her eyes scanned the sea of faces, young, innocent, yet bound by the same fate she had found herself trapped in.

"Good of you to finally join us." The woman clapped her hands, her voice carrying authority. "Children, this is Sister Kallemena. She is new here and will be joining you in your studies."

The children's voices rose in unison, a chorus of polite greetings, before they returned to their food. Mena's senses were bombarded by the rich aromas drifting through the air as she took a seat next to the quiet woman in the white robe. The scent of roasted pig, stewed vegetables, baked chickens, and fruit piled high on gleaming plates filled every corner of the church. It was so overwhelming that, for a moment, she forgot where she was. She forgot everything. Her hand moved instinctively, reaching for whatever was within her vicinity. She shoved bite after bite into her mouth, savoring the richness and juiciness. The food was like nothing she had tasted in so long: warm, satisfying, comforting. She could hardly remember the last time she had eaten anything this good, let alone allowed herself to enjoy it.

It was not until the room grew unnervingly silent that Mena realized something had changed. She froze, a chicken leg still clutched firmly in her hand. Her eyes darted around the room, and she found that everyone was looking at her. Her eyes widen. They were not looking at her, but something behind her. A chill ran down her spine as she slowly turned, the room's stillness pressing on her like a weight. Directly behind her chair stood the woman in the crimson robe, unmoving. Her gaze was mean, calculating. Before Mena could fully process what was happening, she felt a heavy hand land on her shoulder, the weight of it making her stiffen. The woman leaned down, her voice low and stern.

"I will forgive these actions this time, but in the future, I expect you to bow your head and say grace before you consume your food. Here we do not behave like animals."

Mena quickly set the food on her plate, her mind racing as the priestess straightened and turned to address the children.

"Is that not correct, children?" she asked with a grin that made Mena's skin crawl.

The children nodded, their voices coming together in perfect unison: "Yes, Priestess Calwyn."

Mena's stomach churned, the food in her mouth suddenly losing its taste. She glanced around at the children, their faces blank, their movements almost mechanical, as if they had been trained to speak and think as one. An unsettling quiet filled the room, and Mena realized that this place, this Axis, was not just about faith; it was about control. The priestess patted Mena's shoulder before returning to her seat. Her gaze never left Mena, a silent reminder to act with civility. Feeling the weight of her eyes on her, Mena swallowed the remaining food in her mouth and cleaned her fingers on the napkin provided. She bowed her head a moment, her mind blank to what she was supposed to say. She raised her head and then nodded in a subtle gesture of respect toward the woman in charge.

With a slight nod, the room returned to its quiet rhythm, the children continuing to eat without another word. But as the meal ended, Mena felt the familiar, unwelcome pulse of pressure in her temples. The headache throbbed relentlessly. She had been careful not to drink anything, yet somehow, the silvervane had found its way back into her bloodstream. Her gaze drifted around the room. Now scattered in groups, the children were writing or reading books, but none showed any signs of headaches like she was feeling. None seemed to suffer from the ache of the silvervane. Mena pretended not to notice the small girl watching her as she paced around the courtyard. The child's bright blonde curls were pulled back from her face, revealing a constellation of freckles scattered across her cheeks and a pair of wide, blue eyes. The girl smiled, revealing a missing front tooth, then gave a little wave. Mena's heart softened, a slight, bittersweet tug of her emotions. She walked over and sat beside the girl, offering a gentle smile in return.

"Hello," Mena said, the word carrying a weight she had not expected. Ashar's face flashed in her mind. "What is your name?"

The girl tilted her head, her voice sweet and innocent. "Poppy," she said, her smile widening as she said it.

"That is a lovely name, Poppy." Mena paused, wondering if she sounded friendly enough after her time on the ship. "Can you answer a few questions for me?"

Poppy hesitated, then shrugged. "I am not supposed to. Priestess Calwyn said not to talk to you, but I like you. And Sylvie says I should never lie. And I feel like not answering questions I know the answers to is kind of like lying," she added with a small frown, then brightened again. "So, yes. I will try."

Mena smiled, feeling a little more at ease. She tried not to appear too frightening. "How old are you?" she asked gently.

"I am ten," Poppy replied, holding up all her fingers with pride. "But I will be eleven in a few days!"

Mena's heart sank. She did not need to do the math to know that Poppy was not an Echo. The girl was too young, and no celestial event had occurred in over fifteen years. She looked around at the other children, her mind racing. If these children were not Echoes, then why were they here?

"You are very pretty. Are you a real princess?" Poppy's voice was soft, like a bird's song, and Mena blinked in surprise.

Mena nodded, though the word made her feel strange. "Yes, I am a princess," she said quietly. "But Poppy... why did you come here? I thought the Axis was only for Echoes."

Poppy's face lit up as she nodded. "It is. That is why we kids stay here, in the nursery," she explained, her small hand sweeping across the courtyard to include all the others. "We are the kids whose parents or siblings are Echoes. We do not have any other family to watch us. So, we stay here while they go and learn their teachings. My sister entered the Axis when I was just a year old, so in another couple of years, we can leave and go live in a big castle like you did." She tugged at a curl that had fallen in her face, clearly oblivious to the weight of Mena's questions.

In everything Myra had told her about the Axis, she never mentioned the children who were not gifted. Maybe Myra had not known. Mena watched the children mingle with their peers, wondering why they were here if they were not Echoes. If they were not gifted, why were they also being fed the silvervane? Or had it just been her?

"What do you do all day?" Mena asked, returning her attention to Poppy.

"Oh, we say our prayers every morning before breakfast. Then, we have history and math before lunch. After that, we study medicine, and then we have our last meal, the one you interrupted." Poppy smiled, her voice light.

"And now?" Mena glanced around. "Playtime?"

Poppy scrunched her face and shook her head. "The sisters do not like us to play. They say it is too childish, and we make too much noise. A person of the church should learn to be knowledgeable and helpful. Neither comes from play." Poppy smiled as if proud of herself for showing such wisdom. "Now we organize our notes and reread what we learned today."

Mena scooted closer to the girl, her heart softening. "Well, I love to play."

Poppy's eyes widened, and the disciplined ten-year-old smiled a mischievous grin. "What games do you know?"

Mena smiled and held her finger to her mouth, "You will see."

Mena took a deep breath, remembering the feeling from the ship, pushing past the poison that constrained her gift. She pushed past the barrier almost as if finding her way through a maze. She closed her eyes briefly, grounding herself, and then held out her hand. The pressure in her head pounded to the rhythm of her heartbeat, the silvervane's poison pulsing with intensity, but she fought through it. Slowly, a single butterfly appeared. Its silver wings shimmered in the setting sun, delicate and balanced on Mena's palm. Poppy gasped, her lips trembling as she fought to contain her excitement. Her eyes were wide, gleaming with wonder. She was utterly awestruck by what she had witnessed.

"You are one of them? An Echo like my sister?"

Then, she stood suddenly, blocking Mena from the other children, and placed her tiny hand gently on Mena's. Without warning, she snuffed out the butterfly. Her face fell, the joy fading as she looked at Mena with sad eyes.

"They would be terribly angry with you if they knew you could still do that with silvervane in your bloodstream," she said, her voice minor but severe. She clasped Mena's hand and gently pulled her to her feet. "The bunk under mine is vacant. You can sleep there tonight."

Mena's heart tightened as she followed Poppy, her thoughts swirling. She watched as the children formed neat lines and headed to their respective houses, boys in one, girls in the other. The evening routine was swift and efficient. The children cleaned their teeth, changed into thinner robes for the night, and climbed into their assigned bunks. Mena settled into the cramped bed beneath Poppy, but she was grateful it was not a cage. The children sang their prayers in quiet unison before falling asleep. Mena lay awake, her mind spinning with thoughts of the Ministry's layout, the buildings, the courtyards, and the sheer drop on the other side of the wall. Without the key the woman in white carried, escape seemed impossible. At least for tonight.

Chapter Fifteen

A wave crashed over Thaloren, stealing his breath. Instinctively, he inhaled and immediately regretted it as icy water surged into his lungs. He convulsed, coughing violently, his throat raw and burning by the time he managed to expel the liquid. Another wave struck, wrenching him from the plank of wood that had been his fragile sanctuary. When he resurfaced, gasping, he clawed at the water and hauled himself back onto the drifting board. Every limb felt heavy and sluggish, numb from the freezing current that now controlled his fate.

He scanned the wreckage around him, eyes stinging from salt and tears. Splintered wood bobbed on the surface like scattered leaves, and among the debris, bodies floated lifelessly. A sob rose in his chest, but he forced it down. Crying would waste precious strength he no longer possessed. His gaze turned skyward toward the moon. Its silver light, unyielding against the night, shone like a beacon for lost souls. *If only it could guide me to safety,* he thought bitterly. A distant cough shattered the silence. Thaloren's head snapped toward the sound, his hope rising. He squinted into the darkness, but the moonlight made it hard to tell driftwood from flesh.

"Hello?" he called, his voice cracked and hoarse. Pain rippled through his chest with every word. "Is anyone there?"

For a moment, there was nothing. Then, another splash, followed by more frantic coughing. He forced himself upright, his muscles trembling with the effort. A figure emerged in the distance, waving weakly as another wave dragged them under. Thaloren gritted his teeth and pushed off his board. Every movement was agony, but he plunged and pulled at the water with his arms, ignoring the icy numbness creeping through his body. He swam past barrels and jagged planks, his fingers brushing the cold, lifeless forms of sailors as he searched for the voice. When he found a wide piece of wood, likely torn from the deck, he latched onto it and pushed it along with him. He checked each body he passed for signs of life, his heart sinking deeper each time. Finally, he reached her.

The woman clung desperately to a narrow plank, her left arm limp at her side. Her dark blue tunic was shredded, and the remaining glass from her shattered armor glittered in the moonlight. A deep gash ran down her bicep to her forearm, oozing blood into the water, and her face and neck were marred with burns. She gasped for air between waves, her strength fading. Thaloren pushed the larger piece of wood under her and heaved her onto it, his own strength waning. She trembled violently; her lips were blue, and her body pale from blood loss.

"We will die if I cannot find help," he muttered under his breath, desperation creeping into his voice. "Have you seen any others?" his hope diminishing as he scanned the carnage. "Healer Myra?"

The woman did not respond. Her eyes were half-closed, and her breathing grew shallow. Thaloren swallowed hard. Images of his aunt standing beside Ashar on the ship's bow burned in his mind. He clenched his fists, begging his despair not to take hold.

"Please, Gods," he prayed, his voice breaking. "Please let them be alive."

A wave struck him from the side, knocking him against the makeshift raft. Saltwater filled his mouth as he screamed his daughter's name, his voice drowned by the roar of the sea. When Thaloren surfaced once more, gasping for air, he found himself staring into the face of the woman. Her sunken eyes brimmed with tears that carved clean trails down her soot-streaked cheeks. Her body trembled violently, her head swaying side to side as shock took hold. She tried to speak, her lips quivering, but her words came out in broken fragments.

"Healer Myra... she did something," the woman stuttered, her voice weak and halting. "I went below... with them. We were looking for the princess. The prince... he found her. But it was not her, just a trick. Then... then the floor opened beneath him. He fell. I saw snow, and then... nothing." Her haunted gaze locked onto Thaloren, and his chest tightened.

Myra opened a portal; relief swelled within him. *She saved the prince.* The memory of his last moments aboard the ship crashed over him. His heart clenched as he recalled the sight of his friend, King Durnovas, the mast splintering through his chest, his dying words etched into Thaloren's soul: *Save them.* A deep shudder wracked Thaloren's body. Tears spilled freely down his face, their warmth quickly stolen by the icy wind. Myra had spared Prince Ashar from their fate. The thought brought a fragile hope, though it did little to ease the weight crushing his spirit.

"If the prince escaped, then he will come to our rescue," Thaloren said, his voice trembling but resolute.

He turned to the woman, his words meant to comfort her, though he was not sure he believed them himself. She gave no reply, her trembling only worsening as the waves rocked their makeshift raft. They drifted in silence, the sea's relentless rhythm lulling them into a painful slumber. Thaloren repeatedly woke, each time choking on seawater as another wave crashed over him. He checked on the woman each time, her condition deteriorating before his eyes. On the final time he stirred, she was gone, washed away and claimed by the cold waters. A hollow ache settled in his chest as shame gripped him. He had not even asked for her name. The woman who had, if only briefly, soothed his fears with news that Ashar had escaped, and Mena had never been there at all. Anger bubbled in his gut, flaring to life at the memory of the priest's mocking voice, taunting him with promises to "look after" Mena. Her face flashed in his mind, a flicker of hope, now poisoned by dread. The thought of that viper having her, twisting her fate, drove him to the edge of madness. The fury drained what little strength he had left. Slumping against the raft, he stared at the faint glow on the horizon. His breath came in shallow rasps, the effort of living pulling him toward his final moments.

"At least I will see the sun one last time," he mumbled, his voice barely audible over the whisper of the waves.

His eyes fluttered shut, heavy with exhaustion. But the sun did not rise. Time blurred, the glow on the horizon growing steadily brighter each time he wrestled himself back from unconsciousness. It was not the sun; it was something else.

"There! The King!"

A wonderful and familiar voice cut through the haze, echoing across the water. Thaloren stirred weakly, the world around him eerily still. The waves had calmed, the surface of the sea now smooth as glass. Voices surrounded him, calling his name, their urgency pulling him from the brink.

"Thaloren!"

The king recognized his wife's voice, faint but unmistakable. Relief swept over him, his attempt at a smile collapsing into sobs. He wept openly, overwhelmed by the blessing that he would see her face one last time before the end. The water around him grew warm, its icy grip fading as small, glowing orbs surrounded him, casting a gentle light on the darkened sea. The waves beneath him shifted, lifting him higher and higher until he was placed gently onto the stiff boards of a ship's deck. Warm blankets were draped over his shivering frame, their weight grounding him as the glow dimmed.

"We found you, my love! By the Gods, we found you!" Nyssira's voice cracked with emotion as she fell to her knees beside him, her hands trembling as she stroked the wet hair from his face.

She clung to his hand, her grip firm and desperate, as though afraid he might vanish again. Thaloren looked up at her through tear-filled eyes, his voice breaking as he asked, "Have you... found any other survivors? Myra?" His words were fragile, barely audible over the quiet lapping of waves.

"No, my Lord," a guard called from the edge of the ship, scanning the wreckage-strewn waters. At the bow, Ashar stood tall, his hands outstretched. Thousands of his glowing orbs floated over the sea, casting a warm, orange light that illuminated the wreckage. A sea of broken wood, charred remnants, and lifeless forms.

"There!" a crewman shouted, his voice tinged with hope before falling to a mournful whisper. "It is healer Myra…"

Silence gripped the deck as Kivani stepped forward. Her hands moved through the air with smooth, deliberate gestures, and the water obeyed her command. Another column of liquid rose from the sea, bearing a figure with solemn care. The crew watched as Myra's lifeless body was laid gently on the deck. Thaloren's blurred gaze shifted to her. Her once-flowing white hair had been burned to ash, her skin blackened and blistered from the explosions. The pale blue eyes he had known so well were now gray and unseeing. His body trembled as he clenched his fists. He wanted to scream, to curse the gods, and lash out at the High Priest and anyone else responsible. But all he could do was cry. His strength had abandoned him, leaving him a hollow shell consumed by grief. Nyssira cradled her husband in her lap, her tears mingling with his. Their shared sorrow filled the air, drawing quiet sobs from the crew. Even the hardened sailors could not hold back tears for the woman who had cared for them all, who had known the cure for every ailment of the body and heart. Myra's loss would ripple through Glacia like an unending storm.

Ashar approached cautiously, his exhaustion evident in every step. His face was pale, the strain of maintaining his light weighing heavily on him. He stopped a few paces from Thaloren, his voice small and trembling as though the words themselves might break him.

"My father?" he asked, the question carrying the innocence of a child seeking reassurance. "Did you…see him?"

Thaloren squeezed his eyes shut as though the darkness behind his lids could shield him from the truth. The weight of his failure bore down on him, heavier than the sea. So much loss. And for what? Kallemena had never been on that ship. It had all been for nothing, a trap he had led them into. When he opened his eyes, they met Ashar's. The boy who had asked the question was gone, replaced by a man forced too soon into kingship. Thaloren's voice faltered, his words heavy with guilt and sorrow.

"I did," he whispered. "Before the last explosion. He... he ordered me to save you. To save Mena. But I failed." Thaloren admitted, the words crushing his spirits further. His gaze dropped to the deck, unable to meet the weight of Ashar's grief.

"You have my sincerest condolences, Ashar." Thaloren swallowed the anguish, tightening his throat. "He was hurt badly. He went down with one of the ships."

Ashar crumpled to his knees. His face twisted, an anguished blend of grief and rage as he pushed his palms into his eyes, his muscles straining with the desperate, impossible wish to reverse time. Stars danced in his vision as heat radiated from his skin, his body glowing with a fiery hue. The scent of scorched wood filled the air, and the shimmering light on his skin flickered like the embers of an open flame.

"Ashar, ya need to settle ya fire, now!" Kivani shouted, her hands carefully guiding another lifeless body onto the deck.

But her words could not reach him. Ashar's mind was quickly spiraling, anguish flooding his thoughts. Mena was gone. His father was gone. Myra, the one who had saved him from the same fate as everyone else, was gone. He was utterly alone in a world far more cruel than he ever believed. Images flashed through his mind. The ransacked room. Vallorith's portal shrinking before his eyes. The guilt of not running to her faster fueled his remorse. The harsh knowledge that the monster had impersonated him to infiltrate her sanctuary, a place that was supposed to be safe. His father's face came next, etched with determination as he vowed to find the princess. The last embrace they had shared, the memory was now shattered by the brutal truth. And then Kallemena. Her face burned in his mind. The softness of her voice, the wonder in her eyes. The warmth she had brought to his life. The truth struck him like a dagger: he loved her.

Kallemena, the girl he had only just met. The woman he had talked with for hours and shared in laughter with. The person who made his cheeks flush red and his heart skip beats. Then the hideous priest intruded into his memories, tainting their preciousness. The monster that had stripped him of his happiness. Vallorith had taken her away, taken his father away, taken countless people from their families, people who did not need to die. His chest heaved as his misery ignited, fury exploding from him in a violent surge of flame. The inferno lashed out, seeking to consume everything in its path. Flames stretched hungrily toward the ship and its crew, their heat filling the air. Before the fire could reach the others, a wave of water crashed over him. Steam erupted in a hiss as the water boiled and vaporized on contact with his searing skin. Kivani held her ground, her hands commanding a steady stream until Ashar's fiery glow dimmed and his body returned to normal.

"Yuh almost gone and hurt everybody!" Her voice rang out like a mother scolding her child.

She stormed over to him, hauling him to his feet, her grip firm, his body limp. She expected defiance, a stubborn glare, a snapped retort. Instead, she found a broken man. Ashar's knees buckled, and he collapsed onto the deck, his cries wrenching at her heart. Kivani's expression softened. She knelt beside him, rubbing his back in soothing circles as he wept.

"Wi going to get her back, Ashar," she said gently. "And wi going to avenge yuh fatha too."

Oren stepped forward, his armor glinting faintly in the moonlight, its glassy surface a deep blue. "Turn us around and head for Glacia. We need to summon the council immediately." His voice was steady, commanding. He glanced at Ashar, his tone softening. "And the new King must be crowned."

***

Thaloren awoke in his bed, the familiar softness of the sheets a stark contrast to the sharp pain radiating through his body. He tried to sit up, but agony shot from his back through his ribs, and his legs felt as heavy as stone.

"Do not move," Nyssira's voice came, calm and steady. She sat beside him, her hand resting lightly on his arm. "The healer says you must stay still for the next few days. Orentheon is arranging the council meeting, and Kivani is tending to the soldiers' burials and their families."

Thaloren closed his eyes, haunted by the faces of those lost. Brothers, sisters, mothers, fathers, so many lives cut short. He vowed to grieve for each one and to do what he could for their families once he was strong enough. For now, there was a priest to capture. He threw back the sheets, intent on rising, but froze. His breath caught in his throat as his gaze fell to his legs or what was left of them. Bandaged stumps were all that remained, one leg ending just past the ankle, the other nearly gone entirely. Nyssira quickly grasped his hand, squeezing it tightly.

"We will work through this," she said, her voice soothing, though doubt lingered in her tone. "We will find a way to heal you."

Thaloren stared, his stomach twisting violently. He felt as though the world were spinning beneath him. The damage was too severe; he knew no healer or magic that could regrow bone and flesh that had been so extensively destroyed. Swallowing his rising panic, he cleared his throat and forced himself upright. The pain flared, but he gritted his teeth against it.

"Have a guard fetch the best inventors from the village," his voice firm despite the tremor in his hands. "I will stand again."

***

Ashar paced through the snow-covered gardens, his thoughts drowning in memories of Mena. Images of her laughter, her smile, and the way she used to tease him tugged at his heart, making him yearn for the days before heartache consumed their lives. It had been eight days since she was taken, eight long days since he had seen the terror etched on her face. In those eight days, it felt like so much had happened. The call for healers across the continent went out for the king's injuries. The news of the princess's kidnapping broke the hearts of the citizens, and the rumors of Echoes in the royal family tested their loyalty. They had buried Myra. A cedar tree was planted where her body lay so that her sacrifice could produce new life. Her body had been wrapped in soft cotton and silken ribbons, a burial fit for someone of the highest importance. Yet, her pale blue eyes haunted him, staring back from the recesses of his mind. *The reflections are not the end.* What had Myra meant by that? Her words echoed endlessly, offering neither clarity nor comfort.

"Ashar?"

The prince turned at the sound of Oren's voice. The tall man approached along the frosted pathways, his white braid swaying gently against his back. Oren's eyes were shadowed, dark crescents marring his pale skin, a visible weight from the burdens he had taken on since their return. He had assumed full responsibility for Glacia's kingdom while his father was in recovery, an immense task Ashar knew he would face himself once he returned to his own home. Ashar's thoughts shifted briefly to his father. His chest tightened as he remembered the king's body, lost to the unforgiving depths of the sea.

"Kivani said you should eat something before you leave." Oren rubbed the back of his neck. "Though between you and me, I do not think anyone has the stomach for food right now or ever."

A long pause stretched between them, the weight of shared grief settling in the silence. Oren seemed grateful for the quiet, Ashar thought. He had been working tirelessly since their return, and Ashar doubted the man had found even a moment of peace.

"Tell her thank you for the concern," Ashar said at last, his voice steady. "But I will eat when I get home."

The silence lingered before Oren stepped closer, pulling Ashar into a tight embrace. The prince released a faint gasp, caught off guard by the sudden gesture, before returning it. Oren held him like a brother, and Ashar felt a small spark of solace for the first time in days. He had lost his entire family, but in Oren, he found a bond strong enough to anchor him in this storm of grief. As they pulled apart, Ashar quickly wiped a tear from his eye.

"I will burn that man down until he is nothing but a pile of ash," he said, his voice trembling with anger. He felt childish and immature, but the rage was all he had left to hold on to.

Oren gripped Ashar's arms tightly, his dark eyes fierce. "And I will be by your side when you do."

***

The next day, Ashar set sail for Kalyra. He waved goodbye to Oren and Kivani as his remaining two ships pulled away from the ice-covered fjord. The sea was bitterly cold and choppy, but the further away the sails carried them from Glacia, the calmer the waters became, as if nature itself sought to ease their journey. Weeks passed in what felt like a blur. They docked briefly at ports in Thalasson and Aetheria. Messengers were dispatched at each stop to spread the news of what had transpired in the waters surrounding the Glacia continent. Reports of the high priest's treachery, the kidnapping of the princess, and the death of Kalyra's king and more than fifty good men and women began to ripple across the continents. Yet, Ashar grew increasingly frustrated by the people's reactions in these foreign lands. Instead of condemning Vallorith, many seemed more concerned with the actions of the king and queen of Glacia.

"Is it not against the law?" a man muttered. "To have an Echo in a royal family? In any family?"

"Sounds like the priest did his duty," a woman chimed in. "The princess should have been sent to Verdathos years ago."

Each comment stoked Ashar's impatience, his anger growing with every dismissive remark. Their focus on ancient prejudices instead of Vallorith's crimes enraged him. When his ships finally docked near Highspire, Ashar was relieved to find that the news had reached his homeland before he had. It had traveled faster than the waves, sparing him the painful task of explaining his father's sudden death to his people. As he rode on horseback through the town, he was met with bowed heads and solemn condolences. Black flags hung from every lamppost and window, fluttering mournfully in the cold breeze. The people wore black ribbons or scarves, small tokens of their sorrow for the loss of their king. For the first time in weeks, Ashar felt the weight of his grief shift. These were *his* people, and they shared his pain. He clenched the reins tightly, a new resolve forming within him. Vallorith would pay for his crimes, not just for Ashar's family, but for everyone who had suffered under his treachery. For every family who was forced to send their child away to a strange land under the priest's control.

Once welcomed home, Ashar was promptly thrust into the mayhem of court. Discussions of his coronation consumed the room, the council eager to see him crowned immediately. But Ashar demanded they wait. First, there would be a funeral for the late king and all who sacrificed their lives on the icy sea. In the dining hall, he was encouraged to eat. A feast sprawled across the long table, enough to serve twenty if he so desired. The sight of it turned his stomach. He leaned back in his chair, his gaze fixed on the head of the table where his father should have been seated.

"People should be less worried about her being an Echo of royal blood," Ashar growled, his voice shaking with restrained fury, "and more concerned with the fact that a man of the Church *killed my father!*"

He hurled his glass across the table, the pieces breaking and sliding in all directions. Sticky cider pooled on the gleaming surface, its sweet scent turning Ashar's stomach. Servants hurried to clean the mess, their movements quick and practiced. Ashar shoved his chair back and stormed from the room, the smell of roasted meat and spices clinging to his clothes, suffocating him. The halls of Highspire offered little solace. Unlike the gleaming glass castle of Iskaroth, the castle here was built of pale gray stone, its ceilings towering as high as three stories. Every surface was adorned with the legacy of his lineage, portraits of his ancestors, their stern faces watching him with what felt like silent judgment.

The floors were rich, polished wood, and runners muffled the heavy thuds of his boots. He turned down a familiar hallway that led to the gardens, seeking refuge in their quiet beauty. The hedges were neatly trimmed, their greenery reaching the height of his shoulders. The once bright and fragrant blossoms of flowers were now gone, the bushes preparing for the coming winter. Birds sang out as they announced the prince's presence, and squirrels darted across the walkways with seeds packed in their cheeks. At the center of the gardens stood a stone pond. Lily pads floated lazily on its surface, their edges kissed by sunlight, while frogs rested on the rocks, silencing their rhythmic croaks as Ashar approached. His thoughts drifted to Mena. How would she react to his home? He imagined her marveling at the warmer springs and even warmer summers. He could almost see her leaning over the pond, her reflection mirrored in its dark depths, smiling as tadpoles darted below the surface. He longed for her presence, laughter, and hand to rest cold yet comforting in his. He pictured her walking by his side, her scent of fresh snow and starlight filling the air around them.

"My lord." The voice shattered his daydream.

"What?" Ashar snapped, turning sharply, his irritation evident.

The footman flinched, shrinking slightly as he held out a pewter tray with a small, sealed envelope centered on it.

"I-I am sorry to disturb you, my lord," the man stammered. "This has just come for you."

Ashar straightened his vest, feeling rude for his sharp tone. "Thank you."

The servant bowed quickly and hurried away, his eagerness to retreat evident. Ashar turned the envelope over in his hands, his teeth gritting as he recognized the seal. The mark of the Axis was frozen in crimson wax. His instincts screamed to destroy it, to let the letter burn and crumble to ash in his grasp. But the hope that it might hold some information about Mena stayed his hand. He drew a deep breath, forced himself to smother the rage burning within, and went to the study. The halls of the castle were dim, heavy curtains drawn tightly to shroud the interior in darkness. Black flags adorned the premises, the kingdom draped in mourning for its fallen king. Highspire grieved alongside him. His father, King Kaelith Durnovas of the continent Kalyra, had been a brave hero who had led his people through countless battles, holding the Scorvaan desert's threats at bay and ensuring the kingdom's safety. Now, his absence echoed through every corner of the castle.

Ashar paused in the hall, his steps faltering as his eyes found a familiar painting. It was one of his favorites, depicting his parents in a moment of joy. His father stood proudly, his mother's hands resting lovingly on her swollen belly. Her smile radiated warmth, her gaze full of hope. They looked as though they were meant to rule together for an eternity. Ashar stared at the painting, his heart tightening. His father's legacy loomed heavy over him, but it was not just the weight of a crown he felt; it was the emptiness of loss. He let his fingers brush the edge of the frame before turning away. The letter in his hand demanded his attention, but his thoughts remained tethered to the past.

"Not long enough," Ashar whispered, his voice low as he started down the hall again.

Two guards stood stationed outside the study, their silver breastplates adorned with black sashes in mourning. They bowed their heads in respect as they opened the heavy door for their prince. Inside, the warm glow of an oil lamp illuminated a mountain of papers and scrolls stacked with meticulous care on the black wooden desk. The air was thick with the scents of pipe tobacco and ink, a heady combination that stirred memories Ashar was not ready to confront. He cleared his throat, suppressing the flood of emotions, and made his way to the massive high-backed chair behind the desk. Sitting down, he immediately felt out of place. Though he was of sturdy build, with stout arms and legs honed from years of training, the chair dwarfed him. In his mind, it still belonged to his father, a throne of sorts, imbued with a presence he could never fill. He felt like a child playing dress-up, pretending to wield authority he did not yet own. The sudden sensation felt too constricting.

He shot to his feet and crossed to one of the two other guest chairs on the other side of the desk. It felt better, smaller, less grand, more grounded. Unfolding the letter with care, he began to read. The first two lines made his blood boil.

"My sincerest condolences on the loss of your father, the great King Durnovas. I do hope the family is doing well."

Ashar scoffed, the sound bitter in the quiet room. *Family?* Vallorith knew damn well there was no family left. The words were a taunt, a calculated barb meant to remind him of all he had lost. His fists clenched, heat flickering at his fingertips, but he forced himself to breathe, to focus. Letting Vallorith goad him would not bring him any closer to justice. He read on.

"I am calling a meeting of the council to hold the continents of Kalyra and Glacia accountable for their joint deception. The accused will stand before the council and plead their cases for why the Axis was never informed of a royal Echo housed among the royal family in Iskaroth. We will convene on the continent of Nocthrea. I do hope you bring a <u>burning</u> desire for politics.

Well wishes,
High Priest Vallorith of the Axis."

Ashar's breath hitched as he reread the letter, his eyes narrowing at the underlined word *burning*. Twice emphasized, it was not a coincidence. His mind raced. Could Vallorith know he was an Echo? The thought sent a chill down his spine, quickly chased by the memory of that fateful night. *Mena.* She had let Vallorith into her room, believing him to be Ashar. Had she said something, anything, that could have tipped him off? Ashar shook his head, reading the letter once more, his pulse pounding in his ears.

"If the other continents received similar letters, they would surely stop trade with Glacia and Kalyra before this meeting." The sharp and sudden realization slipped from his lips, sending a jolt through him.

"No," a cold fear dawned within him. He turned abruptly, his voice ringing through the halls. "Guards!"

The two men hurried into the room, their boots thudding softly against the wood. Ashar quickly grabbed a sheet of parchment, his pen moving in swift, forceful strokes as he jotted down a message.

"Send this to the kingdom of Iskaroth," he instructed, folding the note and sealing it with wax. "For Prince Orentheon and Princess Kivani."

One of the guards took the letter with a curt bow and hurried off. Ashar's eyes lingered momentarily on the door before he returned to the desk. In the dim, quiet study, his thoughts swirled in chaotic circles. The pieces of a larger puzzle were coming into view. News of the royal Echo would now reach the other rulers badly, and it seemed Vallorith was twisting the narrative to paint himself in the right. If the council agreed to no longer hold treaties with the two accused continents, it would open the gates for a war. Ashar clenched his fists, his anger igniting in his veins. The heat surged, and flames danced to life in his palms, their blue light casting eerie shadows on the walls. The fire burned hot and bright, its intensity warping the air around him. The floor beneath him groaned and popped, the wood straining under the temperature change, but Ashar welcomed the destruction. The flames reflected his fury, his grief, his need for vengeance. If Vallorith thought he could manipulate the world to suit his schemes, he would soon learn otherwise. Ashar would be ready. He would wield his power not just for justice but for the singular purpose it demanded: To destroy.

Chapter Sixteen

It had been a year since Mena had been brought to the Axis. Months spent gazing out to the sea, hoping to glimpse white sails with dark blue flags fluttering on their masts. Every passing day deepened her fear that she would never see her family again, never hear her mother's gentle voice, feel her father's arms around her, laugh with her brother, or embrace Kivani's warmth. And worst of all, she might never look into Ashar's comforting eyes again, the ones that had once set her heart aflutter. With a quiet sigh, Mena tugged a comb through Poppy's golden curls. The small child hummed softly to herself, swaying slightly as Mena separated and braided the strands with practiced care. Poppy had become her constant companion, a bright spot in an otherwise bleak existence. Though she missed her home and family with an ache that never truly dulled, Mena had carved out a place for herself within the intricate machinery that was the Axis. She had learned its rhythms, becoming a seamless part of the sanctuary's operations. Even as her heart longed for the familiar shores of her homeland, she had found some happiness in this strange place.

In moments of stolen quiet, she shared small glimpses of her gift with Poppy, tiny traces of the power that remained within her, unyielding even under the suppressive weight of the silvervane. Nights were spent in the bottom bunk beneath Poppy's bed, the wood creaking under every toss and turn. Each morning, she stretched and relished the satisfying pop of her spine, a fleeting comfort in the endless monotony of her days. Still, Mena's curiosity refused to be silenced. She had poured herself into the study of the Axis, uncovering truths that felt at odds with the stories she had read back home. The Axis, she learned, was not originally a bastion of control or a tool for kings. Her understanding had been that the Axis was created centuries ago by a Darra, whose immense power had raised its walls and forged the golden seals that now loomed over its halls. It had been meant as a sanctuary for young Echoes, a place where they could hone their abilities and live without fear of persecution.

But that was not the whole story. The sanctuary, as Mena came to learn, was built at the behest of the goddess Danira herself. She had envisioned a haven where peace and harmony thrived, a refuge for all beings to heal and flourish. Echoes were meant to mend the damage wrought by the other gods' endless warring, their abilities a gift to restore balance and beauty to the world. Somewhere along the timeline, that vision had been corrupted. What had once been a sacred sanctuary became the Axis, a cold, calculating institution repurposed to serve the ambitions of monarchs. Echoes were sent not to thrive but to be shaped into tools, their will and choices stripped away to better suit the needs of rulers. The weight of this revelation sat heavily on Mena's mind. She exhaled in frustration, her thoughts spiraling once more into the same endless question: how had the purpose of the Axis strayed so far from its origins? And could it ever be restored?

"Time for class, girls." Sister Tressa, the woman who had first escorted Mena to the nursery, appeared in the doorway.

The girls quickly tied their hair and gathered their books, forming two tidy rows before filing out toward the church. Mena followed behind, her steps hesitant at the stare of sister Tressa, until she realized she was not meant to join them. At the end of the line, Poppy turned back with wide, questioning blue eyes before hurrying to catch up with the others.

"The High Priest has requested that you finally join the other Echoes in the sanctuary to learn a trade," Sister Tressa instructed, her voice calm but firm. "He is pleased with your progress and satisfied that your manners have greatly improved since you first joined us."

Mena thought back to months ago when all she did was attempt escapes and refuse to eat. Mena's heart sank, her gaze trailing after the children as they disappeared into the church. Poppy's small face lingered in her mind, her innocent eyes full of trust. Sadness washed over her, quickly followed by a creeping fear. Being sent to the sanctuary meant being molded into an Axis disciple. Being stripped of what made Mena herself. It also meant being closer to Vallorith.

"But surely there is more I can learn here," she stammered, desperate to stall. "I have only been here for four seasons. The children still know far more than I do about the gods and prayers. Tell him to ask priestess Calwyn; she will confirm my inadequacy."

"It was at her confirmation that Vallorith decided on the move. Besides, you will learn more with the other Echoes who share your abilities," Sister Tressa replied, her face impassive, like stone. "I am to escort you to the common room now, where you will meet your brothers and sisters before class."

"Can I say goodbye to the children first? They have all become like family to me." Mena turned toward the church, but Tressa's hand clamped firmly around her arm.

"We have to go now," the sister said, her tone unyielding. "Time is short already."

Mena froze, confused by the cryptic words, but nodded silently. Her heart felt heavy as she let Tressa lead her away. They approached the thick brown door, the clicking of locks should have brought relief, a signal of progress, but instead, it filled her with dread. What lay beyond the door? What would the other Echoes think of her? What would Poppy think when Mena did not meet her for lunch or braid her hair at night? An ache grew in her chest as she stepped over the threshold into a spiraling stone staircase. The door locked behind them with a heavy clang, and Tressa descended quickly, Mena following close behind. The rapid, dizzying descent seemed endless until, suddenly, Tressa stopped. The older woman's face was flushed as she turned and pressed a hand firmly over Mena's mouth. Tressa held a finger to her lips, and Mena nodded, her heart pounding. Her silence was imperative. Tressa then reached into her robe and pulled out a small piece of parchment, pressing it into Mena's hand. It was the tiniest map she had ever seen, walls and twisting corridors crammed onto a space no larger than her palm. Mena looked up, confusion and alarm flickering in her eyes, but Tressa turned and continued downward without a word. When they finally reached the bottom, Tressa paused at the edge of a long, black-stone hallway. A figure in a white robe had just rounded a corner, disappearing from sight. Only then did Tressa speak.

"Things are happening. I am not privy to every detail, but the continents are all in a tiff." Tressa glanced down the hall, relief flickering across her face when she saw it was still empty. "We do not have much time."

She turned back to Mena, her voice dropping into a hurried whisper. "No questions. You listen."

Mena nodded, her heart hammering so loudly it felt like her ears were submerged in water from the pressure.

"The High Priest has called a meeting with the council to occur in a month. There is a rumor that he is planning to banish Glacia and Kalyra from the treaty. He is begging for war. What purpose it serves him, I do not know."

Without waiting for a response, Tressa grabbed Mena's arm and led her swiftly down the hall. As they turned a corner, the rhythmic march of countless footsteps echoed off the onyx stone. Tressa veered sharply into another narrower and dimmer hallway that seemed to lead outside. For a fleeting moment, Mena's gaze fixed on the door at the end of the hall, greenery waving beyond its windows. How she longed to burst through it, conjure a ship, and sail far from this place. But the weight of the silvervane in her system crushed that dream before it could take flight. Even if she tried, she would not make it far. She did not know how to navigate home nor how to survive without supplies. What if her gift failed her? The thought stung her eyes with unshed tears, and she quickly blinked them away.

"Your brother and the new king of Highspire will attend the council meeting to plead their case," Tressa continued. "If it does not go in their favor, your home will likely be one of the first to fall."

Mena's steps faltered. "Wait, the *new* king? What happened to the old king? King Durnovas?"

Tressa's jaw tightened in irritation. "I said no questions."

"Please." Mena's voice cracked, desperation bleeding into her words. "And why Orentheon? Why not have the king, my father, go?"

Tressa hesitated, glancing nervously over her shoulder before answering in a hurried, hushed tone. "There was an accident after you were taken. Your father and King Durnovas set sail after you but were ambushed. I do not know all the details, but the kings died. It is said that your brother now rules over Glacia."

The air seemed to leave Mena's lungs. "No..." Her voice was barely above a whisper as she stared at Tressa in disbelief. Her father? King Durnovas? Both dead? Her thoughts spun wildly, crashing into the stark realization that Ashar was alone now. Tears welled in her eyes, spilling over and streaking her cheeks. Everything was unraveling, all because of her. Her refusal to leave her family, her defiance of the law, and her resistance to coming to the Axis when she was of age had all set this chain of events into motion. The morning bells chimed, their sound hollow in the tense silence. Tressa's face tightened with visible distress.

"We are late. He will know we stopped." Tressa's grip on Mena's arm tightened as they picked up their pace, nearly breaking into a run. "When he leaves Verdathos, that will be your time to escape. They put silvervane in the bread and water served at different times throughout the week. You will have to figure that one out."

Tressa's words fell on deaf ears as they made their way through the halls. They stopped at the base of the stairs, both panting from the hurried pace.

"Did you say escape?" Mena rasped, her lungs sore from the effort of keeping up. "How am I to do that? And why are you telling me all of this?"

Tressa did not answer. At the top of the stairs, the heavy creak of doors opening boomed through the air, followed by a voice that froze Mena where she stood.

"Well, I suppose late is better than not at all. Sister Tressa, I believed you to be a punctual woman. Am I now mistaken?"

Vallorith stood at the top of the stairs, his presence oppressive. His brow arched as he took in the sight of the two women. A slow, cruel smile curled his lips when he saw the tear stains on Mena's face.

Tressa straightened, clearing her throat. "My apologies, High Priest. She was unwilling to leave without saying goodbye to the children. It distressed her greatly, my lord, and she resisted."

Mena shot Tressa a sharp look, but the older woman remained composed.

"Yes, well," Vallorith drawled, his tone deceptively light, "you are here now, and that is all that matters." He snapped his fingers and turned, his voice taking on an imperious edge. "Do come along. You will be late for class."

"You are not the only one from Glacia," Tressa said, placing her hand on Mena's back and giving a subtle push. Then, as she turned to leave, she brought a finger to her lips in a silent plea for discretion. As she walked away, Mena took in her appearance, now seeing something she should have spotted ages ago. Tressa was not old enough for a head full of white hair; she realized the woman was Glacian as well.

Mena hesitated, her stomach churning. Every instinct told her to flee, but she knew there was nowhere to go. With heavy reluctance, she climbed the stairs, step by agonizing step, until she crossed the threshold of the looming doors. Beyond them was a massive library, its walls lined with endless rows of bookshelves that stretched toward a glass ceiling. The clouds outside were thick, smothering what little sunlight might have entered. Vallorith stood in the center of the room, his dark presence a stone in the otherwise airy feel of the library. With a wave of his hand, the scene transformed. The library dissolved, replaced by the icy gardens of Iskaroth. The sudden shift was so vivid that Mena's discomfort abandoned her. The familiar scent of frost and the sharp bite of cold seeped into her senses, easing her tense muscles for a fleeting moment.

"We could go anywhere, you and I." Vallorith's voice broke the spell.

Mena turned, her gaze darting across the garden. For a heartbeat, the sight of the glass statues and hardy shrubs brought a pang of longing, but the feeling quickly soured. This was not her home; it was a cruel illusion. A joke on her emotions.

"I could take you anywhere," Vallorith continued, stepping closer, his tone almost coaxing. "Show you any continent, any world, in an instant." He waved his hand again, and they were now somewhere new. A long sandy beach wash boarded the waves as gulls called overhead. Mena felt the hot sun on her clothes and hair. The smell of the salty sea and fish in the breeze. "Or here." Another wave of his hand gave way to tall trees and soft grass. A canopy of leaves blocked out the sun, and in the distance, a castle sat nestled beneath a mountain. "The kingdom of Highspire."

"Ashar." She whispered as the image faded. Her heart thundered in her chest as she clenched her fists, willing her power to rise. Pain flared behind her eyes, her head pounding in protest as the poison coursing through her veins fought to keep her magic at bay.

"I can feel you are trying," Vallorith said, his amusement evident. "You are indeed strong. I dare say even my equal." They now sat in the frosty glass gardens once more. Vallorith appeared before her as he offered an outstretched hand. "Let me show you what you can become."

Mena batted Vallorith's hand away and reached for her powers again. She felt the magic weaving through her veins, sluggish from the herbal shackles in her veins. Desperation clawed at her mind as she conjured the only thing she could think of. The world around them darkened. Shadows consumed the light, enveloping them in a void where nothing existed, no sound, no warmth, no presence but her own. She could hide here. If she could keep her focus, she could block out everything: the axis, her pain, the time lost with her loved ones.

"Very good," Vallorith hissed, his voice slicing through the silence like a serpent's strike.

Mena's heart broke as she felt her void unraveling. The threads she had struggled to weave began to fray, the edges of her sanctuary tearing apart. And then, with a deafening explosion, it was gone. The world shifted violently. She blinked, disoriented, and found herself standing on the deck of a ship.

"Find my daughter!" Thaloren's voice echoed from nowhere.

Mena spun around, her breath quick as she spotted Myra and Ashar rushing below deck. Relief surged through her, and she ran to meet them, but metal bars materialized around her before she could reach them. The cold steel pressed against her hands as she gripped the cage door, pulling with all her might. It did not budge. Panic rose in her chest as explosions rocked the ship. Screams tore through the air, chilling her to the bone. Tears blurred her vision as she watched while guards in Glacian and Kalyran armor were thrown into the sea by the blasts.

"No!" she screamed, her voice cracking as she saw her father emerge from below deck. Their eyes met, his filled with sorrow and regret.

Then, another explosion shattered the world. Darkness swallowed her again. Vallorith's laughter echoed through the void, a cruel melody that pierced her very soul. Rage bubbled up within her, molten and volatile. She wanted to scream, to lash out, to make him suffer as she had. As her family had. As King Durnovas and Ashar had. The pressure built in her chest, searing and unbearable. It surged through her veins, demanding release. And then it came. Flames erupted around her, brilliant white and blue, burning hotter than anything she had ever imagined. The darkness melted away, revealing the library once more. The fire blazed in a ring around her, and Vallorith stood within its perimeter, unflinching. She collapsed to the ground, sweat dripping from her brow, her breaths shallow and ragged.

"I think I almost felt some heat with that one," Vallorith mused, stepping closer and crouching beside her. His voice was a low whisper in her ear. "I could teach you to burn with that desire of yours. Together, we could take your hate for me and forge it into something unstoppable. You could be the strongest Darra ever to wield such a gift. Well, strongest after me."

"Get away from me!" Mena hissed between labored breaths. "I would never learn anything from you."

Vallorith stood, his smile sharp as a blade. "Oh, my dear princess, you already have."

He gestured to a door on the far side of the library. "Classes are through there. Priestess Liona does not tolerate tardiness."

With a parting wave, he disappeared, leaving Mena alone in the suffocating silence of the library. Her limbs trembled as she pushed herself to her feet. Sweat soaked through her robes, her body heavy and weak. She stumbled to the door, her hands shaking as she fumbled with the handle. The room beyond felt impossibly far away, her steps dragging as though her legs were weighed down by lead. She collapsed into the first chair she found, burying her face in her hands.

"Are you all right?"

The gentle voice startled her. Mena looked up and blinked in disbelief.

"Poppy?" she croaked.

The figure before her came into focus, a young woman with the same blonde curls and piercing blue eyes as the child from the nursery. The girl smiled softly and shook her head.

"Poppy is my sister. I am Sylvie," the girl said with a small curtsy. "I am to escort you to Priestess Liona's classroom. The others were excited to meet you, but unfortunately, classes have already started."

Mena stood and swayed unsteadily on her feet. Sylvie stepped forward, grabbing her arm to help steady her.

"How is she? Poppy?"

The question caught Mena off guard. She could not recall a single family member visiting in the year she had stayed with the children. She frowned, her heart sinking at the thought of Poppy missing her sister just as Mena missed her own family.

"She looks like you," Mena said softly. "She is smart and passes all her exams."

Sylvie smiled, a wistful warmth in her expression. "Good. That is good."

Mena pulled herself free from Sylvie's grip, steadying herself against the wall. "Why does no one visit them? Why did you never visit your sister?"

Sylvie's lighthearted demeanor faltered. Her perfect smile slipped momentarily, replaced by something heavier, more reluctant. "We should get you to class," she said, forcing a brightness to her voice that did not quite reach her eyes. "Punctuality is crucial!"

Grabbing Mena's hand, Sylvie led her out of the common room and into the dim hallway. Doors lined both walls, identical except for the symbols etched onto them. They stopped in front of one with a golden moon carved into the dark wood.

"This is your class," Sylvie said, motioning to the door. "I am just across the hall."

Mena's gaze shifted to the door across from hers. A single drop of water was carved into its surface—a silver lining glinting in the light.

"Is that for Talons?" she asked.

Sylvie's eyes brightened, her face lighting with excitement. "Yes, it is! You are a quick learner!" She patted Mena on the shoulder. "I will meet you after classes."

Without another word, Sylvie knocked on the moon door before disappearing into her own room.

"Enter!" a shrill voice called from within.

Mena swallowed the lump of anxiety rising in her throat. Her hand trembled as she turned the handle, the door creaking as it swung open.

She inhaled sharply as she stepped inside; the heavy door thudded shut behind her. The room was dim, the air thick and stifling. It took a moment for her eyes to adjust to the low light. Rows of tables and chairs crowded the space, though only half the seats were occupied. Every pair of eyes turned to her, their gazes heavy and unblinking. At the front of the room stood Priestess Liona, tall and severe, her presence massive in the room. Her head nearly brushed the ceiling, and her long arms were folded tightly over her chest. They looked as though they could span the entire length of the room. Glacia was known for its tall citizens, but this woman seemed almost otherworldly. A giant compared to everyone else.

"Class," Priestess Liona announced, "It seems a princess has decided to grace us with her presence." She looked down at Mena with thinly veiled disdain. "Introduce yourself."

Mena's mouth went dry. Her muscles tensed as she gave a small curtsy. "Kallemena Vaelora, princess of the continent Glac..."

"No!" Priestess Liona's cry was like a whip crack, making Mena flinch. "Here, you are not a princess. Here, you are a disciple of the Axis. Now, what is your name?"

Mena shrank under Liona's steely gaze. "S-Sister Kallemena," she stammered.

"Very good," Liona said with a curt nod, waving her hand toward the rows of tables. "Now, find a seat so we may continue the lesson."

Mena moved quickly, her legs trembling beneath her. She found an empty table near the back and sat down. The monotone drone of the priestess' voice filled the room as she read from a thick book, her voice grating to the ears. Mena adjusted her robes, keeping her eyes firmly fixed on the desk in front of her. The weight of the other students' stares pressed down on her, but she was too afraid to look up. Her mind swirled with questions. Sister Tressa had warned her to escape when Vallorith left. How? The food and drink were laced with a silvervane. When? Vallorith said I could be his equal. Why? What does he want? Her emotions threatened to undo her.

"And how did the goddess Caerwen create the void that erased the stars?" The question hung in the air while the priestess's brown eyes scanned the room. "Sister Kallemena?"

Mena's head shot up. The entire class was watching her, their faces expectant. She felt her heart pound in her chest as Priestess Liona's stern gaze bore into her. Mena felt her face flush, sweat prickling her skin. The question left her paralyzed. Before arriving at Verdathos, she had learned little of the Gods; such knowledge had never seemed necessary. And her year in the nursery only focused on their names, never what the Gods accomplished, or at least she did not remember such teachings. She swallowed hard as she glanced around the room, twelve pairs of curious eyes fixed on her.

"Brother Mylo?"

Relief washed over Mena as Priestess Liona called on someone else. A slender boy about her height rose to his feet. His ivory skin contrasted sharply with the black of his hair, and his posture was so perfect it seemed almost unnatural.

"She needed to hide from the god Lirian," he began, enunciating every word with care, "because he had become jealous of the praise she was receiving from the citizens of all nine continents. He had threatened to imprison her, for he thought she had been controlling the humans against their will."

"Very good. Thank you, Brother Mylo." Priestess Liona turned her attention back to Mena. "I expect you to know this in the future."

"Yes, Priestess Liona," Mena stammered. "I promise I will."

The rest of the lesson continued in much the same manner. Priestess Liona read fact after fact in her monotone voice, occasionally questioning the class, who repeated the answers in unison. Mena tried to take notes, but the spellings eluded her, and her penmanship was not quick enough to keep up. By the time the bell tolled for lunch, her hand throbbed, the quill having rubbed a raw spot into her finger. Exhaustion weighed her down as she filtered into the hall. Sylvie stood waiting, her bright smile unwavering. The sight of her made Mena's chest ache, thinking of Poppy and the stories she used to tell her sister about life in a castle as a princess. Sylvie led Mena into a large dining hall, its layout a crowded mirror of the classrooms. Long wooden tables and benches filled the space, the room buzzing with chatter. Sylvie waved enthusiastically and pointed Mena out to a group gathered near the center.

"Everyone, this is Kallemena! She is the new Darra."

Before Mena could protest, Sylvie nudged her onto a bench and plopped down beside her. Mena gave a small, sheepish smile as she scanned the faces around her. She recognized the boy from her class and was startled by how oddly comforting his presence was.

"You can just call me Mena," she offered.

"Would you not rather we all call you princess?"

Her eyes darted to Mylo, who wore an exaggerated grin as he let out a nasally laugh that wheezed awkwardly over the group. The tension broke as the boy next to him, a hulking figure with broad shoulders and arms like tree trunks, raised a hefty hand and smacked the back of Mylo's head.

"Ignore him," Sylvie said through clenched teeth. "He can be a very insensitive brother at times." She gestured toward the hulking boy. "This is Slek. He is a Zeph."

"A Zeph?" Mena repeated, her brow furrowed as she tried to recall what she knew.

Before Sylvie could explain, a sudden puff of air whooshed over Mena's head, making her feel as though gravity had briefly doubled. Sylvie laughed.

"Zeph's are wind abilities," she clarified.

"How do you have your power?" Mena asked, curiosity getting the better of her. "Do you not have silvervane in your system?"

Sylvie placed a comforting hand on her shoulder. "We have consumed it for so long that it does not affect us as harshly as it does you. Though we can do small things, it is still better than that of an untrained Echo's powers. Much safer." She wore a smile as if this was a good thing.

Did she honestly value her hindered ability over free will?

Before Mena could question this, Sylvie motioned toward a pair of identical red-haired figures sitting across the table, their pale skin and fiery locks striking.

"This is Finn and Fraya," Sylvie continued. "They are Thorns."

"Nature," Fraya said before Mena could ask. "Boulders, grass, that sort of thing."

Her voice carried a melodic accent, the lilt of her homeland unfamiliar yet captivating. Mena marveled at it, having never heard anything quite like it before.

Sylvie turned her attention back to Mylo. "You already know he is Darra like you. That just leaves Wynna."

A girl across the table regarded Mena with quiet intensity. Her thick, wavy hair framed her face, her dark eyes piercing yet unreadable. Black lines traced delicate patterns along her neck and cheek.

"A Vira," Finn interjected, his accent matching his sister's unique cadence.

Mena nodded politely to each of them, her expression earnest. "It is a pleasure to meet you all." Her words were met with snickers from the group, their muffled laughter rippling around the table.

"You can drop the formality, your highness. This is no palace, and you are no longer a princess." Wynna arched a brow, stretching her arms above her head, causing the sleeves of her robe to fall back and reveal more markings etched into her skin. Mena considered her words and nodded slowly.

"You are right. I do not need to be formal anymore." She looked directly at Wynna. "What are your markings for?"

A collective groan rippled through the group as Wynna grinned. "I do love talking about myself." Her smile widened, promising an endless stream of words. "I come from Sylvara, the land of tribes. These are my markings. We receive our first mark when we are born, and then another each year as we grow. I should be covered in them by this age, but for now, these will do." She pushed her sleeves up past her elbows, revealing the lines stopping just short of her elbows. "I plan to return after this. I do not care if it is against the law. I will learn my trade, but then I am going back. My tribe needs me. We are the mighty..."

"Silver bears, and we rule the forest." Everyone completed her statement in unison.

Mena assumed they had heard it countless times before. Just then, a cart rolled down the aisle, catching her attention. Plates piled high with food were handed out to the students. Mena's meal was beans with bread and cheese, accompanied by a small cup of water. She felt her stomach turn at the sight of the fluffy brown roll and the small cup of liquid her body thirsted for. She dug into the salty, creamy beans, tearing chunks of cheese from the wedge, determined to stay focused. Her goal was clear: escape was possible, especially without the silvervane in her system.

"Are you going to eat that?"

Mena looked up, surprised by the hulking man sitting across from her. His blocky features bulged beneath his white robe. His plate was already empty, and he eyed her roll of bread with eager hunger.

"No. You can have it. However, it probably has silvervane in it, as does the water. Sister Tressa warned me about it."

Slek and the others looked down at their empty trays with disgust on their faces.

"Makes sense." Mylo dropped his last bite of bread.

Sylvie and Wynna pushed their plates away, as did the twins.

"I am going to miss bread." Slek stood and picked up his empty plate.

As he left, Mena's gaze drifted to the table behind him. Seated across from her now was a shadowy figure with a pair of amber eyes fixed intently on her. A sudden wave of unease washed over her; she felt like prey. After finishing her meal, Sylvie nudged Mena, pulling her from the trance. She followed Sylvie to the basin, discarding their plates and heading toward the common room.

"Who was that?"

Sylvie looked back, her ever-present smile fading slightly. "Who?"

"The boy with the amber eyes."

Sylvie's expression shifted into something unreadable. "That is Zepher. He is the only Morin here at the Axis. Most of us stay clear of him."

"The only one? Why?" Mena asked, her curiosity piqued.

Sylvie pulled Mena aside, guiding her toward a new table where the others had already gathered, their books spread out before them. She whispered softly, making sure no one else could hear. "Most Morins do not live past ten or twelve. When their abilities start to manifest, they end up taking the lives of themselves or their family members... accidentally." She shuddered. "Zepher survived, but there are rumors he killed his whole family; he just managed to escape."

A chill ran down Mena's spine as her eyes flicked toward Zepher. She watched him from the corner of her eye, his midnight skin and gray hair, eyes gleaming with a predatory hunger.

Sylvie leaned close, her voice barely a whisper. "He is Vallorith's favorite. So, stay clear of him."

When the classes were over and all the students had finished their evening meal, she followed Sylvie to their room. Just like in the nursery, she would be sleeping in the lower bunk, but she was relieved to find it was a full-size bed, not one meant for children. The room, however, felt engulfed by the dark walls, black as the roof and floor. It was barely large enough for two bunks, with a small desk tucked into the corner and a basket of neatly folded white robes beside it. A candle burned on the desk, its flickering light reminding Mena of her father's study. Fraya and Wynna shared the room as well, and for the first time that day, Mena felt the same warmth she had in the nursery with Poppy.

She crawled onto the flat mattress, curling into a ball. When the candle was blown out, the girls whispered their goodnights before drifting off to sleep. The quiet sounds of their soft breaths surrounded her, and although Mena was exhausted, her mind refused to quiet. Tears slid down her cheeks as Sister Tressa's words haunted her. The news from earlier that day hit her harder than anything before, and a tight ache in her chest threatened to tear her apart. She stifled her sobs, pounding her fist against the mattress in frustration. Her heart ached for her family. For her father. For Ashar. She longed to have been there with them, to have been able to comfort them in their time of need. To have been by her mother's side, helping her through the loss of her husband.

Suddenly, Mena sat up, swiping at the tears on her face. For the first time in months, her mind felt clear, her body alive with energy. She focused, remembering what Myra had warned: the Axis stripped people of their powers. But Mena was not going to be one of those people. She closed her eyes, clearing her thoughts and reaching deep inside. She thought of Ashar, his warmth, the glow of his orbs, the way his hazel eyes sparkled with life. She focused on that feeling, on the love she carried in her heart despite the short time they had known each other. She stretched out her hand and concentrated, straining to pull the magic from within. A faint shimmer glistened, and she saw it. A white snow owl with black-tipped wings was seated on her hand. Its large eyes were watching her with a majestic stare. She let out a held breath, and the owl vanished as quickly as it appeared. The grief returned tenfold.

Her body now shaking. The small room, once a refuge, now felt too small. The three other girls sleeping around her made the space feel even tighter. She needed air. She needed the wind on her face, the moon, and stars above her. Quietly, she grabbed the handle of the door, turning the knob slowly, praying it would not wake her roommates. She peered out into the darkened hall, uncertainty swirling in her chest. She was unsure which direction led outside, but that was the least of her concerns. She just needed air. She needed the cold on her skin.

"Going somewhere, shadow rat?"

The voice cut through the silence, a noise louder than what she was prepared for. Mena froze, heart pounding in her ears. She turned to see Zepher's bright yellow-orange eyes glaring at her from the shadows. He moved closer, each step bringing dread closer to her core. Mena's pulse quickened with the instinctive rush of fear, his presence closing in like a predator on the hunt.

He stopped, his smile cold and knowing. "Someone did not eat their bread today. Tsk, tsk."

Chapter Seventeen

Ashar sat on the throne, his back stiff against the towering silken cushions. The plush seat beneath him did little to ease the dull ache spreading through his hip, a discomfort that seemed to deepen with every passing minute. The throne itself was a masterpiece, its intricate silvery swirls and curling leaf designs glinting softly in the candlelight. Dark green fabrics pillowed his back, but even their luxurious touch felt suffocating under the weight of his thoughts. The high back loomed above him like a shadow, a constant reminder of the burdens he now bore. His gaze swept across the grand hall, the open expanse of plastered white walls interrupted by vivid tapestries. Each one told a story woven with threads of triumph and bloodshed. His eyes settled on a tapestry depicting his father's victory in the Scorvaan desert, the clash that had solidified their kingdom's strength. The memory surfaced like a ghost. He could still see himself as a boy, small and frightened, watching his father ride off to war. He remembered crying himself to sleep those first nights. The mornings were a routine of him clutching a wooden practice sword as he swung it clumsily at his bedpost, pretending to be the hero his father was.

Then the joy, pure and uncontainable, when the warband returned. He had watched the horses gallop into the courtyard, his father at the forefront, armor gleaming under the sun. That moment had seemed eternal, etched into his soul like the threads of the tapestry now before him. His heart ached now, raw and hollow, for his father who had been stolen too soon, for the mother he had never known, for the comforting familiarity of a life that now felt worlds away. The present was louder than his past. The arched ceiling caught the murmur of voices, amplifying the cacophony of the throne room and sending it tumbling back down to his ears. Ashar longed for the stillness that had filled this space only hours earlier. Now, the crowd of nobles, lords, and foreign dignitaries sat shoulder to shoulder in their opulent garb. The air was heavy with perfumes and the rustling of silks and velvets, an unspoken contest of wealth and power that suffocated him more than the room's stifled air.

Some faces he recognized were old warriors who had fought alongside his father and councilors who had served their kingdom faithfully. But the majority were strangers. They hailed from lands he had only read about in scrolls and maps, their names and titles meaning little to him beyond the weight they carried in political games. Many of these same faces, he knew, would be present at the council meeting Vallorith had called for in a few weeks. That thought only deepened the knot of unease in his stomach. The weight of their eyes bore down on him, a relentless tide that made his insides twist. His nerves betrayed him, a fine sheen of sweat rising under the layers of silk and lace that adorned him. The ceremonial attire, with its stiff collar and endless embroidery, felt like a cage. Every breath he drew felt short, as though unseen hands tightened around his throat. Ashar's fingers gripped the throne's armrests, his knuckles paling as he tried to steady himself. He wanted to run, shed the unbearable weight of his title, duties, and regrets, and lose himself in the forest beyond the castle walls. Instead, he sat as still as the throne beneath him, bound by expectations he never asked for.

The space felt like a prison. The heat radiated from the sea of bodies crammed into the room, their collective presence thickening the air with the mingling scents of sweat and fragrant oils. It clung to Ashar's skin, damp and oppressive. The stagnant atmosphere pressed down on him, and the walls seemed to inch closer, the crowd swelling until it felt as though the room itself were alive, squeezing everyone into a tighter space. His chest heaved as his breaths grew shallow, his vision blurring as the high, arched ceiling seemed to lower. Panic clawed at the edges of his mind. Just as he felt he might drown in the racket of murmured voices and shifting people, the clear, brassy blare of trumpets shattered the tension. The sound was sharp, cutting through his rising anxiety like an axe through wood. Ashar seized the moment, pulling in a deep breath of air that tasted faintly of stone and candle smoke. He straightened in his seat, his pulse hammering against his ribs as he focused on the far end of the room. Finally, the moment they had all gathered for was at hand.

The massive double doors at the back of the hall swung open, their tops nearly scraping the high ceiling as they parted with a deliberate grandeur. All heads turned as the doors revealed the procession. At Ashar's nod, the guards stepped forward, their voices ringing out as they announced the names of those entering. The dignitaries entered the room one by one, their titles heavy with tradition. The bishop came first, flanked by his disciples, their robes rippling with each solemn step. Then came the distant relatives, Ashar's blood, though he barely knew their faces, each one draped in finery meant to underscore their importance.

Finally, the name everyone had been whispering about was called—the King of the continent Glacia. A collective gasp rippled through the crowd like the pull of a tide. Heads turned sharply, eager to see if the rumors were true. Ashar's heart lifted as his gaze found the doorway. There, standing tall and unyielding, was King Thaloren. His queen stood at his side, her hand resting on his arm, regal and poised. The hush that fell over the room was almost reverent, as though the crowd were collectively holding their breath. Ashar stood as Thaloren began his march down the aisle. Every step was deliberate and flawless. The king moved with the grace of a warrior, his movements as smooth as flowing water, his form a testament to Glacia's ingenuity and strength. The crowd stared in awe, their eyes devouring every detail of the king's body, marveling at the craftsmanship that could have only come from the icy forges of such a magnificent and foreign land.

Metal and glass intertwined in perfect harmony, forming a figure both beautiful and imposing. His metal bones shone like polished steel, their angular design both functional and ornamental. Glass muscles stretched and flexed with each step, catching the light in dazzling flashes. One leg, covered by a sleek metal shaft that wrapped his thigh like a shield, gleamed with power, while the other foot seemed impossibly perfect in its delicate yet unyielding glass design. His breastplate, polished to a mirror-like sheen, revealed the dark blue of his tunic beneath, a silver crown emblazoned over his heart. His long black hair was braided in a warrior's style, its strands weaving together with precision, while his glass crown rested firmly atop his brow, completing his commanding presence. In his hands, he carried the scroll, the sacred words that had been spoken at the crowning of Ashar's father and his father before him.

The queen, her son, and his wife took their seats as King Thaloren approached the front of the hall. The room seemed to shrink once again, but this time, it was not from suffocation; this was something different. It was admiration. Thaloren's every step carried the weight of history, and the people felt it. Ashar stood rooted to the spot as the king reached him. Thaloren stopped a few paces away, his eyes locking onto Ashar's. There was no cold authority in his gaze, no calculating judgment. Instead, his eyes were deep and full of quiet understanding. They seemed to see past the crown Ashar would wear, past the throne he would inherit, to the boy beneath it all, the boy who, despite everything, would soon carry the weight of an entire continent on his shoulders.

For a moment, Ashar felt the full gravity of his destiny. It pressed against him. He felt like a boy again, standing in the shadow of a man who seemed invincible. But there was also comfort in that gaze, a reassurance that he was not alone, even in the face of such immense responsibility. King Thaloren unrolled the scroll with a slow, practiced motion, the parchment crackling faintly in the hushed silence. When he spoke, his voice was steady and resonant, the words of the ancient proclamation filling the hall, and as Ashar listened, his heart swelled, both with fear and hope.

"The nine continents will recognize a new king on this day," Thaloren's voice rang out, steady and resolute, though the faintest tremor of emotion lay beneath it. "We recognize that Ashar Durnovas of the continent Kalyra will shoulder the responsibility of his people. He will fight for them, protect them, bleed for them, and if the time comes, he will die for them. As his father before him, he will lead with an honorable hand, guided by the wisdom of the council and his court. He will abide by the laws and sacrifices demanded of his station, as the previous king did."

Thaloren paused, his gaze dropping momentarily to the ancient scroll in his hands. The discolored parchment crackled softly as he adjusted his grip, the weight of its words perceptible in the room. "The laws read as such: No Echo to be born from your blood shall stay…"

His voice faltered. The syllables caught in his throat as a wave of emotion threatened to undo him. Thaloren swallowed hard, the tears in his eyes glinting faintly in the light filtering through the towering windows. He shook his head, unable to continue, and rolled the scroll shut with a slow, deliberate motion. His gaze swept over the crowd before returning to Ashar, who stared up at him with wide, curious eyes. Thaloren descended to one knee, his glass prosthetic making a soft, resonant knock as it met the stone platform beneath the throne. He looked at Ashar for a moment, the weight of a thousand unspoken words filling the space between them. Then, his voice lowered, soft but firm, meant only for the boy before him.

"Your father started something the moment he and your mother vowed never to send you to the Axis," Thaloren said, his tone heavy with conviction. "He was a strong and wise king, but I believe you will be stronger. I believe you will grow to be wiser."

Thaloren rose with a commanding grace and gripped Ashar's wrists, pulling him from his seat. His voice dropped further, intimate yet powerful. "The weight of the crown is heavy, but it is not yours to bear alone. We will get Mena back. When that happens, I do not wish for her or you to ever feel the need to hide your gifts ever again. I do not want you, her, or anyone else to live in fear of the abilities they were born with."

He then turned to the restless crowd, his booming voice silencing the murmurs. "Ashar will usher in a new era of monarchs, a time that will surpass all we kings and queens have accomplished. He will lead the world into an age of harmony and peace unlike anything we have ever seen before. I, King Thaloren Vaelora of the continent Glacia, crown the new king of the continent Kalyra. Ashar Durnovas, the first Echo King!"

The words thundered through the hall, reverberating off the white-plastered walls. The gathered nobles and dignitaries watched in breathless silence as Thaloren took the silver crown from the trembling hands of the wide-eyed bishop. He raised it high, the polished metal catching the sunlight and casting streaks of brilliance across the room.

"All hail the Echo King!" Thaloren declared, his voice filled with unwavering authority.

As he placed the crown atop Ashar's head, he firmly gripped the boy's shoulders, grounding him in the moment. "Show them what it means to carry such a title," he whispered.

Ashar turned with Thaloren to face the silent crowd, their dual presence a force against the vast expanse of white and sunlight. Thaloren's dark blue regalia contrasted against Ashar's deep green, their combined presence a storm of strength and unity. The freshly crowned king raised his fist high, his expression fierce with newfound purpose. With a flick of his fingers, a flame burst to life above his palm, roaring and twisting like a living thing. Gasps rippled through the hall as Ashar twisted his wrist, sending the fire into an elegant, swirling dance above the gathered crowd. Then, he spread his hands with a motion as fluid as water. The flame unraveled, splitting into thousands of tiny orbs of light. Each orb flickered with its own small flame, dancing just out of reach of the astonished onlookers. The spheres floated on an unseen breeze, filling the room with an ethereal glow. For a moment, the crowd was frozen in awe. Then, a single clap broke the silence.

An ancient nobleman stood, his polished cane tucked under his wiry arm. His bald head gleamed in the sunlight, and his long mustache and beard swayed as he brought his hands together in a steady rhythm. The sound echoed through the chamber, a defiant break in the stillness. One by one, others joined him, the applause swelling into a thunderous roar.

"All hail the Echo King!" the chant rose, voices united in deafening celebration.

Ashar's chest swelled with emotion, his vision blurring with unshed tears. His gaze flicked to the crowd, and there she was, Nyssira. Her face was a mirror of Mena's, a bittersweet reminder of what he had lost. How he longed for Mena to be here now, standing beside him as his betrothed, sharing in this moment. His jaw tightened, and he turned to Thaloren, his hazel eyes burning with a newfound resolve.

"Gather your armies," he said, his voice steady as a king should be. "We leave at dawn!"

***

A question had plagued Mena's mind ever since she left the comfort of the nursery and joined the common hall with the other Echoes. It lingered, persistent and heavy, until she could no longer contain it.

"What happens to the children? The ones in the nursery who do not have abilities like us?"

The question shattered the comfortable chatter at their table. Slek froze mid-bite, his fork filled with pie hanging in the air as his eyes darted toward the blonde curls hiding behind a book. Quietly absorbed in her reading, Sylvie wiggled uneasily on the wooden bench. Her fingers tightened on the pages as though she might shield herself with the thick tome. Everyone at the table knew the question was meant for her. After all, she was the only one of the friends with family in the nursery. Mena's sharp gaze bore into Sylvie, watching her fidget and avoid eye contact. Her patience, which had been steadily waning, finally snapped. She reached across the table and tapped a finger on the worn leather cover of Sylvie's book. "The Laws of the Sea," the title read in faded gold lettering. Mena had read it repeatedly as she waited for her friend to finish and face her. Sylvie let out a reluctant sigh, carefully setting the book aside to avoid the crumbs scattered from Slek's unmannered eating.

"They get hired out to the kingdoms after their studies," Sylvie said quietly, her words rushed and clipped. "Usually, when they are thirteen, they go away."

Mena raised her eyebrows, prompting Sylvie to flinch.

"I hear it is a good life," Sylvie added hastily, her tone defensive. "Better than the slums of Morbessa."

Mena's stomach twisted at the mention of the infamous continent. Stories of Morbessa were whispered like curses among the Echoes. A land shrouded in constant smoke and fog, its streets gray and lifeless, its people hardened by poverty and despair. Named after the god of death, it was said to be a place where crops withered before they had a chance to grow. Where murderers and thieves roamed freely. The thought made her shiver, her back stiffening. She glanced at Sylvie, who was now staring intently at her folded hands, clearly hoping someone would change the subject. Mena, however, was not so easily deterred.

"You are almost done with your studies," she pressed. "Could you not take Poppy with you when you leave? That would surely be better than leaving her to the fate of a stranger's house." She instinctively pushed her roll to the corner of her tray, only to smack Slek's hand away when he reached for it.

Sylvie's cheeks burned pink as she pulled her book close, her palms flat against the pale brown cover. "Honestly, Mena, I do not want to take her." The admission sent a ripple of shock through the table. "I have not seen her since she was four," Sylvie continued, her voice tight. "I am surprised she even remembers me. And what would I do with her? I do not know how to raise a child. I have no experience and no idea where to even begin. She would be better off with someone else, someone who knows what they are doing."

Mena's jaw clenched. "She is your sister, Sylvie," her voice was low and even, though anger simmered just beneath the surface. "She is your blood."

Sylvie lifted her eyes to meet Mena's, her expression a mix of guilt and defiance. "And what good is blood," she whispered, "when you do not even know the person it ties you to?

Sylvie shrugged, her gaze darting toward Slek, silently pleading for support. Slek, however, was busy shoveling large bites of pie into his mouth, his exaggerated chewing an apparent excuse to avoid speaking. Sylvie rolled her eyes and crossed her arms. "Look, it is just not something I want," her tone was defensive. "Poppy will be fine without me. She will go to a good house, earn a wage, and sleep in a proper bed. That is better than anything I could ever give her, especially as an Echo in some noble's household." She grabbed her book and stood abruptly, her movements tense. "I am done talking about this."

Before anyone could add to her growing guilt, she was gone, leaving behind an uncomfortable silence. Mena sat still, her hands tightening into fists. A burning energy surged through her veins, desperation coiling tightly around her heart. How could Sylvie turn her back on her own sister and leave her to a fate of servitude in a stranger's house? Would Poppy be safe? Her mind spiraled. Memories of her abduction clawed their way to the surface. She could still see Vallorith's cold eyes and feel his unrelenting grip as he tore her from her bedroom and dragged her through his portal. The overwhelming helplessness. The crushing loneliness. It was a feeling she would not wish on anyone, and, least of all a child-like Poppy. Her powers stirred, a restless energy begging for release as her emotions threatened to consume her. A movement caught her attention. Across the table, Zepher watched her intently, his piercing eyes locked on her as though he could feel the storm raging within her. A grin spread across his face, subtle but unmistakable.

"What is he smiling about?" Fraya muttered, sticking out her tongue in distaste. Finn mirrored her, narrowing his eyes at the Morin.

Wynna slid closer to Mena, leaning in conspiratorially and whispering loudly enough for everyone to hear, "Maybe he has a little crush on a certain princess?"

Mylo choked on his water, spraying droplets across the table and onto everyone's plates.

"Ugh, gross," Slek groaned, dropping his fork in disgust. His face turned visibly green as he shot to his feet. "I will go find Sylvie and make sure she is all right."

Wynna doubled over with laughter, slapping Mylo on the back so hard it made him wince between coughs.

Mena pressed her eyes shut and inhaled deeply, willing herself to stay calm. "I will be in the library if anyone needs me," she announced.

Fraya raised an eyebrow. "Still studying everyone's abilities, huh?"

Finn grinned slyly. "If you figure out Slek's weakness, let me know. I have been dying to get one over on that brute."

Mena did not respond. She carried her dishes to the wash basin, discarding her untouched bread in the bin on the way. Every step she took felt heavy, as though the weight of the entire room was pressing down on her. When she reached the hall leading out of the dining area, she glanced over her shoulder. Everyone was still at the table, chatting and laughing, everyone except Zepher. The corridor to the library was crowded with Echoes, their eyes watchful as Mena weaved through the clusters of students. Whispers followed her like a trail of smoke. The hostility was nothing new. Letters scrawled with hateful words were left on her desk. Murmurs of discontent whenever she passed by. The resentment toward a royal Echo was a constant hum in her life. It had stung at first, cutting deep like an invisible blade. But now, she told herself, she had grown thicker skin. She kept her head high, her steps steady.

When Mena entered the library, relief washed over her. The aisles were empty, the tables bare, and the silence welcomed her like an old, familiar friend. She felt her nerves begin to untangle, her lungs filling with a deep, calming breath. The soothing scent of paper and ink lingered in the air, a nostalgic aroma that reminded her of her father's study. She felt closer to home amidst the shelves of ancient knowledge. She had started researching the nine Echo abilities merely to catch up on her studies. But as she delved deeper, her curiosity had grown and blossomed. The skills of the Echoes were far more expansive than she had ever imagined, nearly limitless within their individual domains. Her great-aunt Myra, for instance, had used her Darra gift for sight and healing, a power Mena had always thought unique. But she had learned that even a Cairn could achieve similar feats, channeling their abilities to guide and mend.

Darras, like herself, could project creations born entirely from their imagination, crafting illusions and constructs with endless potential. Then there were the Talons. She had read of one who, in a desperate act, had called upon the sea to protect an entire city, sinking it beneath the ocean currents to protect it from invaders. Legends whispered that the city still lay hidden beneath the waves, untouched by time. The Morin had fascinated her most of all. They were shrouded in mystery, with powers both feared and revered. Rumors claimed they could kill with a single touch or drain the abilities of another Echo, leaving their victim utterly helpless. Her thoughts strayed, unbidden, to the pair of yellow eyes that often watched her from across the room, predatory and unnervingly focused. Zepher.

Why had he not stolen her power when he knew she was wielding it? He had to know she was not taking large doses of poison like the others. Only drinking the water if she did not feel the small ache in her head after swallowing a few drops. Did he actually report to Vallorith, or was that just another rumor whispered through the sanctuary halls? The lack of answers gnawed at her, and her frustration only deepened when she realized how little was written about the Morin. While the histories of other Echo abilities were recorded in painstaking detail, the Morin remained elusive, their legends scattered and incomplete. Her fingers trailed lightly across the spines of the books as she wandered through the tall aisles, their leather covers cracked with age. She read titles softly under her breath, a quiet hum accompanying her search for her next read. The fading orange glow of the setting sun spilled through the glass ceiling, illuminating her path, but she knew the light would not last long.

Mena paused beneath the first stars that began to peek through the twilight sky. She loved the nighttime when the sanctuary was quiet, the halls dimly lit. In those moments, she could almost imagine herself back home, walking beside her mother and father, their laughter echoing softly through the castle corridors. Her chest tightened as the ache in her throat swelled, threatening to spill into a sob. Swallowing hard, she lowered herself to the floor, curling her legs to her chest. She gazed upward, where the deepening black of the night sky framed the stars. The moon was absent tonight, but the thought of the full moon's return in a few days brought a small, wistful smile to her lips. The quiet shuffle of footsteps broke her musings. Someone was lighting the candles on the tables, their faint glow barely reaching where Mena sat. The flickering flames cast long, wavering shadows on the floor, the ladders leaning against the shelves seeming to dance with life.

Suddenly, a book fell from above, slamming flat on the floor with a startling thud. Mena's heart leaped to her throat, and a sharp yelp escaped her lips before she could stop it. Her wide eyes darted to the book, lying face down on the cold stone floor. Its sudden appearance sent a chill creeping up her spine. She hesitated, her breath shallow, before slowly leaning over to pick it up. The cover was old, the leather worn smooth from years of handling. Her fingers traced the faded title embossed in gold as she turned it over in her hands.

"The Shadows of Arvayn." Mena's words still trembled, carrying the startle from the sudden interruption.

"Why are you so interested in me?" A sly, serpentine voice hissed from above.

Her heart jumped as a figure leaped down, landing silently in front of her. The glowing yellow eyes locked onto hers, and she froze, her breath catching in her throat. The figure crouched low to the floor, his movements deliberate, to cause unease.

"Not just you," she managed, though her voice exposed her nervousness. "All the Morin."

"I see." His tone dripped with taunting amusement, his piercing gaze never leaving her. "Still avoiding the poison they slip into everyone's food, I presume?"

Mena swallowed hard, trying to steady her anxiety.

"Who tipped you off about the routine?" he asked.

Shrugging her shoulders, she forced her voice to steady. "I figured it out. It was not exactly subtle. The headaches were... hard to ignore."

Zepher studied her with an imposing intensity before shaking his head. He leaned back and sat cross-legged on the stone floor, his dark skin blending almost seamlessly with the shadows of the library. Only the faint flicker of candlelight illuminated his sharp, otherworldly features: glowing eyes, angular features, and pointed ears.

"Why did you not report me to Vallorith?" Mena asked, clutching the book tighter. "You knew I was using my abilities. You could have told him."

For a moment, Zepher stared, the silence stretching between them. Then, with an exaggerated click of his tongue, he leaned forward slightly.

His features, feline, and unsettling, caught the light, a glint of sharp teeth, slit pupils widening with intrigue, and nails that curved into pointed claws.

"Because I did not want to," he said, his voice laced with indifference. Rising to his feet in a single fluid motion, he turned and began walking down the aisle.

Mena scrambled to her feet, clutching the book against her chest as she hurried after him. "Yet you follow me at his command?" This was just a guess.

Zepher's laugh echoed through the quiet library, a sound that sent a shiver down her spine. He glanced back over his shoulder, smirking. "I do not follow anyone's commands, not even the high priest's. I am his equal."

"Then why are you here?" she demanded, rushing to step in front of him. "Why not leave? You cannot tell me you enjoy it here, pretending to learn a trade, eventually using your gifts to serve others like some obedient servant."

His smirk faded. "That is not why I am here."

"Then why?" she pressed, blocking his path again. "If not to obey your master's orders, then what? Everyone knows you follow his every word. You are Vallorith's spy, nothing more."

The air grew heavy, the tension crackling like a distant storm. Zepher froze mid-step, his back rigid, before slowly pushing her out of his way. "I do not have a master," he grunted coldly.

"Then what are you?" Mena's words grew sharper, her frustration boiling over. "You say you are his equal, but all I see is a pet trained to obey!"

Her final word hit home. In the blink of an eye, Zepher was on her.

His hand closed around her throat with terrifying speed, lifting her onto her toes as he forced her back against a bookshelf.

"I am no one's pet," he snarled through clenched teeth, his face inches from hers.

Mena clawed at his wrist, panic surging as her strength ebbed away. Her lungs burned as she struggled for air, her vision blurring as tears welled in her eyes. Zepher's grip was unyielding, his glowing eyes filled with a dark satisfaction. Then the glow intensified, and Mena felt a strange sensation wash over her, a pull deep within her soul. The pain dulled, replaced by an intoxicating euphoria that clouded her mind. Her hands fell limp at her sides, and her body slackened. Her last coherent thought was of her family and their faces, a fleeting memory before darkness claimed her.

When she awoke, a desperate gasp tore from her throat. She rolled onto her side, coughing violently, each breath ragged and sharp. Her hands flew to her neck, the phantom ache of Zepher's grip still lingering. As her vision cleared, she saw a boot near her face. Zepher stood over her, his usual smile replaced by a cold, impassive scowl. Without a word, he nudged the fallen book toward her with the tip of his boot.

"Some Darra you are," he sneered, his voice biting. Turning on his heel, he began to walk away, his robes billowing behind him. "Just as weak as your family." He continued to mutter as he walked away.

His words cut deeper than the encounter itself, leaving Mena trembling on the cold library floor, clutching the book as tears blurred her eyes once more. But then something took over—something deep within her. Mena's head shot up, her chest heaving as she forced herself upright. Pain lanced through her neck and lungs, but she ignored it. Her steps were uneven as she staggered forward, her pale face ghostly in the candlelight.

"What did you say?" Her voice was hoarse, cracking with effort.

Zepher halted, throwing his hands up in vexed exasperation before spinning to face her. His lips curled, exposing his sharp teeth, and his tone carried deep-rooted hate.

"I said, princess," he spat the word like a curse, "that it is a wonder Vallorith even bothers with you. A *strong* Darra?" He blew a dismissive raspberry. "You are no stronger than that blind aunt of yours. He might have used her instead of you if he had not *blown her to bits!*"

The words struck Mena like a physical blow. She stumbled, the air stolen from her lungs. "Myra?" she whispered, her voice breaking. "No."

Her mind reeled, piecing together the shards of a cruel truth. She remembered the vision Vallorith had shown her the day she left the nursery, Ashar and Myra aboard the ship, engulfed in flames. At the time, she had dismissed it as another one of his twisted manipulations. But now... It was not a lie. Myra had been there. Like her father, she had been consumed by the explosion. Grief gave way to fury, a storm rising from the hollow ache in her chest. She locked eyes with Zepher, her pale, shuddering form solidifying into something unyielding. His mocking grin only stoked the fire raging within her.

"You..." she whispered, straightening. Her head tilted to the side, her dark hair falling like a shadow around her face. Her voice was low, cold. "You will regret that."

The library seemed to darken around her as her eyes turned black, bottomless voids that swallowed all light. She raised a hand toward him, her movements slow and deliberate. Zepher took an instinctive step back, his grin faltering. Before he could act, the world around him shifted. Everything turned to darkness. He stumbled, his arms flailing, his feet searching for solid ground that no longer existed. There was nothing-no floor, no walls, no ceiling—just an infinite black hole.

"What is this?" His voice rang out, but it was swallowed immediately, the sound collapsing into silence.

Panic set in. Zepher screamed, but his cries only echoed in his skull, soundless to his ears. His breathing quickened as he grasped at the empty air, clawing for anything to hold onto. The void was oppressive, pressing against him like a weight he could not shake. The silence was maddening. It was as though the universe itself had ceased to exist, leaving him alone with only the sound of his own thoughts, if even that. He kicked and thrashed, his movements desperate and disjointed. Time stretched and twisted, his sense of it unraveling. Minutes became hours. Hours became lifetimes. His muscles burned, his lungs ached, and every fiber of his being screamed for release. Then came the pain. It began as a faint chill, spreading through his body until it seeped into his very bones. His skin stiffened, the sensation like glass shattering with each movement. He tried to cry out, but the silence devoured him.

He rubbed his arms, hoping to warm himself, but the motion only brought agony. His hands came away wet, slick with blood. Cuts appeared across his flesh, hundreds, then thousands, shallow at first but deepening with every passing second. Zepher clutched at his robe, only to find it rotting away, deteriorating into nothingness. His nails grew long and jagged, his teeth loosened and fell out, and his once-proud form shriveled into something unrecognizable. His body aged rapidly, decades passing in moments. His hair grew long and brittle before falling out in clumps. His skin peeled away, floating like ash into the ether. Death crept closer with every heartbeat. He could feel it, cold and merciless, wrapping its tendrils around him. He screamed silently into the abyss, his mind unraveling. And then, just as suddenly as it began, it stopped.

Zepher gasped, his eyes snapping open. He was back in the library, sprawled on the cold floor. His chest heaved as he pushed himself upright, his hands quivering. He ran them through his hair, relieved to feel the familiar braided strands still in place. His muscles were intact, his teeth whole. But as the panic ebbed, a new sensation crawled across his skin. A scream caught in his throat as he looked down. Thousands of cuts marred his flesh, some fresh and bleeding, others healed into jagged scars. His onyx skin was a tapestry of torment, a haunting reminder of what he had endured.

"What in the gods..." he whispered, his voice trembling.

A violent cough racked his body, and he doubled over. When he pulled his hand away from his mouth, his fingers were stained red with blood. He staggered to his feet, his eyes darting around the now-empty library. The air was heavy and oppressive, as if it still carried her presence. Never in his life had he heard of a Darra capable of such destruction, of inflicting wounds that lingered in reality itself. He stared at the doorway, his mind racing. One thought consumed him, drowning out all others: "What are you, Kallemena?"

* * *

She burst into the shared room, breathless, her face streaked with tears. The door slammed shut behind her, the echo ricocheting off the stone walls. Her head throbbed as she pressed it against the cool black stone, the chill offering a fleeting abatement from the fire raging in her mind.

"Mena, are you all right?" Fraya's thick accent startled her.

She turned, her tear-blurred vision focusing on the three figures staring back at her. Wynna sat cross-legged on her bed, struggling to tame her frizzy hair, while Sylvie and Fraya froze mid-conversation, their expressions wide-eyed with concern. Mena did not answer. Tears streamed down her face as she crumpled to the floor, her body trembling. She pulled her knees to her chest, burying her head in her arms, her shoulders shaking with each uncontrollable sob. A warm hand touched her shoulder, and she flinched, looking up. All three of her friends surrounded her now, their faces soft with worry. Slowly, they sank to the floor beside her, their arms wrapping around her trembling form. The warmth of their embrace broke her further. The ache in her chest doubled as a wave of suppressed grief and anguish poured out of her. The tears came uncontrollably, each sob wracking her body, leaving her gasping for air.

Finally, Sylvie's soft voice broke through the haze. "What has happened?"

Mena wiped at her tear-streaked face with trembling hands. "My aunt..." Her voice cracked. "She is... she..."

The words stuck in her throat, burning like embers. Another sob overtook her, and she shook her head, unable to continue. The others exchanged worried glances, their silence heavy and patient. Hours seemed to pass before the storm in her chest settled enough for her to speak. Her voice was hoarse, barely above a whisper, as she recounted what Zepher had told her about Myra, how her aunt had been killed, how he had taunted her, and how she had lost control of herself and her powers.

"I do not remember how it happened," Mena admitted, her hands twisting in her lap. "It was like... like the anger just swallowed me whole. My power, it just... it took over. It controlled me. I could have killed him."

Wynna huffed, leaning back with a dismissive wave of her hand. "Good for the Morin! Serves him right, pissing off a Darra like that." She gave Mena a hearty slap on the back.

"Wynna," Sylvie seethed, narrowing her eyes at her. "She obviously did not want to hurt him and surely not kill him." Sylvie turned her gentle gaze back to Mena. "Right?"

Mena nodded, her throat tightening again. The conversation lingered late into the night as the three girls comforted her, their words weaving a fragile sense of calm around her. One by one, they drifted into sleep, their presence a reassuring cocoon. Mena did not know how long she had lain there, only knowing that it must have been hours. She woke to the faint sound of rhythmic thuds echoing through the hall. Her head was heavy, and her limbs felt leaden. She rubbed her eyes, sitting up slowly. Wynna was laid across her legs, curled like a sleeping dog, while Sylvie and Fraya flanked her sides, their breaths soft and steady. A pang of gratitude warmed her chest as she looked at them, their comforting closeness easing some of the pain still plaguing her. But the thudding sound continued, louder now, sharper. A second boom followed, vibrating the walls.

Curiosity prickled at her, stirring her from the bed. She carefully maneuvered her legs out from under Wynna, who mumbled in her sleep but did not stir. Despite her slight frame, Wynna felt surprisingly heavy, her limbs draped over Mena like dead weight. Once free, Mena padded quietly across the room. She reached for the door handle, twisting it slowly until the latch was released. Peeking into the dimly lit hall, she found it empty except for the flicker of a single lamp, casting shifting shadows on the slate walls. She hesitated, an unsure feeling took hold in her gut. Something about the silence felt wrong, uneasy. Returning to her bed, she slipped a hand beneath her pillow, pulling out the small, weathered map Sister Tressa had given her. The lines etched across it marked the twisting halls of the sanctuary, a maze she had memorized over time.

Another boom echoed, this one sounding louder and closer. The sound of running footsteps reached her ears. She froze, quickly returning to the door. Quickly, she eased it shut as the noise grew louder. The lock clicked softly into place. Pressing her ear to the cold wooden door, she listened, her breath shallow. The rhythmic thuds continued, punctuated now by hurried voices and the slap of boots against stone.

"They are breaching the main gate. We need to start getting everyone to the cellars."

"What do they want?"

"Someone wake Vallorith!"

Mena frowned at the name, but her heart raced with a flicker of hope. If someone had come to Verdathos, this might be her chance to escape. She reached for the door handle again, but guilt quickly rooted her in place. The soft snores of Fraya reminded her she was not alone anymore. If someone was here, her friends could be in danger, too.

"Everyone, wake up," Mena whispered sharply, shaking Wynna's shoulder and patting Sylvie's cheek.

The girls stirred groggily, blinking away their sleep.

"Is it time for class already?" Wynna muttered through a yawn, her frizzy hair sticking up in all directions.

Mena silenced them by conjuring a glowing orb of light, letting it bounce lazily along the ceiling. Despite having seen her magic countless times, her friends stared in awe at the ease with which she wielded her power.

"Someone is here," Mena said, motioning to the door as another loud bang echoed through the halls.

The three girls exchanged wide-eyed glances.

"What was that?" Sylvie whimpered, clutching the blanket around her shoulders.

"Who is here?" Wynna staggered to her feet, fists raised, though her movements were sluggish from sleep.

Sylvie's voice climbed into a panicked ramble, spilling out a litany of worries as Fraya tried to calm her. Wynna looked ready to charge into a fight, and Fraya struggled to clamp her hand over Sylvie's mouth while shouting at Wynna to calm down. The room grew louder with their chaotic chatter until a door slammed just outside, and heavy footsteps echoed down the hall. Mena acted on instinct. She waved her hand, and a shimmering bubble of magic enveloped her friends. Their voices were muffled instantly as they pressed their hands to the translucent walls in shock. Mena pressed her ear to the door, her heart pounding.

"This should be her room, although she may have already left for the cellars."

Her blood ran cold at the familiar voice, Priestess Liona. The door handle twisted in her hand, and Mena barely had time to step back and project a barrier before the door swung open, slamming over her foot. She bit down on the cry of pain that rose in her throat. Zepher entered cautiously, his sharp eyes scanning the room. Small, deep cuts crisscrossed his face and neck, smearing his white robes with streaks of blood. His expression darkened as he surveyed the bunks, noting the faint indent where Sylvie had been sitting. Fraya pressed her hand harder over her mouth, her wide eyes fixed on Zepher as he looked directly at Wynna. Mena held her breath, her magic trembling at the edges of her control. Zepher turned to the tall figure in crimson robes standing just outside the doorway. Liona was flanked by several white-robed figures carrying swords and torches.

"She must have just left," Zepher muttered, frustration evident in his words. He stormed out of the room, his voice echoing down the hall. "Go and find her. Now!"

The sound of shuffling feet filled the air as Zepher glanced back into the room. Smiling at the three girls playfully before he disappeared. Silence descended once more. Mena waved her hand, dissolving the magical bubble around her friends.

"He could see us?" Fraya gasped, her voice trembling. "How?"

Mena hesitated, scanning their faces. "He can sense my abilities somehow."

"Why not tell Liona then?" Fraya shook off Zephers' creepy stare.

"He looked right at me! Did you see that?" Sylvia squeaked as tears welled in her eyes.

Another loud boom shook the room, silencing their conversation.

"We need to move," Mena said firmly, producing the map Sister Tressa had given her. She took one last look before handing it over. "Take this. Find the boys and follow this path to the docks."

"What about you?" Sylvie asked, her voice rising in panic. "Why are you not coming with us?"

"I am going to get the children," Mena said, glancing at the door. "Once I have them, I will meet you at the docks. Then, we are leaving the Axis behind. Together."

Before her friends could protest, she slipped through the doorway, her steps fading into the growing commotion. Fraya took the map from Sylvie and studied it carefully.

"The boys are here," she said, pointing to a corridor at the back of the sanctuary. "And the children are here."

"If we hurry, we can get the boys and help Mena," Wynna said, trembling with adrenaline as she bounced on her toes.

Sylvie shook her head, tears streaming down her face. "We are supposed to go to the cellar! That is what they taught us, and we are supposed to follow the rules and stay safe!"

Fraya and Wynna exchanged a glance, their determination mirrored in each other's eyes. Fraya grabbed Sylvie's arms, pulling her to her feet.

"We are leaving, Sylvie," Fraya said firmly. "Just stick with us." She nodded at Wynna. "Give us a lift?"

Wynna grinned, cracking her knuckles. "With pleasure."

Her grin stretched wide, her brown eyes darkening into deep, glistening pools.

A ripple passed over her body, silver fur bursting from her skin as she dropped to all fours. The sickening crack of bones twisting and dislocating filled the room, each snap sharp and unnerving. Her frame expanded, muscles contorting under her flesh. Long, jagged claws scraped across the black stone floor, leaving deep gouges in their wake. A guttural growl rumbled from her throat, escaping through a now-protruding muzzle. When she finally stilled, her massive silver frame filled the bunk room, towering over the others.

"W-Wynna?" Sylvie whimpered, shrinking back.

The bear did not respond. Instead, it turned toward the door, rising onto its hind legs. It let loose a deafening roar that shook the walls, a primal sound reverberating in the girls' chests.

"I wish I could do that," Fraya muttered, her voice tinged with awe.

The bear lowered itself, crouching low and dipping its head. Fraya and Sylvie exchanged glances before climbing onto Wynna's broad back, gripping the coarse silver fur for balance. With a pat to her side, Fraya gave the command, "Go." Wynna did not need more encouragement. She took off, her powerful limbs propelling her through the halls. The sound of her claws clattering against stone echoed in rhythmic bursts, adding to the frenzy of booms that shook the walls.

Meanwhile, in the boys' bunk room...

"What do you think is happening out there?" Finn paced back and forth, his hands tugging at his sleeves. His steps were sharp and anxious, each turn of his stride punctuated by a glance toward the door. On the top bunk, Slek sprawled in his usual way, arms and legs dangling off the sides, his broad frame too large for the narrow bed.

"I am sure we will know in the morning," Mylo mumbled, already halfway under his blanket. He yawned loudly, clearly unbothered by Finn's agitation

Finn stopped mid-stride as a louder boom rattled the floor. The door creaked on its hinges as pebbles of stone and bits of wood fell from the ceiling.

"You are still not worried?" Finn asked, spinning toward Mylo.

Before his friend could answer, the sound of boots storming down the hall drew Finn to the door. He pulled it open and was met with boys in various stages of undress spilling into the corridor. At the far end, a priest in white robes barked commands over the clamor.

"All able bodies, come with me!" the priest yelled. "We will stop by the armory to fit you with armor. Everyone else, get to the cellars immediately!"

"What is going on?" one of the boys shouted.

The priest's face was grim, his tone sharp. "Enemy ships have breached the harbor. Cannon fire is already threatening the structure. If you are not fighting, move your feet to the cellars, NOW!"

Finn gripped the doorframe, tension building. His gut twisted as he looked down the hall. Mylo was already slipping on his robe, his movements hurried.

"I am going to help. Come on, get Slek!"

But Finn shook his head. "I have to find my sister, make sure she is safe."

Mylo hesitated but nodded, showing his understanding. "Be careful," he said before running off to join the others. The hallway grew quieter as more boys followed the priest. Finn turned back to the room, his heart racing.

"What is happening?" Slek finally sat up, his massive frame occupying most of the bunk's width.

Finn clenched his jaw, crouching low to the floor. He pressed his palms flat against the cool black stones, focusing his energy. Green light flickered in his irises as he reached out with his gift.

"Someone has come to wage war on the Axis," he murmured. "I need to find the girls; I think I see them, but there is something else." His voice faltered as he straightened, his expression darkening. "Something massive. It is coming this way."

A silver blur shot through the corridor as if summoned by his words. The ground trembled beneath its weight, and a gust of wind followed in its wake. Finn barely had time to duck back into the room as the enormous creature barreled past, claws scraping against the stone floor. His breath caught in his throat. "What in the gods!"

"Wynna, you passed them! Turn around!"

Finn's head snapped toward the sound of his sister's voice. He stepped into the hall just in time to come face-to-face with jagged canines.

The silver bear loomed over him, its black eyes gleaming in the light. Finn froze, his pulse hammering in his ears.

"Wynna?" Slek's voice broke the silence, filled with wonder. He stepped out from behind Finn, his broad hand reaching out tentatively. The bear let out a low rumble, standing tall as Slek's hand brushed against its coarse fur. "That is Wynna?" he marveled. "I am not sure whether to run or bow."

"Slek."

His gaze darted around Wynna's massive frame. Relief flooded him as Sylvie and Fraya slid down from the bear's back, their expressions weary but unharmed. Without hesitation, Slek scooped Sylvie into a tight hug, holding her as if she might vanish.

Finn met his sister with a wide smile. "I felt you coming," he said, his voice soft with relief.

Fraya tilted her head, curious. Finn crouched low, pressing his hands to the floor once more. "Like this," he explained, demonstrating how he had used his gift. Fraya mirrored him, her brows furrowed in concentration. Together, their eyes gleamed an unnatural green as they scanned the sanctuary.

"There are so many," Fraya whispered, her voice breathless with curiosity and fear. "Hundreds... marching from the docks."

"Can you tell who they are?" Slek's arms remained wrapped protectively around Sylvie, though he could not hide the tension in his voice.

"No," Finn replied, his tone grim. "Just that there are so many."

"What about Mylo? Where is he?" Sylvie asked, glancing nervously into the boys' rooms and down the hall.

"He went with the priest to fight the intruders," Finn answered, rising to his feet and brushing dust from his hands. He scanned the corridor. "Wait, where is Kallemena?"

"She went to get the children," Fraya said, straightening up and rubbing her temples. Her expression twisted into discomfort. "That will take some getting used to."

Another deafening boom rattled the walls, now almost on top of them. Dust trickled from the ceiling, and the flickering lanterns swung precariously. Time was running out. Slek looked to the others, determination hardening his features.

"We need to get Kallemena and the children to the cellar. Then we can go help Mylo and the others."

"No." Fraya shook her head, her expression resolute. "Mena said to head for the docks. She said we need to escape." Her voice cracked as she continued, her gaze locking onto her brother. "Let us go home, Finn. Back to our land. Back to our family."

Finn hesitated, his jaw tightening.

"I am with her," Fraya added. "I want a life of my own. Freedom. I do not dream of being a pawn, a tool for some lord." She glanced at Sylvie, her voice softening. "We deserve more than this."

Finn exhaled, his resolve wavering. "I agree. We need to leave." The silver bear nudged him, its warm breath brushing against his arm. Scratching behind Wynna's rounded ears, he muttered, "I am so jealous right now."

Wynna growled low, her sharp eyes fixed on the shadows ahead. Her nose twitched, sorting through the cacophony of scents. Suddenly, her lips curled back, revealing dagger-like teeth. A figure emerged from the darkness.

"What is this?" Zepher's voice rang out, his orange eyes glowing with curiosity and mischief. His gaze drifted lazily over the group before locking onto Wynna. "Leave it to a Vira to make an entrance this dramatic."

Wynna stamped her massive paws against the floor, a warning snarl rumbling deep in her chest. Zepher ignored her, his attention shifting to the others. "Leaving, are we?" His tone was enthralled. "Betraying the Axis already?" His gaze dropped to Sylvie, his smirk widening. "The place that has sheltered you. Fed you."

Slek stepped in front of her, his size imposing.

Zepher chuckled, a low, ridiculing sound. "Where is your little monarch? Has she abandoned you all already?" He tilted his head, his smile sharpening. "Or did she finally decide you were not worthy of her royal presence?"

Sylvie stepped out from behind Slek, her voice steady despite her fear. "None of your concern, Zepher." Her defiance only seemed to amuse him.

"Such loyalty," he sneered, "to someone whose family is perfectly content to destroy us all." His words landed like a blow, and a heavy silence fell over the group.

"What are you talking about?" Fraya demanded, her voice edged with anger.

Zepher's smirk deepened. "Oh, did she not tell you?" He gestured vaguely toward the distant booms of cannon fire. "That is her dear old dad out there, leveling the walls. And the sooner I deliver her back, the sooner the cannons will stop."

Another boom punctuated his words, the floor trembling beneath their feet. Before anyone could respond, a groan echoed above them. Wood creaked and splintered, and a massive section of the ceiling gave way, hurtling toward them in a deadly cascade.

"Move!" Finn shouted, grabbing Fraya.

Before the debris could crush them, a powerful gust of wind surged through the hall, whipping their clothes and stinging their faces with grit. Dust and fragments of stone swirled chaotically as the falling roof seemed to halt mid-air. The slab of wood hovered, suspended just inches above their heads. Slowly, it shifted, carried by the gale, and crashed to the side with an explosive crack. For a moment, no one moved, breaths coming in gasps as the night air flooded the hall. Slek sank to his knees, gulping down the crisp, cool breeze. Welcoming each inhale deep into his lungs.

"You saved us!" Sylvie dropped to her knees, throwing her arms around Slek in a fierce embrace. "We could have died, but you saved us!" Her voice trembled with a mix of relief and gratitude as she planted a quick kiss on his cheek before pulling back, blushing from ear to ear.

Slek blinked, caught off guard, as Sylvie stood and glanced away, her embarrassment visible. Wynna's low growl broke the moment, drawing their attention back to the now-empty hall.

"He is after Mena," Fraya said, her voice taut with concern. "After what she did to him today in the library, I do not think he wants to simply hand her over. Vallorith has a plan for her; he has always had a plan for her."

"What happened in the library?" Finn and Slek asked at the same time, their voices full with urgency.

Fraya did not pause to answer. Instead, she pulled out the small map, her fingers trembling as she turned it to orient herself. "I will explain on the way. This way," she instructed, taking off down the hall.

The others exchanged a glance and then followed without hesitation.

* * *

Mena's fists slammed against the heavy wooden door of the nursery, her hand sore from the effort. Her chest heaved as she gasped for air, her legs burning from the furious race up the spiral staircase. The relentless roar of cannon fire outside the sanctuary walls all but drowned out her cries.

"Hello!" she shouted, her voice breaking as she pounded again.

Only silence greeted her. She dropped to her knees, peering through the keyhole, but the other side was pitch black. There was no moonlight to illuminate the grounds, and no shadows stirred. Her fingers curled around the handle, rattling it in desperation. It was locked.

Frustration boiled over as another thunderous cannon blast shook the walls, the vibrations rattling her bones. Voices echoed faintly in the distance, shouts, the clamor of armored boots striking stone. The enemy was getting closer. Closing her eyes, Mena forced herself to breathe, to focus. She pictured the other side of the door, the exact spot she needed to be. Her hand swept through the air, and a small portal shimmered into existence before her. It was not as large as she had hoped, but it was enough. Dropping to the ground, she crawled through. The gravel of the nursery courtyard dug into her palms and knees as she emerged. With another wave of her hand, she summoned light to flood the area. Shadows retreated, and she caught sight of the church doors standing slightly ajar. Her heart held on to hope as she ran toward the structure, her slippers skidding on the loose gravel. The crunch of each step echoed unnervingly in the eerie silence. Pushing through the doors, concern consumed her. The once-cozy nursery was in shambles. Tables and benches lay overturned, broken, as if a storm had torn through.

"Poppy!" Mena's voice cracked as she called out, racing deeper into the room.

She searched the sleeping quarters, one by one, her dread mounting with every empty bed. The furniture and scattered belongings told a story of hasty evacuation. In her old bunk, she spotted a familiar comb lying untouched at its center. Her chest tightened.

"Poppy!" she screamed again, stumbling back into the courtyard.

"Not here, princess."

She froze at the sound of his voice. Zepher stepped out from the shadows, his orange eyes glinting with cruel amusement.

"You actually thought we would not think to get the children to safety first? What kind of monsters do you take us for?"

Mena's fists clenched, her voice ignited with fury. "I know exactly what kind of monsters you and Vallorith are."

Another cannonball struck the walls, sending a shower of stones raining down. Mena raised an arm to shield her head as the debris scattered around them.

"And yet," Zepher continued, his tone ridiculing, "it is your family that put all of their lives in danger in the first place. There was no concern for the innocent lives here, no hesitation from them to bring war to this sanctuary. Tell me, princess, who is the real monster?"

"You are lying," Mena spat, though her voice wavered.

"Am I?" He gestured grandly toward the wall. "Go on, see for yourself."

Mena kept her eyes locked on him as she edged toward the courtyard wall. She climbed up cautiously, her pulse pounding in her ears. When she looked over, she could not believe her eyes. The sanctuary's defenses were crumbling. The walls had been breached, and amidst the chaos, soldiers clad in the colors of her homeland stood shoulder to shoulder with soldiers in silver and green. Above them, countless orbs of light floated, illuminating their path.

"Ashar," she whispered, her excitement building in her chest.

Relief and fear warred inside of her. Another deafening crash tore her attention back to the courtyard. The door to the stairwell exploded into splinters as Wynna barreled through, the massive bear roaring with feral intensity.

"Mena!" Sylvie and Fraya shouted her name, their voices desperate.

Mena staggered back, confusion flickering in her eyes. "Why are you..."

Before she could finish, Wynna charged. The world seemed to slow as a sharp, excruciating pain bloomed in her wrist. She looked down to see claws sinking into her flesh, feeling like knives carving into the muscle. The air shimmered as a portal formed before her, its edges crackling with unstable energy.

"Mena!" Sylvie's scream echoed as the portal snapped shut, sealing her friends on the other side.

Exhaustion rushed in, swallowing her whole as she drifted to sleep.

Chapter Eighteen

M ena stirred, grogginess weighing on her like a thick fog. A sting-ing, biting sensation in her wrist yanked her back to reality. She could tell her hands were bound tightly behind her back, the rough material biting into her skin as she gave a few experimental tugs. Pain shot through her arms when she tried to adjust, confirming the bonds were not coming loose anytime soon. She knew her ankles were simi-larly restrained when she tried to sit up. The realization hit her like a punch to the gut: she was a prisoner again. Steeling herself, she sur-veyed her surroundings. The room was unlike anything in the sanctu-ary. It exuded a strange, disarming charm.

Cream stone walls, their surfaces softened by wild ivy crawling along the corners and rafters. It stood in stark contrast to the dark, depressing halls she had grown accustomed to. A large desk stood at the far end of the room, its design eerily similar to her father's, a detail that tugged uncomfortably at her heartstrings. Stacks of books lined the walls and spilled haphazardly onto the floor, their worn spines catching the golden glow of candlelight. The scent of old paper min-gled with the faint tang of melted wax, a bittersweet reminder of her childhood spent beside her brother, who was forever poring over the carefully preserved records of her ancestors.

A draft brushed against her skin, forcing her to shiver. She scanned for a window or even a door, but saw nothing. How long had she been unconscious? The disorientation left her uneasy, her stomach threat-ening to empty. She strained her ears but heard nothing beyond her inhaled breaths. The cannon blows were no longer within the range of her ears.

"Oh, good. You are finally awake."

The voice was smooth and immediately chilling. Mena's heart dropped as Vallorith stepped through a shimmering portal, his figure materializing like a specter summoned from the void. Zepher followed on his heels, his orange eyes locking onto her with predatory intensity. Mena struggled to prop herself up on her elbows, but her bonds made the movement clumsy, her efforts futile. Zepher sank into one of the chairs near the desk; his movements were casual, yet his piercing gaze betrayed his suspicion. He was not wearing his white disciple robes anymore. Instead, he was clad in black fighting leathers, a cloak draped over his shoulders, his hood drawn back from his head. The hilt of a dagger peeked from the sheath strapped to his thigh, the polished metal catching the candlelight like a warning.

"Zepher here tells me you have learned a new trick," Vallorith began, his voice laced with amusement. "Nearly killed him in that little void of yours." His words were on the edge of a compliment, a sick sort of praise. "Impressive. Very impressive."

Zepher's jaw tightened at the reminder, but he said nothing. Vallorith, however, was delighted, his curiosity shining in his eyes as he studied Mena. He leaned closer, his face uncomfortably close to hers, his tone almost giddy. "What made you stop, though? How did you learn to damage him with your projection? That mastery takes decades more than you have been alive."

Mena refused to say a word, not that she knew the answer anyway. Her defiance was written in the sharp set of her jaw and the cold glare she fixed on him. Instead of responding, she allowed her gaze to wander again, taking in the room's every detail. Above them, an enormous chandelier hung suspended, its hundreds of melted candles giving it an almost skeletal, ghostly appearance. Their flames flickered and danced on an unseen breeze. Considering the danger she was in, the strange, haunting beauty of it all felt practically ironic.

"Come on," Vallorith pressed, circling her like a dog waiting to pounce on a bone. "Tell me how you did it. You could have killed him with that power. Why did you not?"

Mena's lips twitched into the faintest of smirks. Finally, she raised her gaze to meet Vallorith's, her voice steady and defiant. "I did not stop because I could not. I stopped because I did not need to waste my anger on him." Her eyes burned with murderous anger. "You were the one I would rather kill."

The grin that spread across Vallorith's face was unnerving, like that of a child unwrapping a long-awaited gift.

"We need to hurry this along," Zepher cut in, his tone sharp with impatience. His earlier false calm was gone, replaced by a nervous and irritated edge. "The others will be here soon. I am not a match for all of them, especially without the silvervane in their systems."

Vallorith waved him off dismissively. "Then go. Stand watch or something. Your voice is like a mosquito in my ear." He made a shooing gesture, his annoyance evident.

Zepher hesitated, his expression sour, but eventually stepped back through the portal, leaving Mena alone with Vallorith. The room seemed colder in his absence, the air thick with tension. Vallorith turned back to his books, his fingers gliding over their spines as he plucked a single book from the shelf. A brown cracked leather cover with a marking on it, Mena recognized one of the beloved texts that the Axis cherished. "We will need this," he muttered to himself.

With a wave of his hand, one of the walls faded away, revealing a hidden doorway behind the shelves. Another gesture brought the rug beneath Mena to life. It twisted and flapped like a wounded bird, jerking her forward. Mena fought against it, thrashing with all her might, but her bonds made her efforts futile. The hidden room she was dragged into was smaller, darker, and oppressive. The stone walls were cold and unyielding, their surfaces carved with strange markings she did not recognize. Her eyes darted to one wall covered in dates and names, a crude timeline of battles she had read about in history books.

Another wall bore nine mirrors arranged in a circle, their intricate frames distinguished by the wall next to them, adorned with carvings.

The symbols for the nine abilities. Moon, sun, water, leaf, arrow, skull, spiral, triangle, and paw print. The mirrors' surfaces seemed to shimmer, as though alive with untapped power. At their center, a more significant ruin was carved, its meaning unknown to Mena.

With a snap of Vallorith's fingers, the rug dropped her unceremoniously onto the cold floor. Pain flared in her hip as she landed hard, but she gritted her teeth, refusing to show weakness. Vallorith moved toward the mirrors, his focus entirely on them now. He blew dust from their surfaces and adjusted their positions with painstaking care, his every movement precise. "It is almost time," he murmured, more to himself than to her. "Are they not beautiful?" Vallorith glanced at Mena over his shoulder, his voice dripping with a sinister satisfaction as he relished her confusion. "This is why I have brought you here." With his usual theatrical flair, he turned and placed a pale hand on the ruin at the chamber's center. "With these, I will achieve something no one has ever dared to dream of. The impossible."

His grin widened unnaturally, splitting his face to reveal unnervingly perfect teeth. "I will become a god."

Mena groaned as she shifted, struggling to balance on her hip. The rope bindings at her wrists were now slick with her blood from the gash on her wrist. The ropes loosened ever so slightly, easing the friction on her skin. Her heart thundered with desperate hope; if she could slip free, she might still have a chance at escaping her captor.

"A god?" She forced a laugh, sharp with disbelief. "No one can become a god. Unless they are born as one."

To her surprise, Vallorith's grin did not falter. Instead, it stretched further, his bright eyes glittering with unspoken malice.

"Or," he began, rolling up his sleeve to expose pale, papery skin crisscrossed with inky veins that pulsed faintly, "have the blood of one." He spoke the words with reverence, his voice heavy with self-importance. "And I just so happen to have that very blood running through my body. A gift that elevates my powers far beyond the average Darra."

With a flick of his wrist, a small wooden bowl materialized in midair, suspended as though cradled by invisible hands. Vallorith plucked a knife from a nearby table and held it steady in his other hand.

"Shall I tell you of the prophecy and my plan," he teased, "or see how much you can piece together on your own?"

"I do not believe in prophecies, nor do I care about your plan," Mena shot back, her voice strained but defiant as she twisted her wrists against the rope. "I care about getting away from you."

"Ah, my dear princess," Vallorith said with a smirk, shaking his head as though chastising a petulant child. "There is no getting away. You are part of the plan."

He dragged a blade across his palm with an unflinching motion, leaving a shallow trail that quickly filled with dark, viscous blood.

He clenched his fist, letting the blood drip into the wooden bowl with slow, deliberate plops that echoed unnervingly in the small chamber. "You and so many others like you."

Mena was shocked at his words, her movements halting as unease pooled in her chest. "Others?" she asked. Her heart sank at the thought of more people being imprisoned by this madman.

Vallorith nodded as he began wrapping his wounded hand with a bandage. "Echoes," he said. "Like me, you possess the blood of a god. Descendants of the original nine. And your power is unlike any other Darra I have had the pleasure of encountering."

He carried the blood-filled bowl to the ruin at the center of the wall and dipped his fingers into the thick liquid. Slowly, he traced the intricate markings, his touch bringing the symbol to life with an otherworldly glow. "I need nine Echoes to complete my transformation. One descended from each of the gods. And thanks to my position as High Priest of the Axis, I have had the privilege of finding every last one of you. Special gifts, soon-to-be keys to unlocking my destiny."

"I do not understand. Why do you need nine Echoes?" Mena asked, unease creeping into her voice despite her effort.

Vallorith paused his work, glancing over his shoulder with a smug grin. "Because without them, I will simply stay a Darra. I could never become a god without having each of your abilities. Do you see these mirrors? These wonderfully beautiful mirrors?" he motioned toward the frames lining the walls. "I created them. Each is a realm unto itself, designed carefully to siphon your abilities from you. The process can begin once I have all nine of you contained within them. I will ascend to the heavens, becoming a being more powerful than any mortal or immortal."

Mena's stomach churned. "You are delusional. No Darra can steal powers from another Echo. These mirrors, these realms of yours, will only hold as long as your power does. No Echo can provide endless power like that; you will drain yourself before too long." A flicker of hope rushed through her. "You will lose your ability completely if you attempt this."

Vallorith chuckled, the sound low and mocking. "That is where you are wrong." He touched the frame that sat next to the spiral carving. "Demetra, the Freyla, had the gift of healing, bringing others back from the brink of death. I was smart enough to harness her powers first to ensure I could use my abilities indefinitely." His eyes gleamed with dark amusement as he added, "It is really quite useful."

He dipped his fingers into the blood again and continued tracing the ruins, which now pulsed faintly, his blood bringing them to life. "My offer still stands, you know," he said with a broad smile. "You could always be my equal. Rule by my side. What is a king without his queen?"

Mena glared at him, fury and disgust burning in her chest. "I would rather die."

Vallorith's smile did not waver. He turned to face her fully, his expression softening into something almost pitying. "No, I cannot have you dying. But living forever as a vessel to serve me? Yes, I think we can arrange that."

A chill ran down Mena's spine, dread pooling deep within her. "Forever?" she whispered.

"Enough with the doom and gloom," Vallorith said dismissively, turning back to his work. "Let us focus on the task at hand. Zepher just needs to gather the remaining Echoes, and we will begin. Just in time for the Eclipse Veil."

"The Veil?" Mena pressed, her hands finally slipping free from the rope. She rubbed her raw, bleeding wrists. "What is that?"

"The convergence of all nine celestial events," Vallorith explained, shaking his head. "I swear those teachers do not do their job well." He cleared his throat. "The great wave that makes Talons. The Zenith day that makes Cairns. The rise of the dead that makes Morins. Each event that grants us our abilities will align, flooding the world with enough energy to fuel my ascension."

Mena's breath felt heavy in her lungs. "And when does this happen?"

"A few days' time," he said casually, as though discussing the weather. "But no matter. Before the sun rises tomorrow, I will have everything I need."

He finished tracing the last symbol, and the ruin burst to life, glowing and pulsing like a beating heart. A scream, raw and guttural, echoed through the chamber. Mena's gaze snapped to one of the mirrors, her blood running cold as a face appeared within its glassy depths. A man with brown hair, a beard to match, and eyes heavy with sorrow and despair stared back at her from the mirror labeled with a triangle. His haunted expression made her stomach lurch. The words caught in her throat, her body frozen in a paralyzing mix of terror and incredulity. She wanted to scream. She wanted to run. But she could not move. She could only watch as Vallorith's twisted vision of godhood began to take form.

"Is he not magnificent? Embric here is a direct descendant of the god Tauthen." Vallorith gestured to the man trapped within the mirror, his face shining with pride. "He could have been a legendary captain of the guard, a hero among his peers. But now, he serves me." He flicked his hand, and Embric's haunted face dissolved into nothingness, leaving the mirror blank once more.

"And the Freyla? Who was she?" Mena's voice trembled, though not with fear.

Rage churned in her chest, fierce and consuming, and she welcomed it like an old friend. Her energy was building, thrumming beneath her skin. If she timed it right, she could use her power to drag Vallorith into the void just as she had trapped Zepher.

"Demetra," Vallorith said, his tone almost nostalgic. "A sweet girl. A distant kin of goddess Brynna. She was... cooperative at first. Intrigued by my vision, even." His voice darkened. "But she grew bitter when she realized the mirror was her final destination. How ungrateful." His lip curled in disdain. "Still, her resistance was irrelevant. In the end, it worked out perfectly for me."

"You are despicable," Mena spat, fury lacing every word. Slowly, she shifted her stance, rising to her knees while keeping her unbound hands hidden behind her back. "You imprisoned innocent people. You stole their lives, their futures. You are no god. You are a demon!"

Her final word resonated like a battle cry. She flung her hands forward with a precise gesture, and a black void ripped through the air before her, consuming everything in its path. Loose papers, rugs, even fragments of furniture were sucked into the swirling abyss.

But Vallorith stood unmoving, an amused smile painted across his face.

"Did you really think that would work on me?" he said, almost lazily. With a flick of his wrist, her void dissipated as if it had never existed, leaving the room in chaotic disarray.

Mena barely had time to react before the ground beneath her erupted. Stone and vines lashed out, encasing her limbs one by one. She thrashed and screamed, but it was no use. The roots tightened their grip as they dragged her downward. Vallorith's face loomed above her, his expression a mask of cold anger. "Well, this is inconvenient," he sneered as the ground swallowed her whole.

Mena was plunged into darkness, the damp, cold press of the earth stealing her breath. The roots and stone guided her through a twisting tunnel, pulling her along like a puppet. She fought to stay calm, but the sensation of being buried alive gnawed at her nerves. Panic forced a gasp from her lips, only for dirt to invade her mouth and lungs. Her heart was in overdrive as she struggled to be free of the vines that wrapped around her. Finally, the ground gave way, and she was deposited into a chamber lit by a faint, flickering light. Her bindings released, and she was hauled to her feet.

"It worked!" Fraya and Finn exclaimed aloud, their accents breaking the tension.

"Mena!" Sylvie's arms wrapped tightly around her friend, followed by Slek and the others, each squeezing her in a desperate embrace as she hacked the debris from her lungs.

"How, how did you find me?" Mena asked, her voice raw as she looked at the twins.

"We used our power," Finn replied, still breathless. "We felt the vibrations of your body through the floor."

Mena's heart swelled with gratitude, but there was no time to dwell on it. "It was a hidden room. Vallorith was there. He has mirrors, each one meant to trap Echoes. He is planning something with the Eclipse Veil."

Her words were met with stunned silence. The group exchanged uneasy glances as if struggling to comprehend her jumbled puzzle of words.

"I will have to explain everything later," Mena said urgently. "Right now, we have to leave this place."

A distant boom reverberated through the halls, sending a squeak from the already shaking Sylvie.

"Zepher said Glacia is attacking the Axis. If that is true, I saw the sails, I have to get to them." Mena turned to Fraya, her voice tinged with desperation. "Do you still have the map?"

Fraya frantically patted her robes, her face falling. "I must have dropped it along the way."

A low growl drew everyone's attention. Mena's eyes widened as she noticed Wynna, the enormous bear, crouched nearby. How had she not seen the creature earlier? Wynna's growl deepened as she fixed her gaze on the hallway ahead.

"That usually means someone is coming," Slek muttered, patting the bear's side. "I know this level," he continued, his voice steady despite the rising tension. "Follow me."

As they sprinted through the twisting halls, Mena's skin prickled with unease. Something seemed to watch them. Hunting them. The black walls felt alive, growing darker with every step. Their surfaces writhed and shifted as if thousands of insects crawled beneath the stone. The corridor began to constrict, the walls closing in with ominous intent. Shadows clawed at their robes and hair, whispering threats in the periphery of her hearing.

"Mena!" Fraya's voice was urgent. "Do something!"

Mena thrust her hands forward, summoning a portal just before the walls slammed together with a deafening crack. The group stumbled through, only to be greeted by another dark, writhing corridor. The sanctuary itself had become a living thing. The walls pulsed and reached for them, tendrils of shadow gripping their ankles and tugging at their arms. Mena barely managed to open another portal beneath them, and they fell through in a chaotic tumble. They landed hard, only to find themselves trapped once again. The black walls enclosed them, creeping closer like a predator savoring its prey.

"Open one to the outside!" Sylvie shouted, bracing herself against the crawling wall, Slek at her side.

"That is what I am trying to do!" Mena snapped at her friend. She opened another portal, and for the briefest moment, she glimpsed the courtyard's open sky. But before anyone could step through, the portal twisted, replaced by yet another darkened hall.

"These are not my doing," Mena said, panic creeping into her tone. She glanced down at her trembling hands before trying again. This time, she poured everything she had into the spell. For a heartbeat, the portal showed freedom, only to be hijacked once more, its image replaced by oppressive darkness.

"He is toying with us," she growled, her anger bubbling to the surface.

Wynna let out a thunderous roar, the sound echoing through the encroaching corridor. The massive bear lunged forward, slamming her paws into the writhing wall. Cracks spidered across the surface, and with a final, deafening blow, the wall shattered, revealing a new hallway beyond. This one was still. Silent.

"Go!" Fraya and Finn darted through the opening, motioning for the others to follow.

The group stumbled into the quiet space. Once everyone was inside, the twins dropped to their knees, pressing their palms against the cold stone floor. The air buzzed with energy as slabs of earth rose up with a mighty rush, fresh mud dripping from their edges. The smell of rich soil filled the space as vines and roots sprouted, snaking up the walls and weaving a canopy of vibrant leaves overhead. The once-ominous corridor had been transformed into a verdant haven, a living passage that radiated safety and warmth. It felt like stepping into another world.

"Hopefully, this buys us some time," Fraya said weakly. Finn nodded in agreement. "Although I am not sure exactly how much. We need to move."

The twins took off running, the others following close behind, their footsteps muffled by the soft, earthen floor. Slek led the way, calling out directions as the twins reinforced the walls with every twist and turn. Finally, the cool night air hit their faces as they emerged into the courtyard, only to find chaos awaiting them. Sparks flew in the darkness as swords clashed in the distance, their metallic screeches splitting the night. Waves rose from the sea and crashed over the battlefield, while vines snaked around ankles, hauling the enemy to the ground. The sight was amazing and frightening altogether. The rhythmic pounding of boots and the shouts of soldiers filled the air, illuminated by sporadic flashes of firelight. They had escaped the labyrinth of shadows, but the battle was far from over.

"We have to stop the fighting. Innocent people will die if we do not!" Mena's voice was drowned beneath the roar of battle. The hiss of arrows flying past, the clang of metal against metal, and the shouts of soldiers.

The twins raised dirt walls around the group, their hands pressed firmly to the ground, while Slek shoved everyone down for cover.

"We are going to die out here!" Sylvie whimpered, trembling beneath Wynna's protective bulk.

"This is madness!" Mena pushed past Slek and scrambled to the top of the mound, ignoring his protests.

Crouching low, she peered out at the mayhem below. In the dim light of glowing orbs, figures clashed in a violent tide, their movements blurring into a mass of destruction. She could not tell soldier from disciple, friend from foe, as the relentless sounds of battle hammered at her heart. Taking a deep breath, she flicked her hand, releasing her power. Above the courtyard, an aurora spilled across the darkened sky, its shimmering waves of green and blue casting an angelic glow over the battlefield. The sight took her breath away for a moment as the light revealed the horror below. Bodies littered the ground, blood pooling beneath the fallen. Wounded figures writhed in agony, their cries drowned by the cacophony of war. Her stomach churned. All her life, she had grown up within the peaceful walls of her castle, where her people sang and danced without a care in the world. She had witnessed their joy, their kindness, and their love for life. Now, they were clad in armor, swinging their weapons with feral cries and striking down their fellow men and women. This was a war

they should never have been forced to fight. Her anger surged, a wildfire consuming her from within. To her, there was no difference between her people and those of the Axis. Whether they wore robes or
armor, it did not matter. They were all innocent lives, caught in the
web of a psychopath's delusion.

She raised her hand, her voice firm. "Enough!"

The courtyard fell silent as her magic surged outward, freezing
every limb mid-motion. Soldiers and disciples alike were trapped in
place, their weapons poised to strike or shields raised in defense.
Wide, fearful eyes turned toward her as she stood tall atop the hill, her
gaze sweeping over the sea of faces. So many young men and women.
So many lives that should have been spent with their families, not
spilled on the battlefield for a tyrant's dream.

"Kallemena!"

The voice cut through the stillness, and Mena felt her heart lurch.
Her heart leaped, excitement coursing throughout her body. She knew
that voice. The one who had told her countless stories of adventure
and heroic figures. The one she had fallen asleep to when her nightmares kept her awake. The one she had thought she would never hear
again. She turned, her eyes scanning the crowd until they locked onto
his face.

"Father," she whispered, her voice trembling as an ache erupted in
her chest.

Without a second thought, she leaped from the protective barrier,
her feet hitting the ground as she raced toward him. She weaved
through the crowd, soldiers and disciples alike still frozen as they
watched her move amongst them with a purpose. Her mind spun as
her eyes drank him in. His face had changed in their time apart. Lines
of stress marked his face. Skin darkened by the time at sea. His black
hair was now streaked with white around his temples and through his
beard. Her father had aged decades in the year they had been apart.
Smiles broke across their faces as they closed the distance, mere feet
apart now. Tears flowed freely for the parent she had grieved, longing

to be scooped up in his arms and swung around like he had done when she was a little girl.

"Father," she began, her voice barely above a whisper, "you are here..."

Her words were cut off by a sudden, searing pain in her back. She gasped, her legs buckling as the agony ripped through her. Her eyes went wide as she looked down. The tip of a dagger, bloodied, stuck out from her sternum.

"No!" Her father's cry tore through the courtyard as he turned, his gaze locking onto the man responsible. High above them, Zepher stood atop a wall, his black robes billowing in the light of floating orbs. His amber eyes glinted with malevolence and hatred. His lips set into a satisfied grin.

"No!" Ashar yelled as he forced through the now-thawing crowd. He fell to the ground next to King Thaloren, who held his daughter close in his trembling arms. Ashar's teeth clenched in fury. With a fierce motion, he raised his hand, sending his orbs streaking through the sky like falling stars.

Each one struck the wall where the monster had stood, sending chunks of molten stone and flame crashing to the ground. When the smoke cleared, Zepher was gone, leaving misery in his wake. Mena's breaths came in shallow, ragged gasps, her vision blurred as she tried to take in the faces around her. Her father's dark eyes stared down at her, a smile on his lips as he whispered her name. "Mena, my sweet, sweet snowdrop." He pulled her close and kissed her forehead. His lips were hot against her cold skin.

She shifted her gaze to the stranger near her, his hazel eyes sending a warm, familiar feeling through her body.

"Ashar?" Her eyes drank him in.

His face now wore a beard she did not hate. His hair had lengthened, and a silver crown sat atop his brow. His lips trembled as he came closer, cupping her face in his warm hand. Her chest ached, though it was uncertain if it was from the emotion or the foreign object that was embedded in her back.

"You are both here." She coughed, the taste of blood on her tongue. She looked back to her father, his stoic features cracking before her. Tears welled in his eyes as he turned away.

"Do not hurt them." She gasped through ragged breaths. "They are just doing what they are told." Another cough sent a tremble through her body, the last bit of strength leaving her.

"Ashar?"

"I am here. Stay with us." His hand in hers was familiar and painfully bittersweet

She blinked up at him, her hand trembling as she reached for his face. Her fingertips brushing against his beard, coarse and thick beneath her touch. Tears filled his eyes as he clutched her hand tightly.

"I need a healer!" he shouted, his voice breaking with desperation. "Someone, please!"

Her vision wavered, but she held on, focusing on him. "Ashar..."

His arms tightened around her as he began to pray, his deep voice trembling with each word. She felt his love in every syllable, but the world around her was growing dimmer, slipping further from her grasp. She clung to the sound of his voice, to the warmth of his embrace, and to the memories of the time they had spent together. Mena's body grew weaker, her limbs heavy, and the world around her retreating from her consciousness. Through the haze, she could hear the cries of her friends as they rushed to her side. Sylvie collapsed into Slek's chest, her tears soaking the fabric of his robe as his massive arms wrapped around her. His large hands stroked her golden curls, trying vainly to calm her trembling sobs. Fraya and Finn stood helplessly nearby, their faces stricken with confusion and helplessness as they glanced at one another, silently wondering if their gifts could save her.

The crowd parted in fear as a massive bear lumbered forward, its hulking form casting long shadows in the aurora's glow. Mena did not need anyone to tell her how grave her injuries were; she could feel the warm steel within her, the hilt pressed against her back. Her gaze shifted back to Ashar. His strong hands cradled hers, his lips pressing soft kisses against her palm as if trying to will her pain away. His hazel eyes, so full of warmth and light, were now brimming with tears, the weight of his emotions barely held in check. Leaning close, he kissed her forehead, his breath hot against her numbing skin. She could feel the heat of his body against hers, his trembling arms holding her with desperation. His sorrow radiated through every touch, every whispered breath.

"I love you," she whispered, her voice soft but steady as her eyes closed, her heart beat growing weaker and weaker.

"No," Ashar breathed, his voice thick with grief and barely-contained rage. He pulled her limp body to his and gently pulled the knife from her back. The metal clanged on the stone pathways as he tightened his arms around her, his flames beginning to rise. They danced blue and gold around them. Anger surged through him, burning away his helplessness. He had just found her again; he would not lose her now. The old healer's words echoed in his mind: *From the ashes can come new life.* Ashar closed his eyes, his breathing steadying as he summoned every ounce of his strength. He focused on her wound, on the monster that tried to claim her life. His fire burned brighter, its color shifting to an ethereal blue, hotter than anything he had summoned before. The flames enveloped them both, and the gathered crowd shielded their eyes from the brilliant light and overwhelming heat.

"Come back to me," Ashar whispered, his voice trembling. He poured his energy into her, willing her heart to beat stronger and her breaths to come easier. His power surged from his body into hers, the heat flowing through her veins like a lifeline. And then, he felt it—her heartbeat—growing stronger. Her chest rose and fell with steady breaths. The torn flesh repairing itself, the blood lost being regained. He continued his focus, consumed with his mission to save her. He opened his eyes and stroked her pale cheek. Wiping the dirt streaked across her face away. His flames cooled, his body exhausted with the effort, as he rested his forehead on hers.

"Ashar?" Her voice was quiet, shaking as she opened her eyes.

She gazed upon his face, her cheeks flushing pink, as he held his face close to hers.

Relief flooded him, and he pulled her close, pressing his lips to hers in a tender, desperate kiss. At that moment, no words were needed. The love they had kept buried, the months of longing, the pain of their year-long separation, all of it was poured into that embrace. Ashar had done something he never thought possible. The words of the old healer echoed in his head. *You healed her.* He kissed Mena harder, his passion overtaking him, knowing how close he came to loosening her.

"I love you, too." He whispered in her ear as he pulled her into an even tighter embrace, fearful she would slip away again.

Mena heard the collective gasps of the crowd. She looked up to see her friends' tear-streaked faces, their expressions a mixture of awe and disbelief. Ashar stood on shaky legs, keeping his grip firm but gentle as he eased Mena to her feet. Together, they faced the onlookers, hand in hand, faces flushed, and bodies weak. The courtyard was silent. The war cries had ceased. The clash of steel had faded. The world seemed to hold its breath.

Whispers rippled through the crowd. They had witnessed something impossible, something not taught behind the black walls of the Axis. Mena had been healed by a Cairn, a power thought to be lost to all Echoes. Mena's fingers tightened around Ashar's as she felt a hand on her shoulder. Her fathers. Relief flooded her chest as he turned from the onlookers, his dark eyes filled with pride and unspoken love. As she took him in, her breath caught. His legs. They were no longer flesh and bone but crafted from intricate metal, forged to resemble the limbs he had lost. Her stomach twisted at the sight, the joy of seeing him alive mingling with the anguish of what he had endured. He reached her, pulling her into his arms, his embrace strong and steady.

She buried her face in his shoulder, breathing in the faint scent of jasmine, her mother's scent, still clinging to his warrior's braid.

"Mena. My darling little girl," he whispered, his voice thick with emotion.

Mena felt tears sting her eyes. She wanted nothing more than to be home, to see her mother and brother, to properly mourn her great-aunt, and to find some semblance of normalcy again. But as she stood there, surrounded by her father, her friends, and the man she loved, she knew that the road ahead would not be so simple. The world would change. It had changed. And so had she.

"Your legs…" Mena managed to say as she took a step back, her gaze falling to the sculpted craftsmanship that could only have come from her home continent.

"It does not matter." Thaloren gently tilted her chin up, his dark eyes meeting hers. "Your mother and I have missed you so much, snowdrop."

The familiar name broke something inside her, and tears spilled from her eyes as her father pulled her close again. Memories of a simpler time flashed through her mind, of icy summer mornings, of the little girl he had once cradled in his arms. He had never once hesitated to protect her, to keep her Darra abilities hidden from the world. Now, he smiled at the woman she had become, his heart swelling with pride and relief as he held her once more.

The sound of a slow, mocking clap shattered their moment. Mena pulled away, searching for the source of the disturbance. Her eyes locked onto him, a man cloaked in crimson robes, the crowd parting before him as though his very presence repelled them. Vallorith.

"Family together again. How sweet," he sneered, his sharp features twisting into a cruel grin. He stopped, Zepher flanking him with a retinue of robed disciples standing silently behind. "Too bad it will not last." Vallorith's gaze lingered on Ashar, his expression unreadable, before turning to Thaloren.

"You have two choices, King Thaloren. Surrender now, or watch everyone here die. I will give you exactly *five* seconds to decide before you feel the consequences of defiling the sanctuary of the Axis." He motioned around to the fallen priests and priestesses littering the ground. "Look at them!" His voice rose, sharp and venomous. "Lying around when they have a job to do!" He screamed, his voice cutting through the tense air. Those nearby shrank back, their fear unmistakable.

Thaloren stepped forward, placing himself between Vallorith and Mena. "No more bloodshed. All this fighting was senseless from the beginning. We made it clear that we came only for the princess and that no harm was needed. It was *your* disciples who attacked us without provocation. We defended ourselves because we had no choice. Now you yell at the dead, undermining their sacrifice, those who gave their lives for you, their so-called high priest." The king's voice was calm but firm, his presence commanding. "The ships will leave soon. Anyone who wishes to leave the Axis is welcome aboard. We have plenty of room. This needless violence ends now."

Vallorith tilted his head, his grin stretching wider. "Oh no, dear king, it is only beginning. Five!" He snapped his fingers and vanished.

Zepher dug his claws into the ground, a sickening black smoke oozed from the rubble and cracks in the earth. It crept across the ground in dense, writhing tendrils. The vapor moved with unnatural purpose, curling over fallen soldiers and slipping into their wounds, into their mouths and eyes.

"Get off the ground!" Ashar shouted, his voice barely cutting through the rising screams.

The mist thickened, obscuring their feet as a bone-deep cold sank into them. All around, bodies began to rise, once-lifeless forms, their flesh hanging in tatters, jaws slack, and weapons clutched in lifeless hands.

"That is not possible," Thaloren whispered, his voice barely audible as he watched the dead march again.

"An unnatural ability, the Morin," Mena said, tugging urgently on her father's arm to snap him out of his shock. "We need to get everyone to the ships now!"

Thaloren nodded, his face hardening as he composed himself. He turned to his men, his voice rising above the chaos. "Everyone, to the ships! Help the wounded! Leave no one alive behind!" He turned back to Mena, his expression softening for just a moment. "Go!"

Before she could protest, Ashar pulled her to him. His kiss burned through her, a heat that chased away the cold threatening to paralyze her. "I will always love you," he mouthed silently, his lips curving into a small, bittersweet smile before he pushed her into the hands of a nearby soldier.

"No!" Mena screamed, thrashing against the guard's grip. "He needs me! I can help!"

Ashar had already turned back toward the horror, his flames igniting as he faced back the army of the dead.

Her frantic eyes scanned the battlefield, searching for something, *someone*, to help her. Her gaze caught the great silver bear, Wynna, ripping into a corrupted corpse with a vicious snap of her jaws. With a mighty toss of her head, the creature sent the husk flying before letting out a roar that shook the ground.

"Wynna!" Mena called.

The bear's ears flicked at her voice, and its massive head turned toward her. In a heartbeat, the enormous beast bounded through the commotion, crushing enemies beneath its paws as it made its way to her. Wynna's black eyes locked onto the guard holding Mena's arm. With a low, guttural growl, the bear raised a massive claw and nudged the man, sending him stumbling backward. He hesitated only momentarily before abandoning his task entirely and fleeing toward the ships. Wynna stood protectively by Mena's side, her immense presence radiating strength and unwavering loyalty. Mena's heart pounded as she looked toward the growing swarm of undead and the flames flickering in the distance, Ashar's flames. She gritted her teeth, determination growing. She would return to help, but first, a more critical task captured her heart.

"We need to find the children and get them out!" Mena shouted, her voice straining over the violence that engulfed them.

She turned, frozen in horror, as every fallen body was enveloped by the black mist and rose again. A macabre dance of endless death and rebirth, the bodies fighting, falling, and rising once more, locked in a nightmarish cycle.

"It is never-ending," she whispered, her voice trembling.

Wynna let out a deep, rumbling grunt, almost as if agreeing. An arrow sliced through the air, burying itself deep in Wynna's silver pelt. The bear roared, thrashing as more weapons slashed at her sides. Wynna lashed out, her claws ripping through the nearest husks, but their numbers were too great. A sudden blow sent Mena hurtling from the bear's side. She hit the ground hard, a gasp of relief escaping her lips as she realized she had landed on something soft. But the relief was short-lived. Her stomach turned as she looked down and saw the crumpled body beneath her. The head twitched, its jaw working furiously as if trying to speak. A deep, gurgling sound escaped its slackened lips. Mena screamed, scrambling to her feet as the puppet clawed after her, dragging itself on severed legs. She stumbled backward, narrowly avoiding its grasping hands, before bolting toward the sanctuary. The doors were broken and splintered, hanging askew on twisted hinges. She slipped inside, her breath coming in short, panicked bursts. The once-grand hall was dark; the golden sun now shattered in a mess of broken tiles on the floor, and the angel-like song of the wind chimes was silenced. The oppressive night sky outside, cloaked in thick clouds, offered no light. Though her aurora still rippling in the night, casting a faint glow through fractured windows, it did little to ease he distress.

"Poppy!" Mena shouted, her voice echoing through the cavernous space.

The silence that followed was unbearable. The sanctuary was vast, far too large to search on foot. Her heart raced as she remembered Vallorith's ability to manipulate the walls and turn this very structure against her. She could not afford to waste time and risk being captured again. Lifting her hand, she conjured a flickering orb of light, its faint glow stretching her shadow across the dust-covered floor. Mena inhaled deeply, closing her eyes as she extended her hand and spread her fingers wide. She let her power flow outward, spreading through the halls like invisible tendrils. The air shifted around her as her magic stretched into every corner, brushing against walls, curling through doorways, and searching every room just as her great-aunt Myra had once done.

"Mena!"

Her concentration snapped, her eyes flying open. She turned to see Fraya and Finn pushing through the shattered remnants of the door.

"We need to go!" Fraya panted, her expression grim. "Everyone who falls is rising again. We are becoming overrun!"

Mena shook her head. "Not without the children. Can you feel them?"

The two exchanged a worried glance before crouching low, pressing their hands to the ground. Mena watched anxiously as they reached out with their magic. After a long, tense moment, they stood, shaking their heads. "They are not here," Finn said quietly.

Mena's chest tightened, her heart sinking like a stone. "How? Where could they be?"

"We will have to return for them later," Fraya urged. "Right now, we have to go!"

Reluctantly, Mena nodded, and they moved back into the courtyard together. They froze. The battlefield was a sea of hissing husks, their unnatural movements sending chills down Mena's spine. The reanimated bodies swayed and jerked as they moved, their bones cracking grotesquely with every step. Her eyes scanned the battlefield until they landed on her father and Ashar. They were still fighting, their swords cutting through the relentless tide of enemies as they helped others escape. Mena's mind raced. The mirrors. The two already trapped souls. Her father and mother. Sylvie. Slek. Fraya. Finn. Wynna. Her thoughts were interrupted as her gaze caught on a familiar figure stumbling toward her through the mist. Her heart fell as she watched the figure draw closer. Slow jerking steps, its face shadowed by the rippling aurora above. The three friends stared as recognition struck them like a thunderbolt.

"Mylo," Fraya cried, her voice trembling as the familiar figure loomed closer.

The three huddled together, Finn stepping forward to form a protective barrier around them. With his hands outstretched, he summoned a simple slate wall to protect them, though Mena could see his strength waning. This was not how it was supposed to end. Not here. Not like this. Gritting her teeth, Mena balled her fists, letting her anger and fear coil together like a spring inside her chest. She could feel the weight of the magic surging through her veins, the raw, untamed power begging for release. If the Morin could wield his twisted gift to create such destruction, then she would answer with something far more significant, something good. Something unstoppable. Her hand shot to the sky, fingers trembling as her magic took control. A strange calm washed over her as though she had surrendered herself completely to the storm inside. The air around her crackled, shifting with unseen forces. Fraya and Finn stepped back, their wide eyes reflecting the flickering glow radiating from Mena. Her aurora dimmed, its radiant colors folding into the void of her now-blackened eyes. The dark sky above seemed to ripple, like silk caught in a breeze, and then, from the fading aurora, it appeared.

Massive wings stretched out across the battlefield. Powerful legs, thick with muscle and covered in snow-white feathers, landed with a heavy thud. Sharp and gleaming glass talons curled into the earth, digging deep as the beast let out a roar that shook the ground. Its cry even rivaled Wynna's. It was a primal boast of power and defiance.

Fraya's voice was barely above a whisper. "That is... that is a..."

"A dragon," Mena said, her voice steady despite the storm raging within her.

The dragon was a creature of raw beauty and terror. Its feathers shimmered like frost-kissed snow, and beneath them, scales of frosted glass caught the light in dazzling refractions.

Its glacier-blue eyes burned with ancient intelligence, locking onto the cursed army with predatory precision. Rows of jagged, crystalline teeth lined its maw, and as it drew in a deep breath, its entire body glowed, radiating heat like a forge stoked to life.

"Ashar!" Mena's voice rang out, cutting through the madness that was the dead.

Their eyes met across the courtyard, and the world seemed to fall silent for a fleeting moment. She did not need to say anything else. He understood. Ashar raised his hand, summoning his flames. Brilliant blue fire erupted from his fingertips, twisting and arcing like a living thing through the air.

The dragon inhaled deeply, drawing in the flames, and its body began to pulse with light, brighter and hotter with each second. The dragon crouched low, its wings folding tight against its sides as it unleashed its protective fury. A torrent of blue fire erupted from its jaws, scorching the mist and the twisted bodies it controlled. The flames burned away everything tainted by Zepher's dark power, leaving nothing but ash in their wake. The mist recoiled and shriveled, unable to withstand the purifying heat.

"Shield!" Finn shouted.

Fraya was already moving, her hands carving through the air as she raised a wall of stone and trees around the survivors. Mena ducked behind it, shielding her eyes as the light from the dragon's flames blazed brighter than the sun. The battlefield was chaos, a storm of heat and destruction, but Mena felt a flicker of hope through it all. The dragon roared again, its massive wings flapping as it ascended into the sky. Silent as an owl, it glided above the battlefield, raining fire down on the dead soldiers. The once-imposing horde was reduced to ashes, their bodies crumbling into the ground like forgotten shadows. As the flames subsided, the battlefield fell eerily quiet. Ash drifted through the air like snow, coating everything in a fine layer of gray.

The survivors, what few remained, stared upward, their eyes fixed on the dragon's white plumage as it soared on the currents of the wind. Ashar reached Thaloren, wrapping an arm around him to steady the king as he helped him toward the docks. One of Thaloren's prosthetics had been shattered in the fight, leaving him to limp heavily.

"Let us get you aboard," Ashar insisted, helping Thaloren down the stairs and towards the ship's deck. The king hesitated, looking back toward the battlefield, but Ashar shook his head. "You are in no condition."

The ship's crew rushed to secure Thaloren, and Ashar turned back to the battlefield, his gaze locking onto Mena once more.

She stood amidst the wreckage, her hand still outstretched, her connection to the dragon strong as its glowing form flew in the night sky. Ashar's heart clenched. She looked like a goddess of war, powerful and unyielding but fragile beneath the weight of it all.

"Mena..." he whispered, his voice rough with emotion.

"Get my daughter, and let us go," Thaloren said, his voice strained as he leaned against the ship's railing, pain creasing his brow. His eyes lingered on the dragon, Kallemena's gift, now circling the vessels like a silent, celestial guardian.

Ashar did not need to be told twice. He bolted down the docks, his chest tight with urgency. As he came to the top of the stairs, he came face-to-face with the silver bear, its imposing form blocking his path. In mere seconds, the fur quickly receded, and in its place stood a wobbly girl with thick, wild brown hair. She pressed a hand against her bleeding shoulder, leaning against two fiery-haired twins for support.

"She is back there," Fraya said, her accent foreign to Ashar's ears as Finn moved to scoop up Wynna, who was trembling in his arms.

Ashar gave a quick nod of thanks, sparing no time for words as he sprinted past them. His boots pounded against the pathways of the courtyard. Mena stood under a broken statue that Ashar had recognized as the goddess Danira. He watched as Mena directed survivors toward the ships. Her soot-covered face was calm but focused, her eyes darting between the people and the glowing white dragon that soared high above, its majestic form gliding against the growing pale light of dawn. Even from a distance, she radiated strength, but Ashar could see the exhaustion weighing on her. She looked like a soldier who had carried the weight of a war on her back. He approached her, his heart hammering in his chest. Words, so many words, swirled in his mind, but when she turned to him, her dark eyes meeting his, everything vanished. They stood a breath apart, smeared in soot and ash, their bodies aching from the night's events. The sun had begun to creep over the horizon, casting warm hues across the battlefield's broken remnants.

Slek and Sylvie approached them, their steps hesitant. "That is everyone," Slek said, rubbing the back of his neck, his voice heavy with fatigue.

Sylvie shook as she looked back to what had been her home for half her life. Her gaze was locked on the battered sanctuary walls they were leaving behind. Silent tears rolled down her cheeks as she rubbed her arms, trembling. Mena reached out, stroking Sylvie's back gently, though her own throat tightened. She did not know what to say. What could she say to ease the pain of leaving behind a home she could never return to? After a few moments of quiet, they all turned and walked toward the last ship. A sigh escaped Mena's lips as the ramp was pulled from the dock. The weight of the night pressed down on her all at once, the memories of what had just unfolded feeling more like fragments of a nightmare than reality. Her mind swam with blurred images, fire, screams, and the dragon's roar. Without realizing it, she gripped Ashar's hand. His warmth steadied her, grounding her. She felt his arm wrap around her, his breath brushing against her forehead as he pulled her close. It was a comfort she did not know she needed. Her gaze shifted to her father, Thaloren, sitting on the deck.

Comrades and friends surrounded him; his prosthetic leg shattered, but his spirit remained intact. Relief flooded her chest at the sight of him alive, but her heart ached for what had been lost.

"Ashar," she said softly, her voice trembling as she looked up at him. "I am sorry about your father."

His eyes met hers, and though he said nothing, their grief was unmistakable. A single tear rolled down his soot-streaked cheek.

Mena pressed her forehead to his chest, her tears carving soot canyons on her cheeks. "I should have done more," she whispered, her voice breaking. "I should have fought harder. If I had, Vallorith would have never taken me; your father would have never been on that ship. And Myra..."

Ashar shook his head, his hands covering hers. "No. None of this was your fault, Mena." His voice was steady despite the grief in his chest. He tilted her chin upward gently, forcing her to meet his gaze. "He poisoned you. He kidnapped you. This was all his doing, not yours."

She opened her mouth to protest, but the words died as he leaned down and pressed his lips to her forehead. He pulled her into his arms, holding her close. For the first time in what felt like an eternity, she let herself sink into his warmth, letting it chase away the cold that had seeped into her bones.

"Kallemena," Her name on his lips stirred something in her. She loved the sound. "I have thought about you every day since you were taken." He drew her back to look at her. "I will always fight for you. To be with you."

He swallowed hard, unsure of his next words. He lowered himself to one knee, His hands shaking as he held on to hers. "I know a lot has happened, and this is not the romantic setting I had envisioned for us, but I know I never want to be away from you ever again. I love you with all my heart, Kallemena Vaelora." His eyes were wet with tears as he cleared his throat. "Will you marry..."

"Yes!" she blurted, cutting him off as she threw her arms around him.

Ashar laughed, scooping her up in his arms and spinning her around. Mena clung to him, laughing through her tears. The future seemed brighter and filled with hope, for something she never thought she would have. As the ship rocked gently beneath them, the dragon's distant roar echoed across the horizon, a solemn reminder of all they had endured and all they had yet to face. The cheers and whistles of the crew erupted across the deck as Ashar raised her hand to his lips and gently kissed her knuckles.

Slek clapped Ashar on the back with enough force to make him stagger, his hearty laughter booming. "Congratulations!"

Fraya leaned closer, wrapping her arms around her friend. "He is better looking than you described," she teased.

Finn laughed as he steadied Wynna, her arm now bandaged and in a sling.

"Wait until Mylo hears about this. He is going to be heartbroken. His princess betrothed to another man." She let out a bark of laughter, only pausing when she noticed the look on the others' faces. "What?"

Fraya was the first to speak, her tone subdued. "He... he did not make it, Wynna. He fell in battle."

Before Wynna could respond, a voice cut through the moment. "Who fell in battle?"

The group turned sharply, their gasps audible as a familiar figure emerged onto the helm. Mylo stood there, very much alive. His bright green eyes glowed unnaturally as he smiled with sinister glee. The image of his possessed form, twisted and consumed, rose unbidden in Mena's mind. Then she recognized exactly whose eyes were looking at her now.

"No!" Mena screamed as the air around them warped and shimmered. A portal opened beneath their feet, pulling them all into the cold, unrelenting darkness.

Mena's head throbbed as she struggled to open her eyes. The faint pulse of light danced across the walls of the small, oppressive room, a light emanating from the ruins carved into the stone. Her vision was blurry, but she recognized the space immediately—the room of mirrors. A rough hand covered her mouth, and she thrashed weakly against the bindings that cut into her wrists once more. A gag now tied around her mouth muffled her cries as her strength was drained, her power fading as if pulled from her very core. Around her, she saw her friends, all bound and silenced like her. Ashar was slumped nearby, along with every one of her friends. Her gaze snapped to Zepher, now standing near Finn, his glowing eyes cold as he tightened the ropes around her friend's wrists. He looked at her briefly, a snarl tugging at his lips, a look of disgust for her. Then came *him*.

"I knew she would be the first to wake," Vallorith said, his voice calm and cutting as he moved toward the wall. He plucked a mirror from its place, this one marked with a delicate leaf carving. "I do not really need two," he mused aloud, his gaze falling on the twins. "But they have such an... unnatural bond. It might be fun to keep them together. Yes, I think that is best."

Mena screamed against the gag, her voice muffled. She writhed in her binds, desperate to stop him. Anything to hold off the inevitable. Vallorith raised the mirror high as he chanted unheard words, and in a flash, Fraya and Finn vanished—the space where they had been felt hollow, a crushing void that tore at Mena's heart. Tears streamed down her face as she slumped her head against the cold stone in despair. The ache in her chest was unbearable. She fought with every ounce of her strength, but the ropes held fast.

"Stop!" she tried to scream, but it was no use.

Vallorith moved methodically, taking another mirror from the wall. This one bore the carving of an arrow. Mena's blood ran cold. She could only watch as Slek disappeared, the spot he had occupied now empty. Her screams turned into broken sobs as her will began to shatter. He plucked another mirror from the wall and held it over Wynna.

Mena's heart broke as she watched another friend vanish from the world. Was this how it would end? One by one, her friends stolen from her so easily while she lay here helpless? A sharp cry broke through her hopelessness.

She turned her head just enough to see the door to the next room swing open. Zepher stepped inside, his glowing eyes cold as ice. But beyond him, through the crack in the door, she saw blue eyes staring back at her, Poppy. The children were alive. They were here. Hope flared like a dying ember in her chest, sparking something primal. She thrashed again, inching ever so slowly toward Ashar. She nudged his leg with her head, her movements frantic. His sharp inhale told her he had awoken. His eyes met hers, and though they were weary, there was a fire in them, a fire she clung to.

The high priest's voice cut through the air. "It is almost poetic that you came to me so willingly, dear king of Highspire," he said, his tone dripping with satire. "Can you imagine how bothersome it would have been having you chained and escorted from the council meeting? Who needs that headache? And then that little *display* of yours, healing your precious princess... it was as if you were praying for me to choose you. Begging for me to have you as my Cairn."

Mena's body froze as Vallorith reached for another mirror, this one marked with a sun carving. He moved toward Ashar, his movements deliberate. "Too bad that wedding will have to wait... forever." His grin was pure evil as he watched Mena struggle.

"No," she yelled, the word barely audible through her gag.

The acrid scent of burning filled the room as Ashar's hands suddenly burst into flames, the ropes binding him incinerating in an instant. He lunged at Vallorith, the force of his attack sending them both crashing to the floor. Fire engulfed the room, licking at the walls as Ashar and Vallorith grappled. The high priest screamed for Zepher, his voice unsteady and panicked. Mena gritted her teeth against the pain as a stray flame seared her wrist, the ropes fraying just enough for her to pull free. She ripped the gag from her mouth, her breaths ragged as smoke filled the room. She scrambled to Sylvie without hesitation, shaking her awake and undoing her binds. Sylvie's eyes snapped open wide and filled with fear as she took in the state of the room around them.

"We have to be quick," Mena whispered, her voice trembling but resolute. "This is not over yet."

"What..." Sylvie whimpered back, her voice trembling as she pressed a hand over her mouth, her eyes wide with horror.

Mena gripped her arm tightly. "Your sister and the children are in the other room. We have to get them out." Suddenly, a sharp tug at her hair yanked her head back. She gasped, spinning to find Zepher dragging her toward the mirrors, his glowing eyes cold and merciless. "Sylvie, *go!*" she yelled, summoning an obsidian glass blade into her hand.

With one swift motion, she sliced through her long black hair, freeing herself from Zepher's grip. The blade left her hand in an instant, cutting through the air before embedding itself in the Morin's arm. Zepher howled, clutching the wound as blood seeped through his fingers. Mena did not wait to see him recover; she bolted for the door. The room beyond was crowded with frightened faces, but one stood out.

"Poppy," Mena breathed, relief flooding her as the little girl's face lit up with joy.

Poppy was snug in Sylvie's arms, and Mena's heart felt relieved knowing the children would be safe with her friend.

"Everyone, get to your feet!" Mena ordered, her voice sharp and commanding. "Be ready to catch yourselves; you are about to fall."

With a swift motion, she waved her hands, summoning a shimmering portal beneath their feet. The air warped as the portal expanded. Mena's gaze lingered on Poppy for a brief moment before flickering to Sylvie.

"I am sorry I could not save Slek," her voice cracking under the weight of her failure.

Sylvie's teary, questioning eyes burned into hers, but before she could respond, the portal pulled her and Poppy through. The others followed, vanishing in a flash of light. The last thing Mena saw before the portal closed was Sylvie clutching Poppy on the deck of the ship, her blue eyes searching for her. Then pain exploded at the back of Mena's head, and everything went dark for a heartbeat. She hit the cold stone floor with a gasp, Vallorith's iron grip dragging her back into the room of mirrors. He released her roughly, her knees scraping against the ground as she struggled to regain her balance. Vallorith stood before the mirrors, his furious gaze scanning the wall.

"Now I have to find another Talon with god blood!" he snarled, slamming his fist into the stone. "Do you *know* how rare that is?"

Mena's attention shifted from his rage to the room. Her eyes wide with worry at the sight. Ashar floated midair, his body limp, his skin taking on a sickly blue hue. His eyes were wide with panic; his lips parted in a silent gasp as if the very air had been stolen from him.

"Ashar!" Mena screamed. She scrambled to her knees and waved her hand, her magic surging toward him. The invisible force around him shattered, and he collapsed to the ground, coughing violently as he clawed his way toward her. Mena pulled him into her arms, her trembling fingers brushing against his cheek. His skin was cold, his pulse faint beneath her touch.

"Myra said... do not fear the reflections," Ashar whispered, his voice strained with the effort to breathe. He lifted a weak hand to hers, pressing a kiss to her knuckles, and then he was gone.

Mena's scream tore through the room, raw and filled with anguish. Her vision blurred with tears as she clutched at the empty space where Ashar had been. Her chest ached as if her heart had been ripped from her body, leaving a hollow, gaping wound in its place.

"No, no, no!" she sobbed, her cries echoing off the stone walls.

A sudden, crushing grip around her throat cut off her air. Mena clawed at Zepher's arm as he held her in a vice-like hold, dragging her toward her own mirror. Panic surged through her, wild and consuming, as she watched her reflection grow closer and closer. Her own face stared back at her, pale and desperate, hopelessness painfully evident in her eyes. She lifted her hand, summoning every last scrap of energy she could muster. Her magic burned through her, pulling from reserves she did not know she had. Above Vallorith's head, a mirror materialized, its frame dark and jagged like the obsidian blade she summoned earlier. The high priest turned, confusion flickering across his face for the briefest moment before the mirror pulled him in. The room rippled and warped as Mena felt herself dragged into her own mirror. The last thing she saw was Zepher's wide amber eyes. Then, there was nothing.

Part IV: The Echo From Tirnmoor

Chapter Nineteen

It had been months since Kallemena had shared her story with Nemeah, so long since the farm girl had left the familiar comforts of her home and family to embark on this uncertain journey. Months since she stood at Thornwatch Harbor, the salty air biting her cheeks as she watched the hustle of the docks. Ships swayed on the tide, their crews calling orders as they unloaded crates of goods. Nemeah clutched her meager belongings tightly, nerves fraying as she considered the enormity of what lay ahead. After much procrastination and doubt, she managed to purchase passage on one of the larger vessels bound for Nocthrea. The sailors leered and whistled as she climbed aboard, their coarse laughter adding to her discomfort. Keeping her gaze low, she followed the captain's directions to a cramped storage room below deck, a space he allowed her to use for the duration of the trip. The air was damp and smelled faintly of salt and mold, but it had a door she could lock, and for that, she was grateful.

Once alone, Nemeah conjured a simple bed from her magic, the soft glow of dim orbs illuminating the room's darkest corners. The ship lurched beneath her feet, and her stomach churned in protest. Each drop and rise of the vessel on the icy waves felt like a cruel game, the relentless rocking pushing her to her limits. She pressed a hand to her abdomen, grateful, for the first time, that her father had been a farmer and not a sailor. When the captain knocked on her door to announce their arrival at port, she wept. Nemeah had spent what felt like eons battling the sea's merciless rhythm. Her stomach twisted one final time as the ship slowed to the dock. She stumbled above deck, desperate for solid ground.

Nocthrea greeted her with a stark, wintry beauty. Its cold air stung her lungs, but its towering evergreens and snow-laden rooftops whispered promises of adventure. For the first few days, Nemeah had expected Kallemena to appear, to guide her as she had done in the past. Yet the mirror remained silent, its smooth surface offering no answers. The mysterious princess within had vanished, leaving Nemeah adrift in an unfamiliar land. With no direction, she lingered in the quiet fishing village of Havenwood. The cobblestone streets and quaint cottages became her new surroundings as she wandered aimlessly, learning the twists of its narrow roads and the dense forest that bordered the town. She often found herself pausing beneath the towering pines, their needles brushing the clear blue sky, to listen to the steady drip of melting snow. Winter was losing its grip, and the first hints of spring warmed the earth beneath her boots.

Still, the weight of Kallemena's warning pressed on her. The Eclipse Veil was coming. Discomfort only grew within her, knowing that the day was ebbing closer and closer. Time was slipping away faster than the snow melting around her, and each day that passed without a plan felt like a betrayal of the purpose she had left home to fulfill. A small inn sat perched above a tavern on the edge of Havenwood, close enough to the docks that the scent of salt water mingled with the faint aroma of stale ale and fish. Nemeah had procured a room there, a modest and lonely space that seemed to amplify her homesickness. She often woke in the dead of night, gasping from restless dreams, her cries for her mother and father swallowed by the darkness. She hated to wake this way, but after hearing Kallemena's tale, she knew never again would she consume the silvervane herb that abated the bad dreams.

The small room greeted her with silence, the walls cool and unyielding, and the thin blanket wrapped around her offered little comfort. She missed the days when her sister Orla would crawl into bed with her, their whispered conversations chasing away the shadows. Now, for the first time in her life, she truly felt alone, a feeling she did not welcome. In her solitude, Nemeah found small comforts in the similarities between Havenwood and Fayridge. The bustling docks, more laden with fish than produce, still echoed with the merchants' daily calls. Rain or shine, they sang about their wares, praising their freshness and offering deals to passersby. Nemeah often watched the scene from her cramped room through her small, salt-streaked window.

The mirror rested quietly atop the nightstand while her precious bag of gold was tucked deep within her travel bag, hidden from prying eyes. When the nights grew too quiet, Nemeah practiced her magic. With a wave of her hand, she conjured a floating orb of light, its soft glow casting long shadows across the room. Another gesture brought forth a silver-winged butterfly that flitted through the air, its delicate wings shimmering like moonlight. She practiced the techniques Kallemena had taught her, even recreating the void where she first spoke with the mysterious princess. In the simulated expanse, she gazed upon a sky glittering with stars and streaked with comets, their light sparking an ache in her chest. It felt as though she could create anything, anything but happiness. Her heart ached to be able to show Orla the stars beyond the clouds of Tirnmoor. Or make a portal to go visit her father in his barn, the old mare in the field. Even just to see her mother again, although she was sure she was no longer welcome.

No matter how hard she tried, no matter how much her heart ached for home, she could not form a doorway to the familiar fields and streams of her family's farm. Each failed attempt left her frustrated, longing for one more glimpse of the past. Yet a portal remained stubbornly out of reach. The mornings brought wind that howled through the drafty room, carrying with it the briny tang of the sea. Nemeah watched her orb dance in the air, spinning and gliding as though it had a mind of its own. The movement offered a fleeting distraction from her thoughts. She glanced toward the mirror on the nightstand. Its surface gleamed faintly in the dim glow.

"Where now?" she murmured, lifting the mirror. Her fingers traced its edges as she whispered, "What am I supposed to do, Mena?"

A knock at the door startled her. Heart pounding, she quickly tucked the mirror beneath the covers and extinguished her light with a wave. The room plunged into shadows as she crossed to the door, the hinges groaning in protest as she cracked it open. Relief washed over her when she saw the innkeeper standing on the other side.

"Good evening, Mrs. Donnar," Nemeah greeted politely, though the older woman's pinched face remained unmoved.

The innkeeper leaned against the doorframe, a thin, skeletal figure swathed in a faded dress that hung loose on her frail frame. She raised a cigarette to her lips, the glowing ember casting eerie shadows on her sunken features. As she exhaled, a cloud of sour-smelling smoke curled into the room, burning Nemeah's nostrils and lungs.

"Boarding fees are due," the woman said, her voice surprisingly youthful despite her weathered appearance. Her brown-stained teeth flashed briefly as she spoke, her watery eyes searching into Nemeah's room.

Nemeah blinked, startled. Had another week already passed? A sharp pang of guilt shot through her as she realized how quickly time was slipping by. Soon, the animals back home would be birthing their young, marking half a year since she had left Tirnmoor. Panic fluttered in her chest. She needed a plan, something to bring her closer to freeing Kallemena.

"I will pay for one more week," Nemeah said finally. "I plan to move on now that the seasons are changing, and soon, the nights will be warmer."

She turned to her dresser and began rummaging through it for coins. The clink of gold and silver filled the small room, drawing an inquisitive look from the innkeeper. Nemeah retrieved a handful of coins, sorting through the silvers and coppers until she had enough for a week's board and meals. As she handed them over, the woman's expression darkened. She inhaled greedily on her cigarette, only to choke on its throat-searing burn. A fit of hacking and coughing followed each exhale, releasing small puffs of gray smoke into the air.

Nemeah quickly stuffed the remaining coins back into a drawer, offering the woman a polite smile as she passed over the payment. Mrs. Donnar nodded, her red eyes lingering on Nemeah. The weight of the woman's gaze sent a shiver down Nemeah's spine, and she tightened her grip on the old handle of her door.

"I do not welcome your kind here for so long. Working girls usually bring trouble wherever they go. Thugs following close behind and whatnot." Mrs. Donnar coughed sharply before turning to make her way back down the hall.

Nemeah was shocked at the old woman's words, not knowing how to react. She closed the door softly and returned to her bed, retrieving the mirror once more. A small beam of sunlight filtered through the window, catching on the intricate carvings of its frame. The delicate craftsmanship never failed to draw her gaze. Despite the bitter feelings she harbored toward the high priest Vallorith, she begrudgingly admired the meticulous detail he had put into creating the mirror. Staring into her own reflection, Nemeah let out a groan.

"What do I do?" she muttered, her breath fogging the glass. She wrapped the mirror carefully in its cloth and tucked it back into her bag.

Slipping on her coat, she grabbed some money from the dresser and left the tavern. Outside, the air was brisk, but the sun's warmth danced on her skin, sending gooseflesh down her arms and legs. She welcomed the crunch of cobblestones beneath her boots and the call of gulls overhead. The docks bustled with life, the sharp tang of ocean waves and fish filling the air as merchants hollered their wares to eager buyers. Nemeah moved through the crowd with practiced ease, weaving around bustling bodies and outstretched hands. She stopped at a fruit stand she often watched from her window. The vendor, a diligent woman, always unloaded fresh crates from the morning boats, arranging them with care into bright pyramids of oranges, apples, and pears. Today, something new caught Nemeah's eye.

"Excuse me, what are these?" she asked, pointing to a purplish-black fruit with a thick stem.

The merchant shuffled over, inspecting the fruit before glancing at Nemeah. "Figs," she replied matter-of-factly.

Nemeah felt her cheeks flush, grateful for the cool breeze that brushed her face. She had heard of figs in passing, stories and songs, but had never seen them in person. Offering the merchant a shy smile, she bought a handful, carefully folding them into a small pouch and tucking them into her pocket. After adding a loaf of bread and a few carrots to her purchases, she left the bustling market and headed to her favorite retreat.

She had discovered the clearing by chance during her first days in Havenwood. A terrible storm had blown in, icy rain biting at her skin as she stumbled through the forest. Freezing and disoriented, she had been ready to collapse when a white hare emerged from the trees. Its black, beady eyes had locked on hers, and without hesitation, it had hopped forward, pausing only to glance back at her as though beckoning her to follow. The ground had been treacherously slick, the wind howling in her ears, but the storm melted away when she stepped into the clearing. The air seemed muted, the ground clear of snow, and though the cold remained, the calmness of the place was a balm to her frayed nerves. The hare had sniffed curiously at her boots and skirt before twitching its ears, alert to the distant sounds of the storm. Since that day, the clearing had become her sanctuary. Now, the forest was slowly waking from winter's grip. The snow at the edges had melted into patches, revealing damp earth dotted with tender green sprouts. The clearing itself was alive with early signs of spring. Buds peeked from branches, and the grass swayed gently in the breeze that managed to slip past the towering oaks.

Nemeah settled onto her usual spot, an old fallen tree trunk now blanketed with soft moss and sprouting clusters of mushrooms. She pulled the carrots from her pocket, holding them in her lap as she practiced whistling. Her first attempt came out as a sharp, shrill note that quickly dissolved into a sputtering raspberry. She winced, feeling heat rise to her face, though there was no one to witness her embarrassment but the trees. Still, she tried again, her lips forming the sound with more care. She thought of the hare, wondering if it would return today. The forest seemed to hold its breath, and Nemeah waited, the crisp air carrying the faint rustle of leaves and the chirp of distant birds. Here, in this quiet haven, she could almost forget the weight of her burdens.

The snap of twigs and the rustle of bushes broke the stillness before the white hare bounded into the clearing. Its once pristine white fur had started to shift to soft shades of brown, marking the return of spring's warmth.

"Hello there." Nemeah smiled as she extended a carrot.

The hare sniffed it cautiously before taking the offering, greedily stuffing half of it into its cheek before scurrying a short distance away. She chuckled, knowing it would be back for more soon enough. Raising her hand, she summoned Alban. Her ever-faithful guardian materialized beside her, his towering presence a reassuring weight in the growing unease of her thoughts.

"What should I do, Alban?" she murmured, resting her head in her hands. Her elbows dug into her thighs as she stared at the ground. "It has been almost five months, and I am no closer than I was back then." Her eyes flicked up to his helmeted face, seeking answers that never came. "Where do I go from here?"

The clearing was alive with the quiet hum of spring. Birds peeked from branches, and small pink and yellow flowers had begun to bloom, speckling the grass with color. Bright green leaves unfurled along the limbs of ancient oaks, casting dappled shadows over the soft earth. The world here felt untouched, as though time itself hesitated to intrude. Nemeah tore a piece from her loaf of bread, the crackling crust giving way to its warm, sweet inside. She inhaled its scent, memories of home washing over her like a tide. She could almost see her mother bustling at the stove, the smell of stews and freshly baked loaves filling their little kitchen. And there, under the table, would be Orla, her little sister, giggling as she pretended to hide from imagined monsters.

Nemeah blinked as a tear slid down her cheek. Her stomach twisted. She had been the monster all along. She had brought the Axis to their doorstep, upending their lives forever. A quick nip at her hand snapped her from her thoughts. She startled, looking down at the hare, now nibbling boldly at her bread.

"No, you greedy thing," she said, shooing it away gently. "You get the carrots."

Reaching into her pocket, she retrieved another fat root and snapped it in half with a satisfying crack. The hare's black eyes followed her every movement, its nose twitching furiously as it waited. She held the carrot out, watching as it eagerly grabbed the piece with its tiny paws. Its slender teeth worked quickly to devour it, its ears flicking at every faint sound from the forest.

"Well," she sighed, reaching for her pouch, "I suppose you can share some figs with me. I have never had them before. Do you think they are any good?"

She unfolded the cloth carefully, revealing the dark, plump fruits. The hare sniffed them curiously, selecting one to stuff into its cheek before snatching another and hopping off.

"I guess that is a yes," Nemeah said with a small laugh.

She hesitated before picking up one of the figs, its thick purple skin glinting in the soft light. Biting into it cautiously, she was met with the surprising sweetness of its ruby-red inside. The flavor lingered, rich and almost honeyed. She savored it as she leaned back, letting her gaze drift to the sky.

"I wish I had a map. Or a guide," she murmured, looking over at Alban. "Anything to show me the way."

The sentry stood motionless, stoic as ever, his figure casting a long shadow over the clearing. She let her eyes roam over him, admiring her handiwork. Over the months, she had refined his appearance. Gone was the ragged farmhand and crumpled metal she had first imagined. Alban now stood like a noble warrior, his chest and shoulders encased in polished armor, plates covering his thighs. His helmet gleamed in the sunlight, a design she had crafted to allow his face to show through the slits, a face she had sculpted with care. His long nose and severe brows gave him an imposing air, but it was his eyes that mattered most. She had given him her father's eyes: deep, solemn, and searching as if they could see through any lie. Another tug at her hand drew her from her thoughts.

"Here," she said, tearing a chunk of bread and handing it to the insistent hare. "You are going to eat me out of everything, you little glutton."

They ate in companionable silence, the warmth of the clearing lulling Nemeah into a light, drowsy state. The sun inched across the sky, its golden light giving way to the cool silver glow of the rising moon. Shadows stretched long across the ground, and the air grew noticeably cooler. Nemeah sat up, rubbing her eyes. The hare was gone, and Alban had moved closer, crouched beside her. His gaze was fixed on the tree line, his stance tense.

"We should head back before dark," she said, brushing off her skirt. "Thank you for..."

A sharp snap of a twig cut her off. She froze. The sound of movement grew closer, the rustling of bushes accompanied by faint metallic clinks. Figures emerged from the shadows of the forest, their forms indistinct but unmistakably armed.

"I think we have found our strumpet, boys," a gruff voice called out.

Nemeah's heart hammered in her chest. She spun, hearing another crunch behind her. They were surrounded. The Axis knights advanced slowly, swords gleaming in the faint light. Alban rose to his full height, drawing his weapon with deliberate precision. The blade caught the dusk's last few glimmers of light, a fierce shimmer that matched the protective resolve in his stance. He stepped forward, positioning himself between Nemeah and the encroaching threat. The clearing, once her sanctuary, had now become a cage.

Nemeah's voice trembled as she stepped back, her hands clenched tightly at her sides. "What do you want? If it is money, I can pay."

A ragged laugh erupted from one of the armored soldiers now standing in the clearing. His helmet obscured his face, and his cloak billowed slightly with his movements, hinting at the bulk of his tall frame. Each deliberate step forward tested Alban's patience until his menacing sword tilted to meet the soldier's throat.

"We do not want your money. We want *you*," the soldier sneered, his eyes flicking past Alban to lock onto Nemeah. "We have had reports of a street walker here, defiling our quaint little town's reputation."

"What?" Nemeah's voice cracked, her panic bubbling to the surface. "I am no lady of the night! I am just a traveler staying at the inn."

The soldier's lips curled into a smirk. "That is not what the innkeeper says. And we do not tolerate such a lifestyle in our neighborhoods, do we, boys?" The rest of the guards chuckled. "At least not without us sampling the goods firsthand."

Nemeah felt her stomach drop. The realization of her isolation, far from home and family. Far from anyone who could help. It hit her like a blow to the chest. The soldier's smile widened as he took another step forward.

"Drop your weapon," he ordered Alban, batting at the blade in warning.

But Alban did not flinch. His sword returned to its place at the soldier's throat with unwavering precision, steel gleaming in the sunlight.

"I said drop it," the soldier growled, his voice tinged with frustration. "Or I will make you."

A snap sounded from behind Nemeah. Before she could react, a rough hand clamped down on her wrist, pulling her backwards. Fear spiked through her, her mind reeling, but Alban was faster. His blade plunged into the chest of her assailant, the strike clean and merciless. The man gasped, a wet, gurgling sound escaping his lips as his hand slipped from Nemeah's arm, fumbling for his own weapon. Blood darkened his tunic as Alban twisted his sword free, the motion fluid and practiced. Time seemed to slow as the soldier dropped to his knees and collapsed face-first onto the forest floor, blood pooling beneath him. The air thickened with tension as a battle cry erupted from the trees. Five more Axis soldiers charged into the clearing, their swords glinting as they raised them high. Alban whirled to meet them, his blade a silver blur as he struck down two with a powerful blow. The remaining soldiers pressed forward, their leader shouting orders as he lunged at Alban, his strikes landing futilely against the sentry's shielded back.

"I will have your head for this!" the leader snarled, yanking a hidden dagger from his belt and driving it toward Alban's side.

The blade sank deep through the metal that wrapped his torso, the hilt protruding from Alban's ribs.

"No!" Nemeah screamed, the sound raw and desperate. Panic surged through her veins, her instincts overriding her thoughts.

She threw out her hand, and the world around them seemed to respond. The wind had ceased. Fog erupted from the forest floor, its opaque waves twisting and snaking toward the soldiers. The men cried out as painful numbing cold crawled up their legs, burrowing under their armor. The fog seemed to encase the enemy, holding them in place. Nemeah's chest heaved as she stared at the scene, her breath shallow and rapid. She turned to Alban, her voice cracking.

"What do I do? We need to find a doctor, someone who can help!" Her hands fluttered helplessly as her vision blurred with tears.

Alban's gloved hand wrapped around the dagger lodged in his side. With a quick motion, he pulled it free. Nemeah gasped, expecting a flood of blood, but there was none. The wound sealed itself before her eyes, the armor's surface shimmering faintly as it mended.

"You are not hurt?" she whispered, relief flooding her voice. She threw her arms around him, clinging to his broad frame.

"An Echo! I will see you hanged!" one of the trapped soldiers spat, his words a very believable threat.

Nemeah froze. Slowly, she turned to face the men ensnared in her trap. Her heart hammered in her chest as she took a shaky step forward, her fists clenching at her sides. "Why does the Axis hunt Echoes?" she demanded, her voice trembling but resolute. "Did the Axis not once protect them? What has changed?"

The soldier's dark eyes glinted through the slits of his helmet as he sneered. "Echoes are an abomination. They were never meant to roam amongst the rest of us. We hunt filth like you to cleanse the world of your existence." He struggled against the icy grip, his movements causing the fog to tighten on his limbs. The sound of the men's anguish sent a chilling creaking through the clearing.

Determination welled in Nemeah's eyes as she pleaded, her voice breaking. "Who gave the order to slaughter us like animals? Who is responsible for countless deaths?"

A horn blast shattered the tension, its deep, resonant call echoing through the woods. All eyes turned to the lone soldier who had managed to free an arm and pressed a horn to his lips, sounding the alarm. Alban did not hesitate. He scooped Nemeah up, throwing her over his shoulder, and broke into a run. She clung to him, feeling weightless as they fled through the trees. The bodies of the slain soldiers blurred past her, the memory of this night forever engraved into her memory.

"We need to get to the inn," she called over her shoulder. "I need to grab my bag, and then we have to leave!"

The sun's fading light cast long shadows across the forest as the horizon swallowed the last sliver of daylight. Movement caught Nemeah's eye, a flicker of motion among the trees. Her heartbeat doubled, but the fear she felt soon dissolved into a fleeting smile as she recognized the bounding form of a hare, its long feet kicking up dirt as it bolted past.

"That darn animal," she murmured, a tremor of bitter amusement in her voice.

They reached the inn quickly, the hare trailing them at every turn. Nemeah glanced over at Alban, a small smile tugging at her lips despite the tension in her chest. He had acted defensively without her directing him to do so. He had saved them.

"What would I do without you?" she asked before her gaze dropped to the peculiar little creature at her feet.

Its fur was a muddled blend of white and brown, its long ears twitching as though it were listening in on their conversation. "And you," she said with a chuckle, crouching down to meet the hare's inquisitive stare. "I guess you are a part of our odd group now?"

She stood, placed her hand on the tavern door, and pushed, but it did not budge. A frown pulled at her lips as she leaned in to peer through the window. The interior was empty, except for the hearth's flickering flames casting long shadows over abandoned tables and chairs. Nemeah pounded on the door.

"Hello?" she called. Silence greeted her. "Mrs. Donnar?"

Frustration boiled over as she pressed her forehead against the door's wooden frame. "What I would give to be able to project a portal right about now," she muttered, the chill of the encroaching night pressing against her back like an unwelcome guest.

The shattering of glass jolted her upright. She spun just in time to see Alban pulling his armored arm back through the broken window.

"What are you doing?" she hissed, panic rising in her voice as she glanced over her shoulder.

A few curious passersby turned to investigate the commotion, though most were still engrossed in their own conversations. Nemeah forced a tight, awkward smile at the onlookers before rounding on

Alban. Her mouth opened to protest further, but seeing him gently scooping up the hare and slipping it through the shattered window made her speechless.

"What in the chains are you doing?" she spat, running her fingers through her hair only to find them tangled in a knot of black strands. "Why would you..."

A soft click interrupted her. The door creaked open, and the hare hopped out with an air of nonchalance, its twitching nose aimed smugly in her direction.

Nemeah stared at the animal, dumbfounded. "I am losing my mind," she muttered before stepping inside, brushing past the hare as it settled comfortably on the threshold.

She headed straight for the innkeeper's private quarters, a flimsy wooden door hanging precariously on its hinges. Laughter and the clinking of coins drifted from the other side, accompanied by jubilant voices.

"We will never need to rent another room again, Paul! We are rich! We can go anywhere we want."

Nemeah pushed the door open, the floor creaking beneath her weight. An elderly man and woman froze mid-celebration, their faces pale with surprise. The room reeked of ale and greed; her belongings were scattered across the table in disarray. Her books had been shoved aside to make room for her bag of gold, with her mirror prominently displayed like a trophy.

"There seems to be a thief in this town," Nemeah said, her voice cold.

She raised her hand and twisted her fingers. Ice crackled and spread across the innkeeper and her accomplice, freezing them in place. The woman's mouth opened and closed in silent protest while the man managed to spit out a few drunken words:

"You... You are one of those things! An Echo!"

Nemeah's eyes narrowed as she retrieved her bag, carefully repacking her possessions. "I am not the monster here; you are," she said, her anger evident. She waved her hand again, and a rag wrapped itself around the man's mouth, silencing his calls for help.

She gently wrapped the mirror, tucking it into the bag atop the heavy sack of gold. As she turned to leave, she cast a glance back at the frozen pair.

"I am sure the ice will melt," she said with a half-smile, her tone almost cheerful. "Eventually."

Alban was waiting at the door as he slung her bag over his shoulder. He grabbed her hand without a word, pulling her out into the street. The sound of a distant horn cut through the night, followed by shouts that sent a shiver down Nemeah's spine. She glanced back and spotted the Axis soldiers pouring into the inn.

"We need to blend in," she said, waving her hand. A brown cloak materialized over her shoulders, its hood shadowing her face. Alban's appearance shifted as well. His armor melted away, leaving his travelers' clothes behind. Now perfectly hidden beneath plain, unassuming garb.

The marketplace was bustling despite the late hour, and Nemeah pressed forward, keeping her head low. Her grip on Alban's hand tightened as she navigated through the crowd, her heart pounding in her ears. Another glance over her shoulder revealed the soldiers splitting into two groups, half heading toward the docks, the rest fanning out through the market. Panic bubbled up as she quickened her pace, her movements growing clumsy. She stumbled into carts and people, muttering hurried apologies. Her stomach collided with something solid, and she tumbled forward, somersaulting over the obstacle before landing flat on her back. Dazed, she looked up to find herself nose-to-nose with a braying donkey, its wide eyes staring back at her in what she could only interpret as amusement.

"Rhubarb, get back over here!"

Nemeah sat up as a twinge of familiarity sparked in her chest at the sound of the voice. She scrambled to her feet, brushing dirt from her cloak as her eyes searched the crowd. Standing just a few feet away, there was a stooped yet sturdy figure, the donkey's owner. Recognition washed over her, and her lips parted as her heartbeat quickened.

"Jacob?" she breathed, her emotions caught between disbelief and hope.

The elderly man turned toward her, his brow furrowing at first. Then his face lit up, a smile breaking through his weathered features.

"Well, if this is not an unexpected surprise! Edna! Come and see who is here!"

At his call, a woman with long white hair and a rosy-cheeked face peeked out from behind the wagon's flap. Her soft eyes, brimming with warmth. It was them. Before she could speak, the pair hurried from behind their cart, pulling her into an embrace that smelled of cinnamon and honey. For a brief, blissful moment, the world's problems fizzled away.

"What brings you to Havenwood?" Edna asked, her voice as tender as Nemeah remembered. She ran her hands down Nemeah's arms, clasping her fingers as though greeting an old friend long lost to time.

Nemeah opened her mouth to answer, but the sound of shouting cut through her thoughts. Guards were moving through the market, inspecting wagons and overturning stalls. Her heart sank as she saw the Axis soldiers drawing closer.

"I... I need to hide," she said, her words tumbling out with urgency.

Edna did not hesitate. She grabbed Nemeah's hand and pulled her toward the covered wagon. "Hide in here. Do not come out until they are gone."

Nemeah hesitated as she peeked inside. The wagon was cramped, with just enough room for a small bed on the floor draped in a patchwork of blankets. Herbs dangled from the roof, their strong scents mingling with the musty aroma of old books stacked against the walls.

"There is nowhere to hide," Nemeah whimpered, panic lacing her voice. "They will see me."

Edna waved her hand dismissively, pushing her firmly inside. "That is why I said *hide*."

With a wink, Edna pulled the flap closed and disappeared, leaving Nemeah alone to make sense of her words. Confused, Nemeah looked around the wagon, her pulse hammering in her ears.

"Hide... How?" she muttered. Then her eyes widened as realization dawned.

She lifted her hand and mimicked Edna's gesture, magic stirring faintly at her fingertips. *Did she know?* Her thoughts were interrupted by boots stomping through the marketplace, accompanied by gruff voices barking orders. The soldiers were close. The wagon's flap suddenly lifted, and Nemeah flinched, a yelp catching in her throat. Relief flooded her when she saw Alban crouched at the entrance. He handed her the travel bag before gesturing toward the ground. Nemeah followed his gaze and groaned.

"What are you doing here?" she hissed. The mismatched hare stared back at her, utterly unbothered. "Go home! Shoo!"

She waved her hands, trying to chase the animal away, but it remained stubbornly rooted in place.

"Fine," she muttered in defeat. "Get in here. Quickly."

The hare bounded up the wagon's small steps and hopped inside. Nemeah grabbed the animal and pulled it into her lap, letting its soft fur soothe her nerves. With a wave of her hand, she cast a shimmering veil of magic around the wagon, her presence cloaked by the illusion. Alban disappeared from the wagon's entrance as she hugged the animal tighter in her arms. Nemeah exhaled shakily, her mind racing. Kallemena had warned her to practice staying hidden, especially after the encounter at the antique shop. The memory of the shopkeeper's murder and the assassin's sneer as he called her a "shadow rat" sent a chill down her spine. Her routine had become too predictable. She knew that now, *knew* it was a miracle the Axis had not found her sooner. The sound of Jacob's voice snapped her back to the present.

"We sell all kinds of herbs for all kinds of things," he said cheerfully. "Would you like to try some chamomile? We just brewed it. I promise it will relax you."

"Or maybe something to soothe that armor chafing?" Edna piped in. "Or the lingering rash from midnight excursions?" She gave her husband a laughable nudge to the arm.

"Have you seen a girl or not?" barked a soldier. "Black hair, pale skin. She was with a man, about this tall, wearing armor."

"No girl here," Jacob replied smoothly, his tone as calm as ever. "Except for my beautiful wife."

Nemeah's heart swelled with gratitude, but the reprieve was short-lived.

"Check the wagon," the soldier ordered.

Nemeah's heart thundered in her chest as the footsteps grew louder, the metallic clang of armor ringing out with each step. She clutched the hare tightly, her fingers digging into its soft fur, as the flap of the wagon was suddenly thrown open. A soldier loomed in the opening, his pale brown eyes sweeping over the cramped interior. For a moment, Nemeah froze, unable to breathe, her muscles coiled as if ready to spring. The soldier's gaze lingered, searching every corner of the space before his hand let the flap drop back into place.

"They are not here," he grunted, his voice rough and coarse like it had been dragged through sand.

Nemeah sat frozen as his footsteps retreated. Only when the noise of the guards began to fade did she feel her muscles loosen. She released her iron grip on the hare, which immediately wriggled free and hopped onto the rug. It shook out its fur with a sharp flick of its ears, unbothered by the near brush with danger. Nemeah let out a shaky breath and waved her hand, releasing the shimmering wall of magic she had cast. Relief washed over her as the veil dissolved, the enchantment having held firm against the soldier's scrutiny. She allowed herself to relax for the first time since the commotion began. The warmth of the wagon, combined with the muffled sounds of the marketplace beyond, wrapped around her like a comforting blanket. She settled back on her heels, letting her eyes wander over the small, cluttered space. Books were stacked haphazardly near the wagon door, their spines worn and faded. Nemeah tilted her head, reading the titles that caught her eye: *Herbs and Where to Find Them*, *The Mind and Body Connection*, and *Healing with the Elements*. The sheer variety of knowledge tucked away in this little wagon made her heart ache with curiosity.

As she scanned the interior, a strange sensation pricked at the back of her mind, an almost imperceptible tug, as though something in the room was quietly calling to her. Her gaze shifted, searching for the source of the feeling. And then she saw it. Half-hidden beneath a stack of blankets was a small, unassuming chest. She had not noticed it before, but now it seemed to hum faintly, a whisper of magic radiating from its surface. Her pulse quickened as she crawled forward, drawn to it like a moth to a burning flame. Her fingers brushed over its smooth wooden edges, hesitating for the briefest moment before she lifted the lid. The hinges creaked softly, and as the chest opened, she felt her energy surge within her. Inside, nestled among folds of dark fabric, was a mirror. Shame and excitement twisted inside her, battling for dominance. Her hand trembled as she reached for the mirror, her fingers grazing the cool, polished surface. It was identical to Kallemena's. A chill ran down her spine as memories flooded her mind: Kallemena's cryptic warnings, her enigmatic smile, and the way she had spoken of objects like this with reverence and mystery. Nemeah's chest tightened. How had *this* mirror ended up here, in the possession of Jacob and Edna? Her grip on the mirror tightened as she pulled it closer, her reflection staring back with wide, searching eyes.

Chapter Twenty

Nemeah sat cross-legged on the rough rug inside the merchants' wagon, the coarse fibers pricking her skin through her thick clothing. Her thoughts swirled like storm clouds, heavy with unanswered questions, as her gaze remained fixed on the wooden chest where she had returned the mirror. The merchants' cheerful chatter outside was a sharp contrast to her unease. Jacob and Edna's laughter rose and fell, mingling with the sounds of clinking coins and curious customers, while Nemeah remained hidden, unsure of her next step.

Beside her, the hare had curled into a ball, its soft fur rising and falling with each twitchy breath. Its occasional spasms reminded her that, despite everything, she was not entirely alone. The sun dipped below the horizon, and the bustle of the market gradually faded. The lamps were extinguished one by one, and silence settled over the wagon. Outside, she heard the merchants packing up, their low voices and the shuffle of supplies the last sounds before her heavy eyelids finally won the battle.

Nemeah did not remember falling asleep, but she woke to the gentle rocking of the wagon in motion. The warm, velvety fur of the hare was nestled in her arms. Stretching stiffly, she crawled toward the front, easing open the flap to peek outside. Moonlight bathed the countryside in a soft silver glow, and the slow creak of wooden wheels on the dirt road was oddly soothing. Edna and Jacob sat together on the front bench, silhouetted by the light of the moon. The donkey, its head bobbing rhythmically, pulled them at an unhurried pace.

"It is a tad early for you to be awake, dear," Edna said, glancing back at her with a warm smile. Her face was all soft dimples and knowing eyes that radiated safety. "Go on, back to bed. We will talk in the morning."

Nemeah nodded her thanks, her body still racked with fatigue, and retreated back to the small bed. The wagon rocked gently, lulling her as she listened to the muffled creak of wheels and the soft, distant chirps of the crickets and frogs. She glanced down at the hare, marveling at how the tiny creature had woven itself into her chaotic life. Pulling the warm bundle closer, Nemeah curled around it and let the steady rhythm of the wagon carry her back to sleep.

When she woke again, it was to the mouthwatering scent of breakfast wafting through the air. She stretched and reached to her side, but her hand met only the rumpled blanket. The hare was gone. Panic flickered as she glanced around the enclosed space, now softly lit by the morning sunlight filtering through the canvas flaps. She scrambled to the front of the wagon and peered out. The scene outside was quiet and peaceful. Jacob dozed in a chair near a small fire, his head lolling forward slightly, while Edna bustled around a pot suspended over the flames. A steaming kettle sat nearby, the tendrils of its fragrant contents curling into the crisp air.

"I remembered you liked your eggs scrambled with potatoes," Edna said, her voice warm and cheerful as she swirled her wooden spoon through the hot food in the pot.

Nemeah's shoulders relaxed, and a hint of a smile tugged at her lips. She stepped out of the wagon, the morning sun warming her face as a gentle breeze carried the scent of fresh flowers and herbs. A narrow river gurgled beside their camp, its sparkling surface occasionally broken by leaping fish. On the opposite side, tall trees stood like sentinels, their branches shielding the camp from the wind. Nemeah settled into the chair next to Edna, watching as the elderly woman stirred a pinch of herbs into the sizzling pot. The aroma grew richer, making Nemeah's stomach rumble with anticipation. After a moment, Edna spooned a generous helping into a small wooden bowl and handed it to her. Steam danced upward in delicate spirals as Nemeah cradled the bowl in her hands. The first bite was heaven. Warm seasoned potatoes, and fluffy eggs melting on her tongue. For the first time in what felt like forever, she allowed herself to savor the simple comfort of a meal and the rare feeling of being cared for.

"Thank you so much," Nemeah said, her voice soft but sincere. She gestured over her shoulder toward the wagon. "To both of you, for yesterday. And for lending me your bed."

Edna's face lit up with her usual kind smile as she poured a golden liquid from the kettle into two wooden cups. "Tea?" she offered, holding one out to Nemeah, who accepted it gratefully.

Nemeah ate in peaceful silence, savoring the creamy potatoes and perfectly cooked eggs. Each bite felt like a gift, warm and comforting, grounding her after the turmoil of the day before. The tea was tangy with a hint of sweetness, its golden-green hue glowing softly in the morning light. With every sip, she felt her weariness ebb away, replaced by a steady hum of renewed energy. The quiet gurgle of the river drew her attention. She watched as its gentle currents carried stray leaves and sticks downstream, the sun dappling its surface in golden streaks.

"Your friend left this morning," Edna said, breaking the silence. She gestured toward the woods with her spoon. "As soon as we stopped. Hopped off that way."

Nemeah followed the direction of her hand, noticing a faint trail that wove deep into the trees.

"I do not know if I should call it a friend," she admitted, setting her cup aside. "I do not even know why it followed me." Her gaze flicked back to Edna, hesitation in her voice. "About yesterday..."

Edna waved her off, her warm chuckle putting Nemeah at ease. "No need to explain, honey. Whatever those brutes were after, it could not have been anything good. I am just glad we happened to be there when you needed us."

The old woman smiled as she returned to her meal, her expression as easy as if they were discussing the weather.

Jacob startled himself awake with a snore, his hat tipping back as he rubbed his forehead groggily. His gaze landed on Edna first, softening as he took in her familiar smile. His love for his wife was evident on his old, wrinkled face. His eyes were steady on hers. Finally, his attention shifted to Nemeah.

"Good morning," he said with a slight nod. "Hope you slept well."

"I did," she replied, managing a small smile. "Thank you. Both of you."

Jacob stretched, his joints popping in protest, before helping himself to a generous serving of breakfast. He settled back into his chair with a satisfied sigh, the lines of sleep still faint on his face. The camp was wrapped in a peaceful hush, broken only by the faint crackle of the fire, the occasional scrape of spoons against wooden bowls, and the distant melody of birdsong. It was the kind of tranquility that could almost make someone forget their troubles. Almost. Nemeah shifted in her seat, the weight of her thoughts pressing heavily on her chest. She turned to Edna, the question bubbling to the surface despite her uncertainty.

"Did..." She hesitated. "Did you mean anything when you told me to hide in the wagon?"

The question hung in the air as Edna and Jacob exchanged a glance, their shared look heavy with meaning. Edna set her spoon down and folded her hands in her lap, her gentle smile never wavering.

"Well," she began, her tone light but deliberate, "it seems I did. And it seems like you caught the meaning." She waved a hand in a playful, dismissive gesture, but her words carried weight.

Nemeah felt surprise register on her face. Relief and fear clashed within her, twisting her stomach into knots. "How?" she asked, the word trembling on her lips. "How did you know I was an... an Echo?"

Edna did not answer right away. Instead, she finished her tea with deliberate calm and then set the empty cup aside. She leaned forward slightly, her gaze drifting to a shaded patch of grass beneath the wagon. With a flick of her fingers, tiny mushrooms sprouted from the ground, their delicate caps unfurling in the dappled sunlight. Her hand moved again, this time toward the river. Nemeah's wide eyes followed as underwater plants stretched upward, their vibrant green tendrils breaking the surface like reaching fingers. Finally, Edna turned back to her, her kind eyes meeting Nemeah's stunned gaze. Her usual warm smile softened even further as she let the silence linger. Nemeah sucked in a sharp breath, her mind whirling as the truth settled over her.

"You are one, too," Nemeah said, her voice tinged with awe. "I heard about people who could manipulate nature. The ground and the trees." She racked her brain for the term. "A Thorn," she added, a grin tugging at her lips.

Edna's smile deepened, but her eyes held a glimmer of sadness. "It has been a very long time since I have heard that title."

"How did you know I was an Echo?" Nemeah set her bowl aside and leaned closer to Edna, curiosity brimming in her chest. "Is that part of your gift? Can you sense us? Other Echoes?"

Edna chuckled softly, sipping her tea once more. "In a way, yes. But it is more of a feeling that comes with age and experience rather than just my gift. I can tell when an Echo is near; it is like a change in the air, an old rhythm stirring after years of silence. I had not felt it for decades... until you showed up at the market in Fayridge."

Jacob, who had finished his breakfast, silently gathered the bowls and carried them to the river, leaving the women to their conversation.

"I am a Darra," Nemeah admitted, her tone tentative. "But you already knew that."

Edna nodded. "I had my suspicions that night at the market. You said a monster had been chasing you, and when Jacob returned with you and your cart, it became clearer. But I was certain yesterday after seeing you with that tall fellow."

Nemeah's brow furrowed. "Alban? How did he give me away?"

Edna smiled knowingly. "I could not feel any life from him. Yet there he was, standing with you, moving with you. I figured he must be part of your gift." She winked. "Can we see him?"

Nemeah hesitated for a moment before taking a steadying breath. She waved her hand, and Alban materialized beside her. He stood tall and imposing, his armor gleaming as if freshly polished, his stance exuding vigilance. A shadow stretched long and dark behind him, his presence commanding the space. Edna rose from her chair, approaching the projection with quiet fascination. Her eyes roamed over Alban's metal plating, the sword at his side, the aura of unyielding strength he carried.

"This was the monster from that night," she questioned in a tone of approval and awe. She nodded as though affirming her thoughts. "You turned your fear into your protector."

Jacob returned with the washed bowls just as Edna stepped back, her expression thoughtful. He let out a low whistle as he settled back into his seat.

"He is impressive," Jacob remarked, his tone sincere.

Nemeah flushed under the praise. "Thanks. That is what Kallemena said."

At the mention of the name, both Edna and Jacob froze. Their smiles faded, replaced by seriousness. They exchanged a look before turning back to Nemeah; concern etched into their faces.

"Where did you hear that name?" Edna asked, her voice low and weighted. "Kallemena."

Nemeah's stomach twisted. She sank slightly into her chair, fearing she had misspoken and might have to leave their kindness behind.

"She..." Nemeah hesitated, unsure how to explain. "She speaks to me. From a mirror. She was trapped there by..."

"Vallorith," Edna interjected, the name escaping her lips like a curse. Her hand flew to her mouth as her gaze darted to her husband.

Without another word, Edna hurried to her wagon. The wood creaked as she disappeared inside, rummaging through unseen belongings. When she returned, she carefully cradled the mirror Nemeah had discovered in her arms, its surface glinting faintly in the morning sun. She sat down, her hands shaking as she held the mirror close. Her eyes darted between Nemeah, Alban, and Jacob before she finally spoke, her voice trembling ever so slightly.

"You have it? *Her* mirror?"

Nemeah nodded slowly, her gaze locked on the mirror in Edna's hands. "I found it on the beach," she admitted. Her voice dropped, the memory vivid in her mind. "The same night you and Jacob helped me at the market. It was like... she called to me. I found a box washed ashore, and inside was a mirror that looked just like that one." She gestured toward the mirror Edna held.

Edna erupted into laughter, the sound joyous and full-bodied. Her shoulders bounced with each chuckle, and her eyes crinkled with delight as she held her sides.

"May I see it? Please?" she asked, her voice carrying the edge of a beg.

Nemeah nodded and hurried to the wagon, hoisting her heavy bag down from the bench. She carefully unwrapped the layers of cloth that encased her mirror, unveiling the ornate glass beneath. It glimmered in the sunlight, its frame identical to the one Edna held. Edna handed her mirror to Jacob with a trembling hand before rushing over to examine Nemeah's. She turned the glass in her hands, her fingers tracing the intricate scrollwork etched into the frame. Every detail seemed to mesmerize her.

"Remarkable," she whispered. Her hands shook slightly as she handed the mirror back to Nemeah. "Come," she said, her tone shifting to something more serious. "There is more to this story, something I suspect neither you nor Kallemena knows."

She ushered Nemeah back to her seat and settled in, the air growing heavier with anticipation.

"My great-great-great-grandmother was named Poppy Havander," Edna began.

Nemeah's brows shot up. "I know Poppy! Or, at least, Kallemena did at the Axis. She was someone's little sister... Sylvie?"

Edna's eyes widened with a mix of surprise and nostalgia. "Yes, Sylvie Havander. She was a Talon and the only one to escape from that evil man." Her gaze dropped to the mirror in her lap, her expression softening. "The story has been passed down through every generation of my family. I am the last of them." She reached out to Jacob, who took her hand and gave it a gentle squeeze. The unspoken gesture said everything: no regrets, no sadness, only love.

Clearing her throat, Edna continued. "The story goes that Kallemena used her power to free Sylvie, Poppy, and many other children from the Axis. She opened the ground beneath their feet, and they fell through, landing safely on a ship. The king of Glacia's ship. But when it became clear that Kallemena and the king of Kalyra were not with them, the king insisted they go back."

Nemeah hung on every word, her curiosity peaking as the tale unfolded.

"When they returned, the Axis was in shambles," Edna said. "The room where Vallorith kept the mirrors was abandoned; large claw marks and scorched debris littered the place. But four mirrors remained on the wall. Each had a carving beside it: a leaf, an arrow, a water droplet, and a paw print. Sylvie took them. She said there were supposed to be nine mirrors, but only four were left. She realized the others, their friends, had been absorbed, imprisoned within the glass. Sylvie returned the mirrors to their homelands, except for one." Edna's voice cracked, a tear slipping down her cheek. She smiled, her gaze distant with memory. "Her love."

Nemeah's heart fluttered as understanding bloomed within her. "Slek," she murmured.

Edna's head snapped up, her excitement lighting her face. "She told you about him? It really *is* her, then?" Her eyes shone with wonder.

"We never knew what became of the others, the missing mirrors, or that terrible man."

Nemeah's eyes dropped to her own mirror, her fingers curling tightly around its frame. "She trapped him," she said, her voice quiet but firm. She looked back up at Edna and Jacob. "Before she was imprisoned, Kallemena projected another mirror made of black glass. She watched Vallorith disappear into it before she herself was trapped."

Edna gasped, her hand flying to her mouth. Her words abandoned her as she stared at Nemeah, stunned. "If that is true," she said finally, "why have the others remained imprisoned? How has Vallorith's power lasted all these centuries?"

Nemeah frowned, rubbing her brow as she pieced together what she had learned. "Kallemena mentioned others who were trapped first. Two, specifically. She called them a Glade and a Freyla." She hesitated, catching Edna's confused expression. "The Freyla could reanimate. They could replenish energy to sustain a dwindling power. That is probably how his hold has remained so strong through the years." Her gaze shifted to the mirror in Edna's lap. "Does he ever talk to you? Slek?"

Edna shook her head, her silver hair catching the light. "He only ever spoke to Sylvie," she said softly. "On her deathbed, she made Poppy promise to keep the mirror safe. Since then, it has passed down through the generations, always entrusted to her offspring."

Nemeah began to pace, the mirror cool and solid in her hand as her thoughts raced. "The five that are missing... I am sure he took the Freyla and the Glade. That leaves three." She paused, gripping the mirror tighter. "Two. The Cairn and the Morin." Her sharp gaze turned to Edna. "Where did they go?"

Edna shrugged, her thin shoulders lost beneath her thick wool coat. "Sylvie never knew. She only knew that the mirrors needed to be kept safe, far from the wrong hands. That is why she hid the others on their origin continents."

Nemeah's attention shifted to Alban, standing stoic in his armor, the sun glinting off its polished surface. "If the Axis was in ruins, how did they start hunting the Echoes? Who took over the continent of Verdathos?"

Edna frowned, her eyes fixed on the grass as if searching for answers hidden among the blades. "I do not know who it was. All I know is that it began years after Vallorith disappeared and long after the mirrors had gone missing. The new leader had a deep, unyielding hatred for all Echoes. Some said he was a prince, but most dismissed it as rumor."

Nemeah's footsteps slowed as she digested the information, the weight of it pressing on her. She turned back to Edna, her voice firmer now. "Kallemena also mentioned a prophecy. Do you have any idea what that could be?"

Edna shook her head, her face clouded with regret.

Nemeah felt frustration mounting again. Even with this new information, she was no closer to unraveling the mystery of the Eclipse Veil or stopping an evil god from rising. She looked down at the mirror in her hands, its intricate carvings catching the firelight.

"Sylvie was a Talon," she said suddenly. "And Vallorith could not have trapped another Talon, not after Sylvie hid the mirror, right?"

Edna smiled, a spark of hope in her expression. "Yes, that is correct."

Nemeah nodded, her mind working rapidly. "So, even if we cannot free everyone before the Eclipse Veil, Vallorith still cannot ascend to godhood. There is no one to take Sylvie's place as his Talon." She smiled, a rare moment of calm washing over her. "Then we have enough time to find the rest of the mirrors and free everyone."

"That is where you are wrong."

A voice, low and rough, shattered the tranquility of their camp.

Everyone turned toward the forest. A young man emerged from the shadows, his presence commanding. His lean, muscular frame was evident beneath his brown leather armor, wrapped tightly and trimmed with fur. His boots crunched softly against the forest litter as he approached, his bare arms adorned with intricate markings that stretched from his wrists, up his shoulders, and onto his neck. Nemeah froze, her heart pounding. His angular face was striking, his deep forest green eyes locked on her as he closed the distance. A shiver ran down her spine, cold and sharp, as she glanced toward Alban. She was immersed in a feeling of disbelief while her guard stood motionless, his attention fixed on nothing as if he could not see the intruder at all.

"Alban." A flicker of desperation in her voice, but he did not respond.

The stranger kept walking, his confidence unnerving. Nemeah's pulse quickened, panic spreading through her limbs. She raised her hand, her magic projecting binding threads that coiled around the man's arms and legs.

The threads strung him up like a freshly caught prize, his muscles flexing as he assessed the strength of her spell.

His gaze flicked to Nemeah, then to Edna and Jacob, a slow smile spreading across his face. Then, without warning, he began to laugh, a deep, booming laugh that shook his chest and carried through the clearing.

Jacob chuckled nervously, but the sound died quickly under Edna's sharp glare. The stranger lowered himself onto the soft grass, still bound but wholly unbothered. His complexion glowed in the sunlight, the markings on his skin seemingly alive. He turned his bold, piercing eyes back to Nemeah, his amusement still playing across his features.

"Well," he said smoothly, his voice laced with intrigue, "Is this any way to treat the man you shared your bed with last night?"

Nemeah's face burned crimson. She turned quickly, her eyes darting to Edna in shock before snapping back to the stranger. "Excuse me, sir, but I have done no such thing!" Her arms crossed defensively over her chest, and she refused to meet his gaze, her indignation evident.

The man smirked, his attention shifting to Alban. "Hey, big guy, a little help?"

Nemeah's heart skipped as she watched, horrified, as Alban stepped forward without hesitation. Her stalwart guard, her trusted protector, unsheathed a small blade and cut the bindings away, freeing the stranger.

"Alban?!" she exclaimed, her hands trembling as she glanced between her guard and the stranger. "I did not command him to do that!" She looked down at her fingers as if they might betray her, then back to the man. "How?"

The stranger gave her a playful wink as he shook off the last of the bindings, stretching his limbs leisurely. Without a care in the world, he wandered over to the fire, plucked up the pot of leftover eggs and potatoes, and began shoveling the food into his mouth with his bare hands. Bits of the meal decorated his short beard as he did so.

"Not bad," he mumbled through a mouthful, sniffing between bites like a forager appraising his meal.

Nemeah stared, utterly dumbfounded. Who was this man? Sitting there eating their food as though he owned the camp, he was a whirlwind of audacity. Her eyes roved over him, the cords and braids of his hair streaked white and brown like a mangy animals fur, swaying as he moved.

"No," she whispered, stepping closer. A realization sparked in her mind, her voice rising. "The hare? Are you him? The fat one that was always stealing my food?"

The man grinned wide, his cheeks still full of eggs and potatoes. He swallowed with an exaggerated motion, stood, and dusted his hands off on his pants. Another wink followed.

"Thanks for the meal, Grandma," he said, saluting Edna with a crooked smile.

Edna scowled, her lips pressed in a thin line, but the stranger had already turned his attention to Alban. He slung an arm around the guard's shoulders with easy familiarity, nearly matching Alban in height.

"Good thing *he* recognized me," the man said with a grin, giving Alban a companionable pat. "I have seen what this warrior can do, and I would rather not be on the receiving end of his blade."

Nemeah scoffed as the stranger turned to her, extending a hand. His presence was magnetic, his grin both infuriating and strangely disarming.

"The name is Keanoff," he said, his voice rich with mischief.

Nemeah's gaze shifted from Keanoff's face to his outstretched hand, then back again. Her breath hitched as memories came flooding in, curling up beside the hare in the wagon, its soft fur calming the storm of her anxiety. The realization hit her like a bolt of lightning. Her face burned an even deeper shade of red. She swatted his hand away with a huff and stormed back to her chair, collapsing into it with an indignant plop. *All those times in the clearing. All those shared scraps of food. And yesterday...* Her mind replayed when she held the hare close, finding comfort in its warmth. The mortification was eternal, and her cheeks flared like twin suns. Keanoff, however, was unbothered. He sank to the ground by the fire, rubbing his hands together over the flickering flames as though nothing were amiss.

"Well, this just got interesting," Jacob muttered under his breath, his lips twitching. He avoided looking at Edna, knowing full well the glare she would shoot him for such a comment.

Edna straightened in her seat, her eyes narrowing as they settled on Keanoff. "You said we were wrong," she prompted, her voice cutting through the awkward silence. "How?"

All eyes turned to the stranger, who seemed perfectly at home despite the tension hanging in the air. He leaned back, unstrung his boots, and tugged them off. The same intricate markings that covered his arms and face snaked up his ankles and legs, his feet matching. Ignoring their stares, he wiggled his toes toward the flames before finally speaking.

"I am a Vira," he said, gesturing to himself with an air of casual confidence. "As you have probably figured out by now."

No one spoke. The quiet sounds of the river and the crackling fire filled the space, amplifying the weight of his words. Keanoff reached into a pouch fastened to his belt, rummaging around. "We found that mirror," he said, pulling something out. "The one you are talking about. The one your great-great-whatever returned to Sylvara."

Nemeah and Edna gasped as he produced a mirror identical to the one they held. Its surface shimmered in the firelight as Keanoff twirled it carelessly in his hands.

"Please stop that!" Nemeah yelped, her voice high with panic as the mirror spun precariously, slipping in his grip more than once.

Keanoff chuckled, clearly enjoying her distress. With a smirk, he tucked the mirror back into his bag and secured the pouch.

"So you found the mirror," Nemeah said, her words rushed, her composure cracking. "How does that prove we are wrong about Vallorith not having a Talon?"

Keanoff's eyes locked onto hers. He tilted his head, his grin fading into something unreadable.

"Because I saw it," he said quietly.

The group recoiled, stunned into silence.

"Saw what exactly?" Jacob was the first to recover his voice. "I am sure we all would be most appreciative of whatever knowledge it is you have to share."

Keanoff nodded, his gaze drifting to the fire. His expression was distant, as though he was reliving a memory etched deeply into his mind. "I saw a Talon get pulled into a mirror. One just like these." He gestured to the bag on his belt. "He was practicing his abilities on the beach. Making huge waves and pushing the water away from the shore so the children could play amongst the newly uncovered shells." He paused, his brows furrowing at the thought. "Then this... creature came out of the woods. Black as night, silent as death."

"What kind of creature?" Nemeah asked.

Keanoff's jaw tightened. "None that is known to me, I am a Vira, we know our animals. But this thing...it looked like a demon. It stood on two legs, hunched and unnatural. It slinked up behind him, holding the mirror out. He barely had time to react. The creature said something, some strange, mumbled jargon, and then he was gone just like that. Sucked into the mirror."

"Who?" Nemeah demanded, on the edge of her seat. "Who was the Talon?"

Keanoff's long sigh filled the silence. His eyes finally lifted from the flames, scanning their faces one by one before settling on Nemeah. His voice was steady but heavy with emotion. "My father."

Chapter Twenty-one

Nemeah sat beside Edna, helping peel potatoes for their supper. The small group of misfits worked in an unspoken silence, the weight of their recent revelations hanging heavy over them. The scattered mirrors, Vallorith's imprisonment of the syphers, and the looming threat of the Eclipse Veil haunted them all. Nemeah glanced over her shoulder, watching Keanoff and Jacob by the river. Jacob worked with a long, slender fishing pole while Keanoff waded in waist-deep, pulling fish from the water with his bare hands. His laughter echoed over the gentle rush of the current, a welcomed distraction from the lingering tension.

"Did Sylvie ever tell Poppy about someone named Zepher?" Nemeah asked absentmindedly in her deep trance.

She winced as the small knife slipped, the sharp blade digging into her palm. Gasping softly, she dropped the potato as blood bloomed from the wound. Edna noticed immediately, her eyes narrowing in concern. She moved with practiced grace, swirling her hand in the air. White flowers sprouted from the grass nearby, their thin stems trembling as they rose. Working quickly, Edna carefully plucked a handful and started separating flowers and leaves before retreating to her wagon. She returned with a black stone mortar and pestle, dropping the plant material inside. As she ground the mixture into a thick green paste, the rhythmic crunching sound soothed Nemeah's nerves. "Yarrow," Edna explained, her voice soft but steady. "It will stop the bleeding." Edna tore a clean rag in half and gently applied the paste to Nemeah's wound. The sting made Nemeah flinch, but soon, the ache dulled, replaced by a cooling relief. Once the bandage was secured, Edna leaned back, letting out a tired sigh. Her warm smile did not mask the concern glimmering in her eyes.

Stretching her back, Edna returned to peeling the potatoes, her knife revealing their golden flesh with swift, steady movements. "Sylvie did tell Poppy about someone named Zepher, Vallorith's assistant, or something of the sort. She said he had feline features, amber eyes, and onyx skin." She paused, glancing at Nemeah. "I thought of him as well, after what Keanoff said. The one who trapped his father. But how? He would have to be over five hundred years old. That should be impossible."

Nemeah listened, her hands finding their rhythm again as she peeled beside her older companion. The men's laughter echoed from the river, punctuated by splashes as Keanoff dove after a particularly stubborn fish. Despite the icy spring air, the water's shimmer looked inviting, though Nemeah knew better than to be tempted. Alban stood like a statue near the wagon, his vigilant gaze sweeping the clearing. Ever alert, his ears seemed to catch even the faintest rustle of the trees. Nemeah frowned, her thoughts swirling. She stared at her reflection in the small blade, the evening light catching her worried eyes. "What if it is not impossible?" an idea was brewing in her mind. Edna looked up, one brow raised in silent question.

"What if he used the mirror to keep Zepher alive all these years? Keeping a Morin close that was already one of his trusted followers?" Nemeah's voice grew stronger as the idea solidified in her gut. She turned to Edna, her concern plain. "Sylvie said the Morin's mirror was gone. I bet she never saw the black glass mirror either, the one that holds Vallorith. What if..." Nemeah's eyes darted skyward as though searching for answers in the pale clouds. "What if Zepher took them all and found a place to hide until Vallorith told him when and where to go? Releasing him at the right moment."

Her words trailed off, a storm of unease brewing over the two women. A grim thought spilled through Nemeah's mind, chilling her to the bone. "He would just have to decide when to release Zepher, to do his bidding." She repeated slowly as her gaze shifted to Alban, her thoughts brushing over their shared bond. An invisible tether between them loomed unseen. "If the mirrors are his creation, then he must be able to feel them, the same way I can feel Alban."

Edna's hand shot out, grabbing Nemeah's wrist tightly. She did not say a word, but the realization reflected in her wide, fearful eyes. "Then he would know exactly where the mirrors are," Edna whispered, her voice faltering as her gaze darted to her wagon, where Slek's prison was stowed. "Where they all are."

"And I bet he can see through them, always watching, always listening," Nemeah added, her voice low but firm. Her eyes flicked toward Keanoff by the river. "That is how he knew where a Talon was. If Keanoff's father found the mirror on Sylvara, then Vallorith must have seen him use his ability. He knew where to find him," she said, her tone hardening. "And he sent his dutiful servant to retrieve what he needed."

Edna's trembling hand rose to cover her mouth. Her gaze drifted to the riverbank, where her husband stood, trousers rolled up to his knees, proudly holding a fish as long as his arm. His grin was wide across his face and Keanoff held up a rather small fish in comparison, his only catch for the day. The sight was a fleeting comfort. "We are in danger," she murmured, her voice barely audible over the soft splash of the water.

Later, as they sat around the fire eating their roasted catch and potatoes, Nemeah shared her troubling concern. Keanoff nodded gravely, his plate forgotten as he brought a knee to his chest and stared into the flames. "That makes sense," he admitted, his voice tinged with bitterness. "It was after we found the mirror in Sylvara. My father carried that damned thing everywhere with him." His face darkened, his jaw tightening as the weight of old memories pressed on him.

The moon's pale light crept across the clearing, its ghostly glow heralding a sharp chill. A biting wind swept through the trees, whispering of an impending frost. Jacob rubbed the back of his neck, glancing toward his wagon. "There is not much room in there, but I suppose..."

Nemeah raised her hand, stopping him mid-sentence. She waved her fingers, and an identical wagon materialized beside the first. Jacob's eyes widened with delight as he circled the two wagons, muttering to himself as he searched for differences. His amazement was childlike, his grin infectious.

"Guess I will be bunking with you," Keanoff teased Nemeah, a sly grin carved on his face as he stood and stretched.

She rolled her eyes, her hand waving again. This time, a small crate filled with hay appeared beside the wagons. Keanoff's grin vanished instantly. Jacob tried and failed to stifle his laughter. His booming guffaw echoed through the trees, and Rhubarb, the donkey, brayed loudly in agreement.

"Oh shut it, Rhubarb! It is not that funny," Keanoff muttered, shooting the donkey a withering glare before eyeing the crate. "At least I get hay. What do you get, big nose?"

Jacob's laughter faltered as his mouth fell open. "You can understand Rhubarb?"

Keanoff shrugged, offering no explanation. Instead, he dropped to his hands and knees. Patches of mismatched fur sprouted from his tattooed skin, and his ears stretched upward past his head. A moment later, a hare sat where Keanoff had been, its nose twitching. The hare bounded toward the crate, burrowing into the hay. In seconds, he was hidden, only the occasional twitch of his whiskers betraying his presence. Nemeah shook her head, amused despite herself. The others retired to their wagon, Alban resuming his silent vigil as Nemeah climbed into her own. Lying on the thin mattress beneath a heavy blanket, she stared at the wagon's canvased ceiling. Thoughts of Kallemena and her family crept into her mind, the familiar ache of loneliness tightening in her chest. Sleep came reluctantly, pulling her into restless dreams.

She found herself in a darkened void, amber eyes glinting like distant stars. A pointed claw emerged from the shadows, tracing its way to her throat before slicing her skin. The scene shifted violently, the ambush of the Axis guard being relived, her trusted protector turning his blade against its creator. She saw the flash of steel and felt the cold edge bury itself deep into her gut. Nemeah woke with a start, tears streaming down her face in thick, silent rivers. She gasped for air, her heart pounding in her chest. An arm wrapped around her, pulling her close. Keanoff sat beside her, his forest-green eyes glowing faintly in the dim light. The warmth of his embrace soothed her, his hand stroking gently through her hair. Gradually, her breathing steadied, and her frantic heart began to calm. She pulled away, her eyes meeting his in a silent exchange of gratitude.

"Sorry, I barged in. You were screaming in your sleep, crying out to someone." Gently, he tucked a stray lock of hair behind her ear, his touch hot against her skin. "I just wanted to make sure you were all right."

Nemeah swallowed hard, her throat aching from unshed tears. She shifted away from his touch, pulling the blanket tighter around herself. "Thank you," she murmured, not knowing how to act. "I am all right now."

Keanoff nodded, lingering for a moment before retreating to the door. "I will be in my crate if you need me." he smiled before quietly creeping out, leaving her alone once more.

Nemeah sank back onto the thin mattress, her pulse still racing. She was not sure what had shaken her more, the nightmare that clung to her mind like cobwebs or the warmth of Keanoff's embrace. Shaking her head, she let out a calming breath. "Focus," she whispered to herself. Where do we go from here?"

A loud thud echoed inside the wagon, jolting her upright. Her eyes darted around the dim space until they landed on a small wooden box that sat a few feet away. She crawled toward it cautiously, her fingers brushing the rough surface as she examined it.

"It will not bite," a familiar voice teased.

Nemeah's hand flew to her chest as she whirled around. Sitting near the edge of her bed was Kallemena, her dark figure illuminated by the faint glow of her presence. Her black, feathered dress spilled onto the wagon floor like ink.

"By the chains, Mena!" Nemeah let out a shaky laugh, pressing a hand to her racing heart. "I feel as though I am on the verge of death this morning. Everything has me spooked like a foal."

Kallemena smiled faintly and sat gracefully on the edge of the mattress. "You have been through much," she said softly, her dark eyes filled with a quiet intensity.

Nemeah returned her attention to the box, her fingers tracing the intricate carvings on its lid. She waved her hand, summoning tiny orbs of light that floated around the wagon's interior, illuminating the space in a warm, golden glow. Kallemena clapped her hands together, her expression one of genuine delight.

"You have been practicing," she said, pride lacing her voice.

A small smile tugged at Nemeah's lips. She lifted the lid of the box and found a compass nestled inside. Its weight felt significant in her palm, the metal cold against her skin. She watched the needle spin slowly as though it were searching for something.

"Is it not supposed to point north?" Nemeah asked, her brow arched.

Kallemena's gaze softened as she leaned closer. "It would if it were an ordinary compass," she explained. "This one is different, special. It points to something you are searching for. It will guide you to the remaining mirrors."

Nemeah's eyes widened as she looked back at the compass, a mix of awe and trepidation washing over her. "You made this?"

Kallemena nodded. "It was not easy. I apologize for my absence, Nemeah, but I needed time to craft it." Her voice carried a note of regret, and her ethereal composure seemed to waver for a fleeting moment.

The needle of the compass stopped spinning and pointed south. Nemeah closed the lid and sat back on the floor, pulling her knees to her chest. She stared at the box, her thoughts swirling. "I have much to tell you," she said, her voice heavy. "None of it good." For what felt like hours, Nemeah recounted everything she had learned. She told Kallemena about the mirrors, the people she had encountered, and the creature they believed to be Zepher. She explained their fear that Vallorith could see and hear through the mirrors, her voice trembling as she spoke his name. Kallemena listened intently, her expression darkening with every word.

"I have had these same thoughts," Kallemena admitted. She dropped her face into her hands, her shoulders slumping under the weight of her memories. "I believe Zepher was the assassin you spoke of in Tirnmoor. The one who killed the shopkeeper."

Nemeah's stomach churned, her face falling as the realization sank in. "How do we move forward without Vallorith knowing?" she asked, her voice laced with desperation.

Kallemena lifted her head, her dark eyes burning with determination. "We move carefully," she said. "And we move quickly. But first, you must trust the compass. It will lead you where you need to go."

Nemeah clutched the box tightly, the weight of the task ahead pressing down on her. She nodded, steeling herself for the challenges to come. Somewhere in the distance, the faint call of a bird broke the silence, signaling the start of a new day. Kallemena sat in silence, her eyes scanning the cramped wagon interior before drifting to the growing sounds of the others stirring outside. Finally, she rose gracefully, her voice calm yet commanding. "Let us meet your companions."

Nemeah followed as they stepped out of the wagon, Kallemena's dark, feathered dress trailing behind her like a shadow. Her black hair, woven with golden and silver charms, shimmered faintly in the morning light, giving her an air of regal magnificence. Sitting crouched by the fire with a kettle in hand, Edna turned at the sound of footsteps.

"I have got some lemongrass and ginger tea if you would like..." Edna's voice faltered, her gaze locking on Kallemena. The kettle slipped from her fingers, hitting the ground with a dull thud. Her hands flew to her patched skirt, smoothing it furiously as she dropped into a deep curtsy, her wool coat brushing the ground.

"Your Majesty," she exclaimed, her voice pure delight. "We were not expecting you."

The kettle's contents hissed against the embers, sending a plume of fragrant steam curling into the air, lemon and ginger mingling with the crisp morning breeze.

"Oh! My tea!" Edna exclaimed, snapping out of her reverie. She hastily scooped up the kettle, then waved her fingers toward a patch of grass nearby. Thin, sleek blades of lemongrass shot up, swaying gently in the breeze, followed by the emergence of small, clumped roots. She gathered the ingredients in a flurry of motion and darted toward the river, calling over her shoulder, "Just a few minutes, and I will have more ready!"

Nemeah chuckled softly, a rare warmth spreading in her chest. She glanced at Jacob, who stood frozen, his mouth slack-jawed as he stared at Kallemena.

"Shut your mouth before you catch flies," Edna quipped as she breezed past him, giving his chin a playful pat. She set the refreshed kettle back on the fire and clapped her hands. "There now. Breakfast?"

They ate together by the fire, sharing simple but hearty fare, lumpy dumplings made of flour, herbs, and milk fried until golden in the pan. Nemeah, her belly warm and full, felt a pleasant drowsiness settle over her, though her thoughts flickered back to her nightmare and Keanoff's comforting arms around her. Heat crept to her cheeks as she risked a glance at the Vira. He devoured his food like a wild animal, crouched low with his hands buried in his plate. He sniffed each bite before stuffing dumplings into his cheeks, his nose twitching in satisfaction. Nemeah could not help the small smile tugging at her lips. He looked utterly ridiculous and yet somehow... endearing.

Once the plates were cleared, Kallemena addressed the group, her tone measured and serious. "Nemeah has shared her suspicions about the mirrors and Vallorith's connection to them. I agree. The high priest is using the mirrors to watch and listen, tracking those who possess them." She paused, her gaze steady. "I also believe the creature Keanoff described, the one that took his father, is the same assassin Nemeah encountered in Tirnmoor. Zepher."

A heavy silence fell over the group as Kallemena continued. "I have made something to aid you, a compass. It points toward what you seek. What that may be is something only you will know. I can only hope it is not treasure you desire." She offered a small smile, lightening the tension briefly before her expression grew grim. "Now, for the bad news." Her gaze shifted to Keanoff, sprawled on the grass with a hand over his full stomach. "I can feel your father," she said softly, her voice heavy with meaning. Her eyes swept over the group. "Just as I can feel Slek and Wynna. Their presence is... close."

Nemeah's pulse quickened. "Wait, what do you mean you can feel them?"

Kallemena turned toward her, her expression tinged with sorrow. "It is a bond of sorts, one I have not felt in centuries. It means they are near. And it means danger is near as well." Her dark gaze flickered to Alban, who stood vigilant at the forest's edge. "Trouble is coming," she said gravely. "You must all be ready."

She turned back to Edna, her voice softening. "You do not have to continue on this journey. Nemeah is more than capable of safeguarding the mirrors. She will free Slek when she finds the rest of Vallorith's prisons."

Edna turned to her husband, her eyes searching his face. Uncertainty had carved deep lines into his features, but as she reached out her hand, he took it without hesitation. "Up to you, old girl," he said softly, his grip firm and reassuring.

The old woman smiled faintly before facing Kallemena. "We can take them as far as Mirewood," she said, her voice trembling slightly.

"But I am afraid we cannot go past that." Her gaze swept to Nemeah, her teary eyes pleading for understanding. "We are old, dear. Our time for adventure... it came and went long ago."

Nemeah felt her heart splinter anew, the fissures deepened by forces beyond her control. She wanted to protest, beg them to stay, and shout that they could not abandon her, not like her parents had. But she bit her tongue, swallowing the words that burned her throat. Who was she to demand more of them? They had already risked so much. Her shoulders sagged as she nodded, blinking back tears. She tilted her head to the sky, now a brilliant blue without a trace of cloud, seeking solace where there was none. Kallemena, standing nearby, nodded in silent approval.

"Have no fear, Grandma," Keanoff said with a teasing grin. "I will take care of Nemeah."

Nemeah's cheeks flamed, her hands flying up to shield her face. Laughter rippled through the group at her expense, lightening the heavy mood for a fleeting moment. Kallemena stepped forward, her expression serious.

"I am not certain this will work," she began, raising her hands, "but I can try to shield the mirrors using the compass."

Jacob frowned. "What will a shield do?"

"Hopefully, it will keep Vallorith from using the mirrors to spy on you. Keeping them within the compass's radius should at least distort what he sees and hears." The princess's eyes began to glow faintly, and she spread her fingers wide, muttering words too soft for Nemeah to catch. The air seemed to hum with energy. Then, without warning, a shockwave rippled outward, forcing everyone to shield their faces as the force pushed against them. When Nemeah lowered her arms, the world felt... emptier. Kallemena was gone. And with her absence came a gnawing uncertainty that hollowed Nemeah's chest. The confidence she had felt with Kallemena nearby evaporated, leaving her feeling untethered. For a long moment, no one spoke.

Finally, Keanoff broke the silence, clapping his hands together. "Well? When do we leave?"

Chapter Twenty-two

The night was heavy with silence, the faint creak of the wagon wheels blending with the soft clop of the donkey's hooves. Alban held the reins loosely, his eyes scanning the dark trail ahead, ready to take over should Nemeah succumb to exhaustion. Inside the wagon, Edna and Jacob's gentle snores carried through the quiet, their rhythmic breaths comforting yet bittersweet. Nemeah listened intently, etching the sound into her memory like an anchor against the loneliness creeping into her heart. Her chest tightened. She understood their decision to stop at Mirewood; truly, she did. They had given her so much already, far more than she could ever repay. Yet, knowing they would not follow her beyond the forest felt like the ground being pulled from under her feet. They were the family she had secretly longed for: people who had seen her magic and accepted her, not as a danger or a curse, but as something wondrous. She pressed her lips together as the memory of her parents' rejection surged back like a cold wind through her chest. Alone again. The thought coiled in her mind, suffocating and inescapable.

A single tear slid down her cheek, but she brushed it away quickly. She straightened her back, reached into her pocket, and pulled out the compass Kallemena had given her. She opened the lid, its faint golden glow illuminating her fingers as the needle remained fixed, pointing faithfully south. The steady hum of its magic offered a small comfort, even as the ache in her chest persisted. The soft padding of feet broke the silence, drawing Nemeah's attention. Rhubarb let out a nervous bray, his ears flicking back.

"You know he does not like you in that form," she said aloud, glancing over the side of the wagon.

A flash of fur caught her eye, brown with patches of white, dark green eyes gleamed in the dark. The wolf stared up at her, unblinking, before its gait slowed, and the unsettling crack of bones and rip of flesh followed. Nemeah turned away, the sound of the transformation making her skin crawl. Moments later, Keanoff jogged alongside the wagon, leaping up to join her with ease. He dropped onto the bench beside her, his arm brushing hers as she instinctively shifted closer to Alban. Stretching with exaggerated laziness, Keanoff yawned before settling in.

"I did not see any signs of us being followed," he whispered, making sure not to wake the others. "No sounds but our own. We are safe tonight." He closed his eyes as if the confirmation allowed him to steal a moment's rest.

Nemeah studied him then, letting her gaze linger in a way she had not before. His sharp, angular features seemed more pronounced in the moonlight: the ridge of his nose, the slight curve of his lips, and the faint shadow of his tattoos made his sun-beaten skin appear almost pale.

"Like what you see?" he teased, eyes still closed.

Her cheeks burned instantly. "No!" she snapped, tearing her gaze away as heat flushed her neck and ears. She blew out a frustrated breath and glared at him, but he only smirked.

"Kallemena told me about a Vira she knew at the Axis. Wynna, I think?" Nemeah's voice softened. "Is that whose mirror you carry?"

Keanoff opened his eyes slowly, his gaze fixed on the stars scattered across the endless black sky. He nodded once before reaching into his pouch and pulling out the mirror. The surface glinted faintly, reflecting the light of the moon.

"She only ever spoke to my father," he said quietly, running a finger along the mirror's edge. "Warned him to be careful. I guess she could feel the monster getting close." His voice was calm, but his grip on the mirror tightened slightly. He tilted it to catch his reflection, then gave her a crooked grin. "Just wait until my hair grows back all brown again. You will not be able to keep your eyes off me."

Nemeah rolled her eyes, but a reluctant smile tugged at her lips. "You are insufferable."

Her gaze drifted back to the mirror in his hands, and her thoughts grew heavy. The memory of Kallemena's mirror, the one that had set everything in motion, floated to the forefront of her mind. What would happen when this was all over? Could she ever return to Tirnmoor as if none of this had happened? Would her family accept her then?

"Were you close to your father?" The question escaped her before she could stop it, and she froze, immediately regretting her curiosity. "Ignore that," she said quickly, shaking her head. "I did not mean to pry, sorry. I guess I am just... struggling a little tonight."

She leaned forward, burying her face in her hands as she inhaled deeply. The faint, metallic tang of Alban's armor lingered in the air, grounding her even as the weight of the unknown loomed ahead. Keanoff nodded as he tucked the mirror back into his pouch.

"You will miss Edna and Jacob. That is only natural." He nudged her shoulder gently, his tone unusually soft. "I can see how much they care for you. And it hurt Edna, telling Kallemena they would not be accompanying you. You know that, right?"

Nemeah swallowed hard, fighting the sting of tears as she rubbed her face and forced herself to sit up straighter. "I know I could never ask them to risk their lives for me. If something happened to them, I would..." Her voice caught, and she exhaled sharply, steadying herself. "I would never be able to bear it."

Keanoff's lips quirked into a small smile, his elbows resting on his knees as he laced his fingers together. "That is because you are a good person."

Nemeah flinched slightly at his words, her thoughts flashing to her parents, their faces blank with utter shock and disbelief when they first saw her magic. "How can you be so sure?" she asked, her voice laced with bitterness. "You do not even know me. I could be a terrible person."

Keanoff chuckled, a warm sound that somehow eased the knot in her chest. He glanced over his shoulder at her, his forest eyes glinting in the moonlight. "If you were bad, I would know." He tapped his nose with a knowing grin. "Animal instinct."

The quiet that followed stretched comfortably between them, broken only by the creak of the wagon and the steady clop of hooves. Nemeah leaned her head against the wagon's edge, the gentle rocking lulling her into a haze. She startled awake moments later, her head jerking upright as she rubbed her eyes in a futile attempt to fend off the creeping exhaustion.

"You can lean on me if you need to," Keanoff said, tugging lightly at her coat. "The sun will not rise for a few hours yet. Get some sleep."

Nemeah shook her head, stubborn despite her heavy eyelids. "No... I need to stay awake. Keep watch." Her words tumbled out, slurred with fatigue, each punctuated by a yawn.

Keanoff sighed, shaking his head before pulling her closer, his arm wrapping firmly around her shoulders. "Sleep. You are no good to anyone if you cannot keep your eyes open. I will keep watch with your metal creation."

She opened her mouth to protest, ready to insist that she did not need his help, but the warmth of his arm against her was too inviting. Her head tilted against his shoulder, and before she could fight it, sleep pulled her under.

Her dreams began softly, like a song she once knew. She saw Edna and Jacob with their little gray donkey, the wagon surrounded by a meadow of wildflowers that swayed in the breeze. Edna's arms were open, welcoming her with that familiar, gentle smile. Nemeah ran toward her, a surge of hope blooming in her chest. She wanted nothing more than to feel their embrace, to find her place among people who truly cared for her. But as Nemeah drew closer, the warmth in Edna's expression shifted. Her soft pale green eyes flared a piercing amber, pupils narrowing into predatory slits. Her gentle smile twisted into a snarl, revealing long, jagged teeth, and her fingers morphed into razor-sharp claws.

"I see you," Edna rasped.

Nemeah stumbled back, her heart pounding as Edna's skin darkened, black as night. Her face contorted and stretched until a monstrous feline creature stood before her, its skin marked with shimmering silver scars. The beast lunged forward, gripping Nemeah's shoulder with taloned hands.

"No!" Nemeah screamed, thrashing in vain against its hold.

Her eyes flew open, and her breath came in short, sharp gasps. She jolted back, only to find herself face-to-face with Keanoff, their noses nearly touching. His hands gripped her arms firmly, and his gaze locked on hers.

"You are safe," he said, his voice heavy with concern. He loosened his hold and leaned back.

Nemeah's heart thundered in her ears as she sat up, clutching her head. A dull ache pulsed behind her eyes, the remnants of the nightmare clinging stubbornly to her mind. "What... what happened?" she asked, her voice hoarse.

Keanoff's gaze flicked toward the road ahead. The sun had risen, casting golden light over the trail, and the donkey had come to a full stop. He looked back at her, his expression unusually serious.

"You were crying in your sleep," he said quietly. "And... you said something. You said *he is here.*"

Nemeah's stomach twisted as the weight of her dream settled over her. She did not need to ask who "he" was. She already knew.

"Zepher," she whispered, the name falling from her lips like a curse.

A piercing cry shattered the quiet of the forest. From every direction, golden-armored soldiers emerged from the tree line, their swords gleaming in the dappled sunlight.

"Kill them all!" one of them roared, his blade slicing through the air as he charged toward the wagon.

Rhubarb, braying in a fit of panic, reared in fright, kicking wildly as his harness snapped free. With remarkable speed from a stubby-legged animal, he bolted into the woods and disappeared from sight. Before Nemeah or Keanoff could react, Alban leaped from the wagon with the grace of a predator, his sword hissing from its scabbard. With a flurry of movements too swift to follow, he struck down half a dozen men, their bodies crumpling to the forest floor. Inside the wagon, Nemeah heard Edna and Jacob cry out, their voices shrill with fright. Her heart thundered in her chest as fear and urgency spurred her into action.

"I have to protect them," she whispered, her hand instinctively rising. A tremor rippled through them, and a wall of ice erupted from thin air, encasing the wagon like an impenetrable cocoon.

"Stay inside!" she shouted, leaping from the bench.

The impact rattled through her body as she hit the ground, the air fleeing her lungs. Before she could recover, a deep yell drew her gaze upward, just in time to see a soldier's sword descending toward her.

"Watch out!" Keanoff barreled into her, knocking her aside as the blade sliced into the dirt. They both rolled to their feet, and Nemeah, without hesitation, raised her hand. ropes sprouted like snakes from the ground, twisting around the attacker and ensnaring him in thick tendrils. A sickening crack split the air behind her. Nemeah turned just in time to see Keanoff's body contort. Fur erupted from his skin, his hands elongated into clawed paws, and his teeth sharpened into lethal fangs. A guttural growl tore from his throat as he lunged past her, sinking his jaws into the arm of another soldier. The man screamed, but the chaos around her drowned out his cry. Swords clashed, men shouted, and the forest seemed alive with violence. Nemeah felt the weight of it pressing down on her, fear, adrenaline, and determination colliding in her chest. She threw out her hand again, and burlap sacks gobbled up prey as they flapped around like fish on land, ensnaring the soldiers and pulling them to the ground.

A sudden whoosh split the air. She ducked just in time, the wind of a blade grazing her cheek. Spinning on her heel, she thrust her palm forward, and an enormous flock of birds drove the attacker off his feet. He landed on his back with a bone-jarring thud, his weapon clattering away. She felt the ground rumble and turned to see Edna standing atop a protective stone wall, her hands raised like a conductor commanding an orchestra. Trees groaned and shuddered as their roots twisted out of the ground, trapping the advancing soldiers in an unyielding grip. Grass stretched upward, weaving itself into a dense, living net that slowed the onslaught. More than a dozen soldiers lay bleeding on the forest floor, their wounds too grievous for even the most skilled healer. A blur of fur streaked past her. Another soldier screamed as Keanoff sank his teeth into his leg, dragging the man to the ground. The soldier struggled, his knife flashing as he aimed for Keanoff's back.

"No!" Nemeah cried, her hand slicing through the air. Ice surged from the ground, encasing the soldier in a crystalline prison. His hateful expression froze mid-sneer, locked in eternal stasis.

For a fleeting moment, the battlefield stilled. The wounded moaned weakly, and the imprisoned yelled out insults. But then, another cry erupted from the woods, a sound that made Nemeah's blood run cold. Her fear grew as she turned toward the tree line. The golden glint of armor caught her eye, more brilliant and oppressive under the high noon sun. More than fifty soldiers marched from the shadows, their swords raised and shields braced. Nemeah's heart faltered. She glanced at Keanoff, now crouched low in his wolf form, blood dripping from his maw. Alban stood nearby, sword in hand, armor untouched, and his stance unyielding. Above them, Edna's hands trembled as she continued to summon the forest to their aid.

"We cannot hold them all," dread pooled in her stomach.

She scanned the battlefield, her chest tightening at the carnage and the oncoming attackers. Bodies littered the ground, blood pooling beneath them like crimson shadows as their companions marched over the fallen. Alban's blade cut through the air, relentless and precise, striking two more down, while Keanoff charged into another cluster of soldiers, his growls echoing like thunder. By the wagon, Edna stood firm, her hands raised in fierce determination, roots and branches twisting in her defense. Inside, Jacob stayed hidden and safe. Rhubarb's terrified brays echoed faintly from the trees, the sound barely piercing the cacophony of clashing steel and cries of the dying. Alban swung again and again, blood misting into the air and bodies lying at his feet, but even he was becoming surrounded. Nemeah raised her hand, and a powerful gust sent soldiers staggering back. Another wave of her fingers conjured a stone wall, massive and unyielding, cutting off part of the advancing force. But it was not enough. It would never be enough.

They kept coming, marching forward with an unrelenting purpose. Panic rushed through her. She had never imagined this, this blood-soaked reality, when Kallemena had told her about the journey she would need to take. Nemeah had pictured trials, yes, maybe even danger, but not an endless tide of men trying to kill her. Her heart thundered. She had not asked for this power. She had not wanted to leave her family, her *life*. And now, she was hunted, not for anything she had done but simply for being born on the wrong day. Her gaze flicked to her companions. The weight of their lives pressed down on her, suffocating in its intensity. She let out a brittle laugh that startled even herself, the absurdity of it all snapping against her fraying emotions. Her smile stretched wide across her face, sharp and unnatural, as her fingers tangled in her long black hair. The soldiers kept coming. They just kept coming.

Anger surged, boiling up from the depths of her soul. It crawled through her limbs like fire, lighting every nerve. Frustration, grief, fear, everything she had tried to suppress came roaring to the surface.

She hated this power. Hated this responsibility. Hated the thought of dying at the hands of people who did not even know her. And then something broke. An invisible but immense pulse rippled out from her, violently shaking the air and stilling the battlefield. For a moment, time seemed to stop. Nemeah's hand lifted, trembling with power, and with the slightest flick of her finger, the Axis soldiers were wrenched from the ground and hurled into the air.

Keanoff turned at the sound, his wolfish eyes widening at the sight of her. Nemeah's eyes glowed black, their depths unnatural and fathomless, her smile now a cruel carved thing. Her arms rose, hands weaving through the air with effortless precision like she was crafting an enormous, invisible tapestry. A sound emerged, low and wet, a wheezing gasp. Then another. And another. Keanoff shifted back into human form, his fur retreating and claws retracting. He hesitated as he felt it, a creeping, oppressive energy that pressed against his chest and stole the breath from his lungs. He looked up. Soldiers dangled in the air like marionettes, their swords clattering to the ground in a metallic rain. They clawed at their throats, their faces turning shades of blue and purple as their eyes bulged in desperation. The survivors on the ground watched in horror, their faces pale, their bodies trembling as they tried to crawl away before whatever Nemeah was projecting found them. He watched in horror as, one by one, they dug their nails into the cold ground, desperate to live.

Keanoff's stomach churned. "Nemeah!" he shouted, his voice rough but urgent.

She did not respond. The energy pouring from her was thick and alive, saturating the air around her. Despite the fear that was pulsing through him, he forced himself forward, pushing through the force. He reached out, his arms extended, bracing himself against the sheer power radiating from her body.

"Nemeah?" Keanoff's voice cracked with urgency as he gripped her arms. "Nemeah, stop! You have to stop!"

Her eyes snapped to his, but there was no recognition, only an abyss of seething power. She flung her arm, and Keanoff was sent flying like a rag doll, crashing into the dirt with a dizzying thud. The air started to move around them, swirling and kicking up a dense fog that sucked the warmth from everything within its reach. When Nemeah spoke, her voice was foreign, resonating with an unnatural tone. "Men filled with hate and destruction deserve the same fate they inflict upon their victims." Her body began to rise, her movements fluid and otherworldly. "I am the bringer of death. The one who *can* and *will* end all. The mountains will bow before my feet, and the earth will weep with joy as I cleanse the world of its filth of humans. My reign will be eternal!"

Keanoff groaned, pushing himself upright. He turned to the soldiers, their faces streaked with tears as their bodies convulsed and then fell still, one by one. Frost crept along their skin as their arms dropped limp to their sides, swords holding their reflections on the blood-soaked earth. He looked back to Nemeah, a cold knot forming in his stomach. Her features were almost unrecognizable, twisted by the weight of her unleashed power.

"You need to stop!" Keanoff shouted again, desperation lacing his words as he charged toward her.

Before he could close the distance, a surge of energy struck him like a hammer, sending him sprawling once more. He landed hard on his arm, a sharp crack splitting the air. A cry of pain escaped his lips, but it was drowned out by a scream that shattered the tension. The gut-wrenching sound pierced through Nemeah's storm of power, jolting her out of her frenzy. Her glowing eyes darted to the barricade and froze. In front of the wagon, Jacob's lifeless body lay sprawled on the ground, unmoving. A dark creature loomed nearby, its blade pressed to Edna's throat. Her frail body trembled, her soft whimpers cutting through Nemeah like shards of glass. Nemeah's fury reignited, and thousands of icicles were hurled across the sky, aimed at the monster. But the creature merely smiled, digging the tip of his knife into

Edna's delicate skin, drawing blood. The shards warmed and melted, raining down over all of them as Nemeah collapsed to the ground, drained and trembling. All around her, the soldiers' lifeless bodies hit the forest floor in loud thuds, and silence fell like a blanket of death.

The creature sneered, his slit-pupil eyes and amber irises locking onto Nemeah. He seemed to study her, peeling back her defenses with his gaze as if he were peering directly into her soul.

"How have you survived this long without attracting attention?" he mused, his voice cold. "The Axis should have cut you down ages ago."

Keanoff scrambled to his feet, clutching his injured arm as he prepared to lunge. The creature turned his head slightly, his grin widening. "None of that blind Vira heroics, boy, unless you want to be responsible for this sweet old lady's death."

Keanoff froze, his breath heaving as he steadied himself. The creature's clawed hand grazed through Edna's gray-white hair; his touch was vile and deliberate.

"There is a good lad," he purred, turning his attention back to Nemeah. She struggled to rise, her body trembling with exhaustion, but her legs buckled, and she fell to her knees again.

"Vallorith would be quite unhappy if he knew there was another suitor to his prophecy," the creature said, his voice dripping with satisfaction.

Nemeah's chest heaved as she forced out a plea. "Please, let her go! She does not need to be harmed!"

The creature's lip curled in disdain. "Chains," he muttered. "You noble types and your endless groveling. It is sickening."

Edna whimpered, her frail body quaking with terror as she tried to edge away. The knife pressed harder against her throat, a cruel promise in its sharp edge. Her watery eyes locked on Nemeah's, silently begging for strength. Nemeah's gaze flicked back to Jacob, desperately scanning for any sign of life. She stared at his chest, willing it to rise, to move, anything. But it did not. Her heart sank into the pit of her stomach, the hope draining from her like water from a cracked vessel.

Edna's sobs grew heavier, her knees wanting to give out as grief and fear consumed her. Zepher held her still, his expression one of twisted satisfaction.

"Who does the prophecy warn about?" Keanoff's voice broke the tense silence. All eyes turned to him as he cradled his swollen wrist, his face pale and taut with pain. "What does it say?"

Zepher's grin spread slowly, his blade still hovering near Edna's throat. He seemed to savor the moment before finally pulling the dagger away. Edna collapsed to the ground, trembling so violently that it was a wonder she could move at all. She crawled to Jacob's side, her hands shaking as they pressed into his blood-soaked shirt. Muffled sobs broke from her as she clutched him close, rocking back and forth. Nemeah's throat constricted at the sight, a fresh wave of tears clouding her vision. She had never felt so powerless. Her gaze darted to Keanoff, his shock mirroring her own. Zepher was unmoved. He turned the blade in his clawed hand, running a curved talon over its edge.

"No harm in a quick history lesson, I suppose," he said, his tone lightening, "since you will all be dead soon enough."

A long, ragged gasp erupted from one of the guards, pulling their attention. He struggled to breathe, his face turning a deep reddish-purple as his hands fumbled to unfasten his armor. His helmet clattered to the ground, revealing a desperate man choking for air. Zepher was by his side in an instant, his speed unnerving. Without hesitation, he twisted the man's head with a sickening pop. The guard's body crumpled, lifeless, to the ground. Zepher dusted his hands with exaggerated nonchalance. "I do hate interruptions."

Nemeah flinched, her breaths short as she turned back to Edna. The old woman held Jacob's hand to her cheek, her trembling fingers brushing through his hair. A quiet hum escaped her lips between sobs, a tune so soft and broken it felt like the last flicker of a candle. Zepher's voice cut through the stillness like a blade.

"As I was saying..." He straightened, lifting his chin as a performer stepping into a spotlight. "In the time before mortals claimed this world as their own, the gods themselves walked the lands of Ardoria. One of them, a fierce, vengeful god, was deemed unworthy by her kin. They stripped her of her title and cast her out, banishing her to the moon." He lifted his claw to the sky, his amber eyes gleaming. "From her prison, she wove a spell, a promise that one day her blood-line would rise and set her free. When that day comes, she will rain vengeance upon those who turned against her." He smirked, pacing leisurely as though savoring his audience's silence. "It is said this person will ascend to the heavens and sit amongst the creators. This person will be known as the bringer of vengeance. A god to rule over the nine."

Zepher's eyes locked onto Nemeah, the weight of his gaze heavy and menacing. "I figured it was that damned princess. The one who did this to me." His voice rose as he flung his cape back, revealing the scars crisscrossing his flesh like jagged lightning bolts. Thousands of lines marred his once-sleek skin, running from his face to his clawed feet. He turned his predatory eyes towards Nemeah. "But now I am sensing it is someone else. Someone right in front of me."

Nemeah's breaths were labored, her body shuddering under the fatigue.

"I said we should kill the princess, be rid of her, but no. His high priest insisted on keeping her close. 'A valuable tool,' he called her. Her power is useful." He mocked as he dragged his claws down his face, his sharp nose and large eyes now unmistakably feline. "And look what it brought. A pesky farm girl into the mix. One that happened to escape the blade of the Axis and hold untold potential in her veins. Almost as if she had the blood of that very god within her." His grin disappeared from his face. "Well, not after today."

Nemah froze as her mind flashed with images of her family. "How did you know I was a farm girl?" Her voice was shaking.

Zepher exhaled, a bitter laugh escaping his lips. "Because Vallorith saw it all. Your mother and her love for your puny sister. Your lame father who tends to your cows and pigs. Do you think that was the first time your sister found that mirror?" He rolled his eyes. "She took it from its hiding place every chance she got, and Vallorith just watched. Their daily lives always under his watchful eye, waiting for your return. How pleased he will be when I tell him he no longer has a rival and he can return to being the prophesied one." His teeth were yellow fangs as he sneered. "I may even ride the world of that annoying little girl."

Nemeah's fists clawed at the dirt around her as she tried to get to Zepher, wanting nothing more than to claw his eyes out. Her voice was filled with anger. "I will kill you if you touch her! Any of them!"

"I do not see how you will possibly be able to stop me when you will be the one dying today." He took a step towards her and stopped.

The ground started to tremble beneath them, growing more intense by the second, pebbles and dust skittering across the earth. Zepher looked toward Nemeah, his claws flexing. But before he could close the gap between them, a voice cut through the tension like a blade.

"He was innocent!"

All eyes turned to Edna. Her sobs had quieted, replaced by a calm so cold it sent a shiver down Nemeah's spine. She pressed Jacob's hand to her lips one last time before laying it gently on the ground. The old woman rose slowly, her skirts soaked with blood. The trembling ground mirrored her movements as she slid her foot across the dirt. With a flick of her hand, jagged rocks erupted from the ground, slicing through the air like spears. Zepher darted back, his agility saving him from most of the onslaught... but not all of it. One sharp edge caught his thigh, tearing a deep gash in his flesh. Blood poured from the wound, and his agonized roar echoed through the trees.

"You miserable hag!" he bellowed, his fury a force of its own. He sprang toward her, his blade glinting as it arced through the air. Edna did not flinch.

A flash of light split the sky, a bolt of lightning striking Zepher's dagger mid-swing. The crack of thunder that followed was deafening, sending the assassin hurtling through the air. His body landed in a heap, motionless. Before Edna stood a stocky man with broad shoulders and sandy blond hair pulled back in a leather tie. His glowing brown eyes crackled with power as he extended a hand to her. Edna took it without hesitation, her trembling fingers steadying as their gazes met.

"Slek." Edna's voice, old and weathered, rattled as she spoke his name.

He smiled at her, a warm, almost gentle gesture that softened his sharp features. "I am sorry I could not be here sooner."

Edna looked down at Jacob, tears slipping down her weathered cheeks. "He was innocent."

Slek nodded, understanding etched in his features. He turned back to face Zepher, who was rising to his feet, his amber eyes blazing with fury. Blood poured from the gash in his leg, staining the ground beneath him. His face, half scorched from the lightning strike, twisted in rage.

"You are going to pay for that!" Zepher screeched through clenched fangs, his voice hostile. His twisted smile grew as he wiped spittle from his chin and fanned out his clawed fingers. "New tricks will never beat a classic." Zepher thrust his hand into the dirt, his claws tearing into the earth. Black smoke began to ooze from the soil, creeping like living shadows toward the fallen Axis soldiers scattered around them.

The dark tendrils snaked deep into the lifeless flesh. The bodies twitched violently, their movements jerky and unnatural. Bones cracked and stretched as the dead began to rise, growing to monstrous proportions. Skin sloughed off, revealing grotesque muscles and elongated limbs. Their teeth sharpened to jagged points, their bones revealing themselves as the stench of rot filled the air. What once were soldiers now stood as towering abominations, their twisted forms hungry for destruction.

Slek stepped forward, his voice commanding. "Everyone behind me!" He thrust his arms out in a sweeping motion, a mighty gale bursting from his palms. The wind roared like a hurricane, forcing the monstrous creatures back. They toppled, rolling away as the force grew in strength.

Keanoff rushed to Nemeah's side, hoisting her to her feet and helping her stumble toward the wagon.

"We have to go! We cannot stay here!" Nemeah pleaded, her voice breaking as she reached for the old woman.

But Edna only shook her head, cradling Jacob's lifeless body.

"My journey ends here." Her voice was calm and resolute as she reached into her coat pocket and pulled out two mirrors, pressing them into Nemeah's trembling hands. "You go. Together. You two can stop Vallorith."

"No!" Nemeah's scream tore from her throat, raw and desperate, but it was futile.

Keanoff lifted her effortlessly, carrying her away despite her protests. She kicked and screamed, her weakened body betraying her as tears blurred her vision. She waved her hand, willing her power to summon her loyal guard, but no light answered her call.

Her voice grew hoarse, her sobs choking her as despair settled deep in her chest. Suddenly, Keanoff froze, his grip tightening on Nemeah as he stared into the woods.

Shadows shifted, revealing movement among the trees. Half-rotted, half-formed creatures emerged from the forest—their twisted faces split by jagged teeth, their bodies warped with decay. More of Zepher's horrors followed behind, their grotesque forms unnatural and terrifying.

"We are surrounded," Keanoff whispered, panic threading his voice. A hand fell on his shoulder, and he spun sharply. Standing before him was a small woman, her frizzy brown hair a wild halo around her head. Tattoos coiled up her arms and neck, mirroring his own.

"Let me deal with them," she said, her voice low and calm.

Before their eyes, her body began to shift. Her limbs thickened, her spine curved, and her skin transformed into silvery fur. A deafening roar erupted from her throat as she hunched forward, growing larger and larger until a towering silver bear stood in her place. Nemeah gasped, frozen in awe and fear as the bear's enormous black eyes turned to her.

"Go!" the bear growled before charging into the fray.

The ground shook with each of her thunderous steps as she tore through the advancing monsters. Razor-sharp claws ripped through flesh and bone, sending blood and viscera flying. The bear fought with unmatched ferocity, her massive form a whirlwind of destruction. Keanoff held Nemeah closer, retreating back toward the wagon. Out of the sound of war, a familiar voice rang out.

"You need to get out of here!"

Nemeah felt relief spill through her. Kallemena. The princess swept her hands low across the ground, and a wave of searing light erupted from her palms. The beam struck the advancing monsters, slicing through their legs and sending their massive torsos crashing to the earth. Kallemena raised her hands to the sky, summoning dark clouds that rolled in with unnatural speed. Rain poured in thick sheets, turning the ground into a slick, muddy battlefield. Within moments, the sun was blotted out, and the world plunged into chaos. The silver bear continued its rampage, swatting creatures aside with colossal claws. Bone and flesh were scattered in all directions. Edna, her face a mask of grim determination, slammed her hands into the dirt. Jagged stalagmites erupted from the ground, impaling the abominations where they stood. Nemeah and Keanoff stood frozen, caught between amazement and horror as the battlefield twisted around them.

"We need to do something!" Nemeah shouted, her voice nearly drowned by the deafening roar of rain hammering the ground.

"You are depleted!" Keanoff's voice was sharp, tinged with urgency as he yanked her closer. "We have to do as Slek and Kallemena said! We need to run!"

Nemeah shook her head, her legs trembling beneath her. A stabbing realization gripped her: she could not run. Not even if she wanted to. Then, another roar, this one unmistakable, the sound of sheer power, ripped through the storm, silencing the rain's barrage. Their eyes snapped toward it, widening at the sight. The massive silver bear tore through the reanimated corpses with an explosive speed that left them stunned. Keanoff's lips twitched into a grin, the first hint of relief breaking through his tense expression as he watched Wynna battle through the undead. "That is *amazing*."

The beast was a blur of muscle and fur, its strength and agility carving a path of destruction through the advancing horde. Every swipe of her claws felled multiple mutants, only for them to rise again, black smoke oozing from their wounds. The relentless cycle continued: fall, rise, fall again. The ground trembled as Edna hurled rocks and earth at the enemy. Her arms shook with exhaustion, her power slowly draining, but still, she fought. The Morin's forces pressed closer, an unyielding tide.

"It is never-ending." Keanoff's voice broke with a hollow bitterness. "We are going to die here."

Nemeah's mind raced as an idea, sharp and desperate, flickered through the fog of dread. Her gaze dropped to her wrist, tracing the flowered scar burned into her flesh. Her heart stuttered as she realized this might be the key. "Get us to Edna. I have an idea."

Keanoff's grip tightened, pulling her along through the slew of body parts. They staggered toward Edna, the woman now commanding a snarl of thorned vines to ensnare the approaching monsters. They collapsed at her feet, and Nemeah immediately reached for Jacob's lifeless body, pulling him close. Her eyes swept over the battlefield, the sense of futility crashing over her in waves. The ground churned with the remnants of the battle, but one figure stood out: Kallemena. Her gaze locked with Nemeah's, and in that moment, it was as if the princess had read her mind. With trembling hands, Nemeah fished the compass from her pocket. She flicked it open, watching the needle spin wildly before it finally stilled, pointing south. She pressed her palm into the mud, feeling the texture slide over her skin like slick oil. Her breath quickened, her focus narrowing to a single point. Pain stabbed at her head, sharp and insistent, but she did not waver. Her body felt like it was being torn apart, but she kept going, digging deeper.

Keanoff glanced from Wynna to Slek, both of them struggling under the onslaught of mutants. They could not hold on much longer. Then, a flash of lightning split the sky, striking the ground with energy that sent Nemeah's heart leaping. In that instant, she felt it, a spark deep within her, a force she could not control. A desperate scream ripped from her throat, a sound that *rang* in the ears of everyone nearby, cutting through the storm's fury. And then, the ground gave way. A portal opened before them, expanding in slow motion, a gaping tear in the fabric of reality. They watched it grow, caught by the pull of the portal's raw energy, and fell through. Nemeah's stomach lurched as the air rushed past her, the world spinning. She hit the ground with a jarring thud; the wind knocked from her lungs. The sharp pain made her gasp, tears welling in her eyes as she fought for breath.

From above, a voice rang out, a yell of fury, of hatred. Amber eyes bore down on her, a gaze that sent ice through her veins.

"I will find you!" Zepher's words reverberated in the air as the portal closed, the echo lingering in the charged silence.

Nemeah's heart raced as she struggled to sit up, a sharp ache in her chest as she gasped for breath. Her eyes searched for Keanoff; he was sitting nearby, his face drawn in pain, still cradling his purpled wrist. His gaze was fixed on something behind her. She turned at the soft, strangled cry. Edna was there, her shoulders shaking as her tears fell to the ground, tears that mingled with the freshly fallen snow. The wind howled around them, cold and unforgiving, as Edna's sorrow filled the air. Her cries were gut-wrenching as she clung to Jacob's lifeless body.

Nemeah tried to stand, but her legs trembled, betraying her. She collapsed back down to her knees, the biting cold of the snow sinking deep into her skin, and for a moment, she just sat still. The weight of it all pressing down. She felt her chest heave as tears burst from her eyes, and the cold stiffened her damp clothes.

"It is all right," Keanoff murmured gently. "Breathe and try to calm yourself." He nodded toward the breathtaking view, trying to offer her a glimpse of security. "We are safe here."

They were perched high on a mountain, its jagged peaks stretching out before them like frozen statues, the blue sky hanging overhead in endless, silent glory. The wind sliced through them, a bitter reminder of their new foreign landscape. Nemeah's gaze lifted to the heavens, desperate to ensure there was no way for the Morin to follow them. She let out a breath when she was certain her portal was gone. Her body relaxed ever so slightly, but the pain still gnawed at her insides. She tried to rise again, but her legs were still not yet up to the task. Frustration bubbled up, and a curse slipped from her lips.

Keanoff was quick to his feet, offering her a steadying hand. She hesitated; her pride warred with her need, but she took it. His grip was warm, his fingers strong as he pulled her upright. His smile, small but genuine, was a quiet comfort. He pulled her close once more, his arm snug around her waist as his eyes scanned their surroundings, searching for something in the distance. His eyes flicked to his wrist. "Flying would make finding shelter a lot easier," he muttered with a wince, trying and failing to move his hand. "But it looks like that is not happening today, or anytime soon." With a soft sigh, he helped Nemeah over to Edna, lowering her gently to the snow. "Stay here," he said, his voice soft but firm. "I will see if I can find somewhere to camp for the night."

Nemeah watched him move, the snow crunching beneath his boots as he cautiously navigated the icy rocks and snow-covered ledges. She turned back to Edna, her own tears silently carving paths down her frozen cheeks. Words felt hollow, meaningless, in the face of such grief. What could she say to a woman who had just lost everything? *The love of her life, her partner in the world, her other half.* There were no words for this kind of pain. They sat in silence; the only sounds were the wind's mournful howl and the steady falling of snow. The sun began to sink, casting long shadows across the peaks, the thin mountain air biting at Nemeah's lungs. Time stretched, heavy, and uncertain.

A tremor rippled through the ground, pulling Nemeah from her dark thoughts. She watched, transfixed, as the earth beneath them shifted. The ground opened, a yawning crack splitting the snow and rock. Slowly, Jacob's body sank into the rocks, swallowed by the mountain. Edna whispered something, words Nemeah could not understand, before raising her hand. The grave closed, a slab of stone rising from the earth, Jacob's name etched in neat, deliberate letters.

"He saved me." Her voice was shallow as she stared at the gravestone. "That beast would have stabbed me if he had not gotten in the way. If only he had stayed in the wagon."

Edna wiped the tears from her dirt and blood-stained face before standing and offering her hand to Nemeah. This time, when Nemeah took it, she felt a surge of strength, as if the very act of standing together was enough to pull them both through the weight of their grief. They turned and made their way toward Keanoff, following the faint trail of his footprints in the snow. A cave was not far, its gaping mouth looming ahead like an invitation or perhaps a warning. As they approached, Nemeah called into the darkness, her voice stuttering with her frozen body.

"Keanoff?"

Her words echoed back at her, swallowed by the cave's depths. They entered together, Nemeah drawing on the last reserves of her strength to conjure a faint orb of light. The deeper they went, the warmth in the air shifted, and the smell of cedar and jasmine clung to their skin. The scent was strange here, comforting yet unfamiliar. When they rounded the corner, they found Keanoff standing frozen, his back to them, staring wide-eyed straight ahead.

"There you are, we called your..." Nemeah's voice faltered, her words dying in her throat as her eyes locked on what had caused Keanoff to become as still as stone.

Before her stood a giant beast, its bright blue eyes locking onto hers with an unnerving intensity. The creature's gaze followed her every movement as the two women slowly approached Keanoff, their steps tentative, as if each one might trigger the beast's attack. They all watched, eyes wide, taking in the creature's every detail. Its snow-white wings were tipped with black, feathered but strong, built for flight yet grounded in the cave's cool, shadowed depths. Sharp talons dug into the stone floor, leaving marks as deep as the beast's presence in the room. Protective, glass-like plating covered its massive body, glistening in the dim light of her orbs. Nemeah's lips parted, a soft, knowing smile tugging at her mouth.

"I know this creature," she whispered, her voice trembling with recognition. "This was made by Kallemena."

Keanoff raised an eyebrow, his voice laced with disbelief. "She made that?"

Nemeah did not answer immediately. Instead, she raised her hand slowly, her fingers trembling but resolute. The dragon lowered its head in response, its massive, scaled snout brushing the air as it sniffed her outstretched palm. Nemeah felt the warmth of its breath, hot against her frozen skin, the heat slowly thawing her cold flesh. The smell was intoxicating, rich and earthy, laced with the scent of burnt wood, just like the fires in her family's hearth.

"Keanoff, can you tell it that we are friends with its master?" Nemeah whispered, never peeling her eyes away from the massive creature.

Keanoff stuttered in irritation. "No, I do not speak dragon. That is a dead language. One lost way before my time." He took a tentative step back. "And I am pretty sure the damn thing is going to kill us no matter what I say."

The dragon let out a low, soft growl, its blue eyes never leaving Nemeah as it nudged her hand with its smooth, plated snout. Its glass scales clinking together in an unpredictable symphony as it moved. The faint sound echoed through the cave, revealing how massive its home was.

"It will not harm us," Nemeah whispered, her heart racing as she stroked the beast's warm scales.

Edna looked up in awe, her face still streaked with the remnants of her tears. Eyes, still red and swollen, reflected something different now: curiosity and wonder. "Magnificent," she murmured past the sob that still gripped her throat.

Keanoff nodded toward the back of the cave, his voice a little shaky. "It... umm, it has a mirror."

Nemeah and Edna turned to look at him, confusion clouding their minds.

"What?" Nemeah asked, unsure if she had heard him right.

Keanoff pointed, his good arm shaking as he gestured past the dragon. There, nestled against the far wall, was a massive mound of treasures piled up like a nest, glittering with gold, gems, and relics Nemeah had only ever read about in stories. But what caught her eye was the mirror. A small mirror, its intricate silver scrollwork unmistakable, perched amid the riches. It was identical to the others in their possession. Without thinking, Nemeah slipped past the dragon, moving quickly across the cave, her boots skidding on the golden pile. The dragon growled, its eyes narrowing in warning, but Nemeah ignored it, her mind consumed by one thought: *the mirror*. She did not care anymore. The portal, the lives lost, and the power she had unleashed all blurred together in a single, overwhelming rush. She had nothing left to lose. She reached for the mirror, lifting it with trembling hands.

Her fingers brushed the cool glass, and she felt an unsettling crack against her palm. The mirror was chipped, a jagged crack stretching across its surface.

Nemeah sank down into the dragon's nest, her coat brushing against the golden treasure as she pulled out the other two mirrors from her pockets. She arranged them side by side, staring at their silver frames. The dragon leaned its head closer, sniffing eagerly at the mirrors as if recognizing something in them.

She beckoned to Keanoff. "Bring me your mirror."

Keanoff hesitated, his eyes darting nervously to the back of the dragon. Its long tail swept lazily across the cave floor, and the air seemed to hum with an energy that made him uncomfortable. "I would rather stay over here."

Nemeah rolled her eyes, exasperated. But she moved quickly, hurrying back across the cave. She tugged open his pouch, her fingers rummaging around before pulling out his mirror. She caught a flash of a smile on his lips.

"You are such a child," she hissed under her breath, but she could not help the corner of her mouth that quirked up in amusement. She hurried back to the mirrors, placing his Vira mirror carefully alongside the others. All four mirrors, each one silver, gleaming faintly in the dim light, reflected the ceiling above them. The dragon bowed its head, peering at the mirrors curiously.

"Whose mirror is this?" Nemeah asked the question hanging in the air. She knew no one would have the answer she needed.

The weight of the day pressed down on them. The loss. The confusion. The strange sense of unease that had settled over them all. They made camp in the cave, the dragon watching over them, but the prisoners from the mirrors never showed their faces. No words passed between them. The day had left them speechless and drained. And Nemeah could not shake the feeling that they were standing at the edge of something far darker than they had yet realized. Her mind drifted back to Zepher's words about the prophecy. How someone was meant to undo Vallorith's plans to ascend to godhood. Her thoughts flickered to the power she had felt in the forest, a power so intense it had consumed her. She shivered, but whether from worry or excitement, she could not tell.

"Five more to go," Nemeah whispered to herself, the words barely audible over the crackle of the fire.

Keanoff lifted his head, his wrist now bound tightly with the herbs Edna had conjured. The swelling had gone down significantly, though the bruising was still visible, a dark reminder of the day's violence.

"You still want to go find them?" His voice was edged with disbelief. "Knowing that at least four are in the hands of that maniac who almost killed us today?" His brows furrowed deeply as he looked at her. "No. You will get yourself killed... and us with you if we are dumb enough to follow you. No."

Nemeah shot him a quick glance, her expression unreadable, before her gaze shifted to the dragon, now curled up on its bed of gold. It slept soundly, unaware of the tension between the humans. "Not if I kill Zepher first," she replied, her voice low but laced with a deadly determination. She turned to Edna next. The woman was curled on a bed of soft moss and grass, a makeshift blanket woven from nature's own bounty. Edna had cried herself to sleep hours ago, her whimpers still echoing in Nemeah's mind, each one like a dagger to her heart. Nemeah looked back at Keanoff. "Are you with me?"

Keanoff rolled his eyes before lying back down, clearly irritated.

"They have your father. Are you just going to let that vile man steal his gift and become more powerful than we could ever stop?" Her words hit like a lash, but her voice held no anger, only a cold, calculated urgency.

Keanoff's face flickered through a series of emotions: resentment, disbelief, and a slight hint of concern beneath it all. But when he spoke, his voice was tight, reluctant. "You do not even know how many mirrors they actually have. And how can we even fight someone like that?"

Nemeah did not falter. "We do not know if he has four or five. But we already know where he will go before the Eclipse Veil hits."

Keanoff scoffed, his voice tinged with bitterness. "Do we? I certainly have no idea where a lunatic goes to ascend to godhood." He sat up now, cross-legged, cradling his injured wrist.

Nemeah's eyes narrowed, her gaze hardening as she fixed him with an unwavering look. "The Axis. There is a room there with strange carvings on the wall. Kallemena called them runes."

Keanoff stared at her, blank-faced, his brow furrowing in confusion. "Edna said someone else controls the Axis now. Someone who wants to kill all Echoes. You remember that, right? You are an Echo. I am an Echo. Edna is..." He waited for Nemeah to finish his sentence, irritated by her silence. "An Echo! We are all Echoes, Nemeah." He pushed his hand through his brown and white patched hair. "And what makes you even think they will just let us stroll on in?"

Her attention drifted to the flames, the orange glow flickering and devouring the wood with a hungry roar. The fire's heat clawed at her skin, but it did little to dull the sharpness of her thoughts. Memories rushed through her mind like a fast-moving river: flashes of the portal, Jacob's death, all the lives taken by her hand. The fear she had felt as a child, running from the golden guards. Running again, just days ago. Zepher's golden eyes, Edna's sorrow. Leaving her family. Vallorith's watchful eyes on her home. Her sister's tear-streaked face. Nemeah let the memories wash over her, not to mourn but to fortify herself. She felt the familiar pull from deep within, the darkness of her power growing.

She allowed herself a dangerous smile, the kind that sends a chill through the air. She turned back to Keanoff, her eyes now glowing black as the abyss itself, as her power slithered through her veins.

"Because I am the Echo who will put an end to the purges. Because I am the Echo who will release the prisoners from their mirrors. I am the one who will watch Vallorith and his pet take their last breaths. Because I am the Echo of Tirnmoor!"

Ripley Larrow is a firm believer that stories should take you somewhere new, preferably where dragons fly, castles loom, and heroes rise to meet their destiny. A lifelong reader turned writer, Ripley grew tired of reading the same fairy tales retold with different names and decided to craft fresh, original adventures that readers of all ages could enjoy.

Ripley is always dreaming up the next big quest. When not plotting epic journeys and quiet romances that bloom naturally amidst the chaos, she is hanging out with her family, navigating their own adventure through life. Ripley is on a mission: to write books the whole family can enjoy—stories that spark wonder, inspire courage, and leave readers eager for more.

Also, despite many attempts over the years, Ripley cannot whistle. But dragons do not whistle either, so it will probably be fine.